PRAISE FOR THE
MILLION-COPY
BESTSELLER

M.J. Arlidge

'Helen Grace is one of the greatest heroes to come
along in years' **Jeffery Deaver**

'Chilling' *The Times*

'Addictive' *Express*

'Truly excellent' *The Sun*

'Amazing' **Richard Madeley**

'Chills to the bone' *Daily Mail*

'Mesmerizing' **Lisa Gardner**

'Gripping' *Sunday Mirror*

'This is going to be as big as Jo Nesbo'
Judy Finnigan

Also by M.J. Arlidge

DI HELEN GRACE

Eeny Meeny
Pop Goes the Weasel
The Doll's House
Liar Liar
Little Boy Blue
No Way Back *(an eBook novella)*
Hide and Seek
Running Blind *(an eBook novella)*
Love Me Not
Down to the Woods

OTHER NOVELS

A Gift For Dying

M.J. Arlidge has worked in television for the last twenty years, specialising in high-end drama production, including prime-time crime serials *Silent Witness*, *Torn*, *The Little House* and, most recently, the hit ITV show *Innocent*. In 2015 his audiobook exclusive *Six Degrees of Assassination* was a number-one bestseller. His debut thriller, *Eeny Meeny*, was the UK's bestselling crime debut of 2014 and has been followed by eight more DI Helen Grace thrillers – all *Sunday Times* bestsellers. *All Fall Down* is the ninth novel featuring his much-loved lead detective, Helen Grace.

🐦 @mjarlidge
📘 /MJArlidge
📷 @m_j_arlidge

ALL FALL DOWN

DOWN

M.J. Arlidge

ORION

An Orion paperback

First published in Great Britain in 2020
by Orion Fiction,
This paperback edition published in 2020
by Orion Fiction,
an imprint of The Orion Publishing Group Ltd.,
Carmelite House, 50 Victoria Embankment
London EC4Y 0DZ

An Hachette UK company

1 3 5 7 9 10 8 6 4 2

A CIP catalogue record for this book
is available from the British Library.

ISBN (Paperback) 978 1 4091 8842 1
ISBN (eBook) 978 1 4091 8843 8

Typeset at The Spartan Press Ltd,
Lymington, Hants

Printed and bound in Great Britain by Clays Ltd,
Elcograf S.p.A.

MIX
Paper from
responsible sources
FSC® C104740

www.orionbooks.co.uk

For my father, Anthony,
who knows how to tell a good story.

Day One

Chapter 1

Justin Lanning stared out of the window, his eyes fixed upon the horizon. The sun, which had flooded his office all day, was now starting to descend, its golden glare stealing across the water. There was something majestic, even triumphant, about its progress, the long arms of light seeming to claim the lapping water, the bobbing boats, even the marina itself. It was a sight Justin had witnessed many times, but it still had the power to affect him. Awesome, beautiful, it was also soothing, a moment of release after what had been a very trying day.

Turning away from the floor-to-ceiling glass, Justin glanced at his watch – 17.58 – then marched back to his desk. He was the sole occupant of this vast, well-appointed office, a fact that gave him much pleasure. It was opulent, indulgent, powerful... but it was also a glorious secret. From the outside, Endeavour House looked no different to any of the other office blocks in Ocean Village. The foyer was unexceptional, offering no clue as to the bespoke offices on the top two floors; offices that were designed to dazzle. The expensive Italian furniture, the modern art installations and, yes, the view – everything had been carefully calibrated to pronounce affluence, professionalism and success. Few were allowed in, but those who *were* left reassured and inspired, after a tantalizing glimpse of Redstone Solutions.

Switching off his computer, Justin picked up his phone and crossed to the lift. However demanding or unpredictable his day was, he prided himself on leaving on time. The efficiency of it appealed to him – in by 6 a.m., out by 6 p.m. – and it was also useful in regulating his mood. Whatever the business of the day, if he could leave on time, then assuredly everything was under control.

The lift doors slid open and Justin stepped inside, punching the button for the basement. If he left now, he could be home by half past six, allowing him plenty of time for a workout before Adam returned. Adam – just the thought of him conjured up a bewildering array of emotions: anger, disappointment, lust and much more besides. Things had been so difficult recently, so complicated, that home was no longer the sanctuary it should have been. Their relationship needed to be carefully managed, in a calm frame of mind, hence the importance of a relaxing workout beforehand.

The doors kissed shut and the lift began to descend. The floors flicked by – ten, nine, eight, seven. Justin found himself humming a cheerful tune, celebrating the fact that the working day was finally done. Six, five, four. Justin was losing himself in a pleasant reverie, his cares slowly melting away...

Then suddenly, and without warning, the lift bucked, screeching to a shuddering halt, throwing him backwards. Justin crashed into the mirrored wall, cracking his head against the glass, exhaling an expletive as the wind was punched from him.

A strange silence now filled the metal box, the pleasing hum of progress replaced by lifeless inertia. Stunned, Justin stumbled forwards, stabbing the button for the basement – once, twice, three times. Nothing happened and, even as he continued to jab away, he became aware of something else. The lights in the lift had gone out too. It was as if the whole contraption had suddenly just... died.

Gathering himself, he tried the buttons for the other floors, before giving up, hitting the alarm bell in angry resignation. Somewhere in the distance, a dull ringing sounded, but this gave him little comfort. It would take the office manager an age to summon the lift engineers and longer still for them to free him, as he appeared to be stuck between floors. Would they be able to get the lift working again? Or would they have to haul him up the lift shaft, like a sack of potatoes? Cursing, he kicked the doors, his plans for the evening disintegrating. What the hell had happened for him to be left dangling here like a broken puppet? What was going on?

He felt it before he heard it – his new Samsung vibrating in his pocket, before letting out its familiar trill.

'Thank God...'

Someone was aware of his plight – there was no question in his mind that this call was connected to his emergency. Tugging out the phone, he was surprised by the caller ID – it wasn't Adam or the office, the number withheld – but answered anyway. What did it matter who it was, so long as they could liberate him from this tin can?

'Hello?'

He was met by silence.

'This is Justin Lanning. Can you hear me?'

His voice filled the lift, but there was no response. He was convinced the connection was fine – he could hear something humming at the other end – so why wasn't the caller responding?

'I'm stuck between floors four and three, so if you can...'

Now something made him stop. An intake of breath at the other end, as if the caller was about to speak. Justin wanted to carry on, to explain his predicament, but suddenly he felt powerless to continue, as if something – or someone – was commanding him to be quiet.

And now, finally, the caller did speak, a soft, male voice whispering:

'You have one hour to live.'

Chapter 2

The needle tipped eighty miles per hour, but DI Helen Grace didn't relent. She was on the Fawley Road, speeding south towards the coast, drawn onward by the open road and the glinting water in the distance. This lonely stretch of tarmac could, perhaps *should* have troubled her, flanked on one side by the disused power station and the New Forest on the other, both scenes of crime that had cost her dear in recent years. But today she was untroubled by past trauma.

The Honda Blackbird pulled alongside, manoeuvring to overtake. Helen shot a look at the driver, half expecting DS Joseph Hudson to offer her a triumphant smile, but his gaze remained resolutely fixed on the road ahead, as if he could see a chequered flag in the distance, as if this after-hours race actually meant something. It pleased Helen to see that he was intent on avoiding defeat, that he was willing to respond to her silent, teasing challenge.

Of course, in truth, this pursuit *did* mean something, though neither was prepared to admit it. Joseph Hudson was a relatively new addition to Southampton Central's Major Incident Team and an even newer addition to Helen's bed, but slowly he was becoming part of the fabric of her life. They spent much of their working day orbiting each other and most of their nights engaged in this enjoyable dance. Helen didn't profess to know Hudson well, but he was an exciting, impulsive, passionate man, who shared her lust for speed. The relationship was not without its complications – it would certainly be frowned upon by her colleagues – but Helen couldn't deny that she enjoyed his company and the frisson between them.

Twisting the throttle, Helen nosed ahead, gaining a yard or two on her competitor. The road was running out now – there was only a hundred yards or so before it took a sharp right turn – but still she was not surprised when Joseph drew level once more, refusing to be relegated to second place. On they roared, the sharp bend racing towards them, each rider calculating their next move. The setting sun bathed the coastal road in light and Helen could see that the way was clear, sharpening her sense of anticipation. If she'd spotted a vehicle approaching, she would have killed her speed immediately, the game over, but as it was she pushed the speedometer up to ninety, hurtling towards the turn, before suddenly decelerating and leaning in to the corner. The road on this stretch of the coast was old and tired, a sprinkling of loose gravel coating the surface and Helen's bike slid across it now. She was comfortable, in control, but nevertheless the skid took her further out than she'd intended and her pursuer took advantage. With a satisfied roar, Joseph sped past on the inside, calling out to her as he did so.

'See you back at yours ...'

'As if ...' Helen replied, her bike roaring forward, as her speed tipped one hundred miles per hour.

Joseph was an experienced rider, but had to rely on guile to stay ahead, because when it came to raw power, there was only one winner. With a determined thrust, Helen nosed past him, her Kawasaki Ninja growling happily as it responded to her promptings. Moments later, Joseph Hudson moved alongside her, pushing his ride to the absolute limits just to stay in touch.

This time Joseph did flick a look her way – affectionate, challenging – which pleased Helen. This was an activity she usually enjoyed alone, ripping along the country roads in glorious isolation. But now it was something she was happy to share, showing Joseph secret routes and cut-throughs she'd explored during her many years as a solo rider. This was not just because she'd found an able competitor, but because it felt natural to do so. Their relationship was still in its infancy, but Helen had relaxed into spending time with Joseph in a way she could never have predicted. Since Jake, she had let no one get close to her, deliberately keeping interested parties at bay, but now it seemed pointless pushing intimacy away, ignoring the obvious fit. Oftentimes, it had seemed to Helen as if it would never happen, but there was no denying it now.

Finally, she had found someone who could keep up with her.

Chapter 3

'For God's sake, slow down. You're not making any sense...'

'What part of it do you *not* understand?'

'All of it. You're talking like a crazy person—'

'So would you, if you'd just been through what I've been through...'

'Which is what exactly? *Slow down* and tell me what happened...'

Adam's tone was so condescending, so laced with irritation, that Justin's first instinct was to tell him where to go. But something – a residue of affection? Sheer, naked terror? – held him back, forcing him to rein in his anger.

'I was coming down in the lift...'

'Yes...'

Dear God, shut up and let me finish.

'And my phone rang...'

Once more Justin's voice started shaking, as he tried to articulate his predicament.

'...and this... this voice at the other end started threatening me... telling me I had one hour to live.'

Silence.

'Adam, are you still there?'

'Yes, I'm here, I'm just...'

The condescension had evaporated now, replaced by confusion and concern.

'Did you recognize the voice?'

'No…'

'Do you have any idea who might want to threaten you?'

'No.'

'Could it have been a joke? A prank of some kind?'

'No… no way…'

It was possible, of course, but Justin knew it wasn't. The caller had delivered his chilling ultimatum, then seconds later, the lights had come on and the lift had continued its smooth descent, as if his antagonist was in control of *everything*.

'Do you want to call the police?'

'I suppose so…'

'Justin, if you genuinely think someone intends to harm you, then you *must* call the—'

'And tell them what? I don't know who this guy is or what he wants—'

'OK, OK. Don't bite my head off. Just… just get yourself home and we'll decide what to do then. If I leave now, I won't be far behind you…'

A sudden rush of affection and gratitude flooded Justin. Despite their recent difficulties, more than anything he now wanted to be with someone who really knew him, who could put an arm round him and tell him everything was going to be OK.

'Thanks, Adam. I've called for the car. I'll… I'll see you back home shortly.'

Ending the conversation, Justin turned. Right on cue, the black Mercedes came into view, purring past the long line of cars in the office's basement car park, coming to a halt in front of him. At the same time every day, one of these luxury vehicles ferried him home and their familiarity, their solidity, was comforting now. Yanking open the door, Justin climbed inside, pulling the heavy door firmly shut behind him. On cue, the small red light by the glass partition came on, signalling that the driver was listening.

'Grange House, please. Quick as you can.'

The light clicked off, a silent affirmation of shared intent. Moments later, they were through the security barrier and out onto the street, taking their place amidst the rush-hour traffic. As Justin leaned back against the comfortable leather, taking in the cars around him, he finally felt his heart rate begin to slow. When the lift had ground to a halt, he'd been appalled, convinced he would spend hours in an airless box. But what followed had been even worse. Incomprehension, then unadulterated fear, Justin conjuring up all sorts of awful images – the lift doors springing open to reveal an attacker, the lift plummeting to the ground – before he was unexpectedly released from his ordeal, deposited in the basement car park as if nothing had happened. Confused, disoriented, he'd nevertheless been spared and now had the chance to put the whole awful nightmare behind him. His phone was switched off, he was nestled in the back of a plush Mercedes and he was heading *home*.

Exhaling slowly, he shook his head at the madness of it all, before angling a glance at his watch.

18.08.

Chapter 4

'This is a dead weight. I'm going to have to ask *you* to move it.'

Charlie Brooks collapsed onto a packing case, breathing out heavily. She'd hoped to be of some assistance to Steve in their dusty loft, but her attempt to lift the pieces of Jessica's old cot had ended in abject failure. It weighed a ton and in her current condition, eight months pregnant with a gigantic bump, there was no way she was going to risk it.

'No worries,' Steve chuckled. 'I know I'm the beast of burden here.'

He began gathering the pieces together, as Charlie ran an eye over the cornucopia of baby products that flanked the wooden cot.

'I'd no idea we had so much stuff up here.'

They were surrounded by sterilizers, baby bouncers, a rocker, their old Moses basket and endless bags of baby clothes. When Jessica had become a toddler, then eventually a pupil, they'd packed all this stuff away, out of sight, out of mind. But when Charlie had surprisingly, pleasingly, fallen pregnant again, they'd been forced to venture back into this neglected space. Taking in a slice of their past, which would become their present again, Charlie felt a shiver of anxiety. Would she remember what to do when the baby came? Could they cope with the lack of sleep?

And how would Jessica react to the arrival of a sibling? So far, she had said little about it, despite the studied promptings of her parents and the obvious change in her mother's shape.

'If I head back down, do you want to pass things to me?'

Charlie suddenly wanted to be out of this claustrophobic space. There were too many props up here, too many symbols of her past. Her school books, her Interrailing rucksack, her first police uniform, a bridesmaid's dress, all of which combined to make her feel old, unattractive and bone-tired.

'OK, but be careful.'

Charlie didn't need Steve's warning, taking each step of the loft ladder carefully, ensuring her foot was firmly planted before descending. Her pregnancy had gone well, despite hideous morning sickness, and she was determined not to jeopardize herself or her baby through her own stupidity.

Descending, she headed into the nursery. This had been Jessica's at first and later, when she moved into a bigger bedroom, it had become the spare bedroom. Or, in other words, the dumping ground. People seldom came to stay, meaning the small box room was a repository for stuff they'd been too lazy to throw away. The imminent arrival of their second child had spurred them into action, however, every spare minute spent sifting and discarding. As a result, the room was now clear of detritus, though whether it was fit to be a nursery was still open to question.

'We've got so much to do,' Charlie moaned, as Steve passed her, clutching the headboard of the cot.

'Plenty of time,' he responded breezily, before exiting again.

He was excited, which pleased Charlie, as she was finding it hard to slough off her worries. How would they find time for it all? Now that Jessica was at school, her life outside work had become an endless round of logistical challenges.

Drop-offs, pick-ups, play dates, birthday parties – to these had now been added a long list of baby-related duties: check-ups, scans, decorating, cleaning and shopping. For, however careful Charlie thought she'd been in stowing Jessica's baby equipment, there always seemed to be one key part of the sterilizer or baby bouncer missing.

Looking around her, at the unpainted walls, the naked light bulb and the discarded headboard, Charlie felt overwhelmed. She was genuinely excited by the prospect of the new arrival, but they suddenly seemed completely unprepared. She still had two weeks of work left, so meaningful preparation time was hard to find. She hated the idea of not having everything in place, convinced now that she'd forgotten all that she'd learned about how to rear a newborn. She knew she was being irrational but she couldn't help herself. In all other areas, deadlines could be massaged, timings reset, but not with this. As Charlie rested her hand on her bump, feeling once more the sharp jab of her baby's foot, one thing was painfully clear.

The clock was ticking.

Chapter 5

'Come on, come on ...'

Justin breathed the words to himself, urging the car to get past the temporary traffic lights that had detained them as they tried to leave Southampton. As if the driver could hear his quiet urging, the car sped up, sliding past the lights just as they changed from yellow to red.

Justin afforded himself a brief smile. Finally, they were free of the traffic, on the home stretch to the small village of Wickham, which he and Adam had called home for the past year. It had not always been a welcoming place, some older residents initially unnerved by the presence of an openly gay couple, others put out by the opulence of their purpose-built house, fearing it would prompt a sudden invasion of 'new money'. But over time, Justin and Adam had won over the doubters and they were now as much a part of village life as if they had always lived there.

Another quick glance at his watch: 18.48. In under ten minutes, he would be home, with Adam and Caspar, their recently acquired Yorkshire terrier. Safe, happy, at ease. With each passing minute, his ordeal at the office seemed more and more unreal, to the point that he now began to question whether it had happened at all. He felt silly to have been so terrorized by it

– perhaps it *was* just some idiot calling numbers at random after all.

Closing his eyes, Justin sank deeper into his plush, upholstered seat. He knew using the car service was an extravagance, that he could just as easily have called a cab or, God help him, learned to drive. But he liked the idea of having an account with them, liked the idea of being able to summon a luxury vehicle, liked the feeling of power and prestige it gave him. More than that, he revelled in the comfort of it, as if he was travelling first class to and from work. As they wound their way along the twisting country lanes, he allowed himself to be swayed by the gentle movement of the car, body and mind finally relaxing.

What would he do first? Would he talk to Adam? Or would they take Caspar for a walk? It was mid-October and already the forests were turning russet and gold. Perhaps it would be better to head out and pick through the bizarre events of the afternoon later? Yes, that was the right idea. That way they might even have a relaxed evening together – heaven knows, there had been few of those recently.

Suddenly Justin's eyes flicked open, a tremor of unease rippling through him. He had driven these lanes so many times that he knew every twist and turn, every ascent and descent, his body moving in time with the familiar movements of the car. Usually he loved this ballet, finding it calming, but instinctively he now knew something was off. Rising in his seat, he looked around – to find that they were on an unfamiliar lane, deviating from their well-established route.

'Hello?'

Realizing he'd forgotten to press the communication button, he jabbed it now.

'Sorry? I think we might have taken a wrong turn.'

As if in answer to this, they shot past a signpost, signalling that they were heading west, away from the village.

'This road takes us to Shedfield. The turning to Wickham is about a mile or so back...'

The driver nodded, as if in understanding, but didn't alter his speed or direction. Justin peered at the back of his head, taking in the broad shoulders and neat, clipped hair, realizing for the first time that he didn't recognize him. Was this someone new? Someone who didn't know the area?

'There's a junction up ahead. We can turn there...'

The car sped up, forcing Justin back into his seat.

'There's no hurry. Better to get there in one piece...' he joked, his voice sounding flat and tense.

How fast were they going? Sixty miles per hour? Seventy? Now a creeping anxiety began to steal over him. Why *were* they going so fast? And why wouldn't the driver respond?

'Look, I'm going to have to ask you to slow down...'

No response, the car continuing to roar along the narrow country lane.

'Look, mate, what's the fucking hurry?'

As if in response, the car swerved violently off the road, sending Justin tumbling to his left. Desperately, he grabbed hold of the seat belt and hauled himself upright – to find that they were now speeding along a rough track, the Mercedes bouncing up and down over the uneven surface. Angry, alarmed, Justin unclicked his seatbelt and moved forwards, rapping angrily on the glass partition that separated them.

'I'm telling you to *stop*...'

The car roared on and to his surprise Justin saw chain-link gates ahead, gates which hung open, as if expecting their arrival. Moments later, they swept into what was clearly some kind of building site.

Panic gripped him now and delving into his pocket, he tugged out his mobile phone. He pushed down hard on the 'on' button, but as he did so, the car came to an abrupt halt. Unprepared, Justin was catapulted forwards, his face slamming into the glass partition. The phone tumbled from his grasp and he slumped backwards. His hand instinctively went up to his head, but hovered there hopelessly, body and brain too stunned to function. He was seeing stars, he could taste blood in his mouth, could feel his limbs shaking and there was nothing he could do now, as the door opened and rough hands grabbed him, dragging him from the car.

Chapter 6

Wrenching open the door, Adam marched into the darkened room.

'Hello?'

His greeting echoed through the empty space, dying in the air.

'Justin?'

There was no reply. In fact, there was no sound at all, save for the skittering of Caspar's paws as he scampered across the polished wooden floor. Adam had just picked him up from their neighbour, an old boy who doted on the pup, but as usual Caspar had no interest in Adam, concerned only with finding Justin, the sole object of his affections.

Stepping around the dog, Adam headed into the kitchen. Oftentimes he'd find Justin in here, draining a beer whilst rustling up something imaginative for dinner, but the room was deserted.

'Justin? Are you home?'

His strangulated voice bounced off the walls, but still there was no response. Adam hurried into the master bedroom. This too was empty, so he carried on, completing a tour of the bedrooms and bathrooms, before finally returning to the living area. He'd known it as soon as he'd entered, such was the eerie stillness in the house, but there was no doubt now. They were alone.

Extracting his phone, Adam dialled Justin's number. It went straight to voicemail, his voice shaking as he left a message.

'It's me … I'm home. Just wondering where you are. Call me when you get this.'

The dog was looking at him entreatingly, as if he should be trying harder, but what more *could* he do? He would give it a few minutes – allow Justin time to call him back – then, if he still hadn't heard anything, he'd call the car company to register his concern. It didn't normally take them this long to get home, but it *was* rush hour, so perhaps they'd been held up in traffic? Anxiously, Adam glanced down at his phone.

19.07.

Day Two

Chapter 7

Charlie moved quickly across the kitchen, flicking a look at the clock. It was early morning and as usual she was running late. She'd slept badly, finding it impossible to get comfortable, and was groggy when her alarm went off. Steve had gone to work early, leaving Charlie to feed and dress Jessica, whilst somehow finding the time to make herself look respectable for work.

'Do you want anything more to eat?'

Jessica looked at the remnants of her Weetabix, deep in thought.

'Quickly, please, love, we're on borrowed time...'

After a moment's consideration, Jessica assented, thrusting her hand into the box to pull out another wheat biscuit. Charlie swallowed a sigh – her daughter was a good eater, but *slow* – and they were already behind schedule. Jessica was dressed, which was a blessing, but they'd somehow have to tame her hair before they left – an exercise which Jessica bitterly resented, often threatening to cut the whole lot off with some craft scissors. Some mornings, Charlie was tempted to let her.

In addition to her normal morning duties, Charlie also had to find time to make a packed lunch. This was a new part of the daily routine, Jessica's best friend Mia having recently opted for this over school dinners. Shoving a bag of Hula Hoops and a carton of apple juice into Jessica's lunchbox, she reached for the bread, intending to add a Marmite sandwich as the crowning glory. As she did so, she felt a sharp, stabbing sensation in the centre of her being. The pain seared through her, unbalancing her, and she gasped as she held onto the kitchen surface for support. A moment's fear, a moment's shock, then a flood of relief – it wasn't anything serious, though it was painful, the baby stamping on her pelvic bone. Righting herself, Charlie realized that Jessica was staring at her, concern creasing her face.

'It's all right, sweetheart,' Charlie said quickly. 'Just your little brother or sister getting in some practice for the trampoline...'

It was said lightly, though her innards throbbed. Satisfied, uninterested, Jessica returned to her Weetabix, toying with it, as if considering whether to eat it. For a moment, Charlie didn't move, staring at her daughter, trying to divine her thoughts.

'Jessie?'

The little girl nodded as she finally manoeuvred the cereal into her mouth.

'Jessie, love, are you excited about the baby?'

Another spoonful disappeared, but Jessica didn't respond.

'It'll be fun to have someone to play with, won't it?' Charlie said cheerfully. 'You can show them your dolls, your dressing up, your toys. It'll be like having a friend in the house *all* the time...'

Jessica had now tired of her Weetabix, pushing the bowl away. Still she didn't react, making Charlie wonder if she'd even heard.

'Jessica? *Are you excited?*'

And now finally Jessica looked up, nodding briefly, before saying: 'Can I have sausage rolls at my party?'

Charlie was momentarily taken aback. It was Jessica's birthday party tomorrow and she was sure all bases had been covered during their many conversations.

'And party rings too?'

Jessica rose, heading away from the table, seeking her favourite dolls, which were arranged in a neat line on the living-room sofa. Charlie stood stock-still, saddened. She knew it was foolish to be upset by Jessica's response, but she had hoped for a little more excitement. She'd seen other children who were virtually hysterical at the prospect of having a sibling to mother, dress up and cosset. But so far there had been nothing like that from Jessica. She had asked little, spoken little, about the birth; in fact she seemed supremely unbothered by the imminent arrival.

Lost in her dolls, Jessica was interested only in her party, her friends, her toys … and herself. Such was the perfect self-absorption of youth.

Chapter 8

Helen lay perfectly still, her eyes tightly closed against the morning sunlight. Despite this, she could tell that Joseph was looking at her. She had often woken from her slumbers to find him propped up on one elbow, taking in her firm, battle-scarred body, and she could tell by the rhythm of his movements that he was doing so now. Previously, she'd have tugged the sheet up to her chin, embarrassed by the scarring, but now she was happy to lie there, naked and exposed. She didn't mind him looking, she knew it wasn't lust that made him examine the angry strips of skin that decorated her body. He was intrigued by her, as she was by him.

'Haven't you got somewhere you need to be...?' Helen breathed, without opening her eyes.

'Probably. You see, I've got this nightmare boss. I can't be late for work.'

'Best get a move on then. But you can make me breakfast first.'

'Isn't that the eternal dilemma?' Joseph sighed. 'Ambition versus...'

'Versus what?' Helen responded, rolling over to face him.

'Versus...'

Joseph paused to consider, staring at her, then: '...pleasure.'

'Is that what this is?'

'You tell me.'

Helen smiled briefly, but said nothing, settling down on her back once more. She was enjoying this game, but knew that her light-hearted question would have to be answered at some point. *Did* she have feelings for Joseph? And he for her? And if so, what on earth would they do about it? Romances within the team were frowned upon and if Helen genuinely wanted to pursue a relationship with him, it would mean one of them leaving Southampton Central, a thought that sent a shiver down her spine. But perhaps she was getting ahead of herself. For now, they were just two lovers sharing a bed.

Despite his tacit agreement to make breakfast, Joseph made no move to leave, instead running a finger gently over her most recent war wound, an area of thick scarring on her thigh.

'Don't.'

Helen didn't want to be reminded of her recent brush with death, deep in the heart of the New Forest. Obligingly, Joseph moved his finger up to her stomach, but here too he found remnants of past battles. Moving over her midriff, over her breasts, he brushed the side of her neck, narrowly avoiding another injury.

'How do you do it?' His tone had changed subtly, concern seeping into his affection now. 'How do you keep getting back up?'

'Just lucky, I guess,' Helen replied, with a decent impression of a shrug.

'I mean it,' Joseph continued. 'You've put your body, yourself, through so much. Aren't you afraid that one day your luck will run out?'

Helen turned to him, surprised. She had had a very similar conversation with her superior, Detective Superintendent Grace

Simmons, a few months back, in which she too had expressed fears for Helen. Was that all this was? Genuine, well-meaning concern? Or had they both spotted something she hadn't?

'I don't really think about it, to be honest. If there's a job to be done, I do it.'

'And you've never been tempted to step back, away from the front line?'

'To make way for a better man, you mean?'

'No, of course not. It's just… don't you ever feel that…'

Joseph looked down, staring at the bedsheets, as if trying to find the words.

'…that you've done enough?'

His question struck home. It wasn't something she'd considered before, but now Helen wondered if – when – she would ever be able to stop.

'Not really. I don't know what else I'd do, to be honest—'

'But what if someone had feelings for you…'

Helen stared at him, curious as to what was coming next.

'…wanted to take care of you, say…'

'If they genuinely cared for me,' Helen replied carefully, 'they'd know better than to try to change me. That would be the mark of true affection, the only sort I'd accept.'

'So you are… open to the idea of relationships then?'

'Of course. I'm not a total freak, whatever you might have read.'

Unbidden, an image of Emilia Garanita popped into Helen's mind, but she pushed this spectre away. The journalist had no place here.

'Tell me more…'

Joseph's tone was casual, but he couldn't disguise his interest.

'You probably know a lot of it already, all that I'm willing to share anyway.'

Was that disappointment in his expression?

'The truth is I've never been very good at maintaining relationships. I've … I've always felt that contact with me … harms people rather than helps them. Which … which is why I've made a life for myself alone.'

Another note of disquiet in Joseph's expression.

'Not that I wouldn't say "no" to some company at Christmas, someone to go on holiday with perhaps …'

She wasn't sure she really meant this – whether she would ever be able to go *that* far – but Joseph seemed pleased by the idea, his handsome face breaking into a smile once more.

'What about you?' Helen continued, brightly. 'Are you on the market? Or was once enough for you?'

'Well, I can't say it ended well last time, but never say never …'

Helen said nothing, continuing to look at him. She had answered enough questions and was intrigued to learn more. Joseph seemed to sense this, realizing it was his turn in this game of Show and Tell.

'Karen and I married very young.'

Joseph paused and for a moment Helen thought that was all he was prepared to offer, but then: 'Anyone could have told us it was a mistake – they *did* tell us – but we didn't listen, why would we? The truth is we didn't know each other, not really. You know how it goes, you meet someone, you like the look of them, they're funny, sparky, kind … and that feels enough. But it isn't, of course it isn't … The years pass, life gets serious and suddenly you realize that you have completely different needs, completely different attitudes to family, kids, politics—'

'You had *kids*?' Helen replied, surprised.

'Thankfully not,' Joseph replied, smiling. 'We would have made a pig's ear of that too. To be honest, the more we got to know each other, the more we realized that we were totally incompatible. In the end, we had to chalk it up to experience and move on.'

'A fresh start.'

Joseph nodded and fell silent, continuing to stare at Helen. And now, for the first time, Helen *did* feel self-conscious, as if something had changed. Somehow she felt honour-bound to say something, to respond to Joseph's honesty and openness, but suddenly she couldn't think of anything to say. What could she offer that was honest, sincere and true, when in reality her feelings were changing all the time?

Still he looked at her, as if issuing a silent challenge. Helen could feel her colour rising and was on the point of making a feeble excuse to wriggle out of the situation, when suddenly her phone started ringing. Relieved, and perhaps a little ashamed, she rolled over to answer it.

'Sorry to disturb you early, ma'am...'

DC Bentham was always polite, but never wasted time with niceties when he had something serious to report.

'...but we've found a body.'

Chapter 9

Her wheels bit into the gravel, bringing the bike to an abrupt stop. Helen was off her Kawasaki before the noise of the engine had died, slipping the keys into her pocket and hurrying towards the scene. Selfish thoughts of her own pleasure were already a fading memory – she was a detective inspector once more, energized and focused.

Ahead of her, a uniformed officer hovered by a neat square of fluttering police tape. It was standard practice to erect a cordon around the crime scene, but it struck Helen as faintly ridiculous. They were on a building site in a remote part of the countryside near Curbridge, accessible only by a mile-long dirt track – the chances of members of the public wandering onto the scene were remote in the extreme.

Joseph Hudson had dismounted his bike and was by her side, raising the police cordon. Ducking underneath, Helen approached the attending officer, who looked ill at ease.

'Morning,' Helen said, keeping her tone bright. 'What've you got for me?'

'Lone male, deceased, late twenties, early thirties ...'

'Who found him?' Joseph asked.

'The site foreman.'

For the first time, Helen became aware of a rough-looking

man sitting on the steps of a Portakabin. Unshaven, with greying hair, his weathered face spoke of a lifetime's work in the open air. He was puffing hard on a cigarette and even from this distance Helen could see his hand was shaking.

'There's no work going on here currently, but he still comes down most mornings to check on the site. He opened up at around eight thirty and called us five minutes later. I've got all the details and he's agreed to make a statement...'

As the officer continued his summary, Helen took in the scene. The foundations of a large building – a warehouse, an industrial unit perhaps – were clearly visible, as were cement mixers, wheelbarrows and scattered groupings of breeze blocks. A thin layer of white dust coated everything and this, allied with the discarded Coke cans and crisp packets, should have given the site a feeling of life, of activity temporarily suspended. But actually, the whole place felt dead, as if the crew had given up halfway, abandoning the project to its fate.

'Any idea who the victim is?'

Joseph's question snapped Helen out of her reverie.

'He's not known to the foreman ... and I haven't touched anything,' the officer continued, answering Joseph's next question in advance.

'Anyone reported missing overnight?' Helen asked.

'A couple of people who might fit the bill,' the officer responded hesitantly. 'But until we know more...'

'Shall we?'

Helen gestured to the body and they covered the short distance in a matter of seconds. It was clear that the victim was not a workman – even before Helen noticed his blue silk suit, she clocked the expensive leather brogues. The man was lying face down in the dirt, his arms splayed out in front of him, his head twisted slightly to one side. His eyes were wide open, staring up at the sky in shock.

'He was dragged here,' Helen observed, pointing to the smeared pattern in the dust leading to the body.

'And look there,' Joseph added. 'There's a footwear mark of some kind.'

Helen crouched down, taking in what looked like a bootprint next to the body. It was large – size eight, size nine? – with a distinctive ridged pattern on the sole. An army boot? A hiking shoe perhaps? Turning from the corpse, Helen followed the line of footprints, growing steadily fainter and further apart with each step, suggesting that the killer had dumped the body, then fled.

'Any idea where these go?' she continued, gesturing to the footprints.

'There are fresh tyre tracks in and out of the site. Looks like whoever did this retreated to a vehicle and took off,' the officer replied briskly. 'No idea what sort of car it is, but I've cordoned them off for scene of crime.'

'Good. We're a long way from town,' Helen replied, 'and there's no public transport out here.'

'Which *might* suggest the site was chosen specifically. Remote, deserted, no chance of any witnesses to the crime...'

Mulling on Joseph's words, Helen returned her attention to the body. Leaning in, she removed a pen from her pocket and pulled down the man's shirt collar. She'd spotted markings in this area and her face clouded over as she took in the sight before her. A thick band of purple bruising surrounded his entire neck. Running directly through the centre of this dark, traumatized area, like a neat, scarlet necklace, was a deep cut, which had ruptured the flesh. Whoever was responsible for this awful crime had applied considerable force, the victim's neck so devastated that Helen could glimpse the windpipe inside.

Behind her, Joseph exhaled slowly, echoing her own feelings. This was a brutal, terrifying way to die. Helen could almost feel the choking lack of oxygen, the searing pain as the skin split open, as the weapon – a piece of wire, a garrotte perhaps? – pulled ever tighter. Shaking off her disquiet, Helen slipped on a pair of gloves and gently lifted the man's head, turning the face fractionally towards her. The victim was young, with good skin and strong, handsome features, even though his eyes were now bloodshot, his face dirty and whatever life had once illuminated those features was now extinguished. Replacing his face in the dust, Helen began to pat down the body, her hands alighting on the side pocket of the man's jacket which bulged promisingly.

Carefully, she reached inside, testing the fabric for smaller items that might tumble out, but there was nothing apart from the reassuring bulk of a wallet. Drawing it out, she opened it up. A slew of platinum credit cards greeted her, and tucked in behind them the familiar pink of a UK driver's licence. Withdrawing it, Helen took in the details. And now she got her second surprise of the day. The photo was vaguely familiar, though a little fuzzy, but there was nothing elusive about the victim's identity. This was a name Helen recognized, a name most of Southampton would recognize. A man whose life had been touched by darkness before.

'Was Justin Lanning one of the names on your list?' she asked, turning to the uniformed officer once more.

'Yes, ma'am,' he answered quickly.

'And what do we know about the circumstances of his disappearance?'

Now the officer paused, as if loath to be the bearer of bad news.

'His partner called it in last night. Lanning was picked up from his office around six o'clock, but never made it home. Apparently, he'd phoned his partner around that time, in a bit of state…'

'Because?'

'Because he'd just received a threatening call, telling him…'

The officer hesitated once more, looking unnerved, before concluding: '…telling him that he had one hour to live.'

Chapter 10

Charlie stood on the cold concrete, taking in the deserted space in front of her.

Helen and DC Hudson were at the building site, handing over to scene of crime, but Charlie had headed straight to Endeavour House. Lanning's office was on the top floor, a penthouse commanding stunning views of the water. She would head there shortly, but for now she wanted to run the rule over the basement – the last place Justin Lanning had been seen alive.

He'd been spotted exiting the lift shortly after 6 p.m., heading for the underground car park, where it was his custom to pick up the executive car that ferried him home. After that, nothing – until the foreman's distressing discovery this morning. Lanning's mobile phone was missing and had been turned off around the time he left work, so would be of no use in helping track his movements. The narrative of the affluent executive's disappearance would need to be stitched together piece by piece.

'What time did the car arrive?'

She turned to face Dave Prentice, the block's head of security. Overweight and jowly, he had the physique and demeanour of an ex-policeman. In his day, he would have been an imposing presence, but today he looked cowed.

'At five thirty-one p.m.'

'How can you be so precise? Do you have cameras down here?'

'Unfortunately not,' Prentice responded, his embarrassment increasing. 'But the executive cars have built-in zappers that automatically raise the gates, letting them into the car park. Each zapper has a unique signature, so we can be sure that that was Lanning's car. I gave the number plate and details to your colleague over the phone...'

DC Bentham had already been tasked with chasing down the details of the missing car and its driver – finding the vehicle was crucial – but that wasn't what interested Charlie now. She was more interested in the fact that Lanning's driver – his abductor? – had entered the building half an hour *before* Lanning rang for his ride home. This might simply have been good service – a regular driver knowing that Lanning liked to be picked up at 6 p.m. on the dot – but Charlie sensed a more sinister motive.

'What else is down here?' she asked, scanning the lines of smart cars.

'Not much. Storage rooms, staff changing areas, the substation for the utilities and lift syst—'

'I'd like to see that, please.'

Her tone was polite, but urgent. Prentice didn't linger, leading her to the far side of the car park where a steel door barred access to the utilities area of the building. It was decorated with signs proclaiming 'No Entry' and 'Danger of Electrocution', but someone had not heeded the warning. The heavy-duty padlock that was supposed to secure the door hung limply from its loop.

'What the fu—'

A flustered Prentice reached out towards the padlock, but Charlie stopped him, catching his arm in mid-flight. Stepping forward, donning latex gloves, she removed the padlock. It had been severed cleanly, with bolt cutters or similar, before being replaced in the loop, allowing the intruder free access to this reserved space.

Easing the heavy door open, Charlie stepped inside. An eerie, dim glow illuminated the claustrophobic space, which was filled with the low, satisfied hum of electricity. There were no obvious footprints or dust patterns, but still Charlie proceeded carefully, sticking to the edges of the room as she worked her way to the far wall. Prentice followed in her wake, wheezing gently.

'What have we got here?'

'The mains electricity, the meters, the main fuse box and a separate outlet providing power to the lift system.'

He gestured to a large console on the back wall and Charlie took a step closer. She recognized the brand name – Schindler – but had no idea what any of the buttons or levers did.

'Any idea how it works?'

'Not a clue. Not my area,' Prentice shot back quickly, keen to offload at least some of the responsibility for Lanning's disappearance.

'But if you wanted to kill the power to the lift? If, say, there was a fire and you wanted to disable the system . . .'

'Well, if the fire alarm is triggered, the lifts shut off automatically. But, if you want to do it manually, I think all you do is pull that lever there . . .'

He gestured to a large red lever on the right-hand side of the console. Charlie moved in closer and even in the pale light of the sodium bulb, she could see that this lever had considerably less dust on it than the rest of the box, as if it had been activated recently. It was simple, but effective. Once an intruder had gained access to the substation, it would have been child's play to kill the power to the lifts, leaving Lanning at his mercy.

Thanking Prentice for his help, Charlie ushered him from the darkened room.

'No one sets foot in there until after the scene of crime team have completed their work, OK?'

Prentice nodded forcefully, for a moment back in his role as a beat copper. Leaving him standing sentry, Charlie headed back into the main area of the car park, her eyes falling once more on the main lift doors. The picture of what happened was fairly clear now, seeming to tally with the basics of what Adam Cannon had told the operator when he called in his partner's disappearance. Lanning's assailant had arrived just after half past five, taking up position in the car park, before heading to the substation. Disabling the lifts at precisely 6 p.m., he had then made the call, presumably from this basement, before lying in wait, assuming – knowing? – that Lanning's instinctive response would be to take the car home, to hole up there, until he could make sense of the strange threat he'd just received.

Time would tell who had ferried Lanning to his death. Perhaps one of his regular drivers was involved – bribed, black-mailed, even threatened? Or perhaps his assailant had simply 'borrowed' the car to carry out his murderous scheme. They would discover this in due course, but for now one thing was clear. The attack on Lanning had been meticulously researched, planned and executed. This was no crank call, nor an idle prank.

The killer had made good on his threat.

Chapter 11

They crowded round her, hungry for details. Even the more experienced detectives in the room sensed that this was going to be a major investigation.

'Most of you will recognize the name...'

Helen fixed a head shot to the murder board. She was back at Southampton Central, in the packed incident room.

'Justin Lanning was one of a group of schoolchildren abducted by Daniel King, eight years ago. They were all from the same Southampton secondary school and were doing their Duke of Edinburgh Award on the South Downs when they fell into his clutches. Five teenagers were held captive in his farmhouse near Chilgrove, where they were physically and psychologically tortured. Lanning and three of his friends eventually managed to escape, but their classmate Rachel Wood wasn't so lucky – she was murdered by King in the basement of the farmhouse, before he set fire to the building and fled.'

King had never been apprehended, but Helen didn't need to spell that out. Every officer present knew it – King was an infamous fugitive from justice – and she wanted to keep their attention fixed firmly on the here and now.

'Lanning was seventeen at the time and obviously was severely traumatized by the experience. But he, and the other survivors, have proved to be a resilient bunch. Lanning in particular seems to have made a success of things – at only twenty-five his life seemed a lot more ordered and impressive than mine ever was …'

A chuckle from the team, a moment of levity in what had been a disquieting morning.

'He studied at Southampton University, getting a first in Marine Exploration, then did a post-grad year at Brighton – Business Studies – before returning home. He's from Southampton originally, was brought up in Fordham, and like the rest of his DoE group attended a local comprehensive, St Mary's. He eventually set up home in the city, joining Redstone Solutions in 2016, a company that supplies protection to companies in the oil and gas industry. He lived with his partner, Adam Cannon, in a large house in rural Wickham and seemed to be set fair. But last night he was strangled and his body dumped on a building site, a couple of miles from his home.'

A couple of knowing looks from the team – Daniel King had threatened to strangle the abducted schoolchildren whilst they were trussed up in his basement – but Helen wasn't going to go there. She was interested in evidence, not speculation.

'We believe he was abducted from his office in Ocean Village early yesterday evening. Do we know who was scheduled to pick Lanning up last night?'

'I've spoken to the car service,' DC Bentham offered. 'Prestige Travel, they're based out of an industrial estate in Thornhill. They're a small outfit, who use a rotating roster of drivers for the Endeavour House pick-up. A guy called Leo Bagdadtis was down to pick up Lanning, but his car appears to have been stolen at around three p.m. yesterday.'

'Does that check out?'

'He rang his local police station at around half past three. I've spoken to the team down there – Bagdadtis was in the nick at 6 p.m., reporting the theft. He's got no priors and seemed pretty upset by the loss of his only means of income. I think he's genuine.'

'OK, usual drill then. Send officers to his home address – we're looking for any witnesses, CCTV, anything that might give us a lead on who took the car. Do we have any idea where the car is now?'

'It doesn't have any sort of transponder,' Joseph spoke up, 'so we're going to have to track it down ourselves. We've got some decent traffic cam images as far as Botley. Nothing showing Lanning or the driver, but it does give us the direction of travel—'

'Which suggests they were heading to Lanning's home,' Helen interrupted.

'Exactly. That takes us up to about six forty p.m. No deviations in route, decent progress through the usual traffic, but we lose it when the car leaves the Botley road.'

'So…?'

'From there, it could have gone anywhere, but there's no traffic cam images of it heading back into Southampton, nor was it picked up on any of the nearby A roads or motorways.'

'Anything at ports or airports?'

'No, so our working theory is that it's been concealed locally – in a garage, car park, outbuilding – or it's been dumped somewhere near the crime scene. Obviously we've alerted the traffic police, as well as the local beat coppers, but we're also going to send up the drones – there's a lot of woodland and agricultural units out there that might make good disposal sites.'

'Let me know as soon as you have anything,' Helen responded, turning from him. 'What do we know about the phone call, the one threatening Lanning?'

'It was made from an unregistered pay-as-you-go phone,'

Charlie replied, turning to address the rest of the group. 'The signal was lost shortly after 6 p.m. yesterday and in fact has only ever pinged twice. Yesterday in the vicinity of Endeavour House and once a couple of days before that, in the Northam area.'

'Any idea where the phone was bought?'

'The SIM card's not registered to any of the major domestic providers, so it must have been bought on the black market.'

'Any idea where the first call pinged specifically?'

'We've got an area of about half a mile in Northam, but there's lots of flats, shops, industrial units – we can't be more specific than that.'

'And the call itself, what do we know about it?'

'It was made at 6 p.m. and lasted precisely one minute.'

'To the second?' Helen replied, surprised.

'To the second.'

Helen nodded, but said nothing. Again, she noted looks being exchanged between the team – the precision of the killer's approach was clearly unnerving some of the officers.

'OK, well Lanning's call and message history is obviously important. We only have a second-hand account of the content of the call, from Lanning's partner. So, we need to see who was contacting Lanning in the run-up to last night. Were there other threatening messages, any unusual call patterns, new contacts?'

'We're on it,' Charlie confirmed.

'While we're on the subject of contacts, I want the rest of you to trawl over Lanning's life. Let's run the rule over his current partner, Adam Cannon. Talk to neighbours, see if we can find out what manner of couple they were, but let's also look at his financial situation, his emails, his messages. Also, chase down family, friends, colleagues, people Lanning may have interacted with overseas. Protection in the oil business is a dangerous game – Lanning will have come into contact with all manner of dictators, corrupt officials, mercenaries and common-or-garden mobsters. Let's see if Redstone – and Lanning especially – had had any issues. Contracts terminated, accusations made, people paid off or *not* paid off. Was Lanning himself experiencing financial problems? Had he overcommitted himself with the move to Wickham? Was he content in his personal life? Let's lift all the rocks and see what crawls out.'

There was a brief silence, some of the team scribbling down notes, then DC Malik spoke up.

'And are we looking into whether his death might have any link to his previous experiences?'

Malik didn't need to spell out what she was referring to and privately Helen commended her for having the balls to ask the question.

'That's not our principal line of enquiry,' Helen replied. 'Though we should keep an open mind. There have been three "sightings" of King in the last eighteen months, the most recent one about four weeks ago in Southampton...'

A ripple of interest passed through the group, but Helen was quickly upon it.

'But all of them were unsubstantiated and were either made anonymously or by those seeking publicity. One of the survivors – Maxine Pryce – has just published a book about their ordeal, meaning that their abduction is very much in people's minds – suddenly folk are seeing King everywhere. So, we treat such unsubstantiated claims with caution and interrogate the method of attack too. Yes, it appears Lanning was strangled, but there could be any number of reasons why he was murdered in that manner. It *may* have a link to his past experiences. It may be entirely coincidental. Or it might be deliberately designed to throw us off track, to lead us down a blind alley.'

She let this thought settle, before continuing: 'Daniel King was a highly disturbed individual, clearly capable of killing. And he may, or may not, be alive. But we have to look at the nature of his attacks. Before the incidents at his farmhouse, King attempted to strangle two individuals, both of them schoolchildren walking home down remote country lanes. Neither attempt was successful, both victims managing to fight him off and raise the alarm. These attempted murders were not particularly well thought out or executed – they were crude and amateurish. Even his treatment of the Duke of Edinburgh kids was bungled – he had them all at his mercy, trussed up in his cellar, yet a simple mistake on his part allowed them to escape. So, yes, King was violent and motivated to murder, but he was not a clinical killer. Justin Lanning's murder feels different – clean, precise, even professional.'

'Are we saying it's a hit, then?' Malik replied.

'That's for us to find out,' Helen answered, determined not to let the team get ahead of themselves. 'So let's get to it, shall we?'

The meeting broke up, the team hurrying off to do Helen's bidding. She could have carried on the conversation, but what they needed now was hard evidence. Even so, as she watched her officers scurry back to their stations, her mind continued to turn on the manner of Lanning's death. On the face of it, it had all the hallmarks of a hit – well planned and ruthlessly executed, the assassin making good his escape with ease. But if that was the case, then one intriguing question remained.

If this *was* a professional assassination, why had Lanning been given advance notice of his death?

Chapter 12

'Justin Lanning?'

Emilia Garanita couldn't conceal her astonishment. She'd hurried to the remote building site hoping for something juicy, but what she'd been told beggared belief.

'Are you *sure* that was his name?'

PC Marvin Hayes suddenly looked concerned, as if he'd overstepped the mark or said the wrong thing. He'd seemed keen to get rid of Emilia, hoping that by giving her *something* she might be satisfied, but now realized he'd miscalculated. She was going nowhere.

'How did they identify him?'

'Wasn't hard,' the uniformed copper continued, casting a nervous glance over his shoulder. 'He had his wallet on him. Who is he anyway?'

Emilia was tempted to laugh, but suppressed the urge. This kid was obviously fresh out of police college. He'd only have been twelve or so when Justin and his schoolfriends were abducted, so perhaps it was understandable he didn't recognize Lanning's name, but still... such had been the publicity surrounding the case surely *something* would have registered?

Five teenagers, young, naive and full of hope, abducted and tortured by a crazed loner in a remote farmhouse. It was every parent's worst nightmare – one that was still fresh in people's memory, but should anyone be hazy on the details, Maxine Pryce's misery memoir would fill in the gaps. Emilia had read *One Dark Night* in preparation for their recent phone interview and, at over five hundred pages long, it had more than enough heartache, pain and tragedy for even the most mawkish reader. Perhaps she should buy a copy for this callow young man?

'Just someone I've come across,' Emilia replied, just about keeping a straight face.

This was a lie. Emilia had *tried* to gain access to the traumatized schoolchildren back then, but the families and the police had thrown an impenetrable, protective cordon around them. Emilia was a rookie reporter, lacking the audacity or cunning she now possessed, and had been left chatting to uncles, aunts and distant acquaintances, none of whom could offer up anything decent. Now it appeared the wheel had come full circle and there had been no one to protect Lanning this time.

'Who found him?'

'Site manager. Don't know his name though.'

These final words were delivered sharply, definitively, as if ending the conversation. This time Emilia *did* laugh. Once a copper had bitten, once they'd given you information that could be used against them, they were hooked on the line. It would be *she* who decided when this interview ended.

'One final question, then,' Emilia continued. 'How did he die?'

This was what she really wanted to know. She already had *far* more than she'd been expecting on arrival at this remote scene, but the impact of her article – and of Justin Lanning's death – hinged significantly on what Hayes said next.

'Look, I can't tell you much ...' the officer continued nervously. 'I'm just here to secure the scene ...'

'But ...?' Emilia replied, coaxingly.

'But I overheard DS Hudson saying he'd been strangled.'

And there it was. If she was honest with herself, Emilia had been hoping for this answer, but hadn't thought it remotely possible. She would have to follow this up with her contact at the mortuary, of course, but if PC Hayes was telling the truth, then a sensational story had just dropped into her lap. Justin Lanning had escaped death once, but not a second time. Was it possible the two events were connected? Had the darkness returned to claim him?

It was a tantalizing thought. Daniel King was hardly the world's most *successful* killer – he had twice tried and failed to strangle lone schoolgirls, before the Duke of Edinburgh Award participants fell into his lap. Nor did his body count of one put him in the big league. No, it was what he'd done to those poor kids that fascinated people; that and the fact that he'd vanished into thin air. Following the fire at the farmhouse, he'd been spotted soon after the children's escape in the village of West Ashling, then later in Chichester. King was presumed to have killed himself – his hat, clothes, wallet and phone had been found near a remote cliff, a day after the inferno at the farmhouse. But how could anyone be sure? His body had never been found, nor had he been seen entering the water. Was it possible that he was still out there, consumed by evil thoughts, biding his time to strike again?

Pryce rubbished this notion in her book, but there had been several 'sightings' of him over the years and there were plenty of internet conspiracies, offering details of King's 'subsequent murders'. And now Justin Lanning had been strangled, right here in Southampton. If anything was going to reignite specula-tion about Daniel King's whereabouts, this brutal crime was.

'Thanks very much, Constable Hayes. You've been very help-ful.'

The policeman seemed unnerved, but Emilia didn't linger to enjoy his discomfort. She had a story to break. She'd major on last night's murder, underscoring the cruel, ironic tragedy of Lanning's death, but there would be plenty of room for Daniel King too. He was the real draw and she would not stint on bringing him to life for her readers, making sure to include the one official photo they had of him, the one that still sent shivers down her spine. Crookedly handsome, with beguiling green eyes, straggly fair hair and a sly expression, he was a seductively sinister monster.

A phantom killer who continued to haunt the collective imagination.

Chapter 13

'I can't believe it. It doesn't seem real...'

Maxine Pryce fingered her necklace anxiously, toying with the heart-shaped pendant. Charlie noted how ashen her face was this morning and wondered if she was always this pale.

'I mean, I spoke to Justin a couple of days ago...'

They were seated together in Café Belmondo, an upmarket coffee and croissant outlet in the city centre. The stylish, art-deco-inspired interior was lavish and impressive – all ironwork and stained glass. It was the kind of place that made you feel trendy and successful just by being there. Needless to say, it had been Pryce's choice.

'And how was he when you spoke?'

A slight pause before Pryce answered, then: 'Same old Justin...'

It was hard to say whether this was said with affection or not.

'And you and he were close?'

'Of course. When you've been through what we went through, you can't help but be.'

'You were friends, then?'

'Yeah. Friends with history. But, yes, friends.'

It was said warmly, but had an undertone of irritation, as if Pryce was already tiring of the questions. She had been reluctant to meet up at first – claiming, truthfully, that she had a very busy promotional schedule, given her book's release today. She was a resilient, tough young woman, who was clearly used to getting things her own way, but she'd quickly acceded to Charlie's request to meet, once the latter had relayed the shocking news of Lanning's death. Pryce had promised to help in whatever way she could, but exuded a mixture of shock, grief, irritation and discomfort. Charlie was keen to explore this and was about to continue, when Pryce's phone started ringing. The latter snatched it up quickly, but her face fell when she saw the number and she placed it back on the table, allowing it to ring out.

'If you need to take that …?'

'Just a journalist I know. A very *tiresome* journalist …'

Charlie could guess who and silently cursed Emilia Garanita. Whenever tragedy struck, she was never far away.

'Did you see each other much?' she continued, pushing all thoughts of the journalist from her mind.

'Not that much. Justin had his life and I had mine, but we kept an eye out for each other …'

'You spoke on the phone?'

'Now and again.'

'How often, on average, would you say?'

Now Pryce hesitated, as if sensing a trap.

'As often as we needed to. Why do you ask?'

'Well, following his death, we went back over his call history …'

Charlie hadn't divulged their knowledge of the threatening phone call – there was no need for that yet.

'…and we were intrigued by the fact that he called you every day last week. Prior to that he hardly ever called you – once every couple of months at the most …'

Charlie let this anomaly hang in the air. Once more, Pryce

pushed her hair away from her face, then conceded: 'He wanted to talk about the book, that was all. He knew it was coming out today, so …'

'He was very persistent.'

'That's Justin for you,' Pryce replied ruefully, deflecting the question.

'He called you on Monday and you spoke for…' Charlie made a play of checking her notepad for accuracy, '…fifteen minutes. The following day you spoke for eight minutes. Then on Wednesday and Thursday, he called you a couple of times, but these calls went straight to voicemail.'

'I've been very busy.'

'Did you argue about something?'

There was a hint of steel in Charlie's voice, cutting through Pryce's attempt to flannel.

'Clearly there was something exercising him,' Charlie continued, as if stating the obvious. 'No contact for a couple of months, then suddenly he's bombarding you with calls, which you initially take, then ignore.'

For a moment, Pryce said nothing. Her forced good humour was evaporating. She clearly wanted to avoid having to lift the lid on her relationship with Justin Lanning, but now she had no choice.

'We had an argument, OK? One he was keen to continue.'

'But you weren't?'

Pryce nodded slowly, then said, 'He wanted money.'

Not what Charlie had been expecting. Yes, Pryce had been paid a healthy advance for her book, but there was no question that Lanning was the wealthier of the two.

'He thought that because I was partly telling our story in the book he was entitled to a share of the spoils.'

'And you didn't agree?'

'I told him that if he felt that way, he should write his own book.'

'And what did he say to that?'

'He told me to fuck off, if memory serves.'

'And after that, you blanked him.'

Maxine shrugged.

'There was nothing more to say. I had my view, he had his. What you've got to understand about Justin is he loved being the leader, loved getting his own way. On top of that, he loved money. So when someone else took the initiative, made some cash, culled something good from what was an extremely shitty experience, well, he didn't like that.'

'So it wasn't what you said in the book that worried him?'

'I'm not sure he'd even read it, to be honest. For him it was about the fact that I was getting all the attention, and, yes, the cash, from the book. He wanted his slice.'

'And how did he take your refusal to play ball?'

'He wasn't happy, but what could he do?'

Once again, Charlie spotted the strength – the steel – that lay behind Pryce's attractive demeanour. Like Lanning, she'd managed to survive her ordeal, growing up to become an articulate, successful young adult. Whatever ties of loyalty she felt towards Lanning, she was clearly not going to be bullied by him or let his protestations knock her off course. She was determined to own her success, come what may.

Which made Charlie wonder about the root causes of Lanning's brutal murder. On the face of it, it seemed unlikely that Pryce would go to extreme measures to protect her hard-won prize, but there was clearly a lot at stake. Pryce had signed a lucrative two-book deal – she was rumoured to be working on the sequel right now – and had already had much copy and airtime in the nation's media outlets. She had taken possession of the group's ordeal to the exclusion of the others, perhaps, none of whom had been heard from recently. Had this caused resentment? Anger? Alienation even? It was impossible to tell yet, but as Charlie concluded their interview, she was left to wonder if Pryce's book – and just as importantly the money associated with it – had played an important part in Lanning's death.

Tragedy was a valuable commodity these days.

Extract from One Dark Night *by Maxine Pryce*

I can't remember when we lost sight of them. Up until late afternoon we had been keeping up a brisk pace, determined not to
let ourselves – or our school – down. None of us would admit
it, but there was a definite sense of competition with the other
groups, many of whom came from fee-paying schools. We, the
rough and ready Southampton comprehensive, were going to
show those chinless wonders that we could hack it, that we
were hardier than them. Justin in particular seemed energized by
this idea – his brother had earned his Duke of Edinburgh Gold
Award two years earlier, bringing his team home safe and well.
Perhaps Justin wanted to get one over on his brother, perhaps
he just wanted to impress the girls with his leadership qualities.
We were all in love with him back then, little realizing we were
wasting our time.

We'd been tracking the group ahead of us all day – not
purposely, it was just the way things worked out. We all had
slightly different routes, yet somehow whenever we crested a
hill, there they were, in their distinctive purple raincoats, doggedly
maintaining a lead of half a mile or so. We wondered whether
purple was their school colour, entertaining ourselves by inventing
all manner of obscene mottos for our well-heeled competitors. It
was good fun and despite the blisters, fatigue and plummeting
temperatures, we were happy – a small group of schoolfriends
battling the elements on the South Downs.

Justin, the leader, me the organizer, Callum the joker, Rachel
all laughter and profanity and capable Fran, who was basically
good at everything. We were making a decent fist of it too, more

than holding our own against our more 'illustrious' competitors, but as night fell things started to go wrong. Rachel, who'd been a late addition to the group, had been doing well, matching the brisk pace Justin set, but her concentration must have wavered for a second. Or perhaps it was fatigue. Either way, she missed a rabbit hole and stuck her foot right down it, spraining her ankle badly.

'Jesus Christ. Jesus effing Christ...'

Rachel had a colourful way of expressing herself and was cursing vigorously, clutching her injured foot. Concerned, we crowded round her, wanting to offer what help we could. She put a brave face on things, as she always did, but it was clear she was in serious pain. We would have to rethink our plans.

'Sorry, guys. I know you wanted to stick with them others...'

We were all a bit disappointed, but there was no point grousing about it. We were a team. We would just have to adapt, make a new plan.

Disaster Number Two followed soon afterwards. Callum got the map out – our sole map – to work out where we might camp nearby. But his timing was off, a large gust of wind ripping the map from his grip and, before we could react, it was beyond our grasp, dancing over the moorland and away into the distance.

It's hard to describe how crushed we felt at that point. We weren't in any immediate danger – we had tents, provisions – but night was approaching and suddenly we had no means of navigating our way. Would we have to abandon our attempt to complete the challenge? Summon help? We pulled our phones from our packs, but there was nothing – no signal, no 3G, no way of pulling up a map or contacting the outside world.

A lengthy discussion followed, before Justin made the decision. We'd press on, stick to the original plan, trying to make it to our scheduled stopping point. The tor that we'd planned to camp by was pretty distinctive and easily visible from afar and, though it would be tough for Rachel, we would take it in turns to support her. If we were lucky, if the gods were on our side, we could still make it there before nightfall, then figure out what to do.

The gods were not on our side. If I could turn the clock back, change one thing about my life – about all our lives – it would be that moment. I would insist that we stay put, set up tent and see the night out. So much pain, so much misery, so much tragedy could have been avoided, if we'd just stayed where we were and given up on our ambition to complete the exercise.

But instead we ploughed on, making faltering progress over the uneven ground. Conversation tailed off, to be replaced by sullen silence and the occasional grimace or sigh. Ironically, this was the best it was going to get for us on the night that would change our lives forever.

You could almost sense the fog before you saw it. There was a leaden, damp heaviness in the air that seemed to wrap itself around you, chilling you to the bone. Then we spotted the first wisps, gossamer-thin slivers of vapour, dancing in the air like a spell from a Hogwarts wand. Little was said at this point, though I saw Fran and Callum exchange nervous glances. They were proper outdoor types and knew what to expect. Predictably, we were soon swathed in a thick blanket. Which was when panic really set in.

The girls – myself included – were distressed, whereas the boys just looked pale, which was worse. A couple of feeble jokes were attempted, but the seriousness of the situation was plain to all. We were utterly surrounded by the dense fog, wrapped up tight like a Christmas present, barely able to see our feet, uncertain where – or on what – we were treading.

'I feel like I'm standing in a swamp . . .' Fran complained, surveying her sodden boots.

59

'Any second now, I'm going to do the other foot...' Rachel warned, hobbling on through the pain.

They were right. We should have stopped there and then. But the ground was saturated and there was no obvious point of sanctuary. So, we kept going as best we could. We had our compasses, knew roughly which direction to head in, and besides, if we kept moving, we might keep warm. In truth, I suspect we were putting off making a decision, because no one really knew what to do. We prided ourselves on being mature sixth-formers, full of bravado, but in reality, we were just kids.

Who started crying first? Me? Fran? Rachel? I don't recall, but I do remember that our mood was soon black. We stuck rigidly to our compass direction, but kept encountering serious obstacles – gullies, streams, steep, slippery slopes. With each setback, morale plummeted further; none of these obstacles had been marked on our prescribed route, so carefully detailed on our missing map. Conversation ceased entirely, everyone depressed and locked in their own dark thoughts, most of which – if I'm honest – were focused on Callum's stupidity in losing the map. Slowly, the mood was shifting. Justin had been keen to press on – and his arguments had made sense at the time – but now you could sense people's reluctance to keep going, the pace slowing with every passing minute.

'Come on, guys. We can't be far away...'

'Fuck's sake, Justin. We can't even see our noses, how can you possibly know where we are...?'

It was Rachel who'd spoken. Direct as always.

'Even so, I'm sure if we—'

'We should stop. Wait for the fog to lift. I can hardly walk another step as it is.'

'It's freezing fog,' Justin countered. 'We're not equipped to be out in it. We need to find higher ground, like we agreed—'

'So where *is* this higher ground? We've been on the flat for ages,' Fran interrupted, taking up the fight.

'It should be just up ahead. I'm pretty sure it's just up ahead.'

'Well that's fucking marvellous, isn't it?'

'Shut up, guys. I think I see something.'

It was Callum who'd spoken. We turned to follow his gaze, assuming that he was hallucinating – there was nothing here but thick, all-consuming fog. But then we glimpsed it, a pinprick of light, shifting in and out of sight.

'Is it a torch?'

'Yes, I think it is a torch, it's moving...'

Silence, as we all strained to see more clearly.

'No, it's not moving,' Rachel intervened, her voice suddenly high-pitched and excited. 'The fog is moving, but the light isn't.'

She was right. What was it then? A vehicle perhaps? There *were* tracks up on the Downs. Or a dwelling of some kind? A silent decision was made and we hurried towards the light, certain that it could only mean good things. In less than five minutes, we were there, amazed by the apparition before us. It was a farmhouse, a tumbledown farmhouse in the middle of nowhere. The light that we'd seen came from inside, a lantern illuminating the kitchen window.

Justin didn't hesitate, marching straight up to it and rapping on the front door. Immediately, a chorus of barking started up inside, which gave a few of us pause for thought, but now that we were here, Justin was intent on leading us to safety. The door remained resolutely closed, however – we could hear the dogs barking, but no movement within, no sign of any human presence. Then, softly at first, we heard them. Muffled footsteps approaching.

Now the door creaked open and a man appeared in the

doorway. He was peering at us suspiciously, even as two Dobermanns appeared at his feet.

'Yes?'

He was young and handsome in an odd way, like a youthful Joaquin Phoenix. His eyes flitted between us and he seemed nervous, his voice wavering slightly as he spoke. Justin quickly outlined our predicament, asking if we might take shelter with him until the fog lifted. The man seemed unsure, as if scenting deception, even danger, so Justin offered to pay – for food, drink, anything he could offer – and that seemed to decide things.

'You'd ... you'd better come in, then.'

He stepped aside and one by one we trooped in, our new friend waiting until we were all past, before shutting the door firmly behind us. We were all so grateful to be inside – out of the dark, out of the fog, out of the cold – that we could have cried.

We had no idea then that we'd just entered the lion's den.

Chapter 14

Justin Lanning lay on the metal slab, covered below the waist by a thin white sheet. Helen knew what to expect – she'd haunted the mortuary for over ten years now – but still the stark sight in front of her hit home. By all accounts, Lanning had been a vital, successful young man, buzzing with entrepreneurial energy and youthful zeal. Now he was a pallid corpse, lifeless and grey, save for the livid ring of bruising around his neck.

'Asphyxiation due to ligature strangulation.'

The gruff voice made Helen turn. Head pathologist Jim Grieves was lumbering towards her, anxious as ever to dispense with formalities.

'But I guess you already knew that…' Grieves continued, a wry smile appearing, then vanishing, on his lips.

Helen smiled back; she could never resist Grieves's odd mixture of persistent irritation and curmudgeonly good humour.

'Pretty much. Any idea how it happened? What was used?'

'I'd suggest it was probably a two-stage process,' Grieves replied quickly, taking his place beside the body. 'He was disabled first, then killed.'

Helen turned to him, surprised.

'He was assaulted, you mean? Knocked unconscious?'

She gestured to the bruising on Lanning's cheeks and fore-head.

'No, they're just impact injuries, probably sustained in the car or elsewhere. There's no dirt or dust in the cuts.'

'So he was drugged then...?'

Grieves smiled, pleased to have Helen at a disadvantage. Then he pointed to the right side of Lanning's neck, where the skin had a blueish yellow mark on it.

'The bruising's not dark enough for a chokehold,' Helen said, leaning in to the body.

'Look closer...'

Helen obliged and now she spotted puncture marks at the centre of the bruise.

'He was injected with something?'

But even as she said it, she knew she was wrong. There were *two* tiny puncture marks side by side.

'He was *tasered*...' she continued, unable to conceal her surprise.

'That would be my guess,' Grieves confirmed. 'The spacing of the puncture marks makes it highly likely.'

Helen thought back to the crash site. The tyre markings sug-gested the car had come to an abrupt halt, the drag patterns on the ground outside the vehicle, the bootprints, the fact that Lanning's suit had been coated in dust.

'So maybe the car braked sharply, then Lanning was dragged from it, disabled with a taser...'

'Quite possibly. If he *was* successfully tasered, then he would have been in no state to resist further attack.'

Helen nodded, her expression grim. Tasers disabled their victims for over ten minutes, during which you had very little control of your limbs or your faculties. The idea of someone in such a vulnerable state being slowly, deliberately, strangled was awful to imagine.

'Any idea what was used during the second stage of the attack?'

'Hard to say,' Grieves responded ruefully. 'We can tell it was ligature strangulation because of the neatness and uniformity of the bruising and the comprehensive nature of the compression – the entire circumference of the neck was affected, as if something had been looped round then tightened. Very different to manual strangulation...'

'But whatever was used must have been very thin,' Helen responded, gesturing to the narrow red line that ran down the centre of the bruising.

'Normally with ligature strangulation, the article used is something readily to hand, a scarf, a belt, an item of the victim's clothing like tights or a bra...'

'But this is what? A garrotte of some kind?'

'Probably not, that would have cut deeper, perhaps even severed the windpipe, but it *is* wire of some kind.'

Helen digested this calmly, but her stomach tightened.

'I can do more tests, see if I can ascertain what type of metal it was, but that's all I've got for now.'

'Any defensive wounds? Any skin cells under the nails? Any clothing fibres?'

'You'll have to talk to Meredith about his clothes, I've sent them all to her. But I haven't found anything suggesting any kind of struggle. By the looks of things, he was taken by surprise, with little chance to react before he was murdered...'

This fitted with Helen's own conclusions, but was hardly cheering. The killer had been swift and precise, Lanning standing little chance of saving himself from this savage attack. That was perhaps a blessing, as he wouldn't have suffered, but it made Lanning's death all the more macabre. The killer had apparently made the threatening call, before calmly driving Lanning out to a remote site of his choosing to murder him. Such self-possession, such assuredness – all these appeared on the face of it to be the hallmarks of a determined, experienced killer.

'I'll let you know as soon as I have anything more.'

Grieves had already turned away to continue his examination. Thanking him, Helen left the mortuary, a dozen conflicting thoughts tumbling through her mind. The sophisticated, methodical nature of the execution seemed to run counter to the possibility that Daniel King might somehow be involved ... yet it *was* possible that he had struck subsequently in the intervening years, honing his skills. The taser was also an odd addition. Police officers and security guards frequently used them, but then so did all manner of criminals and lowlives – Border Force had recently confiscated three crates of them from a Dutch cargo vessel docked at Southampton. Of course, it was perfectly possible that whoever was responsible just felt such a precaution was necessary to subdue Lanning, no longer a callow adolescent but an athletic gym-toned young man, but it was an intriguing detail nevertheless.

The truth was that none of this would necessarily have set alarm bells ringing were it not for the use of the wire. It had been impossible to tell what horrors Rachel Wood endured before her death, her body consumed by the farmhouse inferno, but what *was* clear – both from the victims King targeted on country lanes *and* the unfortunate troupe of schoolchildren – was that he'd used a loop of galvanized farming wire to attack his victims, wrapping it round their necks and pulling it tight as they struggled for breath. The choice of weapon could be a coincidence but, given Lanning's history, it seemed unlikely.

Helen was almost out of the building when her phone rang. She answered it quickly and was pleased to hear DC Bentham's voice on the other end. Bentham was a diligent, determined officer and Helen detected a hint of excitement in his voice.

'I'm with the team in Wickham. They've turned up some interesting anecdotal evidence from neighbours and I've just taken a call from Lanning's bank which might be significant.'

'Go on.'

'His partner withdrew twenty thousand pounds *in cash* from a joint savings account three days ago. It doesn't fit with his normal spending practices; neither Lanning nor Cannon had made a withdrawal from that account in *months...*'

'And?' Helen replied, sensing there was more coming.

'I spoke to the bank where the withdrawal was made. A restriction had been put on the account recently, ensuring that *both* account holders had to be present when withdrawals were made, but in this instance Cannon managed to sweet-talk an inexperienced employee into coughing up, spinning her a sob story that his boyfriend was stuck in hospital and was in urgent need of funds...'

Helen suddenly felt herself relax. It wasn't a definitive break-through, but it *was* an important lead and a timely reminder not to get ahead of herself. There was no point imagining phantoms, it was *evidence* that would lead her to the truth.

Thanking Bentham, Helen rang off, pushing through the doors and out into the sunlight.

Chapter 15

'I don't know why you're so interested. It was a simple with-drawal...'

'For a very large amount.'

'It's *our* money. What we do with it is nobody's concern but our own.'

'Not in this case. So can you tell me what it was for?'

Helen watched Adam Cannon as he paced the room, his leather loafers sliding across the polished wood. He was distracted and agitated, clearly debating how much to share and how much to hold back.

'Look... a few months back, I had some issues as a result of... of gambling. I got in a little over my head and had to use part of our savings to clear my debts.'

'Is that why there's a double lock on your account?'

Cannon looked up sharply. Having voluntarily agreed to meet Helen, he was now concerned by the extent to which she had penetrated his private life.

'The savings were for our wedding. Justin... Justin wasn't happy about what I'd done, which is why I moved out for a couple of weeks.'

'And your recent arguments?'

Another darted look towards Helen.

'Justin was heard shouting the house down last week. Your neighbours were going to come and say something, to see if everyone was all right, but then the argument suddenly stopped, so...'

Helen could tell that Cannon was tempted to swear under his breath. Exhaling slowly, he replied: 'Recently... I had a bit of a relapse. With the gambling...'

'How much are you in for?'

Cannon couldn't bring himself to look at Helen, as he replied, '£50,000, give or take...'

Helen omitted a low whistle.

'I didn't mean to get in so deep, of course I didn't, but... being down here, in Southampton, I mean... Well, it never quite worked for me. Justin never saw it that way – he always talked about the *choices* we have – but I'm not sure he ever understood how I felt. How *bored* I was in this bloody place.'

Helen should have been surprised by this, but somehow this perfectly quiet house, in its perfectly quiet rural isolation, did seem oddly lifeless, even a touch suffocating.

'I gave up a good job in London to move here. I set up on my own, but I couldn't get enough clients, so I was left *here*... A house husband and dog walker...'

He shot a dark look at Caspar, who ignored him.

'I was bored. Bored out of my tiny mind, so I did whatever made me feel a bit more alive.'

'But how did you rack up new debts so quickly?'

'Justin had spoken to all the local bookmakers and plenty more in Southampton. That, and my bad credit history, put paid to most outlets...'

'So you gambled with black market bookmakers?'

Cannon nodded.

'I'm assuming Justin discovered you'd fallen off the wagon?'

'One of the people I owed money to came here. Justin answered the door.'

'When was this?'

'A week ago.'

'So your relationship was in trouble then ...'

'We were having our difficulties.'

'Had he threatened to call off the marriage?'

'We'd discussed it.'

'Had he asked you to leave?'

'No!'

'But you must have feared it?'

Cannon's silence spoke volumes.

'How much money is in that savings account?'

'Five hundred thousand, give or take. Justin had been doing well...'

'And this place is worth, what, the best part of a million?'

'I guess so ...'

'And am I right in assuming that you are Justin's next of kin?'

'Piss off.'

The words were launched at her.

'But you can see my thinking?' Helen continued. 'Your relationship is foundering because of your gambling. You could be kicked out on the street, left to face your creditors alone. But with Justin gone, your debts are cleared—'

'That's an outrageous thing to suggest. I would *never* have harmed Justin.'

'Yet you betrayed his trust *repeatedly*. And a few days before his death you withdraw twenty thousand pounds without his knowledge or consent.'

'It was just to keep my creditors at bay. They'd threatened me.'

'But surely it would have made better financial sense to pay someone to murder Justin? That way all your problems would have been solved. Twenty grand would certainly cover an attack of that ki—'

'No, no, no, a thousand times, no.'

'Then what happened to him?'

'I don't know …'

His tone was anguished, but there was anger there too.

'Yes, I was a rubbish boyfriend – a rubbish human being – at times. But I am *not* a killer. I would never do anything like that and every second you spend accusing me is time wasted, time which could be spent tracking down his real killers.'

'Killers?' Helen asked.

'Come on, Inspector,' Cannon shot back. 'This wasn't a madman … or someone after revenge. This was to do with his work. It was a hit, you must see that?'

'Because?'

'Because his actions cost people millions of dollars, he had enemies in numerous countries …'

'But you told my colleague that there weren't any specific threats that you knew of?'

'Exactly, that I *knew* of. Doesn't mean they weren't there – Justin seldom talked to me about his work, said it was safer that way.'

He was talking nineteen to the dozen now, but whether this was borne of conviction or desperation, Helen wasn't sure.

'He worked in a world full of fixers, crooks, middlemen. If he helped one outfit thrive, then other people would miss out, people who wouldn't take kindly to being denied a fortune they felt was *rightfully* theirs.'

'That might all be true, Adam. But we have no evidence of a specific threat—'

'Then look harder. And look around you.'

Cannon gestured to the ceiling and Helen now noticed that

there were small cameras, tucked away up high in the corners, discreetly covering every room.

'Justin took his security *very* seriously. For one reason and one reason alone: he worked in a dangerous business, a business in which people would *kill*. On a couple of occasions, people have tried to gain access to this place. No one else in the village has had any trouble like that, so why Justin? Why us?'

Cannon stopped now, his manic performance robbing him of breath. Helen looked up at him carefully, weighing up his words.

'Do you have CCTV everywhere?'

'In every room and at several points around the perimeter of the property.'

Helen paused, then looked directly at Adam Cannon.

'Then we'd better take a look.'

Chapter 16

It nestled in the centre of the screen, demanding his attention. The car was moving fast, bumping over the rough ground, making it hard to focus on the fuzzy image, but Joseph kept his attention riveted to it, convinced they had unearthed their first concrete lead in this strange case.

On leaving the incident room, he'd joined up with officers from the tech team, initiating the hunt for the missing Mercedes. The motive for Lanning's murder was still shrouded in mystery, meaning that the missing vehicle remained their best lead. There might be DNA or fingerprints inside, whilst the car's navigational system might furnish them with valuable information about where the killer had been before the car was dumped.

Taking the building site as their starting point, Joseph and the team had pored over the local area, identifying every road, track and byway, every forest, lake, quarry or fly-tipping site that might have offered an opportunity for disposal. They had employed all the drones they had, half a dozen all-seeing insects winging their way through the sky, beaming their images back to the control consoles. All means necessary would be employed to find the missing Mercedes.

The search had been long and fruitless, revealing abandoned shopping trolleys and a handful of bicycles. It was possible that the killer still had the vehicle, though Joseph doubted it, given the efficiency of Lanning's murder. Finally, after three hours of gruelling searching, they got a break. In a dense area of woodland north of Shedfield, Joseph made out a shape – a large, dark shape. Keeping the drone at a safe distance above the trees, he'd zoomed in, his heart beating fast as the distinctive form of a Mercedes saloon filled the screen. Most abandoned cars were Fiestas and Corsas, lifted by joyriders before being dumped in the countryside. The car on his screen was no hatchback; however, it was powerful, sleek and long. Moreover, it was in an area of woodland that was just five miles from the crime scene.

The pool car slowed, pulling up on the track at the edge of the wood. DC Roberts was driving, while Joseph flicked his eyes between the screen and the woodland beyond. Just above the treetops, he could see the drone dancing in the wind, drawing him towards their prize.

'Hold it in position,' Joseph said, handing the console to Roberts. 'I'll call you if I need directions.'

Roberts took the console from him. Joseph wasn't part of the tech team and was glad that babysitting drones wasn't the limit of his remit. Moving away from the car, Joseph cut through the long grass, his eyes scanning for signs of disturbance – flattened grass, discarded items, footprints – but he could see nothing of interest. The ground here was muddy and cloying but still he kept up a swift pace. Reaching the fringes of the wood, he took a breath and pushed inside.

The truth was that this wasn't any ordinary investigation for him. He'd tried to pretend it was, but knew he was kidding himself. It had been six months since the conclusion of their last big case and since then he'd been kicking his heels, cursing the tedious parade of domestics and street stabbings that had landed on his desk. Only a fool would fail to close those cases – there was little chance for a detective to shine, to show what he was made of.

Joseph was deeper in the woodland now, his eyes darting here and there, searching for the dark form. He could hear the drone above, so he must be close, but where was it? On he went, cresting fallen logs and ducking low branches. Momentarily it reminded him of his adventures with Helen in the New Forest, when they were hunting a vicious killer together and anything seemed possible. Since then, there had been definite highs, not least his burgeoning relationship with Helen, but nothing that relieved him of his sense of frustration and shame.

That investigation had been a disaster for him. Yes, he had played his part as a team member in the successful conclusion, but he had also let himself down publicly. He had failed to help Helen in that final, terrifying confrontation, but worse – much worse – he had been bested by a suspect and would perhaps have died at his hands, were it not for Helen's intervention. She was his superior officer, more experienced in tackling vicious killers, but still his shame burnt at the memory of having to be rescued by her. He was certain other members of the team talked about it, principally because they all seemed intent on pretending it never happened.

This investigation would be different. As soon as he'd laid eyes on the brutalized corpse at the building site, he'd sensed that this case would be an opportunity for him to show his mettle. Or was it? Scanning the thickets that surrounded him, he'd expected the missing car to come into view, but still it remained hidden. Where the hell was it? The drone couldn't be wrong, it must be virtually under his feet...

Now he spotted it. A small glint of metal in the middle distance. Craning his neck round the thick foliage in front of him, he made out first the contour of bumper, then the body of the car itself. Now he didn't delay, skirting the edge of the bushes as he hurried through the woodland. He moved speedily but stealthily – it wasn't impossible the killer was nearby – sliding his baton from his belt, just in case of surprises.

He was thirty feet from it and closing fast. He could see no signs of movement, but still he kept alert. Twenty feet, now ten, then finally Joseph burst into the small clearing. The Mercedes, which appeared to have got there via a scrubby track at the far side of the forest, was definitely the car they were looking for, its damaged number plate still partially visible. But that was all that Joseph could make out, for the car had been completely burnt out. The chassis was buckled and battered, the windows shattered, even the boot yawned open, blackened and charred inside. It was a thorough job – the tang of petrol still sharp in the air.

Joseph slumped, sickened by the sight in front of him. He had dreamed of affirmation – of redemption – through his work on this case, but in this scorched clearing, those fond hopes had just been reduced to ashes.

Chapter 17

She stared at the screen, drinking in the details. Helen was cloistered away in the boot room at Lanning's house, sitting cheek by jowl with Adam Cannon in front of the flickering CCTV monitor. They'd been at their task for over an hour and had spotted nothing of interest, no unwelcome presence inside or outside the house, save for the fleeting appearance of a fox.

The room was close, the atmosphere uncomfortable. Helen maintained a healthy suspicion of Cannon, the only person currently who stood to gain from Lanning's death, and her host knew it. He said nothing, sitting quietly, rigidly, by her side, as Helen spooled back through hour after hour of footage. Occasionally, Cannon would sigh or look away as an image of his dead lover sprang up on screen. Most of these snapshots were innocent – Lanning eating his breakfast, talking on the phone, working in his study – some were more intriguing. On a number of occasions the arguments between Lanning and Cannon had been sustained, occasionally even aggressive, Lanning grabbing Cannon by the lapels at one point, shoving him forcefully towards the front door. When this scene of domestic drama played out, in staccato black and white images, Cannon dropped his head, staring at the floor. Whether this was out of a desire to hide his distress or to conceal something else, Helen wasn't sure.

She spooled on, her eyes drifting between one screen show-ing the interior feeds, and another covering the exterior of the property. The latter was potentially more useful, if Cannon was telling the truth about their property having been targeted previ-ously, but it was harder to focus on, especially at night when the darkened garden offered little for the eye to engage with.

'Look, I don't want to hurry you, but I need to head down to the solicitor's today. There's a lot to sort out…'

'I'll keep going a little longer,' Helen replied, politely. 'If you need to get off, feel free. I can secure the house on my way ou—'

'I'll stay.'

Helen resumed her surveillance. The small-change of their existence continued to play out – groceries being unloaded, meals shared, even moments of the two men in repose, snuggling into each other as they watched TV. Reaching forward, Helen sped up the flow of images. She had taken it slow to begin with, keen to gauge the rhythm of Lanning's day-to-day life, but these recordings went back weeks – she could spend days locked away in this tiny room.

Now the figures sprang to life, scurrying in and out of rooms in comic fashion, going about their business at quadruple speed. The contrast was strange – the lifeless dark of the exterior feed and the manic energy of the interior cameras – but now Helen spotted a change in the dynamic. Now there *was* movement outside. Punching the controls, Helen rewound the exterior feed, before setting them in motion once more, now in real time.

She glanced at the info line at the bottom, which gave date and time. It was 28th September, over three weeks ago now, and the time was 11 p.m. A figure, dark and indistinct, was moving steadily towards the house. He was lean and tall – Helen meas-uring his stature by the full-length statue he passed – and he seemed intent on his task.

Pausing the footage, she turned to Adam. He looked pale, frightened even.

'Where were you on the evening of twenty-eighth of September?'

Cannon shot a look at the info bar on the screen, then pulled his phone from his pocket, anxiously scrolling back through his calendar.

'I was in London with friends, at a restaurant in Covent Garden.'

'And Justin?'

'He ... he was at a gig. At the Joiners.'

Helen hit play once more. It was true that the figure didn't resemble Lanning, he was too slight to be the gym-toned executive. Moving in closer, Helen took in the intruder. He was dressed in black, with a dark beanie hat on top of his head. He appeared to be Caucasian, a flash of skin occasionally visible through the gloom, but beyond that it was hard to say. What was clear, however, was that he intended to gain access to the property. He had reached the rear of the house now and was proceeding with greater caution, creeping up to the back window and peering inside. Satisfied that the property was empty, he set to work on the rear door, testing the handle, before pulling a crowbar from his jacket.

Now he came unstuck. As he raised the crowbar to force it into the door jamb, he triggered one of the security sensors. Immediately, the wall-mounted lights sprang on, illuminating the intruder. Startled, the figure looked up, frozen for a minute, as he stared up towards the camera. A moment's indecision, then he turned and fled, eventually vanishing into the gloom.

Helen hit rewind again, the figure running backwards across the garden, before coming to a halt at the back door once more. Carefully Helen teased the footage forwards, pausing it as the intruder stared up at them. It wasn't a perfect image – the tech team would have to clean it up – but it *was* their first concrete lead, an unsettling image of an attempted home invasion. Was this gaunt figure their man? Had he deliberately targeted the property that night, knowing Lanning's lover would be away? And, having failed to gained access to Lanning's home – for the purposes of ambush, murder? – had he then targeted him at his office?

Was Helen looking at the face of a killer?

Chapter 18

He stood stock-still, barely able to breathe. It was as if his world had suddenly collapsed, as if all he was capable of doing was listening to the words that filled his tiny kitchen, words that shook him to the core.

'Obviously, we'll bring you more on that story as soon as we have it. Now it's time to find out what the traffic is looking like...'

He switched it off, jarred by the sudden change in tone. Moments earlier the newsreader had been sober and measured, now she sounded positively ecstatic at the prospect of the traffic report. Callum couldn't bear to listen – what right did he have to be so happy, when the world had suddenly turned so dark? Who gave a damn about the traffic, when Justin had been killed? No, not killed, *murdered*.

Callum felt his legs give and he reached out, grasping the kitchen table. Easing himself down, he collapsed into the chair, a sob escaping from him. He didn't know what to do, whether to cry, whether to scream, whether to curl up in a ball on the floor. Justin, his friend, his inspiration, who'd made a far better fist of his life than *he* ever had, was dead. The details had been scant – a body had been found on a building site on the outskirts of

Southampton – and Callum hadn't really been listening anyway, until the reporter had confirmed the identity of the victim.

Justin Lanning. The words had gone through him like an electric shock. He had spoken to Justin not two weeks ago and he'd seemed full of life, as always. Now that had been snatched from him. It seemed improbable, no impossible, made weirder still by his final resting place. A building site. What the hell? If Justin was ever to run into trouble, Callum would've expected it to be a domestic – he'd never really liked or trusted Adam – so what was his old friend doing all the way out there? It was near his home, but still…

What Callum needed now was information. Propelling himself out of his chair, he hurried into the living room. Grabbing his phone, he searched for local news feeds, willing the radio station to have got it wrong. But there it was in black and white – the headline declaring that the body of local businessman Justin Lanning had been discovered that morning and that police were treating his death as suspicious, journalistic code for murder. Callum scrolled through the meagre details, before searching other local sites and then the BBC news website. But they offered nothing more than the name of the victim and the location of his discovery.

What was going on? What had happened? The desire to know pulsed through Callum – he knew there was no question of doing any work today, of honouring his afternoon appointments. He would just have to hunker down, waiting for Hannah to return home, hoping for some information – any information – about Justin's death.

Should he call Adam? No, it was too soon and besides, how could he possibly ask what he was aching to know? Calling Adam now would only in part be about expressing his profound grief. What Callum really wanted was reassurance – reassurance that this was a botched robbery or a crime of passion. What he needed was *facts*, nice solid facts proving that Justin's sudden death was in no way connected to their previous ordeal, that it was just a cruel, ironic act of God.

Callum knew he was still processing what had happened back then – his terror, his utter conviction that he would die – and the thought of it made him shudder. He had handled things less well than the others, which was a source of shame and distress, black moods descending upon him with alarming regularity, moods that even his beloved Hannah found hard to shift. But it was not past trauma, nor even depression that was laying him low now.

No, it was ignorance that was killing him today.

Chapter 19

Knowledge is power. This was a maxim Emilia lived by. If she had the facts before anyone else, then *she* would be the one to break the story. But these days knowledge was nothing without *speed* – it was how quickly you could deliver your scoop that counted. This was the core of modern journalism, when every newshound worth their salt tweeted and posted. You could no longer wait for the ten o'clock bulletin or the next print run, the story you'd unearthed had to be out there, grabbing attention. This meant processing information and delivering it swiftly, something Emilia was adept at. And she needed those skills now – Maxine Pryce's book launch was due to start in just over an hour and Emilia would have to file her copy soon if she was to make it in time. Given the day's revelations, there was no way she could miss it.

Even so, urgency was no excuse for bad copy, especially when the story was so juicy. So she took a moment to review her work. Overall, the tone of her piece was respectful and heartfelt. She had lauded Lanning's strength and courage in rebuilding his life after his teenage ordeal, focusing on all the things – the new home, marriage, perhaps even kids – that he still had to enjoy. She then switched focus to Daniel King, reminding her readers of his cruelty, his inhumanity and the continuing mystery over his fate. Only once she'd done that had she moved things on, posing the question of motive and culpability.

She'd had to judge this part carefully – she would never want the paper to be accused of being irresponsible or sensationalist, but there was no question of *underplaying* the story, especially now she'd broken the news that Lanning had been strangled. It was a question of flirting with possibilities without ever committing to unverified facts or theories. Fortunately, after many years in journalism, Emilia was a practised tease.

She'd explored the possible explanations for Lanning's murder, asking who might stand to gain, who might have an axe to grind. So far there had been no statement from the police about arrests and, by the look of his Twitter feed, Lanning's boyfriend remained at liberty, suggesting that Helen Grace and her team had no obvious suspects. This suited Emilia down the ground. She'd phrased it artfully, but she'd left her readers with one nagging thought. Given the method of the murder, given the fact that Lanning and his friends escaped King's clutches, given that their former attacker was still missing, was it possible that the key to unlocking this dreadful crime lay in the past? She wouldn't say it outright, but no one could miss her meaning.

Was it possible Daniel King returned to finish the job?

Chapter 20

After the darkness, it was time to embrace the light.

That had been Maxine Pryce's motto for several years now. It also happened to be the tagline she'd used when pitching her second book to her publishers. *The Next Chapter* would take her story on from the awful events at Manor Farm, allowing the readers a glimpse of what happened to her and the others after they'd made their daring escape.

It was a book about positivity. Her previous publication had ended with the traumatized teenagers stumbling back to civilization, this one dealt with the emotional and psychological ramifications of their experiences, but not in a grim or depressing way. It was about how it was possible to survive, even when beaten, abused and degraded. Or as she'd put in their meeting, how you could still embrace life when you've been frightened half to death.

It was an uplifting idea and Maxine had enjoyed writing it, until today at least. There had been so much interest in the run-up to her first book that initially she'd found it hard to concentrate, distracted by emails, phone calls, even hopeful journalists knocking on the door. Keen to capitalize on the apparent success of her first book, she'd complained to her agent, who'd immediately provided a solution. A friend had just headed off to New York on a six-month assignment, leaving a discreet, well-appointed, city-centre flat unoccupied.

Maxine had been using it for a few weeks now, quickly settling into a productive rhythm. Coffee brewed, mobile switched off, she would sit down early and have a couple of thousand words done by lunchtime. She would review what she'd done, honing and editing her prose until she was happy. Then she'd head to the gym, have dinner with friends or take a trip to the cinema. It was a routine she'd become comfortable with and, in idle moments, she wondered whether it might actually be worth renting the flat herself, making it her office for the next six months.

Today, however, things were not going well. Maxine felt unsettled, unable to think clearly. This was partly because of Justin's death, the timing of which was disquieting to say the least, but also because of her interview with the police. DS Brooks had been polite enough, but their conversation had left Maxine feeling vulnerable and exposed. The police officer was clearly interested in her arguments with Justin, searching perhaps for a financial motive for his murder. It was absurd – as if she would be so vicious, not to mention stupid and reckless – but the suggestion had left her feeling unnerved. Was it possible that this was a genuine line of enquiry? One that she would have to defend herself against? If so, the timing could hardly have been worse.

Rising, Maxine crossed to the galley kitchen and fired up the coffee machine. She had hurried to the flat after her conversation with Brooks, hoping that the calm atmosphere and the cathartic effects of writing might restore her equilibrium. But she couldn't settle – managing only two hundred words – which irritated her further. Perhaps she should go for a walk? Or to the gym? But would that do any good? She would probably just dwell on things. The truth was that life had been going her way of late, she was full of hope and ambition for the future, yet the events of the last twenty-four hours had shaken her badly. Now when she sat down to write her uplifting narrative, she felt fake, even misguided, sensing that there were enemies out there ranged against her, waiting to bring her down. It was irrational, an overreaction, she knew that, but it was a feeling she couldn't shake.

'Come on, girl...' she muttered to herself, as she settled herself down in front of her laptop once more. 'Five hundred words more, then you can go...'

Her fingers rested on the keys, but still she hesitated. Thoughts of Justin, of DS Brooks, tumbled over one another, clouding her mind. She was due at her book launch shortly – she wanted to arrive there feeling upbeat, able to speak with confidence about her future ambitions – but the more she tried, the more rattled and distressed she became. Perhaps, after all, it was best to forget today, chalk it down to experience and concentrate on the job in hand – selling *One Dark Night* to an expectant public.

Saving her work, Maxine snapped her laptop shut. Rising, she checked her watch – 18.59 – then scooped up her coat and bag. As she did so, however, she was startled by a loud noise behind her – a shrill cry, peeling out, then suddenly falling quiet again. Now it rose up again, ebbing and flowing rhythmically. Her heart thumping, Maxine now realized what it was – a phone trilling. Confused, she shot a look at her mobile. But it was turned off, as usual, so presumably it must be a landline. But who has a landline these days?

Slipping on her coat, Maxine prepared to leave. It was a short walk from here to Waterstones and she would be on time if she set off now. Still the phone continued to ring, but Maxine didn't linger – surely the answer service would click in at some point.

Her heels, bought for tonight, made a satisfying click-clack on the solid wood floor as she made her way to the door, grasping the handle gratefully, suddenly keen to escape, to grab some fresh air before the evening's duties. But, as she pulled the door open, she paused.

The phone was still ringing, harsh and insistent, demanding her attention. She probably should leave it, it could hardly be for her. Yet the caller clearly was very keen to get through and the one person who *did* have this phone number was her agent. Barbara knew Maxine always had her mobile off when she worked, so was it possible that it was her trying to get in touch? Had there been a last-minute change of timings for tonight? Maybe she had news of a new deal, perhaps even some foreign sales?

Marching across the room, Maxine spotted the wall-mounted phone and plucked it off the receiver.

'Hello?'

She was met with silence. Irritated, she tried again.

'Hello?'

'Hello, Maxine.'

It was a man's voice. She'd been expecting her agent, but was taken aback by the soft, lisping whisper.

'Who is this?'

He didn't reply, but she could hear him breathing.

'How did you get this number?'

There was another long pause and Maxine was about to hang up, when finally the man spoke again, his measured words taking her breath away.

'You have one hour to live.'

Chapter 21

'Do you recognize him?'

Helen leaned in closer, peering at the ghostly face on the screen. Charlie's question hung in the air, but Helen took her time, examining the features closely. Alice Wright, a leading light in their tech team and expert in digital enhancement, had spent the past hour manipulating contrast, reducing glare, magnifying and refocusing the image, with the result that they now had a decent shot of their intruder. Rangy and slender, unshaven, with high cheekbones and a gaunt, haunting expression, he stared out at Helen, caught in perpetual surprise as he looked up at the camera.

'I don't think it's King …'

She turned to Charlie and Joseph, soliciting their opinion. Alice dropped her gaze, wanting to be an invisible presence amongst the detectives.

'The face is too thin …' Charlie murmured.

'He might have lost weight, I suppose. It's been a long time …'

'Even so, the shape of his face doesn't look right …'

'And look there,' Joseph piped up.

He tapped the screen, gesturing this time not at the man's face, but at his left hand, which could be glimpsed in the darkness, hanging by his side.

'I'm counting five fingers. Can you see five?'

Helen resumed her scrutiny. She knew exactly what Joseph was referring to – one of King's oddities was the fact that he only had four fingers on his left hand, the legacy of a childhood accident on the farm. It was hard to see precisely on the monitor, as the fingers were bunched together, but the overall size and shape of the hand did suggest that there was nothing missing, that there *was* a sliver of flesh next to the man's ring finger. Helen felt instant relief – she had never really believed Lanning's attacker was King – but even so it felt good to rule him out at this early stage. Gathering herself, she continued: 'So, who is it?'

The trio leaned forward again, searching the man's features for clues.

'I've never come across him,' Joseph breathed, sounding a little deflated.

'Me neither,' Charlie concurred.

'Can we run it through the system?' Helen asked, turning to Alice.

'There's not enough detail for facial recognition, I've already tried. And there's no one I've seen recently who fits the bill. I did run a check for anyone who's been convicted or charged with this kind of attack – strangulation with a wire, garrotte or such like ...'

'And?'

'Nothing, I'm afraid. If you want knives, baseball bats, bricks, that's a different matter. But this is a very specific MO ...'

'Which tells us what?'

Helen's question was directed at everyone, but Alice immediately withdrew. Her job was to assist with analysis of the evidence, not to offer theories.

'Could be coincidence,' Joseph offered, but even he didn't

sound convinced. 'Or it could have been deliberately staged to mask the identity of the real killer?'

'Or it could be a copycat killing?'

It was offered tentatively, but Charlie's suggestion hit home. Helen presumed, like 99 per cent of her colleagues, that King *had* taken his own life after the schoolchildren's escape, torching the family home before throwing himself off Butler's Point. The fact that his body hadn't been found meant nothing – many corpses failed to wash up, disappearing forever in the Channel – and Helen was disinclined to believe the hoaxes and conspiracy theories. She was, however, troubled by the method of Lanning's death – right from the start she'd wondered if someone might be deliberately trying to ape, even recreate, King's crimes, though as yet she hadn't voiced this out loud. Charlie, so often her sounding board, had now done it for her.

'To what end?'

'Notoriety,' Charlie responded simply. 'King's famous, a phantom killer. Maybe whoever did this wants to make us think he's returned…'

'Or perhaps they want to outdo him?'

Joseph's offering was not a comforting one, but nor could it be discounted. In an age that revelled in true crime, where podcasts and documentaries on killers and their victims were common, the theory of copycats could not be ignored. It was surely not beyond the realms of possibility that someone had become so obsessed with King – with the *idea* of King – that the lines between fantasy and reality had become blurred.

'You could check out fan sites and murder forums,' Alice offered now, 'but to be honest most of the scary stuff is on the dark web and that'll take you a long time to penetrate.'

'Do we have anything else?' Helen countered, trying her best to sound upbeat.

'Not really,' Alice responded, with an apologetic shrug. 'That's the clearest facial image we have. Your best bet is probably to share it with the public, see if it jogs anyone's memory.'

'And there's nothing in the rest of the footage?'

'Nothing that stands out...'

Alice resumed typing and the image on her iMac now changed, the man's face disappearing to be replaced by a wider shot of the intruder gaining entry. As she punched play, the intruder resumed his activities, trying to gain entry to the house, before fleeing the attention of the security lights.

'He tries, he fails, he does a bunk,' Alice continued. 'A minute or so later, he departs in a vehicle of some kind.'

On the edges of the frame, the far end of Lanning's garden was briefly illuminated by twin beams of light, before they moved off, leaving the lawn in darkness once more.

'Is the vehicle picked up on any of the other cameras?'

Alice shook her head, dashing their hopes.

'The best we've got is this...'

She paused one file, then pulled up another. This time the file showed footage from the security camera at the front of the house. Immediately, it was apparent that the camera's eye was pointed firmly down – at the front steps, the pathway, the pond in the front garden – rather than at the road.

'You see the headlights as the vehicle goes past, then...'

The lights disappeared from view, a fleeting footprint of the intruder, then darkness, the still calm of an autumn evening in the sleepy village.

'Play it again...' Helen said.

Alice obliged. The quartet took in the footage, wishing they could crane round the limits of the camera's viewpoint to gain a view of the departing vehicle, but it was hopeless.

'Again...'

Helen saw Charlie shoot her a look, as if questioning the wisdom of repeat viewings, but Helen ignored her. And this time, her persistence was rewarded.

'There.'

Alice froze the footage.

'Back a bit, slowly now...'

Alice did as she was asked, winding back the footage frame by frame.

'Stop.'

As soon as she did so, the others saw it too. Something small and indistinct reflected in the pond at the front of the garden.

'Can you go in closer?'

Alice obliged and now the reflection became larger, clearer. It was the back of the departing van, caught as it sped away. Because of the angle, it wasn't a perfect image, but the rear bumper of the vehicle was partially visible, as were the last three characters of the number plate – VZL.

'What is that? A Ford?' Alice asked.

'No,' Joseph countered. 'It's a Vauxhall Vivaro. You can tell by the way the bumper juts out.'

'Then we need to check out all Vivaros, registered locally, with those letters on the plate.'

They had all risen, excitement – hope – pulsing through them.

'Well? What are you waiting for?'

Joseph and Charlie hurried off. Helen paused to thank Alice, asking her to print off copies of the partial plate, before heading back to the incident room. Once more, Helen felt that familiar buzz, the feeling that always accompanied a new lead. It wasn't much, but it was something.

Something that might lead them directly to Justin Lanning's killer.

Chapter 22

She had chosen her vantage point with care. From her position in front of the Self-Help section, Emilia had a clear view of the doorway but, shielded by the bulky bookcase, was not herself visible. She could loiter here undetected, hidden from the staff and hopefully from Maxine herself.

The fans, journalists and gawpers had been traipsing in for half an hour now. Some paused to chat to the manager or investigate the displays, but most headed into the store, towards the chairs laid out in readiness for the star attraction. Many had arrived early in the hope of finding space in the front row, keen to be within touching distance of the woman of the hour – even now the rows were filling up with excited groups of readers. But Emilia had taken a different tack, preferring to stick close to the entrance.

Having finished her article, she'd raced over to Waterstones, intent on gauging the lie of the land. Some writers had publicists, agents and editors in tow at these events, a dedicated support team who would quickly become a protective phalanx, if someone unpalatable intruded on proceedings. Emilia often found herself in that category and tonight was no different. She'd not come here to buy the book – she'd already read it – or to get Pryce's autograph. She had come here to quiz her about Justin Lanning's death.

She had already tried calling Pryce on a number of occasions, but her calls had been rejected. Pryce was growing into her celebrity, courting the national papers and media, with little time now for local press. Emilia would therefore have to resort to doorstepping her, something she'd done many times in the past, though not usually in a bookstore. Pryce's agent seemed to be here, but no one else official, which was good news, but still she would have to move fast. As soon as Pryce penetrated the main body of the shop, she would be drawn into the loving embrace of an event designed solely to showcase herself and her work. She would be surrounded by store staff, fans and well-wishers, all of whom would look unkindly on Emilia's intervention. No, the key was to grab Pryce as soon as she entered the building. She would be off guard and Emilia could probably get two or three questions in before her agent intervened. Anything of note that Pryce said would immediately be disseminated on Emilia's Twitter feed, then recycled for tomorrow's edition. There was nothing like a quote from the horse's mouth.

The audience was continuing to troop in – mothers and daughters, groups of chattering young women, the token bloke – but still there was no sign of Pryce. This wasn't like her – Pryce was something of a professional at this – but Emilia reasoned that everybody would want a piece of her today, especially after the morning's distressing events, so she would cut her some slack.

Keeping half an eye on the shop entrance, Emilia ran her eyes over some of the Self-Help titles – *Learn to Love Yourself, Think HAPPY* – before turning away in disgust, amazed that anyone was duped by these snake-oil peddlers. Instead, she amused herself by running her eye over the front page of the *Evening News*, which was still tucked under her arm.

As she did so, taking in the beaming, handsome face of Justin Lanning, a shiver ran down her spine. This guy had it all, so much to look forward to, but he'd ended his days having the life choked out of him on an isolated building site. It was a hideous way to go. Emilia had not stinted on the detail and it was already having an effect – her Twitter feed buzzing with comments and questions. How would they react, she wondered, to first-hand testimony from someone who knew him intimately, who'd escaped from hell with him, only now to have her friend snatched away? Emilia already felt excited about the upcoming encounter and was hopeful for its outcome – it was raw emotion, raw grief that her readers wanted now.

The flow of fans was ebbing now and Emilia shot a look at her watch – 19.08. Maxine was late for her own launch. Emilia clocked a huddle of store stuff, chattering earnestly, concern on their faces. Had something happened? Was it possible that Maxine wasn't coming? That she'd pulled out? Surely such a thing was impossible on her big day…?

The staff were separating, moving back into their position near the chairs. Emilia watched them closely, trying to read their body language. They seemed tense, but calm. Did that mean that they'd had news that Maxine was on her way? Or were they just putting a brave face on things?

Either way, there was no point abandoning her post now. She would blend into the background and stick to her plan… waiting for her moment to pounce.

Chapter 23

'Is this to do with Justin?'

He tried to keep his voice steady, but Charlie could sense the anxiety that lay beneath the surface.

'That's right. I'm doing the rounds, speaking to friends and colleagues, trying to get a clearer sense of his life...'

This wasn't entirely true, but it seemed to put Callum Harvey at his ease. He'd looked like a frightened rabbit when he'd opened the door, peering around it as if expecting a nasty surprise, but now seemed to relax a little.

'You'd better come in then.'

Soon they were huddled together in his small sitting room, cradling cups of tea. With each passing minute, Harvey's anxiety levels seemed to ease a little as he gradually opened up to her. In fact, Charlie was of the impression that he was *glad* of her company, that he wanted to talk to someone.

'We were close,' Callum was saying, in between sips of tea. 'We both joined the school in year seven and we hit it off. He liked football, NFL, Xbox, all the stuff I liked. He was a Portsmouth fan, of course, but I let him off that one...'

He smiled at the memory and Charlie was surprised by the effect it had. Callum was pale and thin, with a permanent frown, as if expecting the sky to fall on his head. But when he smiled, his face lit up, revealing a warmth and humour that had been hidden.

'We were very different. He was louder, more confident perhaps – but we were good mates...'

'*Were?*'

Callum looked up, but there seemed to be no irritation at the question.

'What happened... with King... changed things. Afterwards, we were looked after by our families, shepherded off to counsellors and... and we didn't see so much of each other. Justin's parents decided to pull him out of school, sending him to a sixth-form college in Dorset where he'd get less attention. But we still kept in touch, as much as we could anyway.'

'How often were you in contact?'

'Once a month, with a call or a message...'

'And how would you characterize your relationship?'

Callum thought for a while, then replied: 'Supportive. Justin was doing well, I could see that, so every time I saw him mentioned in the local press, I sent him a message. When he built the new house, I went around to see it. I was glad that he was happy and I wanted him to know that.'

'And he?'

'He was the same. I... I haven't had as much to shout about as him, if I'm honest. But for me it was always just about being on an even keel, about... not letting our past experiences define me.'

It was said bullishly, determinedly – clearly this had been a hard-fought battle.

'Justin encouraged me every step of the way. He always said we have a choice in life, whether to be happy or not. That at the end of the day, it's down to us. He was right and I was grateful to him for forcing me to make changes to my life. So we didn't see each other regularly, but we were *close*.'

Charlie nodded, scribbling down a couple of notes.

'Do you have any idea what happened to him?'

Charlie looked up, surprised by the question.

'I mean, do you have any idea *why* he was killed or who—'

'We're still pursuing several lines of enquiry.'

Callum's eyes narrowed slightly, as if suspicious he was about to be fobbed off.

'But there is something I'd like to show you.'

This was the real reason for her visit. Reaching into her bag, Charlie took out the A4 printout.

'I'd like you to take a look at this photo and tell me if you recognize the subject.'

Callum took the photo from her, staring at the grainy black and white image of the intruder at Lanning's house.

'That's Justin's house . . .' Callum said, sounding shocked.

'That's right.'

'And this guy was trying to break in?'

'I'm not at liberty to disclose that,' Charlie apologized, 'but I will say that we are keen to identify him.'

That was an understatement. This sinister figure was their best lead and, given that there might be a copycat element to this brutal crime, Helen had been keen to talk to Lanning's former schoolfriends, in case *they* had any concerns for their safety or could offer any pertinent information. DC Osbourne had headed off to talk to Fran Ward, whilst she had been asked to talk to Harvey.

'I . . . I don't know,' Callum said, suddenly tense. 'The light's pretty bad and there's a shadow across part of his face . . .'

Charlie watched him closely, intrigued by his reaction.

'But I *might* have seen him.'

'Go on…'

'There was a guy out in the road a week or so back. I didn't recognize him and he didn't seem to be waiting for anyone. Just hanging around…'

'Did you talk to him?'

'No, I went to the shops to get some milk and by the time I got back, he'd gone.'

'And how sure are you that it *was* this guy?'

'I'm not…'

Callum looked up from the photo.

'It *could* be him. The face is a similar shape, the physique too, but I saw him in broad daylight, this is the dead of night… I'm sorry, I just can't be sure…'

He handed the photo back to her, but seemed almost reluctant to return it, Charlie having to tug slightly to release it from his grip.

'Is there a problem?' There was a slight tremor in his voice. 'Am I in danger?'

If anything, he was paler now than when she'd arrived, so Charlie moved quickly to reassure him.

'Absolutely not. As I said, we're just doing the rounds. The man in that photo may or may not be relevant. We're talking to Justin's friends, seeing if he mentioned any concerns, any worries…'

'Apart from the obvious?'

'Meaning?'

'Meaning Maxine.'

His tone was uncharacteristically harsh.

'You and she didn't get on?'

'Well, we used to be pals – friendly enough anyway – but recently…'

'Because of her book?'

Callum nodded.

'None of us wanted it written…'

'Because it was your story too, because she'd taken it from you?'

But he was already shaking his head.

'Was it do with money then? The fact that she was profiting from—'

'No, it was nothing like that. I don't give a shit about money.'

It was almost as if it was a dirty word.

'I … I just wanted what happened to us to stay in the past. I wanted it to stay *buried*…'

His voice shook as he said it. Even now, all these years later, the legacy of Callum's trauma wasn't far from the surface.

'Justin … he had his own issues with the book, but for me … I just didn't see why we had to keep talking about it, why Maxine felt she had to bring it all up again, just when I was getting back on my feet…'

He shot a brief look at a framed photo on the mantelpiece – a nice picture of a smiling young woman.

'I'd made a new life for myself. A nice girlfriend, a new home. When people looked at me, talked to me, they saw that – an ordinary bloke making his way in the world. But after Maxine did all those interviews, then wrote the book, suddenly people only saw the other me … That dirty, half-naked victim, the boy who wet the bed every night for three years afterwards, who couldn't speak for stammering … That's what people think when they look at me. They think of th-that little boy, that sad little boy…'

His tone was angry, but beaten, as if all his recent progress was just a mask concealing his bleeding trauma. Perhaps he *was* still a boy at heart, after all.

'I just wanted it to be done with, gone. That's not too much to ask, is it?'

His appeal was direct, passionate. Charlie's heart went out to him. He had clearly tried hard to chart a new course for himself, but in truth he was still defined by events that had taken place eight years ago, still in thrall to the ghosts of his past.

Chapter 24

She scurried along the road, firing accusing glances at the faces passing by. Was the guy with the short dark hair staring at her? Why had the old man suddenly stopped as he walked past her? Was one of these strangers scoping her even now, choosing his moment to strike?

For a while after the call, Maxine had remained rooted to the spot, unable to move, incapable of processing what had just happened to her. It didn't seem real … yet the caller had been so assured, so confident that he could carry out his threat, that she had no doubt he could deliver on his promise. Fear seized her, her hand shaking so much she'd eventually dropped the phone, even as tears pricked her eyes. She was not naturally a timorous person, but the things he'd *said* to her …

Eventually, she'd gathered herself. Her heart was still thumping, but her mind had started to clear. She knew the launch was about to start and that she should probably cancel it even at this late notice, staying safely locked up in the flat. But the thought of that terrified her even more. He knew where she'd been hiding out, knew the flat, knew the phone number. It was impossible, but he *knew*. Which meant she was in danger.

Suddenly, she knew she had to leave. Had to put one foot in front of the other and get herself somewhere where there were people, bright lights, safety. Her dimly lit, discreet bolthole now seemed like the very worst place to be. So, teasing open the front door, double-, triple-checking that the hallway was deserted, she'd run. Past the lifts, down the emergency stairs and out onto the street.

It was early evening and there were plenty of people about, hurrying home from work, heading into town for a night out. At first Maxine felt reassured by their presence, but slowly, a feeling of dread had stolen over her. Had the caller been lurking outside the flat? Was he following her even now? She spun around, but there didn't seem to be any immediate danger. In fact, the world seemed to be going about its business, utterly unconcerned by her plight.

Picking up her pace, Maxine stole a look at her watch – 19.22. Twenty-two minutes had passed since she received the call, but thus far she was safe, she was alive. It felt good to keep moving – surely that made her a harder target? – and she felt herself break into a jog. She wasn't dressed for it, wearing heels and a tight-fitting dress, and no doubt looked ridiculous haring down the busy street, but she didn't care. Waterstones was only a couple of minutes away and the fact that she was late for the launch might actually be a good thing – hopefully there would be a big, safe crowd there to welcome her.

The thought energized Maxine and now she started to sprint. Crossing the road, she spotted the sign for the Westquay Centre and hared in that direction, darting off the main drag. This side street was less busy, lonelier, but there was no other way to reach the bookshop, so Maxine pressed on. She was more vulnerable to attack, but was flying now, which gave her a chance. She didn't break stride, powering towards her destination, towards *safety*, scouring the blank faces that passed by, as she raced away down the quiet street.

Chapter 25

They drove in silence. Helen was behind the wheel, navigating her way through the evening traffic, while Joseph sat in the passenger seat, staring out the window, lost in thought. When he zoned out like this, Helen had no idea what was going through his head – was he thinking about himself? About her? About the task that lay before them? She found it impossible to tell, comforting herself with the knowledge that, when the time came for him to engage, when she needed him by her side, he would be there.

They'd run the partial number plate through the PNC and soon had a shortlist of three – three grey Vauxhall Vivaros, registered locally. The efficient DC Bentham had already tracked two down, talking to the owners first, before sending officers round to verify the recent movements of both vehicle *and* driver. One van belonged to a courier, the other to a florist and neither had set any alarm bells ringing. The final van was more interesting, however.

This vehicle was registered to a Simon Collins, currently living at an address in Freemantle. The address was real enough, but Collins himself appeared to be a fiction. He appeared nowhere on the electoral register and the driving licence and V5 form were forgeries, albeit convincing ones. Clearly someone needed a van – legitimately taxed and licensed – which wouldn't attract attention, but *would* conceal the identity of the person driving it. It had been a long day, but even so Helen had decided to head out to the address herself, rather than farming it out to one of her DCs. Joseph had volunteered to accompany her.

'You know you didn't have to come,' she offered, keeping her eyes on the road. 'It's getting late and DC Reid would have been more than happy to step in.'

'I'm intrigued.'

'By me?'

'By the owner of the van,' Joseph replied, smiling at Helen's provocation. 'We've no idea who he is, what his game is or how dangerous he might turn out to be.'

'He probably won't even be there,' Helen countered.

'Even so.'

They had reached a crossroads. Helen waited for a lorry to trundle past, then pulled out, turning onto Paynes Road. They were proceeding at speed, but anonymously. There was no immediate threat to life, so the blues and twos had been dispensed with. Helen wanted to arrive unannounced.

'Obviously, I appreciate having my leadership team at the forefront of the investigation,' Helen continued, ignoring Joseph's attempt to shut the conversation down. 'But we've got a long road ahead of us—'

'I appreciate that.'

'And, as we've discussed, I *can* take care of myself.'

'I know.'

It was said simply, even affectionately, as if he was completely relaxed about the whole thing, yet the fact remained that he *had* been insistent on accompanying her.

'And there won't be any overtime in it...'

Joseph laughed easily and turned away, looking out of the

window at the traffic. Helen stole a look at him, trying to gauge his thoughts. For some time now she'd felt that there was a tension inside him, a frustration lurking within. Joseph seemed keen to be at the heart of everything, driving the investigation, never far from her side. At first, Helen had thought this was simply borne of a desire to spend time with her, but lately she'd changed her mind. There was a restlessness to him, an impatience, and even a hint of competition between him and Charlie, as if he wanted to match her in importance or even supplant her. Did Joseph feel he hadn't proved himself yet? Was there something bothering him, some ghost that he needed to exorcize? Or was there a genuine issue between her two deputies?

Since Charlie had announced her pregnancy, she'd slowly been winding down her front-line activity in favour of less dangerous pursuits. She was still key to each investigation, but had a more tactical role now, gathering information, running theories and helping Helen direct operations. The running, jumping and kicking would be left to others. Was Joseph suspicious, even envious, of the friendship between the two women? Or was this old-fashioned station politics, an ambitious DS aiming to take advantage of a colleague's impending absence? He wouldn't be the first officer to exploit another's maternity leave. Helen didn't approve of it – and would certainly guard against this happening – but if it *was* that, at least she'd know what she was dealing with. Currently, she hadn't a clue what was going on, which unnerved her. Often, she'd been tempted to ask Joseph straight out, but had always run shy of it for fear of having misread the situation. She wanted to penetrate the heart of Joseph's unease, to understand the tension within him, but any further examination of the issue would have to wait.

They had arrived.

Chapter 26

'How do you want to play this?'

Joseph lowered his voice, even though there was little chance of them being overheard. Helen peered through the windscreen towards the house opposite, whose ragged curtains were drawn tightly shut against the world. There was no sign of the van on the street, but a dim light burnt within, just visible through the curtains on the upper floor.

'I thought I'd knock on the door and see if anyone answers.'

It was said with a smile, Helen amused by the notion that Joseph might have been expecting her to catapult herself through the window.

'I like it. It's simple, effective ...' he replied, smiling.

'But if you want to position yourself around the back, that would be appreciated. There's no need to be subtle, park yourself by the back door and see if anyone comes out.'

'Roger that.'

Joseph had already opened the car door and was on his way. Helen gave him a couple of minutes' head start, then followed suit, exiting the car and crossing the street. It was a busy road, a local cut-through, but curiously nondescript, the peeling Victorian houses having so far avoided gentrification. Most of them had been divided up into bedsits and flats and appeared to be unloved, discarded toys and junk littering the tiny front gardens.

Rapping sharply on the door, Helen listened intently to the reaction within. She waited for ten seconds, then ten more, but there was no obvious response to her intrusion.

'Police. Open up...'

She rapped again, three, four times, then resumed her vantage point. And this time there *was* a response. A slight fluttering of the curtains on the upper floor, the shadow of a figure beyond. Helen strained to make out the voyeur, but the apparition now withdrew, disappearing from sight.

Ten seconds passed, then ten more. There was no noise within, no creaking floorboards, no groaning stairs – no sign at all that the occupant was willing to admit her. Helen went to knock again, but this time noticed something. The front door was old and warped, bowing away from the doorframe at top and bottom, meaning that it was held in place only by the aged Yale lock. Helen had thought about knocking again, but now simply leant in, applying steady but powerful pressure. The door protested meekly, a gentle squeal as the wood strained, then splintered, before the lock gave way. The door now swung open, revealing a gloomy hallway within. Gathering herself, Helen took a breath and stepped inside.

The floorboard creaked loudly as she shut the door behind her. Helen froze, straining to hear. Was that movement she heard upstairs? She darted a look into the downstairs living room, but there was little there, save for discarded newspapers and a TV that appeared to have had its plug ripped off. The kitchen that led to the rear garden was also swathed in darkness, so Helen didn't delay, walking slowly up the stairs, scanning the landing above, in case anyone was lurking there.

Cresting the stairs, she stepped onto a narrow landing. A

squalid bathroom lay immediately in front of her, mouldering and unpleasant, as if the drains had given up the ghost. Curiously, the light pull was still moving, swaying gently back and forth, which immediately put Helen on her guard. Had someone just vacated the room, or was it just the breeze that rattled through the ventilation flap? Stepping inside, she tried the window, but it refused to budge, seemingly painted shut.

Stepping back out onto the landing, she surveyed the interior. There was a small bedroom to the rear, whilst a larger one looked out onto the street. Helen chose the former, stepping decisively into the small room. Her body was tensed, she was braced for someone to fly at her... but the room was deserted. There was a wardrobe, a single bed, but little else. Turning, she hurried to the master bedroom.

The door was ajar, meaning she couldn't see inside. This made her hesitate – there was nowhere else their suspect could be hiding now. If Helen was right the ghostly figure caught on Lanning's CCTV was just a few feet from where she now stood. Using the tip of her boot, she eased the door open. It obliged, swinging easily on its hinge before coming to rest. Taking a breath, Helen stepped inside.

She moved fast, her eyes darting around the room. She was expecting trouble, perhaps even a personal attack, but this room was also deserted. Moving forwards, she pulled back the curtains, thinking someone might be hiding behind them, but here too she was disappointed.

Turning, she took in the empty room. It was cold and bare, a stained mattress lying on the bedstead. The wardrobe hung open and empty and there was little of interest... except for a dozen small boxes that lay on the unused bed.

Crossing to them, Helen picked one up. She clocked the brand name – Samsung – and quickly opened the box, to find a brand new Galaxy S10 inside. Putting it down, she investigated the others, discovering they were all the same make and model.

Pulling out her radio, she pressed down the call button.

'No sign in here. You got anything?'

'Nothing. No movement at all,' Joseph replied, his crackling, disembodied voice filling the room. 'What's in there?'

'Nothing. Unless you count a dozen knock-off Samsungs. All brand new, but in slightly dented boxes from where they fell off the lorry...'

Joseph laughed and Helen clicked off to continue her investigations. But now she heard it. A tiny creaking sound, like a small door opening. And instantly she realized her mistake. The wardrobe in the back room. She hadn't checked the wardrobe.

She burst towards the door, just in time to see a flash of black disappearing down the stairs. She didn't hesitate, tearing across the landing and arriving at the top of the stairs, just in time to see the front door cannon into the wall. Helen leapt down the stairs, taking them three at a time, landing gracefully in the hallway. And then she was after him, sprinting through the doorway and out into the street.

He was dressed from head to foot in black, but even so was visible beneath the meagre street lights. He had a head start on her, but was only thirty yards away, so Helen gave chase. She had always kept herself fit, pushing her body hard during her daily workouts, and she hammered the concrete now, her muscular legs powering her forward. Her quarry was fast, but she was faster, already the gap between them was diminishing. The question was whether she could get to him before he reached the busy road ahead. There he might be able to jump on a bus, dart into a shop or lose her in the crowds. It was imperative she apprehended him before he got there, so Helen redoubled her efforts, ignoring the burning sensation in her lungs.

The gap between them was fifteen yards, now ten. The fugitive could sense the danger, briefly upping his speed in response, but Helen had been expecting this, taking her speed a notch higher too. She could almost reach out and grab his black hoodie, but now he surprised her, suddenly darting left through parked cars and onto the street. Helen skidded to a halt, but even as she did so, she heard the piercing squeal of brakes, then a dull metallic 'thunk'.

Their suspect had misjudged his escape attempt and even now was rolling across the bonnet of the braking car. It happened in a flash, the vehicle lurching to a sudden halt, depositing the unfortunate fugitive on the other side of the street. Helen froze for a moment, shocked, but even now her quarry wasn't done, struggling to his feet. Spotting the danger, Helen burst forward, leaping clean off the ground and sliding across the shiny bonnet of the car. The suspect was now on his feet, but it was too late. Helen landed on the tarmac just beside him, grabbing the front of his hoodie and pinioning him against a parked car.

The concerned driver was already emerging, even as a breathless Joseph arrived on the scene. But Helen ignored them both, pulling back the hood of her struggling captive. Breathless, confused, Helen stared at the startled face looking back at her.

The disappointment was instantaneous and crushing. For this was not their suspect, the ghost from Lanning's house; in fact, the fugitive was not even male. The person standing in front of Helen was a terrified teenage girl.

Chapter 27

'I'm sorry, I'm sorry, I'm sorry...'

The words came out in a torrent.

'That's all right, there's no need to apologize. We're just glad you're *here*...'

The store manager's face was a picture – relief at Maxine's arrival coupled with evident concern for her state of mind. Maxine could hardly blame her – not only was she very late, she was sweating, flustered and dishevelled. So much planning had gone into tonight – she had bought her outfit over a month ago – and now it was all unravelling.

'We've got a huge crowd,' the manager continued, encouragingly. 'It's going to be a great night.'

Maxine nodded, but said nothing.

'Could I get you a glass of water?' the manager persisted. 'Something stronger, perhaps...?'

'No, I'm all right, honestly...'

She exhaled long and loud, trying to release the knot of tension inside her.

'I... I was just running late, so I had to dash over. I'll be totally fine, I promise...'

And perhaps she would. This place was packed with people. Surely nothing could happen to her here?

'Well, just say the word then, and we'll begin. If you're *sure* you're OK...'

Maxine stole a look at her watch – 19.32. Over half an hour had passed now since the call.

'Yes, I'm good. Let's do this.'

The manager led the way through the store towards the events space. Rows of heads turned to greet her. Maxine was suddenly intimidated – yet pleased – by the number of people who'd turned out. Several people were standing, unable to find a seat, and the realization that she had filled the place gave her a jolt of happiness, of optimism. Everything would be fine. Surely the call was a hoax? A horrible prank from some jealous prick who wanted to rain on her parade?

Keeping pace with the manager, she rounded the chairs at the front and stepped up onto the low stage. Pleasingly, a ripple of excitement, of anticipation, was audible, further boosting Maxine. Sadly, it was short-lived, the manager now opening proceedings, thanking the assembled throng and giving a short summary of Maxine's journey to this point, to this evening, to the launch of her much-anticipated book. Now people were clapping and Maxine found herself stepping forward to face them.

'Thank you, Samantha, and thank you all for your patience. Timekeeping has never been my strong point...'

A gentle murmur of laughter. Maxine's heart was still beating fit to burst, but she felt a little more in control.

'In a moment, I'd like to talk about the background to this book, about my life during the last eight years...'

Her voice was croaky, so she cleared her throat, wanting to sound as calm and composed as she could.

'About what I've been through and what I still hope to achieve...'

An elderly woman in the front row was staring at her,

seemingly entranced by her every word. And now Maxine became aware of the sheer number of eyeballs that were glued to her. Row upon row of people gawping at her, as if they knew her, as if this was the most natural thing in the world. She'd done TV and radio before, but that was different. Here your audience was close at hand and it was impossible to escape their attention. She knew she should be talking, teeing up her reading, but now she found her eyes wandering over the crowd. To the young man in the second row. To the middle-aged guy five rows back, who seemed to be studying a notebook. To the gaunt, bald figure at the rear, staring unblinkingly at her.

Suddenly she had no idea what to say, or what to do. She was gripped by the idea that the caller had made his way *here*, that he was even now in this room.

'Maxine?'

Samantha was by her side once more and Maxine realized she had petered out, distracted by her dark thoughts.

'Sorry, just having a mind blank. I must be nervous...' she lied, earning an indulgent smile from the elderly lady at the front. 'Like I said, I'll talk about my journey in a moment, but I'd like to start by reading a short passage from the book.'

Picking up her book, Maxine opened it at the relevant page. Then, taking a breath, trying hard to swallow down her growing dread, she began to read.

Extract from One Dark Night *by Maxine Pryce*

The honest truth is that we were glad to step into that farmhouse. It was foggy and unpleasant outside, the thin drizzle clinging to us, somehow finding its way through our waterproof layers. We were cold, wet, frustrated and scared. Which is why the house, with its dancing lanterns and cosy range cooker, seemed like a sanctuary for us.

Our host was odd – I think we all felt that – but he wasn't unwelcoming, telling us to hang our wet things by the oven and sit down at the kitchen table. I remember he wouldn't look at us at first – as if there was something intimidating or contagious about our troupe – but initially I assumed he was just shy. He asked us the odd question, keeping the conversation meandering along, even as he rustled us up something to eat. In truth, it was lean pickings, some bread and butter, some apples and a few stale crackers, but they tasted good to us. We were tired, hungry and nearing the end of our tether.

The whole expedition had been a disaster. We would probably complete it, but we would limp in last, the butt of other schools' jokes for our inability to hold onto a map. Even now, Justin was examining Rachel's swollen ankle, the latter wincing and moaning at his prodding, a fitting image, perhaps, of our ineptitude and misfortune. Even when the fog cleared, would we be able to find our way? Or had we strayed so far off track that we would have to give up the pursuit altogether?

'So where are we exactly?'

Fran, always polite, was working hard to engage our reluctant host.

'Manor Farm.'

'Which is?'

'Near Chilgrove, if you know where that is.'

None of us did, which seemed to amuse him.

'Where are you from anyway?'

Now it was his turn to ask questions.

'Southampton. We're doing our Duke of Edinburgh Award. Well, we *were*...'

This was from Callum, who seemed even more pissed off than the rest of us.

'And where are you heading?'

'The nearest A&E probably...' Rachel responded ruefully.

'But the final destination is supposed to be Midhurst,' Justin clarified.

Our host just nodded, saying nothing in response. We were all hoping he might direct us there, but he seemed more interested in watching us eat. Now that he too was seated at the table, I could take a proper look at him. There was no question, he was a weird one. Slight, lean, with unruly, fair hair, he could have been handsome, but there was something awkward about him. His delicate, feminine features were hard to read and his lip was curled up on one side, in an expression which looked now ironic, cruel.

'I'm Maxine, by the way,' I finally said, keen to fill the silence. 'And this is Fran, Callum, Justin, Rachel...'

'I'm the one who ballsed the whole thing up,' Rachel confirmed unhappily, easing her foot onto the floor.

If she expected gallows humour to open him up, she was mistaken. Our host stayed resolutely silent, but not one to be deterred, Rachel continued: 'And you are...?'

'Daniel,' he conceded. 'Leassst that's the name my mother gave me.'

We all picked up on it. He was slurring his words, only slightly, but he was definitely slurring his words. Was he drunk? If so, how pissed was he? As he lounged awkwardly on his chair, he seemed amused – though whether by his guests or their predicament, she wasn't sure.

'So what're you going to do now?'

It was a good question. I turned to Justin, but he shrugged, then turned back to Rachel. There was little we could do, other than wait for the fog to clear.

'Is there someone you're supposed to c-call?' our host continued falteringly. 'I haven't got a landline and the reception is shit here . . .'

I surreptitiously slid my phone from my pocket. You weren't supposed to use them, except in dire emergencies. This situation might well qualify – we were, after all, in a stranger's house – but there was little chance of that. No bars, no 3G, nothing.

'We're OK,' I replied. 'We'll just sit it out until things improve, then we'll be on our way. We don't want to intrude.'

I was trying my best to be polite, confident, assertive, but I couldn't fully disguise the tension in my voice. For reasons I couldn't explain, I didn't feel comfortable. Maybe it was our host's languid manner, or the way he stared at you unflinchingly. I couldn't say for sure, but I know others were beginning to feel it, especially the girls.

'No rush,' Daniel replied. 'No rush at all.'

He rose, crossed to the doorway, stooping to pet his Dobermanns who responded to his touch, nuzzling him with their wet noses.

'In fact, the weather is going to get worse before it gets better.'

This time it was Rachel who shot a glance at me, discomfort and guilt evident in *her* expression.

'So, you're welcome to ssstay the night... I've plenty of bedrooms.'

A brief, telling silence followed.

'We don't want to put you to any bother,' Rachel replied, as casually as she could.

'Yeah, we should be on our way,' I agreed. 'So if it's OK with you, I'll just use your bathroom, then we'll get out of your hair.'

'But... but your clothes won't be dry...'

'We have to press on,' I insisted.

'Well... if you're sure. The toilet's second on the left.'

I hurried into the corridor, suddenly pleased to be out of the room, out of his orbit. I passed doors on either side of me, the rooms inside concealed in darkness, then darted into the loo. The room was freezing, the toilet seat colder still; I realized now that there seemed to be no central heating, nor even any electricity in the house. Illumination was provided by paraffin lamps and the range seemed to be the sole source of warmth. What was this place? Why was it so... backward?

Finishing up, I washed my hands hurriedly and left the bathroom. Heading back down the gloomy corridor, I made my way towards the kitchen... but as I did so, I noticed something. The first door on the right, which moments earlier had been ajar, was now closed. I had only been a couple of minutes, so what had happened? Had our host ventured down here to shut it? And if so, why?

I paused on the threshold of the room. I thought for a moment he might be inside, but now I picked up his voice in the kitchen. I'm not quite sure why I did it – perhaps it was some nagging sense that something *was* badly wrong here – but I turned the handle and opened the door. The interior was shrouded in darkness, so pulling my phone from my pocket, I hit the torch.

It didn't look like much, just a junk room full of trinkets and little models. What kind of geek was this guy? But as I looked closer, curious as to what keepsakes this oddball treasured, I noticed something. The little white structures, which I'd assumed were wooden models, were actually . . . skeletons. Tentatively, I picked up the nearest one – it was the skeleton of a small bird, a sparrow, perhaps, or a wren. Putting it down quickly, I investigated the others. There were plenty of other birds, but bigger skeletons too. I had no idea what these were – stoats? weasels? foxes? – but the combination of them, plus the numerous animal skulls that littered every surface, was chilling. This was a room steeped in death.

Why would you hoard such things? Were they the remains of animals he'd found around the farm? Animals he'd trapped? My nerves were jangling now and I was about to turn and run, fearful I'd be caught, when my eye fell on something else. Amidst all the bones was a scrumpled piece of cloth. Knowing I shouldn't investigate – that I didn't really *want* to know – still I couldn't help looking closer. It was a torn fragment of material, white cotton, perhaps from a shirt, and as I picked it up, I was surprised to feel something inside. Opening up the fabric, I discovered a locket. Fingering the pretty mother of pearl piece, my mind was full of questions. Had it belonged to his mother? To a girlfriend? If so, why did he keep it in *here*?

Turning it over, I noted some initials etched on the metal – 'LK'.

The echo of a memory. The initials were strangely familiar to me for some reason, though I couldn't say why at first. LK, LK, why did those letters mean something? What was their significance?

Then it hit me. And suddenly my blood ran cold.

I remembered having read about the locket in the local paper. A young schoolgirl – Laura Kietly? Lorraine Kielty? – had been attacked on a country lane. Some guy had come out of nowhere, had dragged her into the bushes, had tried to strangle her. She'd escaped, thank goodness, but her clothing had been torn in the attack and she'd lost her locket – a locket her grandmother had given to her for her sixteenth birthday, inscribed with her initials.

'LK'.

My heart was racing, my head pounding, my whole body gripped by fear. I didn't know what to say or what to do, but one thing was clear.

As long as we remained in this house, we were all in grave danger.

Chapter 28

'We need to get his picture out asap. See if we can engage the public's interest.'

'*That* shouldn't be hard,' Joseph replied drily. 'Lanning's murder has been keeping the hacks busy all day.'

'Then let's see if we can harness their enthusiasm. We've got precious little else.'

Joseph Hudson didn't disagree with Helen's downbeat summary of the situation. They had journeyed to the house in Freemantle full of optimism, hopeful for a break in the case, but all they had unearthed was a low-level hustler, a kid who'd been kicked out of her home and was surviving by selling stolen Samsungs. She'd sworn that the house in question had been empty for weeks – an assertion confirmed by the neighbours – and that she was just squatting there until she found somewhere better. Nor was it likely that she was the driver of their missing van. She was too young to have a licence and wouldn't have the cash to buy a transit van anyway.

Which meant the elusive Simon Collins remained just that. Traffic cameras hadn't picked up the van and the ghostly CCTV image of their suspect hadn't jogged memories in any of the other departments at Southampton Central. So they were at a loss, clueless as to the man's identity and location, with little option now but to widen their search. This would mean a slew of mistaken identifications, hoaxes and fake leads, but it might be worth it in the end if it helped them identify their man.

The police station now reared into view, Helen swinging the pool car into the sole remaining space. It was late, but by the looks of things the team were still hard at work. Helen was pleased by this, but knew it was time to send them home. Odds on, they still had a long road ahead of them in this investigation. Climbing out of the car, the pair walked swiftly through the atrium of the glass and limestone building and were soon in a lift, heading for the seventh floor.

'Meet in the bike park in fifteen?'

Wrenched from her thoughts, Helen turned to him, surprised. 'What's the rush?'

'Well it's nearly eight o'clock,' he replied, genially. 'And you know what they say about all work and no play…'

'Even so, I've got to get that screen shot to media liaison—'

'Osbourne can do that, or Bentham…'

'I'd like to do it myself, make sure the message we're putting out with it is the right one.'

'OK,' Joseph replied, glancing at his watch. 'Half an hour, then? I've got stuff I can be doing in the meantime.'

'Don't let me keep you, I might be a while…'

Joseph was still smiling, but some of the warmth had gone from his expression now.

'Is that a problem?' Helen asked, curious.

'No, no… though I did have plans for us.'

'Really?' Helen replied, surprised.

'Dinner plans, I mean. I've booked somewhere I think you'll like…'

He was working hard, trying to reel her in. And there *was* a part of her that was tempted, but still… they were in the middle of a major investigation. A man had been brutally murdered and they were no closer to discovering why or by whom – it didn't seem right to be putting her own needs first. Helen knew this was most likely *her* problem, not his. She always had trouble switching off during an investigation, couldn't rest while there were unanswered questions, yet she couldn't deny that this was how she felt. Even if she did go out with Joseph tonight, she knew she'd be tense and distracted. Poor company for a man who demanded her full attention.

'We can bike it, be there in half an hour. It's a nice pub hidden away in the countryside, without a copper in sight…'

The lift slowed as they reached the seventh floor. Helen knew it was decision time, so placing her hand on his arm, she said: 'I'd love to, but it'll have to be another time.'

She smiled at him, but it was not returned. She looked into his eyes, hoping to see that familiar sparkle, perhaps even a little good-humoured resignation, but instead she saw a flash of anger, as if her polite refusal was a pointed rejection.

'I might not offer again…'

There was a hard edge to his voice that Helen didn't care for.

'I'll take my chances,' she replied evenly. 'You get off, I'll see you in the morning.'

She walked away towards the incident room, the lift doors kissing shut behind her. She had no idea what Joseph was feeling, if this minor set-to might provoke an argument later, but she wouldn't let outside concerns cloud her judgement or stop her doing what she needed to do.

Whilst there was a killer at large, she wouldn't rest.

Chapter 29

From his elevated vantage point, she looked minuscule. Like a tiny little ant that he could reach out and crush.

The bookshop was closing, the last few customers having been shepherded from the store in the wake of Maxine Pryce. The star attraction had done her duty briskly, scarcely engaging with the Q&A and dashing off the signatures without conversation, before hurrying out the door with her agent. The Waterstones staff were visibly unimpressed, but Pryce didn't seem to care. She had quit the shopping centre and was currently in the courtyard below, huddled in conversation with her agent.

The customers were drifting away, clutching their copies of the new book and chatting animatedly. He lingered, however, waiting until the last reader was out of sight, before dumping his own copy in the bin. It had been an extremely pleasurable experience – the harassed writer dedicating a copy to *him* – but he didn't need to read the contents. He knew everything about her.

In the background, he could see the bookstore staff stacking away the chairs, a dumb show of quiet efficiency. But he was alone now in the mall and he shot nervous glances around him, looking for CCTV cameras or patrolling security guards. He had chosen his spot well, however – there was little chance of detection here. Still, it wouldn't do to linger and he was pleased to see the women move off together, hurrying away into the night.

'One, two, three, four, five ...'

He counted quietly to himself, enjoying the feeling as the seconds ticked past. He was methodical, careful, but he *was* liable to get overexcited, to rush in. Better to take his time, be patient, enjoy the moment. As hard as she tried, Pryce couldn't escape his attentions now.

Casting around to check that there were no obvious witnesses, he left his vantage point from behind the pillar, moving fast down the escalators. From there it was a short march to the revolving doors, then out into the fresh air.

The night was crisp and fresh, the cold draught hitting the back of his throat, sharpening his senses and filling him with energy. Surveying the darkened street, he spotted the diminutive Pryce and her companion up ahead. Quietly, he padded after them, intrigued to see where Pryce would go next. Would she head home? Dive into a bar? Or did she have somewhere else in mind?

His movements mirrored his quarry's, his pace matching hers. They were locked together in silent communion, yet Pryce seemed blissfully unaware of this, engaged in intense conversation with her agent. She still seemed flustered, agitated even, constantly stealing glances at her phone. What was she looking for? What was she hoping to find? It amused him to watch her distress, her disorientation.

He was gliding along happily, lost in the moment, so wasn't expecting it. Without warning, Pryce slowed down. Her body looked tensed, coiled even, as if sensing danger. And now she paused, turning to steal a glance back down the street towards him. Had he been a second slower, had his reflexes been dulled, she would have clocked him instantly. As it was, he saw her ful-some hair shift, saw her head begin to turn, so flattened himself against the wall, praying the long shadows would conceal him.

He hardly dared breathe. Pryce scanned the street quickly, hunting danger. Had she heard him? Seen him reflected in a shop window? Or was she just being cautious? To be caught now would ruin everything, all his carefully laid plans…

No, she was turning once more, satisfied that she was alone. Now she was moving away, shaking her head at her own stupid-ity, though whether this was genuine or for her companion's benefit, he couldn't tell. She was hurrying away down the street, approaching the corner. He was tempted to give her a head start, but couldn't risk losing her. He would have to take a chance to stay in the game.

Moving away from the wall, he picked up speed, his rubber-soled shoes dulling the sound of his steps. Pryce and her com-panion had reached the top of the road now, vanishing around the corner. Upping his speed, he pursued them, slowing only as he reached the end of the road, darting cautious glances around the corner, before following his prey.

The street was quiet once more, as if the whole mini-drama had played out unobserved. But now, a fourth figure emerged from the darkness. A young woman, petite in stature with visible scarring down one side of her face, who had watched the whole thing from *her* hiding place behind a clutch of wheelie bins. Cursing herself for wearing heels, she hurried away down the street on the balls of her feet, picking up pace all the while, determined not to let the tall, gaunt figure out of her sight.

Chapter 30

'So we've no idea who he is?'

Helen stood in front of the murder board with Detective Superintendent Grace Simmons. The pair were alone in the incident room, taking in the evidence in front of them. The murder board was filling up – images of Justin Lanning, Adam Cannon and their suspect, flanked by a rough timeline and several active lines of enquiry – but there were too many blank spaces for Helen's liking.

She shook her head now, in answer to Simmons' enquiry.

'And your trip to Freemantle didn't yield anything?'

Helen shook her head once more.

'I get the feeling this guy exists beneath the radar. There are no obvious real world links, and he's obviously going to great lengths to conceal his identity. He seems kind of… invisible, suggesting perhaps that he operates in the margins – the black economy, the dark web – whatever his business or intent might be.'

Simmons was nodding, but didn't look cheered by this news. In truth, Helen's boss looked washed out, even a little defeated tonight. Helen was keen to buoy her up – to give her something – so carried on briskly.

'However, he's obviously someone's son, someone's mate, so

our best bet now is the public appeal. He's bald, which narrows it down, plus he has quite distinctive features, so *somebody* will recognize him. The question is whether they'll feel like telling us. Lanning's death has already provoked a lot of media coverage, so we'll get the exposure. We just have to hope that someone out there has a conscience and is willing to pick up the phone.'

'There won't be any shortage of people willing to do that,' Simmons added, a touch ruefully.

'In the meantime, we'll obviously keep looking for the van. We've no reason to think he's got rid of it, so we've got patrols out and we're keeping a close eye on the traffic cams...'

Simmons continued to stare at the board, looking a little like Helen felt. The truth was that, despite their best endeavours, they were still a long way from working out who this mystery figure was.

'Well, we've got the press conference scheduled for tomorrow morning,' Simmons said eventually. 'Hopefully that will yield something. In the meantime, we should all get some rest, *you* included.'

'Five minutes, then I'm gone.'

'I'm glad to hear it. You know better than most that it's a marathon, not a sprint.'

Smiling wanly, Simmons turned to go. It was late and the best thing Helen could do now was let her friend go, then pack up and go herself. But instead, she found herself speaking once more.

'Are you OK?'

The question took Simmons by surprise, and she paused now. 'I'm fine... why?'

Simmons turned as she spoke, her expression a mixture of curiosity and confusion. Helen wouldn't normally have spoken to her superior so directly – and never in the incident room – but they were alone and in truth she *was* concerned about her friend and mentor.

'It's nothing really,' Helen replied, brightly. 'It's just that you're very pale and ... perhaps a bit subdued. I was wondering if anything was bothering you, if you weren't feeling well or ...'

'No, I'm fine,' Simmons responded, gamely. 'Just dog tired, that's all. It's old age, Helen, I wouldn't recommend it.'

'You're not old.'

'We both know that's not true. I should have retired two years ago.'

The thought filled Helen with dread – Simmons was the only boss who'd ever had her back – but there could be no question of her carrying on at the expense of her health.

'Look, if you need to step back for a bit, I'm happy to help out, do what I can—'

'I wouldn't hear of it,' Simmons countered, warmly. 'You've got enough on your plate and I can hardly take a sabbatical when we've got *this* on the books.'

She gestured towards the murder board, drawing Helen's gaze to it once more.

'I'll be fine, just need a good night's sleep, that's all. Don't worry about me.'

Rubbing Helen's arm, Simmons flashed a final smile, then headed on her way. Helen watched her go, feeling oddly disquieted. She was grateful for her friend's support, but knew that she wouldn't be able to settle tonight. There were too many unanswered questions in the investigation and now some concerns about Simmons too. She hid it well, but Helen was convinced her boss had been struggling of late – anxious, distracted – which made Helen uneasy. Grace Simmons had always been frank with her, but now Helen felt a barrier growing between them, an evasiveness that was totally out of character. For reasons she couldn't explain, Helen suspected that for the first time in their long-standing friendship, she wasn't being told the full story.

Chapter 31

She slammed the door shut, sliding the chain on. It was a flimsy thing, so she flicked down the latch lock and bent to secure the deadlock. Satisfied, she hurried across the living room towards the window – Barbara was waiting for an Uber outside and waved at her – before turning away once more. She had contemplated inviting her in, but Maxine knew she wouldn't feel happy until she had checked *every* inch of her flat. And how could she have explained that away? Barbara was suspicious enough as it was, sensing that Maxine was lying when she'd suggested her strange behaviour tonight was the result of exhaustion. Maxine knew she'd only just got away with it and was keen not to excite her suspicions further. The last thing she needed now was awkward questions.

She glanced at her watch – 20.38. Exhaling slowly, Maxine tried to calm herself, to convince herself that she *really* was safe. She was sweating, having marched all the way home, but didn't bother to remove her coat, scurrying from the living room towards the back bedroom.

Entering the small space, she was pleased to see that nothing was out of place. Walking over to the window, she checked the latch and the security locks, then gave it a hefty tug. Happily, it wouldn't budge, so she moved on.

Her own bedroom was also as she left it, but she took her time, checking under the bed and in the cupboards before confirming that the window was securely locked. What she was expecting to find she wasn't sure, but she knew she wouldn't be happy until she had completed a full circuit. On she went, into the bathroom, then on into the living room. The windows here were not in the best nick – why hadn't she replaced them with modern ones before now? – but seemed secure enough. They would hold.

Heading back to the front door, she rechecked the latch and the deadlock. They were still in place, as she knew they would be. Relieved, Maxine leant against the door, closing her eyes and breathing out. She had made it.

Only now did her heart rate begin to slow. She had been rigid with tension for the best part of two hours, fearing the worst, but now she could finally relax. This evening had been hideous, awful, thrusting her right back into a nightmare she'd thought was behind her, but now it was over, she'd made it through. She had survived.

It seemed crazy, but it was true – the caller had been as good as his word, honouring the deal they'd made. She'd hardly believed it possible – fearing he was merely toying with her, prolonging her agony, before her brutal death – yet here she was, alive and well. In truth, she hadn't hesitated when he'd made the offer, seizing the chance to save her skin. In other circumstances, she would have wrestled with her conscience, perhaps even rejected his vile suggestion out of hand, but tonight it had been a price she was willing to pay.

If another had to die, so she could live, then so be it.

Chapter 32

'Please, Callum, just tell me what you want me to do.'

Hannah was staring at him intently. She was being sympathetic, as always, but couldn't completely disguise the irritation she obviously felt.

'If you'd like me to stay, I will. I know you were close to Justin... But if you feel you're going to be OK, then I'll go.'

He knew that he should tell her to go, to pretend that he was robust enough to spend the night on his own, but still he hesitated. Stella's hen night had been months in the planning and Hannah was one of the bridesmaids – of course she couldn't miss the revelry. Yet Callum *was* feeling badly shaken, not only by Justin's awful murder, but by DS Brooks' subsequent visit. Was he just imagining he recognized the suspect she showed him? Or had he really been out there in the street, not fifty yards from their house?

'Look, you're clearly in a bad way,' Hannah said briskly, interrupting his train of thought. 'I'll call Stella and tell her that I might make it to the club later.'

She crossed the room and started rummaging through her bag. She had said it decisively and with no hint of self-pity, but her body language gave the lie to her apparent equanimity. Her shoulders were hunched, her body sagging, as if finally capitulating after a long battle. Suddenly, Callum felt a rush of love, but also a piercing sense of shame. This was *his* fault. It was always his fault. This patient, loving, vivacious woman was always there for him. Whatever else she had going on, however gruelling her shift at South Hants Hospital had been, she always had time for him, for his problems, providing just the right amount of comfort, love and inspiration. He knew he was hard work, he knew that many lesser women would have walked away by now and, all of a sudden, he felt terrible guilt for the deadening effect he had on her life.

'Hold on ...'

She paused, looking up. And in that moment, despite her studiedly neutral expression, he saw it. A flash of hope in her eyes – that she would be released, that she would be able to go out and get drunk with her pals, dancing the night away with the girls she'd known since school. He had it in his power to give her this, this small token of his love, and suddenly he was determined to do it. Yes, Justin was dead and it was true he was badly shaken, but he'd get by somehow. In truth, what right did he have to be alarmed, to be scared? No, he would not see demons where they didn't exist. He would be strong.

'You must go. Of course, you must go,' he asserted, sounding much more confident than he felt.

That seemed to do it. Hannah crossed the room to him, wrapping him in one of her trademark hugs, pulling him close.

'Thank you, love,' she whispered.

He could tell that she was emotional, that she perhaps had tears in her eyes, convincing him that he'd done the right thing. She clearly needed a break – from work, from life, from *him* – and tonight she was going to get it.

'You run along and have fun. I'd hate you to miss the cocktails,' he said jovially, as she extracted herself from him.

'Love you,' she replied, giving him an affectionate peck on the lips. 'I'll call you in the morning.'

Scooping up her bag, she headed for the doorway.

'Don't do anything I wouldn't do,' he replied breezily.

She raised her hand in mock-acknowledgment and two minutes later she was gone, the front door shutting firmly behind her. Crossing to the window, Callum pulled back the curtains, watching her walking away down the street. As she slowly disappeared from view, heading for the taxi rank, he suddenly felt a profound emptiness inside him. It was as if he could only function, only be cheerful and constructive, when he was in her orbit. All the false levity he'd exhibited when sending her on her way suddenly evaporated – now he felt lonely, fearful and unnerved. The silence in the house surrounded him, goading him, threatening him. Images of that ghostly, gaunt figure shot into his mind. He could imagine the man climbing the garden fence, forcing the back door, coming for him...

A loud bang outside made him turn... but it was just his neighbour slamming his car door. He knew he should do something – cook dinner, watch TV, anything – but suddenly he wasn't capable of doing *anything*. So, he remained where he was, clutching the window ledge, staring hopelessly out of the window. He had tried so hard to get better, to be stronger, more resilient, but tonight he felt like that traumatized teenager once again.

Lost, confused and scared.

Chapter 33

Haring down the road, Emilia scanned left and right. But the road was empty, so picking up speed, she carried on towards the junction. And now, as she approached the busy crossroads, she spied salvation.

'Taxi!'

The car cut across the road towards her. It had barely stopped before Emilia yanked the door open, leaping inside.

'Do you see that van?'

The driver looked perplexed, so Emilia persisted, gesturing frantically.

'Do you see that grey transit van?'

'Yes…' the driver replied hesitantly, looking down the road.

'Follow it. I'll give you double the fare, if you can stay close.'

Flicking the meter on, the driver obliged, setting off after the van. Sweating, Emilia sat down, strapping herself in, without once taking her eyes off the vehicle. It would be disastrous to lose it now.

'You a private eye?'

The driver, who'd seemed concerned at first, now appeared more at ease, even a touch excited, sensing that he might be part of some unfolding drama.

'No,' Emilia replied, tersely.

'Husband playing away then?'

'Just drive. I'm not paying you for conversation.'

Reluctantly, the driver returned his attention to the road. Emilia was glad of the respite – she needed a moment to catch her breath and gather her thoughts. It had been a curious evening. Pryce's off-colour performance at Waterstones had been odd, but more intriguing still was what followed. Most present had crowded around the reluctant star after her reading, clamouring for selfies and autographs. But a couple of people had held back: Emilia and a pale, bald man, who'd entered late, taking his place at the back of the crowd. He seemed intently interested in Maxine, but made no attempt to engage her. Truth be told, he seemed barely concerned with her book or the launch, buying his signed copy, but binning it shortly afterwards.

It was possible, of course, that there was a perfectly innocent explanation – there were plenty of oddballs in the world. But some instinct told Emilia that there *was* something different about this guy. So she'd hung back, keeping a close eye on him as the store emptied, and was eventually rewarded for her patience. This guy *did* have an interest in Maxine, though what it was she couldn't say. He'd waited until Maxine had left the store, then began to follow her, clinging doggedly to the shadows.

He, meanwhile, seemed blithely unaware that *he* was being followed. The trio had made solid progress, covering the ten-minute walk to Pryce's flat in good time. There the man had paused, watching as the lights came on inside. He made no move to approach her, to ring the bell; instead he loitered near the entrance, looking at the front door, the adjoining properties, though what his interest was in them, Emilia couldn't say.

She had watched this silent drama play out, debating what to do for the best. Though it went against her instincts, she'd primed herself to call the police if he made even the slightest attempt to enter Pryce's flat. But in the end it had proved unnecessary, the man moving off, hurrying away from the scene. Emilia had immediately resumed her pursuit, tailing the man down the darkened streets, until he suddenly darted down an alleyway. Moments later, a grey transit van had emerged, cruising away down the darkened street.

Emilia had given chase, chancing on this taxi, and because of her speed of thought and deed, the van was still in sight. They had now left the city centre and were pushing deep into Portswood. This was an area frequented by students and young couples – fun, lively, if a little rough around the edges. Emilia kept her eyes fixed on the van and was intrigued to see it pull off the main drag, heading deeper into the less travelled parts of the neighbourhood. Here there were numerous industrial estates, all of which would be deathly quiet at this time of night.

'You want to carry on?'

The driver shot her a glance in the rear-view mirror. Was he now starting to wonder what he'd got himself into?

'Yes. I'm sure I'll be quite safe with you here to protect me.'

Shrugging, the driver obliged, though he looked far from happy. Ignoring his discomfort, Emilia kept her eyes glued to the transit van. It was slowing now, which intrigued her. Moments later, it came to a complete halt, pulling up outside a tired-looking warehouse on the fringes of a down-at-heel industrial estate.

'You can stop here.'

The taxi driver pulled over, Emilia watching intently as the driver climbed out of the van, hurrying away into the warehouse. Emilia made a note of the address, then asked the driver to take her home. She'd done enough detective work for one evening – she made a note of the van's licence plate too – the next stage of her investigation would best be carried out in the morning, when there were more people about.

Settling back in her seat, Emilia allowed herself a brief smile. It had been an intriguing end to the day. She felt certain that she had witnessed something significant, something that might yet throw light on Justin Lanning's brutal murder. Important questions remained unanswered – what was going on with Maxine? Who was her stalker? And, crucially, what did he want with her? – but those were questions for tomorrow.

Tonight, she could simply reflect on a job well done.

Day Three

Chapter 34

There were days when she loved her job. There were others when she wished she could turn her back on it, pretending she didn't have duties and responsibilities to attend to. Today was definitely the latter.

Mornings were a time for multitasking and as ever Charlie was spinning a dozen plates. She was dressed, which was a start, but she hadn't managed to eat, which was probably why she felt so unwell. Jessica, meanwhile, was making several last-minute party demands, which reminded Charlie that she still had to organize a time for the cake to be delivered, even as Steve continued to fire questions at her.

'What time do you think you'll be back?'

'I can't say for sure. But I *will* be back in time, don't worry about that.'

'And we're sure about the bouncy castle?'

'Yes...' Charlie replied, a touch vaguely. 'But I'll ring them to double check.'

'And what about the party bags? Have we done those?'

Charlie swore silently. She'd bought all the necessaries, but had completely forgotten to make up the party bags. Truth be told, she'd been too exhausted to do anything last night.

'The stuff's in our bedroom, on top of the wardrobe, but it'll need sorting and bagging. I don't suppose you'd have time...'

Steve was giving her that look, so she shot a glance at the clock, hoping it might have miraculously slowed, that there might be time enough to do the job. But, as she'd expected, she was already running late.

'I'm sorry, love, I really have to go...'

'On a Saturday? On the day of your daughter's birthday party?'

'You know what we're dealing with here,' Charlie countered euphemistically, aware that Jessica was listening. 'But the sooner I'm in, the sooner I'll be back.'

'OK, go then.' Steve exhaled, puffing out his cheeks, even as he shepherded her towards the door.

'Thanks, love,' she responded, pecking him on the cheek, before turning to Jessie. 'And love you too. You be good for Daddy...'

Bending down, she kissed her daughter's cheeks, ruffling her hair as she did so. Then, scooping up her bag, she hurried out into the hallway before she could be waylaid again. Even as she opened the front door, she could hear Steve organizing the day, spelling out to Jessica what they would have to achieve in her absence. She was pretty sure this wasn't aimed at her – Steve wasn't that kind of guy – but even if it had been, it wouldn't have landed. Huff and puff as he might, Steve always took up the slack willingly, enjoying spending time with his daughter. He'd never been under any illusions about the demands of Charlie's job and, as long as she was safe, he was happy. It meant a larger role for him, running the house, looking after Jessica, a role he embraced. And grouse as he sometimes did, Charlie instinctively felt that he had the better half of the bargain, that somehow it was always *she* who ended up grabbing the short straw.

Perhaps it was her general sense of exhaustion, perhaps

it was the significance of Jessica's last party before the new arrival, perhaps it was just what she'd experienced yesterday, but instinctively Charlie felt reluctant about stepping back into the investigation, with all its inherent darkness and danger. Today she would much rather be at home in the bosom of her family, relaxed, happy and safe. But there was nothing for it, no way she could welsh on the team when they were up against it, so summoning her courage, she pulled the door shut behind her, stepping out into the cold.

Chapter 35

Helen sat alone at the kitchen table, swallowed by the silence. Her laptop was in front of her but apart from its dull whirring, everything was still. Normally her flat was her sanctuary, a welcome respite from her troubles, but today it had a heavy, lifeless air, a far cry from the previous morning when she'd woken entwined in the arms of her lover.

She had spent the night alone. This had been her choice, but she wondered now whether it had been the right one. Often, she craved isolation, needing to retreat from the world, from people, but occasionally this was her undoing, magnifying her fears and underscoring her loneliness. She wasn't sure what Joseph meant to her and knew she was playing a dangerous game, allowing herself to become involved with a member of her team, but there was no doubting that he was a healthy distraction, dragging her attention away from her own anxieties. Last night, however, he'd provided no such relief. Questions about him – his actions, his character, the wisdom of their relationship – had continued to swirl around her brain, even as more pressing questions, about Lanning's murder, about the investigation, jockeyed for position.

The night had crawled by. Hour by hour, minute by minute, the dark clouds had slowly descended, conjuring demons out of shadows, cutting Helen off from light and hope. In times gone by, she might have resorted to desperate measures to drive the darkness away – seeking out punishment in the city's S&M clubs or taking a razor to her own skin – but she was trying hard to move beyond that, so she'd stayed where she was, tossing and turning, as she desperately sought sleep.

Had she drifted off at any point? She felt disoriented and faint, but whether that was the result of fractured sleep or none at all, she couldn't say. Eventually, she'd given up the fight, hoping a shower might revitalize her. But half an hour later, washed, dressed, with a strong cup of coffee in front of her, she scarcely felt any better. Because those same questions remained.

It was early, but she still had half an hour before she needed to leave. Normally she would have used this time to force herself to eat something, but today she couldn't summon the enthusiasm. Instead, she'd fired up her computer and, in spite of her misgivings, despite the little voice inside telling her to stop, she'd begun to search.

She'd started with the obvious 'Joseph Hudson' and 'Detective Sergeant Joseph Hudson' but had discovered nothing that she didn't know already. Before she'd interviewed him, she'd done a thorough search of his past professional triumphs, and the odd censure, and that was all rehashed online, in various local newspapers. That wasn't what she was after. She wanted some insight into Joseph Hudson, the man.

She realized now that she knew very little about him. She had a handle on his tastes, his desires, his passions, but their odd encounter last night proved that she knew little of his character. He seemed a decent, enlightened, committed man, but there had been something in his expression last night – a naked anger – that had alarmed her. As if she had been given a fleeting glimpse of the inner man, before the veil descended once more.

Altering her tactics, she now typed in 'Karen Hudson'. Scores of names, scores of Facebook enthusiasts immediately sprang up on the screen and Helen's first instinct was to snap the laptop shut and give up her quest. But her curiosity was aroused – she'd heard tell of Joseph's ex-wife, but had never seen her in the flesh. So she began to scroll, faces whizzing by in an endless blur. Soon growing tired of this, she refined her search: 'Karen Hudson, Birkenhead.'

She knew that this had been Joseph's last posting before he upped sticks and headed south. This time many fewer entries filled the screen and it didn't take long to identify the woman in question, only one of the women on screen identifying themselves as being the ex-wife of a Merseyside police detective. There she was – a pretty, petite woman with short, cropped hair. She was nothing like Helen, in build, looks or attitude, but there was nothing to dislike about her – on the face of it, she appeared to be a pleasant, warm type.

Once again, Helen was tempted to cease her search, but her desire to hear Karen's side of the story, to corroborate Joseph's account of their break-up, compelled her to continue. So, she scrolled through the various Facebook posts, taking in the small-change of this stranger's life. Karen appeared to be happy, she now had a young son whom she clearly adored, which cheered Helen, suggesting the break-up had not been too unpleasant. But as she scrolled on, a couple of things became increasingly apparent. Firstly, that there was no new partner on the scene. And secondly, that she was still deeply upset by the behaviour of her ex-husband.

Helen felt awful, like she was spying on someone's anguish, but she couldn't turn away now. She read on with growing disquiet, realizing very quickly that the little boy in question – Kieran – was Joseph's and that her current lover had abandoned them both.

There was no question of it having been an amicable break-up. A frustrated Karen didn't hold back on Facebook, telling anyone who'd listen that Joseph had turned his back on his responsibilities and had cut them out of his life, to the extent that he didn't even send a card on the little boy's birthday. Some of her posts on the subject were angry, some upset, but all had the same theme: a loving wife and child abandoned by the man who said he'd loved them, who'd sworn to nurture and protect them.

Helen's hand hovered over the cursor, wanting to read on, but unable to do so. She felt like she'd been punched in the gut. It was possible, of course, that none of this was true, that Karen was deliberately exaggerating his faults, but the fact that Joseph had failed to tell her of the existence of his son made Helen doubt this. She suddenly felt adrift, as if she'd lost her hold on things, as if all the certainties and hopes she'd clung to were now proving to be illusory. When she felt brave enough, when the opportunity presented itself, she would challenge him on this, to see if he'd been deliberately misleading her. But it was not an encounter she was looking forward to.

The truth was that Helen didn't know what to think any more – if Joseph was basically a decent man or a wolf in sheep's clothing. If nothing else, the morning's unpleasant search had reminded her of something she should have known all along.

History is just one person's side of the story.

Chapter 36

Pushing through the doors, Joseph angled a glance towards Helen's office. He didn't want to be obvious about it, but he needed to know if she was in.

To his relief, the office was empty. The door was ajar, but there was no sign of his superior – in fact the incident room was largely deserted this morning, save for the presence of the ever-eager Osbourne and a couple of data handlers. Immediately, Joseph felt himself relax, the tension that had been building inside him all morning dissipating.

He'd wanted to get in early, to prove his commitment and worth to the team, but he'd known that might leave him alone with Helen. Since their awkward exchange last night, he'd been debating what to say to her, tying himself in knots. He knew he'd messed up, his temper getting the better of him, when a cool head had been required. He'd debated ignoring the problem, then decided that the only possible response was an outright apology. This didn't fit well with him, but perhaps was a price worth paying if it got them back on track. Now, however, it appeared that this might not be necessary after all. By the time Helen got in, the day's work would be well under way, the room full of their colleagues – perhaps last night's discomfort could be glossed over and forgotten.

Cheered by this thought, Joseph was about to head to his desk when he heard a phone ringing. Normally, this wouldn't give him pause, but the phone had now rung eight, nine, ten times without being answered. Experience had taught him that an unanswered phone in an incident room was usually a bad thing, so he sought out the source of the sound. To his surprise, he realized that it was coming from Helen's office. Now he hesitated, nervous of crossing the threshold in her absence, but still the phone rang, strident and insistent. So, swallowing his reservations, he strode into her office.

'Incident room?'

There was a pause, then the voice on the other end replied: 'I was after DI Grace? I thought this was her direct line?'

'And you are?'

Joseph dispensed with the pleasantries, irritated by the caller's tone.

'Emilia Garanita. I wonder if you could ask her to call me when she gets in—'

'If you have any questions, call media liaison. DI Grace doesn't have time to—'

'Actually, I was calling with some information, about the Lanning case.'

'What sort of information?'

There was another pause, then: 'May I ask who *you* are?'

'DS Joseph—'

'Hudson, yes, I thought it was you.'

Still she made no move to enlighten him, which angered him further.

'So?' he demanded.

'So, if you could get her to call me ...'

'I'd be delighted to. But she's not here and I'm the senior officer in charge, so if you have information that's relevant—'

'DS Brooks not in?'

'No, she isn't,' he shot back angrily.

'I see ...'

Joseph had the impression that the wily journalist was toying with him. His first instinct was to tell her where to go, but for once common sense prevailed, as another possible route opened up for him.

'I don't need to remind you that withholding information from the police is a criminal offence ...'

'Don't threaten me, Joseph. I've been working this patch a lot longer than you have.'

'Nevertheless, I'm the one that can arrest you for obstruction, so ...'

'Ah, men. Why are they always such blunt instruments?'

'Because that's the only language some people understand. Now am I going to have to bring you in or are you going to tell me what you've got?'

A long, pregnant silence, then: 'Well, I suppose I *could* tell you what I know. It would be interesting to get to know you a little better.'

'Meaning?'

'Meaning you scratch my back and I'll scratch yours. I believe I know the current location of the man you're searching for.'

Joseph said nothing, stunned by this casual bombshell. He knew he was being played, but there was no question she had his interest now. If she *did* know where this guy was hiding out, then she was one step ahead of them.

'And I'm prepared to share it with you, to help the investigation, if the terms are right. So the question is ...'

The journalist paused, her words hanging in the air. Joseph could almost see the smile on her face, as she concluded:

'...are you ready to make a deal?'

Chapter 37

Maxine stared out at the skyline, as if seeing it for the first time. The sun was climbing, bathing the cityscape in a brilliant light, making everything appear shiny and new. Southampton was not Florence nor Paris, but this morning it seemed to her as if it was the most beautiful city in the world. As she looked out at the glistening roof tiles, she actually felt tears fill her eyes. Maxine hadn't cried in years, not since she was a teenager, but now tears slid down her cheeks and she welcomed them, because of what they meant.

There were plenty of things she should be doing, book-related duties, but she stayed where she was, standing by the window. She wanted to bottle this moment, to remember it, so she could call on the memory when darker emotions set in. She had already spent a restless night, plagued by nightmares, waking just before dawn, sweaty and scared. She'd come to with a violent start, her head pounding, her mouth dry, consumed by fear. Scrambling from her bed, she'd done a circuit of the flat, checking once more that she was alone, but even as terror and paranoia started to recede, other more troubling emotions took their place. Now she was haunted by waking visions of what was still to come, of the bloodshed and agony that she was complicit in. In the cold light of day, there could be no avoiding the consequences of her actions, prompting urgent, unavoidable questions. Would she be able to live with herself? Even if she could, would she be *allowed* to? Or would someone find out what she'd done?

Even as anxiety assailed her, Maxine fought hard to resist, clamping down on the doubt, the self-loathing, through sheer force of will. The decision had been made, the die cast. Was she really going to torture herself for the rest of her days, when the matter was out of her hands? Perhaps this was the way it was meant to be, the way it was *always* going to be. Perhaps it was her destiny to live, to prosper, to grow?

Buoyed by these thoughts, Maxine had swallowed her fears, taking up a position by the floor-to-ceiling window. And, drinking in the sunrise, she had begun to see only promise and possibilities, energized by the intoxicating beauty of the world. She knew that there would be dark days ahead, that a reckoning *would* come. But that was for the future; for now she just wanted to savour the exhilaration, the surging sense of optimism.

Today was the first day of the rest of her life.

Chapter 38

He hadn't slept a wink. Despite the crippling exhaustion Callum felt, despite the two double whiskies he'd forced down his throat, respite had eluded him.

Had he managed to sleep, would his nightmares have been any less horrific than his waking thoughts? He'd worked hard to banish his fear, conjuring up all sorts of happy memories. His mother singing to him as a child, playing cricket with his dad, his go-karting victory at his twelfth birthday party, the day he met Hannah – a panorama of happiness, but the relief was only ever temporary. Before long, anxiety, paranoia and, eventually, panic seized him, poisoning his mind and whispering of dangers to come.

In the dead of night, it had all felt so surreal. He craved Hannah's company, her reassuring warmth, yet she was out partying. Laughing, drinking and joking with her oldest friends. How could one person be having so much fun when another was experiencing such anguish? Many times he'd been tempted to summon her home, but somehow he'd managed to hold off. That was the only good thing to come out of his night of hell. Perhaps he was a little stronger than he gave himself credit for.

The sun was up now, he could see it peeking through the blinds, and he should be rising too. Darting a look at his watch, he saw that it was almost ten o'clock already... but still he didn't stir. For reasons he couldn't explain, he felt safe under his duvet, as if the flimsy cotton fabric was an impenetrable shield. It was laughable, of course, but in the absence of any other support, it was a valuable crutch to keep him from going mad, from imagining phantoms that didn't exist. He knew he had an overactive imagination – it had been both a blessing and a curse throughout his life – and he was determined to rein it in. If he let fear assail him, he knew he'd be lost, years of counselling undone in an instant.

If only Hannah was here. Dear, beautiful Hannah. They had met three years ago at a housewarming party, their mutual attraction obvious from the start, and they'd been virtually inseparable ever since, despite his best attempts to drive her away. She was his rock... no, she was his *life*, the other half of his beating heart, and he was never happy when they were apart. Even now he wished he hadn't let her go out, that he had persuaded her to stay with him. And even as he thought this, something amazing happened. His phone started ringing.

Callum sprang into life. There was no caution, no reserve – he flung off the duvet and hurried over to the dressing table, where his phone was vibrating. Looking at the caller ID, his heart soared – it *was* her. She was calling to ask him to pick her up, she was coming *home*.

'Hello, love, how are you?' He was trying to speak calmly, but he knew his words sounded desperate and garbled. 'How was your night?'

There was silence at the end and suddenly – crushingly – he wondered whether this was a 'pocket call'. But then a voice spoke, low and measured.

'You have one hour to live.'

For a moment, Callum said nothing, confused and alarmed. It was a man's voice on the other end.

'Sorry...? Who is this?'

Silence.

'Where's Hannah...? Why have you got her phone?'

'You have one hour to live, Callum.'

The voice on the other end was so knowing, so intimate, that it rendered him speechless. Callum almost felt pained, as if the words were arrowing into his soul.

'Unless,' the man's voice continued, 'you'd like to trade your death for somebody else's.'

'*What?* What the hell do you mean?' Callum spluttered, disbelieving.

'Maxine and F-Fran always were such... *pretty* girls,' the voice continued, stumbling slightly. 'Would you like to make a dea—'

The phone bleeped loudly, as the call ended. Callum was surprised to find his thumb clamped on the red button. He hadn't felt himself do it, instinct had taken over, so horrified was he by this awful, twisted call. Collapsing back onto the bed, he dropped the phone, a dozen terrible questions pulsing through his brain. Why did this man have Hannah's phone? Why was he threatening him? Was it possible that this call had some connection to Justin's murder?

And if so, did it mean that *he* would be next?

Chapter 39

'Where did this come from?'

Helen was in her office, flanked by Charlie and DC Reid. There were several sheets of paper spread out on her desk, a full breakdown of the 'sightings' and 'leads' that had poured in since they released the image of their suspect, but the trio only had eyes for the mobile phone clutched in Helen's hand.

'A neighbour of Callum Harvey's, a Mrs Louise Marks...' Reid offered. 'She spotted someone behaving oddly in the street, so decided to film him.'

'Did she bring her phone in?' Helen replied, surprised.

'She's head of the Neighbourhood Watch team in that area, so was on the blower first thing this morning. When I told DS Brooks what she'd described, she decided to call Mrs Marks in, so we could see the footage first-hand.'

'She's in the interview suite now, if you want to talk to her,' Charlie added. 'But she seems on the level to me.'

Turning away from her friend, Helen looked at the footage once more. The clip was about twenty seconds long and appeared to show a thin, bald man hovering on the street, just beyond Mrs Marks' front hedge. Five seconds into the clip, he started to move, crossing the street to the other side. As the camera phone tilted up to track his progress, Harvey's house came into view. The man walked past, apparently casually, but Helen noted that his eyes never left the house. He then disappeared from shot, but moments later he reappeared, walking back in the other direction, his eyes once more glued to the property. Then he decided it was time to leave, but before he did so, he shot a glance across the road towards the Marks house, as if checking that he hadn't been seen. There was no question it was the same sinister figure who'd tried to access Justin Lanning's property – even at that distance, on this small screen, the shape of his head, the angular features, the willowy frame were unmistakable.

'When was this footage taken?' Helen demanded.

'Three days ago,' Reid answered.

'And Harvey himself said he thought he'd seen this guy hanging around?'

'Yes,' Charlie confirmed. 'But that would have been three or four days before that...'

Not the answer Helen wanted. It looked like this man was scouting the property and his repeat visits suggested serious, even deadly, intent.

'OK, we need to talk to Harvey again asap,' Helen said, straightening up. 'I'll head there now. In the meantime, cross-reference this with the other tip-offs we've had...'

She gestured to the list of names and phone numbers on the desk.

'See if anyone else from that area has called in with a sighting that matches this guy. Where did he go afterwards? Was he on foot? Did he have the van with him? Check out CCTV from local shops too, that might give us a steer on what direction he went in. Anything from the traffic cameras?'

'The van *was* sighted in the city centre briefly last night, on Oxford Street.'

Helen looked up, intrigued, but Charlie was swift to dampen her enthusiasm.

'But it went off grid somewhere in the Harefield area. I've sent extra uniforms down there, but so far there's no sign.'

'Keep on it.'

Helen was almost through the doorway, but paused on the threshold, adding: 'We need to bring this guy in.'

Chapter 40

'Are you sure we should be doing this?'

Joseph let the question hang in the air for a moment, carefully guiding the car around the corner into Lodge Road, before answering.

'What exactly is it that's worrying you, DC Malik?'

It was customary to address colleagues by their rank, but this time Joseph lingered on the young woman's title, signalling his displeasure at being questioned in this way.

'Well, shouldn't we check in with DI Grace? She'll be in by now, so—'

'To what end?'

Malik, a spirited young woman who was new to the team, paused, unnerved by her superior's terse tone.

'To ... to let her know that we've got a lead on the suspect's whereabouts.'

'Do we have a lead?'

'Isn't that why we're here?'

This was shot back at Joseph, suggesting Malik was not going to be a walkover. Irritated though he was, Joseph nevertheless felt pleased by her response. He'd written her off as a rule follower, a wallflower. Perhaps she did have some grit after all.

'We have Garanita's *word* that she knows where this guy is. And you know what that's worth...'

'So why are we here, if you think she's spinning us a line?'

'Because this time I think she *might* be telling the truth. But I'd like to be sure before I bother DI Grace with it. She's got enough on her plate as it is.'

Malik said nothing, but it was clear she wasn't happy. Her fingers rapped repeatedly on the armrest, beating out the rhythm of her anxiety.

'Should we at least let the team know where we are? Won't they be wondering...?'

Was she scared of getting into trouble? Or worried about missing out on something? It was hard to tell.

'I told DC Reid we were popping out for an hour to follow up a lead. That'll be enough for the boss.'

Malik nodded, seemingly reassured, though Joseph could tell she was uneasy. Most officers who joined Southampton Central MIT did so purely on the basis of Helen's reputation and were naturally wary of incurring her displeasure. Joseph had known Malik might kick up and had been tempted to meet Garanita alone, but it was better this way, in spite of Malik's attitude and the accompanying questions. He didn't want there to be any suggestion of him going rogue or of cosying up to Garanita, which he knew could get him fired. No, better to have a wing-man, someone who could confirm that everything was above board and on the level.

'But if you'd like to radio in, let DI Grace know that I've waylaid you, feel free...'

They were on the outskirts of Portswood now. Joseph wanted to shut the conversation down, wanted to focus on how he was going to handle Garanita. His offer was genuine, but was also loaded, suggesting as it did that DC Malik somehow doubted him, despite his superior rank. In spite of her discomfort, there was no overwhelming reason to go against Joseph in such a pointed fashion, meaning she would have to play ball for now.

'Of course not. I know I'm in capable hands...'

It was said brightly, but lacked sincerity, leading Joseph to wonder exactly what the nature of her problem with him was. No matter, the debate was over, her reservations stilled. And right on cue, even as they approached a collection of industrial estates hidden away in the back streets of Portswood, Garanita came into view, leaning on her red Corsa and looking pointedly at her watch.

This was it then. The moment of truth. Was the wily journalist just stringing him along? Or was she about to hand him the prime suspect on a plate?

Chapter 41

'What *exactly* did he say?'

Helen was speeding along The Avenue, heading north along the busy road. Cars roared past in the adjacent lane and building works were in full swing nearby, meaning she had to strain to hear Osbourne's reply through her Bluetooth helmet.

'He said he'd received a threatening phone call and needed urgent assistance.'

Osbourne's response came through clearly enough, despite the background noise.

'And you're sure it *was* Callum Harvey who was calling?'

'It was his phone number and, besides, DS Brooks took the call – she's convinced it was him.'

Helen swore under her breath. She was on her way to talk to Callum Harvey now, but suddenly her mission to Lordswood had become a lot more urgent. Justin Lanning had been murdered within an hour of receiving a similar call.

'Scramble uniformed officers to the house—'

'Already done it.'

'And tell them to sit on him until I get there.'

Helen ended the call, pulling back hard on the throttle. Her bike bucked, then sped on, eating up the road in front of her. The Avenue, which flanked the common, was one of the main routes north in Southampton and was either totally clear or utterly clogged, depending on the time of day. It had been easy going so far, but now Helen spotted a problem. A sign for roadworks ahead and beyond it a long queue snaking back from temporary traffic lights.

'Shit…'

It would be easy to ride down the side of the traffic, but the lights had just changed to red and Helen wasn't minded to get into a discussion with the workmen about why she needed to pass. So, she made an instinctive decision. To get to Lordswood, she would need to crest The Avenue, then hang a left down Burgess Road. There was a quicker, though less travelled route, however, and Helen now took it. Steering her bike up onto the pavement, she drove swiftly across it, then down the shallow bank onto the grass on the other side. The wide expanse of the common, the lungs of the city, now spread out in front of her. What she was about to do was certainly illegal and potentially dangerous, but Helen didn't hesitate, tugging back the throttle and roaring across the grass. She would never normally be so reckless, so cavalier with public safety, but today was an exception.

This was a matter of life and death.

Chapter 42

He marched back and forth, desperately trying to control his breathing. He'd hoped his call to the police might have calmed him a little, but neither his spirit nor his body were at rest. Callum was now in the middle of a full-on panic attack.

'Come on, keep it together...'

He wheezed the words, weak and fractured. In the aftermath of his ordeal with Daniel King, he had been assailed by a whole host of psychological horrors – night terrors, panic attacks, leaden bouts of depression – none of which had been helped by his asthma, which he'd had since he was a toddler. Over time, he'd managed to get a grip on these awful visitations, though not his asthma, which still affected him badly.

He put the inhaler to his lips and pressed down hard on the trigger, sucking the medication into his mouth. The cool blast gave him a temporary feeling of relief, the memory of previous tokes instinctively cheering him, but his respite was short-lived. For some reason, the Salbutamol didn't seem to be doing its job today. His chest felt tight, his lungs were heaving – panic was assailing him.

Sitting back down on the sofa, he put his head between his legs and inhaled slowly, trying to regulate his breathing. It was going to be OK. Any minute now the police would be here and then things would start to improve. He would explain what had happened, they would find Hannah and bring her home, then they would get to the bottom of this twisted prank. Because that must be what it was, just an awful, cruel joke ...

Yet still they didn't come. Why were they taking so long? Every second seemed to last a lifetime, ratcheting up the pressure, cranking up his terror. Was it possible that his lungs would pack up? That he would have a heart attack? That he would lose his mind before they arrived? Anything seemed possible, even probable now, and suddenly Callum felt utterly abandoned. Why could he not hear sirens? Why were they not rushing to his door? Why was someone not putting him out of his misery?

And then he heard it. Snapping his head up, he listened intently. Was his mind playing tricks on him? No, he could definitely hear it – footsteps coming up the path. Measured, confident footsteps. Relief burst forth and he laughed out loud. This was it, they had arrived. This was the rescue party.

Seconds later, the doorbell rang, long and loud.

Chapter 43

Her tyres tore into the turf as the Kawasaki roared across the common. She was making good progress, speeding in a sharp diagonal across the park, hopeful that she would make it to Harvey's residence in less than five minutes. She was drawing lots of strange looks – no doubt Southampton Central was receiving numerous phone calls about a lunatic biker on the loose – but Helen didn't care. Speed was all that mattered now.

She was racing towards the ornamental lake, but now spotted an obstacle – a high-vis snake of schoolchildren up ahead, heading for the play park. She couldn't risk driving close to them, the turf was soft today and she was liable to skid, so changing tack, she angled back onto the tarmac path, heading directly north. Soon she was roaring past the artesian well and the old racecourse, before angling back onto the turf, having bypassed the knot of schoolchildren. Now she cut left, skirting the path, as she rounded a small stream, heading fast towards the north-west corner of the common.

It was soon upon her and she lowered her speed, manoeuvring herself through the narrow entry gate and back onto the road. Mercifully it was clear and after a few swift turns, she found herself on Lordswood Road. Gently upping her speed, she leaned into the bike, intent on making swift progress.

She hadn't had any update yet, which unnerved her. Uniform had been scrambled, so why hadn't she heard anything? Thanks to police cuts, beat patrols were quite wide-ranging now, so it was possible it would take them fifteen minutes to get there, but still... The fact that she'd heard nothing suggested that they were still making their way there or had arrived and were dealing with an incident. Neither of which was good news.

She was moving fast, approaching the crossroads with Coxford Road. Once more the traffic was building, so Helen mounted the pavement quickly, cutting off the corner. A pram suddenly came into view, and Helen had to brake hard to avoid it, wiggling around the obstacle then back onto the road, before speeding away, the surprised mother's expletive hanging in the air.

She was close now. Cutting down Coxford Road, she angled right into Greywell Avenue, then right again onto Wonston Road. Harvey's house was number fifty-two and she roared towards it, swallowing up the last few yards, before coming to an abrupt, skidding halt.

Leaping off, she spotted them – two uniformed coppers pounding on Callum's door. Sprinting up the path, she took in the modest house in front of her, looking for signs of trouble, but on the surface everything seemed normal.

'What's happening?'

The officers turned at the sound of her voice.

'Nothing, ma'am. We just got here, but haven't managed to raise anyone.'

Where *was* he? Harvey had said he would sit tight and wait for them. So what was going on? Stepping off the path, Helen peered in through the front window, searching for signs of life. Even as she did so, her blood froze.

'Get away from the door.'

The startled officers hesitated, then backed away. Composing herself, took two steps back, then sped forward, launching her boot at the door. It immediately burst open, the flimsy latch catapulting into the room beyond. Helen followed it, racing into the house to the prone figure lying half-hidden behind the sofa.

Kneeling down, she turned the body over, praying that she wasn't too late. But the sight in front of her put paid to that fond hope. Callum Harvey lay in her arms, lifeless and pale, a nasty, livid ring of bruising around his neck.

'Call for assistance,' Helen barked, as the horrified officers joined her. 'And check the rest of the rooms.'

Helen was already on her feet, hurrying towards the back of the house. Callum's body was still warm, suggesting the attack had just taken place, but the house itself was cold and as she approached the rear, Helen saw why. The back door was hanging open.

Helen barrelled through it, charging across the grass to the gate. This too lay open and Helen pushed through it. There was a small alleyway beyond, leading back to the road, but it too was deserted. Harvey's attacker had escaped.

Breathing heavily, Helen leaned on the fencepost, cursing. She had been close, but not close enough.

Chapter 44

He stared at her, disbelieving.

'No way. That was never part of the deal.'

But the journalist seemed utterly unabashed.

'We agreed the main points, this is the small print.'

'I said I'd help you out where I could,' Joseph shot back angrily. 'Not that you could ride along with us.'

'Joseph, I have loads of other sources who can give me titbits of information. What I need is someone who can cut me in on the *action*.'

'Are you nuts? I can't have you following me around when I'm bringing people in. It'd be dangerous for you and would compromise our investigations.'

His voice was raised now and looking up he clocked DC Malik staring at him from the car. He'd hoped his conversation with Garanita would be short and sweet, but still he'd taken the precaution of leaving her behind. Now he was glad he had. It was obvious, however, that they were not completely out of earshot, so tugging the journalist behind a large municipal bin, he continued to press his case.

'What if something happens to you? I would be responsible for that.'

'I can take care of myself.'

'Like you did with Daisy Anderson?'

This provoked an immediate reaction – Garanita didn't enjoy being reminded of her hostage ordeal.

'That was a mistake, one I don't intend to repeat.'

'Be that as it may, I can't have you as my shadow. It will cause too many problems, raise too many questions.'

'Then we're done here.'

Emilia turned to go, but Joseph stopped her, laying a restraining hand on her arm.

'I *will* arrest you for obstruction of justice.'

'Then I'll say I was mistaken. That I got it wrong. And maybe I have…'

Her tone was teasing. Joseph didn't have a leg to stand on and he knew it. He faced the unenviable choice of playing ball with Emilia or losing their lead. It infuriated him to be put in this position, but he didn't have the power here.

'If we do this, we're going to do it my way,' he eventually replied.

'You're the boss.'

'You stay well back. You can get your pictures when we have someone in cuffs, when *I* say it's safe to do so.'

'Fair play.'

'And this is a one-time deal.'

'We'll see…'

She smiled once more, as if she knew each move in advance. Infuriated, Joseph was about to hit back when a loud noise made him pause. A vehicle was roaring down the road, careless of safety or noise. Instinctively, Joseph put his arm out, easing Emilia further behind cover. Seconds later, a grey transit van sped past. It was gone in a flash, but Joseph was sure he'd read the number plate correctly. This was their van, the one they'd been searching for.

Finally, the prime suspect was in their sights.

Chapter 45

She spotted it as soon as she entered the room.

Callum Harvey lay where she'd left him, his face contorted in agony, his body twisted into a strange position, one arm tucked underneath him, the other stretched helplessly out across the carpet. At first, Helen thought he might have been trying to claw himself across the room to safety, but now realized that a mobile phone was clamped in his fist.

The uniformed officers were securing the scene, so slipping off her boots and sliding on latex gloves, Helen picked her way across the springy carpet towards the corpse. With luck, the thick, absorbent fibres would contain useful forensic evidence for Meredith, but that was for later – now Helen's sole priority was to find out exactly what had happened here.

Kneeling down next to Harvey, she slid her fingers between his, easing open his fist. The phone – a Huawei – fell into her outstretched palm. It was still on. More than that, it was still warm, the screen covered in smudged fingerprints. They were presumably his own, though they would have check, so taking care not to smear them, Helen opened up the main menu. Selecting Call History, she took in the list of numbers. She recognized the most recent one – it was the call Harvey had made to Southampton Central at 10.05 a.m. Scrolling back, Helen was not surprised to find another call immediately preceding it – *incoming* this time – clocked at 10.02 a.m.

The identity of the caller, however, was confusing. It appeared Harvey had been called by someone from his own contact list – 'Hannah'. The name immediately chimed with Helen – she was sure Harvey was engaged to a Hannah Bradwell – and flicking back through his call log and messages, taking in the numerous calls and affectionate texts, it was soon clear that the call *had* come from his absent fiancée.

Quickly, Helen double-checked this morning's call history, but she'd been right first time – Harvey had received no other calls. Worried, she now scanned the room for a landline, another mobile – some other means of contacting Harvey – but there was nothing. And now a new thought occurred to her. Returning her attention to Harvey's mobile, Helen sought out Call Duration. And now she ground to a halt. Hannah's call to Harvey had lasted exactly fifty-nine seconds – a strikingly similar duration to the call Justin Lanning had received on the day *he* was murdered.

The odds of this being a coincidence were small, which set Helen's alarm bells ringing. Lanning had been contacted via an unregistered phone, his killer deliberately concealing their identity, whereas Harvey had been threatened via a call from his fiancée. This meant that either *she* was their killer – suddenly reckless and self-advertising – or that something had happened to her and the killer had her phone in his possession. Either way, Helen's priority was clear.

She had to find Hannah Bradwell. And fast.

Chapter 46

'How sure are we?'

Simmons' tone was unusually brusque, so Charlie got straight to the point.

'Meredith Walker will send through photos as soon as she has them … but DI Grace's description was pretty clear. It was ligature strangulation.'

Simmons didn't respond, staring into a space just above Charlie's shoulder, almost as if she hadn't heard her, leaving the junior officer unsure how to proceed. A breathless Helen had called in the news, even as she hurried from the scene. As a result, the rest of the team were engaged in frantic attempts to track down Callum Harvey's missing fiancée and it had fallen to Charlie to update the chief super. Normally, Simmons was calm, decisive, unruffled. But today she looked rattled.

'And the victim …' Simmons continued. 'Did he have any professional connection to Justin Lanning?'

'No, he's a maths tutor.'

'Were they still friends? Did they see each other much?'

'Too early to say, but there was nothing in Lanning's calendar or call history that suggested they were in regular contact.'

Charlie could tell this was not the answer Simmons had been hoping for.

'Then, we're saying what...?' her superior responded, her agitation clear. 'That someone is deliberately targeting this group of survivors?'

It seemed crazy – the small band of teenagers had escaped certain death, only to now find themselves hunted – but there was no denying that, on the face of it, this was the obvious conclusion. The lives of Justin Lanning and Callum Harvey had diverged markedly since leaving school – in terms of affluence, professional success, personal lives, everything. The only thing that appeared to link them was their past trauma and, now, their deaths.

'That has to be a key line of enquiry,' Charlie confirmed. 'But we're keeping an open mind.'

'I'm not sure the press will be so circumspect,' Simmons muttered darkly. 'This is a bloody gift for them. And you can bet your bottom dollar they'll waste no time in dredging up old history, whipping up hysteria...'

'Let them. We've dealt with worse before.'

Charlie meant it and her quiet strength seemed to buoy Simmons.

'You're right, I'm sorry. It's just a bit of shock. I guess I was assuming... *hoping*... that Lanning's death might be linked to his work, a deal gone wrong or...'

'We were all thinking that, but...'

'But you have to follow the evidence.'

'Exactly.'

Simmons considered for a moment, then replied: 'OK, then, I'll talk to media liaison, decide on a line to take. In the meantime, I'll let you crack on, but I *would* like to hear of any developments as soon as you have them. From here on in, we're facing a shit storm.'

Charlie thanked her superior and left, hastening towards the incident room. As she marched briskly over the faded carpets, dodging detectives heading in the opposite direction, Simmons' words remained with her. The media *would* make great play of the coincidence of their deaths ... and who could blame them? The individual murders were brutal and shocking, but put together they presented an altogether more chilling narrative. It wouldn't do to get ahead of themselves, but Charlie already had the feeling that they were being pulled into a dark vortex that promised only further bloodshed.

Pushing into the incident room, she was pleased to see that the team were hard at it, hammering the phones in pursuit of Harvey's missing fiancée. Finding her could help unravel much about this mystery and Charlie had been loath to abandon coordinating the search in order to update Simmons. But it had to be done and it had to be done by her, as Joseph Hudson was conspicuous by his absence. He *had* been spotted first thing this morning but had vanished around nine and hadn't been seen since. It seemed a curious, inexplicable, time to go missing, reducing the chain of command at a critical point in a fast-moving investigation. At first, Charlie had been irritated by his absence; now she was growing angry, so tugging her phone from her pocket, she tried his number again.

'This is Joseph Hudson. Please leave a mess—'

Charlie hung up, a sliver of concern now mingling with her anger.

Where the hell *was* he?

Chapter 47

He stole across the dirty floor, praying he wouldn't be heard.

As soon as the van had passed, Joseph was on the move, abandoning Garanita to rejoin DC Malik. Together they'd set off after the van, but the pursuit was short, the suspect pulling up by a warehouse at the far end of the industrial estate.

Lingering a short distance away, the officers glimpsed a figure hurry into the dark interior of the building, pulling the door firmly shut behind him. Malik's natural instincts kicked in once more, suggesting they call it in, but Joseph had scotched that idea. They would do *nothing* until they were 100 per cent certain that this *was* their suspect – the memory of last night's disappointing failure was still fresh. For his own piece of mind – not to mention his standing in the team – it wasn't one he wanted to repeat.

Sending Malik around the back to cut off any possible escape routes, Joseph had moved cautiously towards the main door. To his relief, it was shut, but not locked, opening silently as he eased the handle down. Inching it open a fraction, he slipped inside, pulling it to behind him.

The gloom of the interior contrasted sharply with the sunlight outside and for a moment Joseph stood still, blinking, trying to penetrate the surrounding darkness. Slowly his eyes became accustomed to the murk; however, a small roof light overhead provided a modicum of illumination, and he began to get the measure of his surroundings. There was no sign of the suspect, nor any sound either. The whole place was deathly quiet, which was perhaps no surprise, as the warehouse was filled with cardboard boxes. Towers of them, piled high, creating tall corridors that cut out light and swallowed sound. The cavernous space had a lifeless, intimidating feel to it, the corridors seeming to crowd in on you, but Joseph had not come this far to chicken out. Summoning his courage, he pressed on.

The concrete floor was grubby but solid, his soft-soled shoes making no noise as he padded down the gloomy corridor. He had no idea where their suspect was, but instinct drew him towards the back of the building. Moving swiftly but silently, he scanned around him, searching for signs of life. But there appeared to be nothing here except boxes – all of which had names on them. At first, these labels meant nothing to him, but slowly they became more familiar – shadows of past investigations drifting across his mind – before finally, as he reached the rear of the warehouse, they became instantly recognizable. Rose West. Jeffrey Dahmer. Peter Sutcliffe. Then, most surprisingly of all, Charles Manson. What the hell was this place?

Joseph suddenly had the feeling he'd stumbled upon something dark, something unexpected. Now, for the first time, he wondered if perhaps Malik had been right, that they *should* have called for backup. But even as he paused, contemplating retreat, he heard something. A noise towards the rear of the warehouse.

Slowing his progress, he inched forwards, keeping his back to the cardboard wall as he glided towards the end of the corridor. Reaching a junction, he peered round the tall wall and suddenly he saw him. His back was to Joseph, but there was no doubting that this was their man – the gaunt, bald figure who'd tried to break into Lanning's home. He was bending over a table, examining something, though what Joseph couldn't see.

What should he do? Protocol demanded he withdraw, summoning help before proceeding. But the entrance was much further away than the suspect – would he be able to retreat without alerting the suspect to his presence? No, better to proceed. Capitalize on the element of surprise and have the suspect in cuffs, before he knew what had happened to him.

Carefully, Joseph took a step forwards. Then another. Still the figure remained preoccupied by what lay on the table, unaware of the danger he was in. Joseph took another step. Then another. He was only ten feet from the man, who now began rummaging in a box beneath the table, distracted and oblivious. Easing his cuffs from his belt, Joseph took another decisive step towards the fugitive.

And now the man spun round, turning to face the intruder. Joseph hadn't seen this coming – he was startled by the man's sudden movement and only had a second to react as the suspect's hand shot towards him. For an awful moment, Joseph thought his attacker might have a knife, or even a gun, but now he realized the man was clutching a taser – a nanosecond before its metal coil rocketed towards him. If it hit him, Joseph would be paralyzed, utterly at his attacker's mercy, but diving to the right, he felt the charge speed past, missing him by an inch. Joseph collided roughly with the floor, the breath punched from him, but instantly he scrambled to his feet, his hands slithering over the dust. It was graceless and lumbering but he righted himself, turning to face the suspect, ready for a fight. But the attack was already over, the suspect haring away down the corridor, sprinting towards the main exit as if his life depended on it.

Without hesitation, a furious Joseph sped off after him, determined not to let him escape. He was dirty, breathless and at a distinct disadvantage, but he would not be beaten.

The chase was on.

Chapter 48

She sprinted across the polished floor, dodging loitering tourists, before skidding to a halt by the front desk. Pulling her warrant card from her jacket, she confronted the startled receptionist.

'Hannah Bradwell. Which room is she in?'

The young woman looked stupefied, unable to speak.

'I'm with Hampshire Police,' Helen continued, enunciating very clearly. 'And I need to find Hannah Bradwell. Which room is she in?'

Now the receptionist grasped the urgency of the situation, fumbling with her computer. Helen took a moment to take in her surroundings – their search for Bradwell had led her to a Travelodge near the Westquay, where the hen party was staying. Helen had raced here, making it to the hotel in less than twenty minutes, but on the face of it nothing seemed amiss. The lobby was full of happy, relaxed people enjoying their weekend, oblivious to the drama playing out under their noses.

'Room 612. It's on the sixth—'

But Helen was already on the move, racing across the atrium and sliding inside the lift, just as doors slammed shut. Ignoring the startled looks of the American tourist inside, Helen stabbed the button for the sixth floor.

'Come on, come on…'

Slowly the lift began its ascent, before coming to a halt on the fourth floor. The doors now slid open, Helen's companion eyeing her warily as she exited. Helen watched her go, but even as she prayed for the doors to shut, she saw a large family party readying themselves to enter. Even now the father had reached out his arm to hold the doors, so Helen didn't hesitate, pushing past her American friend and sprinting towards the stairs.

Barrelling through the door, Helen took them three at a time, driving up, up, up. Spilling out onto the sixth floor, she took a moment to get her bearings, then raced on.

606, 607, 608…

She tore past the doors, sprinting down the long, airless corridor.

609, 610, 611…

Killing her speed, Helen came to a halt outside room 612. Rapping loudly on the door, she cried out: 'Hannah?'

Silence from within.

'Hannah. Are you in there?'

Still nothing.

'Are you OK?'

Helen's voice sounded strangulated and unnatural, her words dying in the hushed corridor. She regretted now not having thought to get a master key from reception, but dismissed the idea of returning there. Time was not a luxury she had.

So, for the second time today, she took a few steps back, readying herself to break down the door. She counted down from three, then launched herself forwards – only for the door to suddenly swing open. Instantly, Helen put the brakes on, but still she was just an inch away from taking out the startled woman in front of her. Righting herself, she stumbled slightly to avoid contact, even as an aggrieved Hannah Bradwell advanced upon her, tugging her robe around her, as she demanded, 'What the bloody hell is going on?'

Chapter 49

'What the hell are you playing at?'

They had missed the journalist by a few inches, Emilia Garanita just managing to jump out of the way as they sped past.

'If we catch our man *and* take out Garanita in the process, I'd call that a result...'

Joseph shot a look in his rear-view mirror. Even now, he could see the aggrieved journalist hurrying to her car, but he had no interest in her now. His sole focus was on bringing their man in.

'Just don't get us killed in the process...' Malik grumbled, as she slid the blue light out of the window, fixing it to the roof.

Joseph ignored her, his eyes glued to the speeding van ahead. Their siren was already blasting out its clarion call, but so far it didn't seem to be helping. It was scattering the traffic, allowing them easy progress, but they didn't seem to be gaining on the suspect, who weaved expertly between the cars, changing lanes constantly. Having been surprised by Joseph, he'd fled the warehouse, jumping straight into his van and roaring off. Joseph wasn't far behind, Malik joining him at the front of the building, but their vehicle was parked twenty yards away, meaning their suspect had a healthy start. It was clear that he intended to make good use of it.

'Officers in pursuit of suspect, heading east on Thornhill Park

Road. Suspect is driving a grey Vauxhall Vivaro, registration number oscar, echo, one five, victor, zulu, lima...'

Joseph noticed that Malik hadn't checked with him before radioing in. He felt a flash of anger, though he knew she was only following protocol. Nevertheless, there was something in the way she did it – a tightness in her voice, the way she turned away from him – that signalled her irritation. Was he making an enemy of the young DC?

Pushing these thoughts away, he returned his attention to the grey van, which continued to dart in and out of view, changing lanes erratically and violently. Horns were blaring, cars were braking – already there had been several near misses. Gripping the steering wheel tightly, keeping the acceleration steady, Joseph followed in the van's wake, determined to stay with the fugitive. But it was no easy task – the grey van seemed to be speeding up, undaunted by the obstacles in front of it, or the pursuing officers behind.

Now, however, Joseph spotted an opportunity. Thornhill Park Road merged into Bitterne Road East, as you headed towards the centre. There was always traffic where this major artery merged once more with Maybray King Way and so it proved now – a line of slow-moving cars coming into view. Sensing victory, Joseph pressed down on the accelerator, speeding towards the fleeing van.

But the fugitive sensed the danger. Without warning, the van now lurched right, cutting across the oncoming traffic and swinging a hard right into a side road. Braking sharply, Joseph followed suit, just missing a braking bus. Malik shot him an angry look, hanging onto the handrail.

'Suspect now heading north-east on Somerset Avenue...'

The operator responded, offering details of patrol cars being scrambled to intercept. Joseph hoped they wouldn't be long.

The fleeing suspect was careless of the danger, ramping up his speed to over eighty miles an hour, despite the fact that they were moving into a heavily residential area. Instinctively, Joseph felt his jaw tighten. The sooner this pursuit was over, the better.

'What are we going to do?'

Joseph ignored Malik, determined not to be distracted.

'We've got Woodlands Community College up ahead and beyond that there's a children's play area...'

It was just like Malik to sound like a talking map.

'There's not a lot we *can* do,' Joseph replied, as calmly as he could. 'We follow the protocol, we bring this guy in.'

'But at the speed he's going, if he hits someone...'

'So we should let him go?'

'No, of course not. But if we ease off a bit, let the other cars box him in—'

'They're still half a mile away and if we lose sight of him, there's no telling when we'll find him again. If he abandons the van, we'll have no mark upon him at all. We need to keep him in view...'

Joseph pressed down on the accelerator, bridging the gap between the vehicles. It was risky, but he could see no other way. Once more the fugitive responded, raising *his* speed. Startled pedestrians flashed by in the corner of Joseph's vision, spinning on the pavement to watch the desperate pursuit, but he kept his eyes fixed on the road.

Was Malik right? Should he ease off? No, they had to stay with the suspect, had to bring him in. Joseph teased the accelerator once more and now, to his surprise, he saw the van's red brake lights flick on. For a moment, Joseph thought their fugitive was about to stop and make a break for it. But, no, he'd killed his speed in order to negotiate a bend in the road, riding over the kerb and away, as he sped down Somerset Avenue towards the next junction.

The children's play area was just up ahead. This presented an obvious problem, with parents and carers regularly crossing the road, but Joseph was pleased to see the siren doing its work. Even from this distance he could see heads turning, parents retreating from the road, as the cars sped towards them.

Looking ahead, Joseph now saw that the way was clear. It was two hundred feet or so towards the intersection with West End Road. From there, the van could swing right towards the cricket ground or left towards Bitterne and, as if sensing this opportunity, the fugitive sped up once more. He was hurtling towards the junction, Joseph just behind him, still showing no sign of giving up the fight.

'Where the hell are they...?' Joseph muttered angrily, furious that they were still alone in their pursuit.

The patrol cars were supposed to be attending, cutting off any escape routes, so where were they? Was he going to have to bring this guy in alone?

The junction loomed large in front of them. They were fifty yards from it, now thirty, now ten. With another burst of speed, the van roared into the junction, then suddenly ground to a halt, skidding wildly as it tried to avoid an articulated lorry directly in front of it. The fugitive broke hard, but too late, slamming into the side of the moving vehicle, before stopping dead.

Immediately, Joseph pulled his foot off the accelerator, slamming it on the brake pedal, but even as he did so, the grey bulk of the van seemed to fill his windscreen. A sickening impact was imminent, so acting on instinct, Joseph wrenched the steering wheel hard to the left. He was thrown into Malik, who herself connected hard with the window, as the car leapt sideways. For a moment, Joseph thought it'd worked, that they had avoided a collision, but then the car shook violently as it clipped the side of the van, cannoning off it.

Now time seemed to stand still, Joseph watching in horror as the car left the road, rearing up on its left side, before toppling over completely. Blood rushed to his head, his ears filled with the sound of screeching metal as the roof of the vehicle slid across the ground. Then another juddering impact, the car coming to a shuddering halt, glass shattering all around them. Then there was silence.

Joseph hung there, stunned. His vision was blurred, he couldn't hear properly and there was no movement at all from Malik.

'Malik?'

Nothing.

'Malik. Are you OK?'

He tried to turn to her, but found he couldn't move. And now he started to panic. Would she be OK? Would *he* be OK? And what had happened to their suspect?

There was no way of knowing, so he hung there, powerless, suspended in the battered vehicle, fear assailing him. He had started the day with high hopes, determined to make a difference, to bring their suspect in, but all those hopes had now disintegrated. Suddenly his world had turned upside down.

Chapter 50

She stared at her in utter disbelief.

Hannah Bradwell, nursing a hangover and still groggy, had not held back, berating the strange, leather-clad woman for disturbing her sleep, after what had clearly been a wild night out. But Helen's warrant card had had a sobering effect, as had the shocking news that she'd just imparted.

Bradwell sat on the edge of the bed, her eyes blinking regularly, rhythmically, as she tried to take it in. Her fiancé, her love, was dead.

'What... what happened?'

She could barely muster the words, she looked nauseous and her head was clearly pounding. Whether this was a result of shock, or last night's indulgence, was hard to say. Placing the waste-paper bin strategically in front of her, Helen took a seat on the bed.

'We're still trying to piece that together,' Helen replied, gently. 'Callum rang us just after ten o'clock this morning, concerned for his safety. We think he was attacked shortly after that, before we could get there...'

Hannah shook her head, apparently stunned that all this could have played out while she was tucked up asleep in this quiet hotel room.

'Why was he worried... what had happened?' she asked, turning to Helen now.

'I was hoping you'd be able to help with us that. He received a phone call just before he rang us, from someone making direct threats to his life. That call was made from your phone, Hannah.'

Another sledgehammer blow, the bereaved woman reeling now.

'No, no way. That's not possible...'

She snatched up her handbag and started rummaging through it. With each passing second, her investigation became more urgent – make-up, jewellery, a novel tumbling from the bag as she dug deeper.

'It's not here. My phone's gone...'

Ashen, she offered the empty bag as evidence. Helen took it from her, sifting the remaining contents and inner pockets. But there was no doubt she was telling the truth.

'When did you last have it?'

'When we went to the club. I checked it while I was there.'

'Where was this?'

'The Moon Lounge... on Dorchester Road. We had a VIP area. My bag was on the floor, my phone was *definitely* in it. I remember I checked it around eleven o'clock. After that we had more drinks, then we went dancing and... and I suppose I didn't look at it again...'

She petered out, horrified by the implications of her drunken carelessness. She looked like she was about to recede into herself, overwhelmed with grief and shock, so Helen moved quickly to keep her on board.

'When did you last speak to Callum?'

'When I left the house last night.'

'How did he seem to you yesterday? During the last few days...?'

'Generally, he's been fine...' she replied slowly, a cloud descending over her expression now. 'Callum-like, but fine. Then last night...'

'Yes?'

'...he was uptight, upset. It was because of what happened to Justin...'

She petered out again, connections seeming to form in her mind.

'Do you think he might have *known* he was in danger?' Helen prompted.

'I'm not sure, I don't think so, but he *was* nervous about being left alone.'

She was speaking slowly, a dozen nightmarish possibilities distracting her.

'...I offered to stay with him, more than once, but he insisted I go, said he didn't want me to miss the cocktails...'

Her voice shook, her eyes filling with tears.

'You mustn't blame yourself, Hannah. There was nothing you could have done and, had you been there, you might have been harmed too...'

The young woman said nothing, staring at the floor, making no attempt to brush away the tears that slid down her cheeks.

'How...' she eventually gulped. 'How did he die?'

It took everything she had to get these last words out. Helen didn't want to answer her, but had no choice.

'He was strangled. I'm very sorry.'

Bradwell didn't react at all at first, as if the words hadn't registered. Then she seemed to collapse in on herself. Burying her head in her hands, her whole body shaking, she began to moan – deep, long, agonized expressions of pain. Helen wanted to comfort her, to try and stop her slipping into a vortex of agony, but now her phone started to ring, loud and urgent. Helen hesitated for a moment, then rose gently.

'I'm really sorry, I have to take this...'

Bradwell didn't answer, continuing to stare at the floor. Guilt-stricken, Helen hurried away, stepping into the adjoining bathroom.

'DI Grace...'

'It's DC Osbourne, ma'am.'

Helen had assumed it would be one of her team and hoped it would be good news. But Osbourne's tone put paid to that fond notion.

'I'm afraid there's been an incident...' He paused, raising Helen's fears still further. '...involving DC Malik and DS Hudson.'

Chapter 51

'What in God's name were you thinking?'

Normally, Helen would have held back, given that there were members of the public nearby and that Joseph was obviously badly shaken, but her blood was up. Joseph's reckless pursuit had put numerous lives at stake – it was a miracle nobody had been killed.

'We had eyes on him, I felt we had no choice but to try and bring him in.'

The suspect was in custody, which was one small mercy. It might even save Joseph from suspension, but the fugitive's apprehension had come at a considerable cost. The suspect would probably be fine, though he was currently getting checked out at South Hants hospital, as was DC Malik, who had a nasty case of concussion. Joseph seemed to have escaped largely unscathed, which was more than could be said for his pool car. It, like the van it had been pursuing, was extensively damaged, badly bent out of shape. All in all, a bad morning's work, given the risks they'd run in this heavily residential area.

'And you felt you could do that alone, did you?'

'Of course not,' Joseph countered. 'We radioed in our pursuit, followed all the protocols *to the letter*—'

'DC Malik will confirm that, will she?'

Joseph said nothing, telling Helen all she needed to know. DC Malik was badly shaken, but had nevertheless found time to make her anger known to her attending colleagues, once the fire service had cut her free.

'You know the rules,' Helen continued, tugging him away from the prying eyes behind the shattered carcass of the pool car. 'If you have eyes on the prize, you call it in first.'

'I didn't have time,' Joseph protested. 'The guy tried to take me out with a taser and then he ran. If we hadn't given chase, we'd have lost him.'

'That may be true. But why were you even in that position in the first place?'

Now Joseph hesitated.

'The team couldn't raise you this morning, despite several attempts to do so. The chain of command was compromised, nobody had a clue where you were. Then suddenly you're chasing the prime suspect through a kids' playground—'

'It wasn't like that—'

'So what *was* it like? How had you managed to get a bead on this guy, when the rest of the team hadn't been able to find him?'

Another moment's hesitation, before Joseph responded.

'I got a tip-off.'

'From whom?'

'A source.'

Helen stared at him, stunned that he was thinking of holding out on her.

'And this source is...?'

'A contact, that's all.'

'When did you get this tip-off?'

'Early this morning.'

'And you chose not to share it because...?'

'I wanted to verify it really *was* our man.'

'And having done so, you decided to play the hero, despite the grave danger you would put yourself *and* your colleague in, not to mention innocent members of the public—'

'I've told you it wasn't like that,' Joseph countered, his volume rising.

'I think that's exactly what it was like. You had your phone, your radio, hell, you even had a colleague with you, who could have called it in, when you first spotted him. Instead, you *deliberately* went off grid—'

'No, I didn't—'

'Even as the rest of the team were dealing with a second murder, one you were *blissfully* unaware of, because you were playing Boy Wonder. Do you deny it?'

Joseph eyeballed her, but said nothing.

'So I'll ask you again, DS Hudson. What on earth were you doing? And don't even think about lying to m—'

'I was doing my job, *ma'am*.'

It was not the hostility in his expression which shocked Helen. It was the way he said that last word, investing it with venom, bitterness and deep, deep sarcasm. As if he was mocking her right to criticize him, as if he was mocking *her*.

'Now if you'll excuse me, I'd like to see how DC Malik is doing.'

Without waiting for a response, he stalked off, heading away towards a gaggle of concerned colleagues. Helen stood still, shock bleeding into her anger. She knew Joseph Hudson was a rough diamond when she took him on, knew he'd had his brushes with authority before. But even so, she'd never expected such open hostility, such an obvious flouting of hierarchy and rank, nor such a personal attack on her. Did he just hate having a boss? Or was it the fact that she was a woman that riled him?

Given his attitude, and her surprising discoveries earlier this morning, Helen suddenly realized that she didn't know this man *at all*. A man whom she'd thought she liked, was perhaps even developing feelings for. Everything suddenly seemed up in the air, as if the foundations of the team, of her relationship with Joseph, had been shaken to the core. Should she have listened to her first instincts after all? That little voice inside her telling her that pursuing a relationship with Joseph was a reckless, foolish idea? As Helen watched her agitated deputy haranguing his juniors for news of the stricken colleague, one thing was abundantly, painfully, certain. There would be trouble ahead.

Chapter 52

She flicked through the photos, a wide smile stretched across her face. This was better than she could possibly have hoped for.

Having promised Hudson that she'd remain at a safe distance, Emilia had waited all of five minutes before setting off towards the isolated warehouse. She'd hoped to get a better vantage point, somewhere close to the building where she could get a decent photo of the suspect emerging in cuffs, but she'd barely walked ten yards before the grey van came roaring towards her. Deciding discretion was the better part of valour, she'd stepped aside, glimpsing the gaunt figure at the wheel as he shot past. Emerging from her hiding place, she got off a few good shots of the departing vehicle, before she heard a noise behind her. Turning, she saw Hudson's pool car on top of her, only just making it out of the way in time. The car must have missed her by inches – something Emilia felt was deliberate on Hudson's part.

Less determined journalists might have counted their blessings and given up at this point, but Emilia knew fortune favoured the brave, so she'd joined the pursuit. Down Bitterne Road, up Somerset Avenue, past Woodlands College and then the cherry on the cake – the spectacular crash on West End Road.

The violence of the two impacts – first the grey van ramming a passing lorry, then Hudson's epic flip – had taken her breath away. For a second, she'd hesitated to approach the carnage, wary of what she might discover, but then her better instincts took over. Grabbing her Nikon, she'd abandoned her Corsa and hurried towards the scene, calling for an ambulance as she went. Whatever Grace might think, she wasn't a monster.

By the time she got there, shocked motorists were helping Joseph Hudson from the car, even as the fleeing suspect half stumbled, half fell from the cab of his vehicle. He was trying to escape, but was too disoriented to make a decent fist of it and was soon in custody. Hudson, torn between attending to his stricken colleague and keeping an eye on their suspect, seemed not to notice Emilia. Meaning she was free to snap away at her leisure – taking in the details of the handcuffed fugitive, the wreckage of the cars, the shocked members of the public and the bruised, bloodied figure of Joseph Hudson.

Eventually, traffic officers arrived, forcing her to retreat. Which was a pity as shortly after that, DI Grace roared up, looking like she wanted to take someone's head off. How she would have loved to be a fly on the wall when she tore a strip off Joseph Hudson, but the pair of them were soon closeted away out of sight, so Emilia had returned to her car to examine her haul.

'Police are saying West End Road may remain closed for the rest of the day, while they carry out investigations...'

Local radio was full of the accident, rehashing the details they'd managed to glean, but Emilia wasn't interested. They only had half the story, having no clue as to Hudson's identity, nor who he was chasing, so she concentrated instead on the images in front of her: images of bloodied officers, mangled cars, the dazed prisoner – a pleasing collage of a police operation gone badly wrong. Any number of people might have been killed or injured and Emilia already had a double-page spread in mind, half of which would major on the captured suspect, the other half on the police recklessness and incompetence. The articles seemed to be writing themselves, so replacing the camera on the passenger seat, she reached for the ignition, intending to drive straight back to the office. But even as she turned the key, she paused. She had zoned out the radio broadcast, too involved in her own life, but the tone of the newscaster's report had now changed, sounding suddenly urgent and excited. Reaching over, Emilia turned up the volume.

'Police have so far declined to identify the victim, but local sources have named him as twenty-five-year-old Callum Harvey.'

Emilia sat bolt upright in her seat, electrified by the news.

'Along with murdered oil executive, Justin Lanning, Harvey was one of five teenagers abducted by Daniel King...'

Ramming the car into first, Emilia executed a wild U-turn, barely checking for oncoming traffic as she roared away down the road. All thoughts of returning to work were now forgotten. Thanks to her research into Maxine Pryce and her friends, she knew exactly where Callum Harvey lived and she was heading there now, keen to find out more. If it was true, if Harvey *had* been killed only a day after Justin Lanning, then a major story was breaking.

And Emilia was determined to be at the heart of it.

Chapter 53

'A house in Wonston Road has been cordoned off and we understand that forensic officers are on site. The police have made
no official statement as yet regarding the precise nature of the
incident, nor the identity of the alleged victim, but the property
belongs to Callum Harvey—'

Fran Ward turned it off, unable to listen to another word.
She'd been preparing to head out to the gym, idly listening to
the radio as she got her gear together. She was due to teach a
class at two o'clock, but all that was forgotten now. She would
have to call in sick, lie her way out of the obligation. Now she
needed time alone, time to *think*.

She was tempted to turn the radio back on – to check she
hadn't been daydreaming – but she couldn't face listening to the
ghoulish excitement of the newscaster, so checked local news
feeds instead. To her dismay, they were carrying the same story;
they even had a picture of the house, flanked by police tape and
uniformed officers. It was unquestionably 52 Wonston Road, a
house she'd visited on several occasions.

At first, she used to dread her visits there, but she'd endured
them nevertheless. Callum was unrecognizable at first from the
chirpy, cheeky teenager he used to be – now withdrawn, fearful,
bitter. But over time, through the patient help of Hannah and his

fellow survivors, he had begun to turn things around, discovering some of his old spark. Increasingly her visits to Callum's house had been fun, Fran had even taken her ex there, when things were good between them and it seemed that there might be mileage in their relationship. Laura was long gone now – they were totally incompatible – but her friendship with Callum had endured. Until now.

What had happened? Fran had been knocked for six by Justin's murder. She was not that close to him, but was pleased he'd made a good fist of his life. To die like that, alone and scared on a remote building site, was too awful to contemplate, but as she processed what had happened, dissecting the news reports and local articles, she'd begun to convince herself that perhaps something in his personal life had gone wrong, that his death was *not* linked to their past experiences. But now Callum was dead and there were no certainties any more.

Had Callum also been targeted? Or had he perhaps taken his own life? Was it even possible that he was somehow mixed up in Justin's death and had ended it all as the police closed in on him? It scarcely seemed possible, Callum wouldn't hurt a fly. Nor did it seem likely he would throw in the towel whilst engaged to be married. He loved Hannah, no, he was *obsessed* with her, and was looking forward to their big day. Did that then suggest that he *had* been killed, that both men had been murdered in the last forty-eight hours?

Fear arrowed through her. Fran was not naturally timorous – her dad always said she was made of stern stuff – but her heart was pounding now. She had spent the last few years living alone and she was used to it, but she missed the presence of someone now. Someone to talk to, to give her a hug, to protect her. She had been in danger before and had lived to tell the tale, but this was something else. A slow, sinister feeling of dread was gradually consuming her. Looking down, she saw her hands were shaking, her body reacting to the shocking news.

'Come on, Fran...'

She needed to regain control, to marshal her fear. More than that she needed clarity, solid information about what had happened, confirmation that Callum was genuinely dead. She would contact the police – demanding information. If they wouldn't give it to her, she'd contact local journalists; they were always interested in talking to her and were generally happy to trade information. But there was someone else she needed to talk to first.

Picking up her mobile, she dialled the number and waited. Barely a second later, it was answered, a cautious, female voice greeting her.

'Maxine...' Fran responded, keeping her voice as steady as she could. 'I think we need to meet.'

The smile was fixed on my face, but I was quaking inside. I'd resumed my place at the kitchen table, trying to be as unobtrusive and inconspicuous as possible, pretending *nothing* had happened. But my world had just turned on its axis.

We were in danger. As I'd felt my way down the corridor towards the kitchen, I'd wracked my brains for details of the attack on Lorraine Kielty – yes, that was her name – but I could remember nothing about the alleged attacker, other than that he was a young man. Even so, as I re-entered the room, my eyes falling on our host, I felt certain that it was him. *This* was the violent psycho who'd tried to strangle that defenceless girl.

Sitting down, I clamped a cheerful expression on my face, as my eyes sought out Justin. It had never been articulated, but he and I were the leaders of our group and I felt it was up to us to remedy this dire situation. But he was still tending to Rachel, who for once was subdued, looking more than a little deflated. I longed for Justin to look up, to engage, but his attention was firmly focused on the injured party, so instead I turned to Fran.

She was sitting across the table from me, cradling a cup of tea. Next to her, Callum was keeping up conversation with our host, but it was fractured and faltering – certainly not loud enough for me to engage Fran directly. So instead, I felt out her leg with my foot, giving it a sharp kick. Fran jumped, surprised, then recovering, turned her gaze towards me. She looked relaxed and happy enough, but as soon as she saw me, a cloud passed over her face. She told me later that I looked deathly pale, as if I'd just seen a ghost, which was pretty much how I felt. She looked at me quizzically, so instinctively I darted a look at Daniel King. He seemed distracted, picking his nails, whilst talking to Callum, so I took my chance, mouthing 'we need to leave'. I was worried that Fran wouldn't understand my dumb show, but she understood immediately, her frown deepening. But she made no move, didn't respond in any way, so I followed it up with a distinct 'now'.

The briefest of nods from Fran, as if she appreciated the urgency. Inside, I felt myself relax, pleased to have an ally. Exhaling slowly, I turned back to the general conversation – to find our host looking directly at me. Had he seen me? Had he clocked our silent conversation? My heart was in my mouth once more, but he seemed relaxed, even amused. And now he was looking away, distracted by Fran rising to her feet.

'Do you mind if I use the bathroom?' she said brightly.

'Sure it's down the—'

'I'll show her.'

I hadn't planned to do this, but now found myself on my feet, determined to seize this opportunity. Our host shrugged and let us go, Fran following me out of the room and into the darkened corridor.

'What the fuck's going on?'

Fran's fierce whisper filled the darkened space. She was hanging onto my arm, gripping it tightly.

'We need to leave. We need to get our stuff and get as far away from here as possible.'

'But what about the fog?'

'Fuck the fog. We're safer out there than in here.'

I wasn't trying to frighten her, but there was no time for niceties. Quickly, I explained what I'd discovered, why I thought our host was potentially dangerous. Fran, lovely, angelic Fran, lost all her colour. She looked stunned, no, she looked *terrified*. I could tell part of her wanted to believe I was making it all up, but she knew I wasn't prone to flights of fancy. Moreover, when I told her to look into the room herself, she refused, sensing the darkness that lurked behind the closed door. My testimony was enough for her – she too was now convinced that we needed to go.

'How do you want to play it?'

Once more, she seemed to be looking to me for leadership. Why was it always me?

'We just get our things and go. Say we want to try to complete the journey, do our school proud, whatever, it doesn't matter. We just need to leave.'

'And what if he tries to stop us?'

'What can he do? It's five to one. We just get out of here, any way we can.'

Fran nodded, but looked rigid with fear. Taking her by the arm, I pulled her back down the corridor with me. There was no point stringing this out, the longer we prevaricated, the more likely it was that our nerve would fail. The floorboards underneath our feet creaked noisily, exacerbating the silence that emanated from the kitchen. Just our bloody luck, I thought to myself. I'd been hoping that the conversation would still be going, allowing us a few seconds' distraction, before we announced our departure.

Stepping back into the kitchen, I was immediately struck by the atmosphere. Heavy, silent, almost crestfallen, the remaining kids were quiet now. All conversation had ceased and our host was no longer at the table, stationing himself near the door. Confused, but determined not to be distracted, I snatched up my wet anorak and announced: 'Come on, guys, we need to get going.'

They looked up, but made no attempt to move. And it was then that I saw it – terror, no, *despair* in their eyes. Which is when Daniel King turned around, levelling a shotgun directly at me.

'You're going nowhere, bitch.'

Chapter 54

Helen slid a copy of *One Dark Night* across the table. It was inside an evidence bag, but was still plainly visible – well thumbed, with a torn cover and numerous Post-it notes protruding from the pages.

'Where did you get this?'

The sullen figure opposite looked up at Helen briefly, before dropping his eyes to the book. It sat on the chipped Formica table that hovered over the hospital bed in which he lay. The suspect had somehow managed to escape serious injury – save for a nasty case of whiplash – but as the medical staff wanted to monitor his condition, Helen had decided against dragging him back to Southampton Central, conducting the interview in a private room at the hospital instead. It was a more congenial, less threatening, arena perhaps, but the suspect could be under no doubt of the seriousness of the situation – two armed officers guarded the door and Helen sat opposite him, focused and determined.

'It's a proof copy of *One Dark Night*, printed over two months ago, and not available to the general public. So how come yours is so well thumbed? I take it you don't work in the publishing industry?'

It seemed unlikely. The gaunt figure was unshaven and

covered in tattoos, with a long, distinctive scar on his neckline. You certainly wouldn't want to meet him in a dark alley and even here, in the bright, comfortable surroundings of the hospital, he appeared brooding and hostile. So far he'd resisted all attempts to prise him open and now shook his head, smiling ruefully as if this was all a massive waste of his time.

'You seem very interested in Maxine's story. In fact, you seem interested in *all* of Daniel King's captives.'

The suspect's sarcastic smile faded slightly now, as Helen slid a photo across the table towards him.

'This is a CCTV image of a man attempting to break into the home of Justin Lanning three weeks ago. Do you recognize the face?'

The man was staring at his likeness, but didn't move a muscle, determined not to give any clue as to his feelings.

'What about this, then?'

She slid another image towards him.

'This is an e-fit provided by a witness, a neighbour of Callum Harvey's. She's provided us with a statement, confirming that a man matching this description was seen casing Harvey's house a week ago. Does *that* ring any bells?'

The man didn't react, staring blankly at the image. Nevertheless, there was a coiled quality to him, his body rigid with tension.

'Now I'd love to put a name to this face – to you – but I think that's going to be a little tricky...'

Helen produced her final prop – an evidence bag containing no fewer than six UK driving licences.

'These were recovered from your wallet at the time of arrest. Now I don't know if you're... Mark Samuels... or Peter Frith... or Steven Abram...'

She leafed through them.

'...or Simon Collins – and from our preliminary discussions, it's clear you're not minded to enlighten me, so let's focus instead on the nature of your interest in the Daniel King case.'

Helen let her words hang in the air, but still her adversary didn't respond. She had seen this before – suspects shutting down, hoping that if they kept their head down, saying nothing, that all their troubles would miraculously disappear. But there was no chance of that – not with two bodies in the mortuary.

'The book is heavily annotated, all sorts of small details picked out. The kids' nicknames for each other, what they were wearing when they were abducted, how they survived on the Downs, what they said to the police, what they're doing now... Shall I go on?'

'If you like.'

It was loaded with sarcasm, but sounded weak.

'Because the book is just the tip of the iceberg, isn't it? My colleagues are currently taking apart your Aladdin's cave...'

A definite flinch this time, as if the idea of her officers crawling over his lair was physically painful to him.

'...and they've already found some very intriguing stuff. A school bag that belonged to Callum Harvey, a diary that was once Rachel Wood's, a dog collar with Daniel King's name written on it, even a brick that allegedly came from the destroyed farmhouse—'

'So what? I'm a collector.'

It was offered tersely, his anger at her intrusion punching through.

'I can see that. I'm not entirely sure why anyone would *want* to keep bedsheets that belonged to Rose West, or Charles Manson's doodles, but that hasn't stopped you, has it? What is it that particularly interests you about these killers?'

Now the suspect paused, as if uncertain how to answer.

'I ask because I'm genuinely interested,' Helen continued.

'There's not a single modern killer of note that you've over-looked. You've got them all: their artwork, their prison files, their underwear, their porn collections. You're like a one-man encyclopaedia of murder. Why?'

Another moment's hesitation. Her question wasn't a direct accusation, which seemed to tempt him to answer.

'Because they're not like ordinary people.'

'I won't fight you on that one.'

'They act without boundaries.'

'Without conscience,' Helen corrected him.

'Without *boundaries*. They do what most people couldn't countenance. And they do it without fear.'

'And you admire them for that?'

'They intrigue me.'

'And their victims? You seem very interested in them, judging by your collection. One of my officers said you had a lock of hair belonging to Alice R—'

'They've been touched by something,' he interrupted. 'Something bigger than themselves. Something that's *changed* them.'

'Permanently, in some cases,' Helen remarked, failing to conceal her distaste.

'Either way, their experiences have transformed them. They're part of a different story afterwards, someone else's story. They have a legacy.'

'And that excites you? That intersection between killer and victim?'

'I'm a collector, that's all.'

'Like hell you are.'

Now, finally, he looked up, stung by the aggression in Helen's voice.

'I'm sure you'd like us to believe that you spend your days

closeted away in your little hideaway, fingering your unpleasant collection of keepsakes...'

Anger flashed across his face. He didn't like being held up to ridicule.

'...but you've been pretty active, haven't you? Your van was clocked near Justin Lanning's house on the night you tried to break in—'

'Bullshit...'

'And I've no doubt that in time we'll be able to place you near his office block, on the day he was abducted and murdered.'

Another angry shake of the head.

'And you were also seen near Callum Harvey's property, three days before *he* was killed. And as if that wasn't enough...' Helen paused for effect, enjoying the suspect's evident discomfort, 'we now have testimony from the staff at Waterstones that you were at an event featuring Maxine Pryce *last night*, that you were loitering long after the other customers had gone. Was she next on your list?'

'Piss off.'

'Are you denying that you were stalking her?'

'Yes.'

'That you intended her harm?'

'This is crazy talk. I've never hurt anyone.'

'So why do carry a taser?'

There was no comeback this time.

'Justin Lanning was disarmed with a taser, before he was strangled. And I'm betting Callum Harvey was too.'

'I need it for protection,' the suspect shot back quickly.

'Protection from whom?'

A long silence, then once again, the suspect broke eye contact, unable – or unwilling – to answer.

'You know, for an innocent man, you appear to have a lot

stacked against you. An obsessional interest in killers. Clear evidence of your desire to penetrate the lives of King's former victims. Possession of a taser. And to top it all, you resisted arrest, assaulted a police officer and driven like a maniac in an attempt to evade capture.'

The man maintained his silence, glowering at her.

'So I understand why you'd like me to believe that you're just a humble collector, a student of the darkest human impulses, but I don't buy it. I think you're obsessed with murderers. With the idea of killing. Obsessed with Daniel King in particular...'

He was staring directly at her, but he made no attempt to deny the thrust of Helen's accusations.

'Why is he such a pin-up for you?'

Nothing in response.

'According to my officers' reports, your warehouse is packed full of gruesome items. It's like a who's who of the depraved and the insane, but your collection of King's effects dwarfs all the others. Why is that?'

The suspect stared at his hands, which Helen could see were shaking.

'You've got sketches he did of his mother, his old school reports, even clothing that belonged to him. You have numerous personal effects from his victims, not to mention an official school photo of the children he abducted, with their heads neatly ringed in black ink. Why? What is it about him that you so admire?'

Still, the suspect refused to meet her eyes.

'Does it turn you on, what he did to those kids? Did you like the idea of bringing him back to life? Of *finishing* what he started?'

'You're sick...'

'From the off, I wondered whether this was a copycat killing, someone resurrecting the phantom of Daniel King for their own twisted ends. Now I'm sure of it. So tell me...'

Helen fixed the suspect with a steely glare.

'...what was it made you cross the line? When did you finally stop dreaming about killing... and actually do it *for real*?'

Chapter 55

'This is the man we're interested in.'

Charlie handed the manager the mugshot. It had been taken in the hospital and was well lit and crisply focused. It was infinitely superior to the grabbed CCTV still they'd had previously and Charlie had high hopes that the owner of the Moon Lounge, or one of his employees, would recognize this mystery figure.

'When did you say he was in here?' Chris Bridges shot back, his thick Portsmouth accent punching through.

'Around ten, ten thirty last night.'

Hannah Bradwell was convinced she'd had her phone with her when she entered the club. She remembered checking the time at around eleven, before heading off dancing, leaving her bag unattended. If she was telling the truth, then someone had stolen her phone in this club last night. If they could get a positive ID of the thief, then they would have a clear link to their killer.

'I can't say I recognize him, but I was out back most of the night. You're better off speaking to our front of house, Lisa. Let me get her...'

Handing back the photo, he walked off in the direction of a slender woman with exuberantly frizzy hair, who was busy berating the cleaning staff. Charlie took the opportunity to look around her. In the cold light of day nightclubs always seemed soulless and down-at-heel – the leather banquettes looked tired, the dance floor heavily marked and without the clouds of perfume to hide the aroma, you couldn't miss the stench of stale alcohol. It was a very different place at night. It was a massive club, hugely popular with locals and visitors alike, always drawing huge crowds at the weekend. Someone had used this human shield to ghost into the club and lift Bradwell's phone. But to what end? Bradwell had faithfully promised to ring Callum Harvey in the morning, so the latter would have been expecting a call. Had Harvey's killer known this? Had he reasoned that the reclusive Harvey might not answer if it was *someone else* calling? Just how deep did his knowledge of their lives go?

The front-of-house manager was now approaching, so Charlie wrenched herself back to the present.

'Lisa McGee, how can I help?'

It was said politely, but without warmth. Charlie suspected that the flinty manager had had dealings with the police before – these clubs were a mecca for dealers – and didn't welcome the intrusion.

'We believe this man was in the club last night.'

'Let me see.'

She took the photo and surveyed it, but said nothing.

'Do you have CCTV?'

A curt shake of the head. Charlie could guess why, but didn't push it.

'Would the bouncers have seen him? Ticket staff?'

'We can certainly ask them, but a thin, bald guy is going to be hard to pick out, the place is full of his sort at the weekend, working man having a few beers, sniffing around the girls…'

'What about the bartenders? Or the waiting staff? We think

this man would have been circling a group of women in the VIP area?'

The manager shot a look towards a small roped-off area in the far corner of the room. Once again, it didn't look like much in the daylight. Whatever glamour or prestige it had last night was long gone.

'Well we can ask, you might get lucky. But honestly, this place was heaving last night and what with the flashing lights and the sheer mass of bodies, it's hard to see anyone clearly unless they collar you specifically. My staff are run off their feet – I need more of them, to be honest – and if your man wanted to keep a low profile, then I'd say he stood a fair chance.'

She seemed oddly cheered by this thought, as if anyone evading the long arm of the law was somehow a good thing. Charlie was sorely tempted to haul her over the coals for her attitude, but she knew she wouldn't get anywhere without McGee's co-operation, so decided to play nice.

'When will your staff – the ones who were working last night – be back in?' she continued, politely.

'We work a rota system, so some'll be in tonight, some will be in tomorrow.'

'Then I'd like to have a couple of officers present until we've managed to talk to them all.'

The manager's face was a picture.

'Don't worry, they don't have to be in uniform. They can be plain clothes if you'd prefer, but it is vitally important we talk to everyone who was working here last night.'

McGee looked like she'd prefer the officers to be *anywhere* but here, but there was sufficient steel in Charlie's request – not to mention the tacit threat of uniformed officers patrolling the club – for her to decide not to kick up.

'Do what you need to,' she eventually responded, with the

minimum of grace. 'But honestly … given the state of this place, and the amount of folk we had in last night, well … it'll be like looking for a needle in a haystack.'

And with that, she was gone.

Chapter 56

He felt claustrophobic, like the walls were crowding in on him. More than anything, he wanted to escape this place... but there was no question of that now.

Joseph's 'discussion' with Helen had ended badly. It was partly his fault – he was still shaken from the accident and hadn't appreciated being taken to task in front of other officers. It was unprofessional of her... but even so he shouldn't have stalked off like that. It made him look insubordinate, as well as reckless, and he knew he would pay for it. In truth, he already had. Not only was he the butt of jokes and gossip around the station, he'd also been assigned this grunt work, a job beneath even a DC, Helen having decided to interview the suspect alone.

It made his blood boil. It was *he* who'd got the tip off from Garanita, *he* who'd escaped being tasered by a hair's breadth, *he* who'd risked his neck chasing the suspect through the Southampton streets. And what was his reward? Auditing the suspect's effects – this extraordinary collection of murderabilia – and supervising its transfer to Southampton Central.

He had been intent on visiting Malik, to check on her well-being and smooth things over between them. But this too had been denied him, blocked by Helen as another element of his punishment. She was insisting on having all the evidence logged and analysed asap, a perfectly reasonable request given the importance of the investigation, but not one that required the presence of a senior officer. No, his presence here was a statement, a very public statement.

How had things gone so wrong, so quickly? A couple of days ago he was lying in her bed, content that his career and their relationship was heading in the right direction. He knew he still had to prove himself to her and the rest of the team, but she wouldn't have let him get so close to her if she thought he was a bluffer. No, she'd obviously rated him, thought he had potential, in more ways than one. But now he was out in the cold, imprisoned in this oppressive and sinister retreat.

Only now did Joseph realize that one of the other officers – a PC who was even greener than Malik – was staring at him. Snapping out of it, he resumed work – there was no point drawing further attention to himself by staring into space like an idiot. He had a job to do and the sooner it was completed, the sooner he would be out of this grim place.

It was not a task he went to with any relish. The good stuff – the extensive haul of keepsakes linked directly to King and his former captives – had already been itemized, bagged and dispatched to the station. There was little or anything in the way of personal items, anything that might help them identify their ghoulish prisoner, so what was left was a treasure trove of misery and suffering. Dental braces worn by Alan Carter, a degenerate killer who used to bite his victims as he murdered them, the shiv that was used to stab Charles Bronson during an attack in Strangeways, a signed letter from Ted Kacyznski, the notorious Unabomber – there seemed no gruesome oddity that didn't interest their suspect. These Joseph could just about handle – to each freak his own – it was the items purloined from the victims that really sickened him. Mementoes, keepsakes, even love tokens of innocents who had been brutalized, abused and murdered. The discovery of a child's teddy bear that she was allegedly cuddling when her mother murdered her made him feel physically sick. What kind of freak took pleasure from owning that?

How he would have loved to have been in an interview room with him, face to face across the table. He knew from experience that criminals both feared and respected the coppers who brought them in and he would have used that to his advantage, applying just the right amount of pressure to convince the recalcitrant suspect to cooperate. At the very least, he'd have had a chance to let him know exactly what he thought of him, something that would have given him no little satisfaction.

But he would be denied the opportunity. Helen had chosen to go it alone, leaving him to play the part of a glorified removals man. It was not what he was trained to do, it was not what he was *born* to do, but there was no question of abandoning his post, not after this morning's catastrophe. No, there was nothing for it now but to knuckle down and get the job done, hoping – praying – that his stint in purgatory would be a short one.

Chapter 57

'I've done nothing wrong.'

The suspect continued to protest his innocence. But Helen instinctively felt his resolve was weakening – he seemed weary now and less quick to contradict her. The question was whether she could get a confession out of him before the medical staff intervened. Even now, Helen could glimpse the doctors hovering outside, anxiously discussing whether – when – they should step in.

'So you keep saying, but here's the thing. I don't believe Daniel King did this. He's a phantom. But *someone else* could carry on his work. What a story that would be, what a feather in your cap...'

'King was nothing special—'

'You don't need to tell *me* that,' Helen countered. 'But I'm not sure you believe it. You've got an extensive collection of his personal items, not to mention numerous books on him.'

'I'm interested in a lot of killers.'

'But this guy was local, his captives still live in Southampton, so it would be easy – tempting – perhaps. I've no idea who you are, but your accent says that you're from around here. Simple then for you to run his former captives to ground, target them at their homes, their offices—'

'No.'

'And having done so, you could disappear into the ether. We've no idea who you are, where you live, what your history is. Maybe you've got form for violence, abduction, murder. I couldn't say for sure, because you live entirely off grid, in the shadows. You're *invisible*. A phantom able to ghost into people's lives, then disappear. To strike at will, making the world think that your hero, Daniel King, had returned from the dead—'

'No, no, no...'

'Then where were you on Thursday night? Between the hours of 6 and 7 p.m.?'

A moment's hesitation, a cloud passing across the suspect's face.

'I was at the warehouse.'

'Can anyone verify that?'

'No, I was alone.'

'And this morning? Between 10 and 11 a.m.?'

A brief pause, then: 'I... I was with someone.'

'You were with Callum Harvey.'

'No way...'

'At least try and sound convincing. Where were you?'

A long, heavy silence. The suspect continued to stare at the bedsheets, as he nervously picked at his fingernails.

'OK, so you've no alibi for either murder,' Helen continued briskly. 'Which is not surprising as you've been aggressively stalking both of them, planning exactly *when* and *how* you were going to target them.'

'I've never hurt anyone—'

'You tried to taser a police officer...'

'I had no idea who the guy was, he was creeping up on me.'

'Why did you even have a taser in the first place?'

'For protection.'

'Protection from *whom*?'

The suspect, who'd briefly looked up to engage Helen face-on, now dropped his gaze once more.

'Look, owning a taser is illegal. I can charge you with possession of a firearm, not to mention resisting arrest and assaulting a police officer. There's more than enough to keep you in custody whilst we trawl over your life, your possessions, your movements, piecing together exactly *how* you gained access to Lanning and Harvey, what you used to kill them—'

'It wasn't me!'

'So you keep saying, but in the absence of any evidence to the contrary—'

'It *wasn't* me.'

'Look at me...'

The suspect made no attempt to do so.

'LOOK AT ME.'

Helen shouted it, making the suspect jump and provoking a reaction from the worried staff outside. Despite his evident hostility, the suspect slowly raised his eyes, reluctantly meeting Helen's.

'I'm investigating a double murder. The sentence for double murder is life imprisonment, with no the chance of parole. It's game over...'

His eyes didn't flicker, but Helen could see fear there now.

'Now, you clearly have an unhealthy obsession with King and his victims, were seen attempting to access the latter's properties, possess the type of weapon that was used to subdue them, have the physical strength to strangle them... You can see where this is going, can't you?'

There was no doubting he could.

'I need a conclusion to this investigation. It's a high-profile case and you are the only man in the frame...'

Helen paused briefly, before continuing: 'So unless you can offer me something, something that *proves* that you are innocent of these crimes, then I will have no option but to charge you with—'

'I was with another collector.'

It was mumbled, almost inaudible.

'Excuse me?'

'This morning. I was with another collector.'

'Where?'

'At an industrial estate in Duke Street.'

'Who?'

'I can't say, that's not how it's done.'

'For God's sake...'

'And you won't find any CCTV, not round there. But I took the van. You can track it on traffic cameras. I drove through the centre of town.'

The team were already busy tracing the vehicle's movements through ANPR. If he was lying to her, Helen would know soon enough.

'And the address I was going to is in the sat nav.'

'What was the nature of this "meeting"?' Helen replied, failing to conceal her scepticism.

'A guy was interested in some of my King memorabilia; I was showing him a sample of the merchandise.'

'*Merchandise?*'

'Prices have gone through the roof recently, given the media interest in the case...'

'You were selling him parts of your collection?'

'That's what I do. There's a big market for it – stuff that belonged to notable killers, or their victims. Lots of people are interested and'll pay good money—'

'That's how you make a living?'

'Sure.'

'And if we look into your computer, your messages, we'll find evidence of this?'

'Course not. It's all on the dark web. These people, they don't want to draw attention to themselves, neither do I. It's all done off grid, with people who may or may not be who they say they are. As long as they pay, that's fine by me. I meet them in industrial estates, pub car parks, NCPs, wherever. But I always take a taser with me...'

'Why is it so cloak and dagger if you've *nothing* to hide?'

Now the suspect hesitated – his brain whirring – before eventually continuing: 'Look, most of this stuff is pretty hard to come by. The police take all the evidence, or the family of the perpetrator makes sure the personal stuff is destroyed, locked away, but there are always ways, if you're inventive...'

'Meaning you steal it.'

'Meaning you take your opportunities when they come. With Daniel King, the place had been made safe, but was too dangerous for the forensic team to go in, so I took my chance, got what I could...'

'Because you could profit from it?'

'King's a good seller, cos he's never been found, because the case is well known, because people remember the images of those kids on the Downs...'

Helen couldn't contradict him there.

'That's... that's why I was interested in Lanning, Harvey, Pryce. They have things of value...'

'That you wanted for yourself?'

Again he paused, knowing that he was talking himself into a jail term.

'Yes.'

'That's why you were following Maxine Pryce last night?'

'She has a necklace – a heart-shaped thing that she was wearing when she was found on the Downs. She still wears it and... and, well, I know I could get good money for it. Someone contacted me directly, asking me to acquire it, but she hasn't been at home, she's been working at another place. I needed to know where, which is why I followed her.'

Helen's disgust for this parasite's activities was writ large on her face, because the suspect now continued: 'So, think what you like about me. Call me a thief, a peddler, scum, whatever you like. But I am *not* a killer. My interest in these people, it's not personal, it's not even unpleasant, for me.' He fixed her with a stare. 'It's just business.'

Chapter 58

They were surrounded by bodies, yet Fran still felt exposed, darting nervous glances around as she spoke. She'd chosen this Caffè Nero because it was always rammed, but now she regretted her choice. Every face that passed by seemed suspicious to her – as if they knew something, as if they might be dangerous.

'Had you seen him recently? Callum, I mean ...'

Maxine shook her head. Fran noted that her former school-friend seemed thinner, older even, since they last met.

'Not for a couple of months. You?'

'A couple of weeks back. He was in a good space, he was happy, for God's sake.'

'I heard he was getting married,' Maxine replied, ashen. 'And I was *pleased* for him. After everything he'd been through, he deserved a bit of happiness ...'

Her words seemed to hang in the air, hollow and worthless now.

'Jesus Christ, what a fucking mess.'

Fran's voice shook, fear and distress punching through. Maxine reached out and took her hand in hers, but she felt no comfort, her nerves jangling wildly.

'First, Justin. Now Callum ...'

'There'll be an explanation for it, there *has* to be,' Maxine insisted. 'Someone they've pissed off, someone they've managed to antago—'

'They were *strangled*, Maxine.'

Fran had said this too loudly, other coffee drinkers turning to look at the pair.

'They weren't run over,' she continued quickly, lowering her volume. 'They didn't fall down the stairs, they were *strangled*.'

'Look, I know it's scary,' Maxine continued, clutching Fran's hand still tighter. 'But whatever this is, it's not *that*. The police said as much when I spoke to them.'

Fran looked up, surprised that the police had been in touch with her already, but Maxine pressed on.

'And I'm sure that whatever sick fuck is responsible for this, they'll catch him. Until then, we just have to stay vigilant. I'm sure we're not in any direct danger.'

'But why is this happening?' Fran insisted. 'What had they *done*?'

'I've no idea, but the police *will* find out. They've got a suspect, someone who was seen trying to break into Justin's house. *Somebody* out there will know who he is, they'll identify him, then the whole thing—'

'So Justin had *already* been targeted? Before he was killed, I mean?'

'It looks that way, though I don't know all the details...'

'Do you think he *knew* he was in danger then?'

Fran felt her fear rising once more.

'It's possible, though he certainly didn't say anything to me,' Maxine replied, carefully. 'We spoke last week and he was uptight, but not about that...'

'What about Callum? Did the police say anything about him?'

'We didn't talk about Callum. But if this guy was targeting Justin, then it's possible he was doing the same with Callum.

Maybe Callum noticed something, maybe he didn't. Either way, the police will talk to Hannah, they'll find out what's going on, then they'll *deal* with it.'

'And you?'

'Me?'

'Have you noticed anything suspicious?'

Maxine looked surprised, even disconcerted by the question. 'Should I have done?'

'No, of course not,' Fran continued quickly. 'It's just that everybody knows who you are – because of the book, the stuff in the media... Have *you* noticed anything?'

Fran was aware that she sounded needy, desperate. But she had to know.

'No, nothing.'

Fran felt the knot in her stomach relax a tiny bit.

'I've had the odd comment on Twitter, Facebook,' Maxine continued, managing a rueful smile. 'But that's just the usual trolls, nothing sinister.'

'You're sure?'

'Totally. So, try not to worry. I'm not in any danger and neither are you. What's happened to Justin, to Callum, it's... beyond hideous. But it's got nothing to do with us. So, be sad if you want to be, cry as much as you like, God knows you've the right. But try not to worry. Daniel King is where he belongs, in the past...'

She gave her hand another little squeeze.

'And that's where he's going to stay.'

Chapter 59

She would only get one shot at this, so she didn't hesitate. Joseph Hudson was finally alone and if she was to make her move, it had to be now.

Emilia had stationed herself at the rear entrance of Southampton Central. Out of sight, out of mind, this discreet doorway had been used on many occasions to shuffle suspects in, or police officers out. Often times, Emilia had been lying in wait, snatching the odd off-the-record comment or an incriminating photo and something had told her that Hudson would use this entrance now. In all honesty, there was nowhere else he could go, given the sheer number of boxes he was bringing back from the warehouse. They seemed to engulf him now – a lonely figure amongst the orange packing crates – as he stood in the open courtyard.

The gates had just reopened, a patrol car slipping out, affording Emilia a clear view of the detective sergeant. She was sure he had junior officers helping out, but they were absent now, so even as the doors started to close, Emilia darted between them, hurrying towards him.

'You can't be here.'

He barked the words at her, looking even more pissed off than usual. Emilia noticed the scratches on his face, the shadow of bruising around his eyes – he was clearly in a bad way following his recent accident. So much the better for her.

'I'm not staying. I just need a minute of your time...'

'We've said all we need to say to each other. You've got your story, you've got your photos. Print them and be damned.'

He flung the words at her – his frustration palpable – but he couldn't look at Emilia, which pleased her. Despite his bluster, he seemed embarrassed rather than angry. And who could blame him? This morning's catastrophic escapade could have cost lives, could still cost him his career.

'I will but first I need your help. I'm not entirely sure how to frame the story...'

Hudson arrowed a dark look towards her, clearly not liking her teasing tone, nor his sense that there was more to come. He shot a look towards the rear doors of the station, as if fearful of discovery.

'You see, I've got so much good stuff,' Emilia carried on quickly, 'that I don't know what to put in and what to leave out. Obviously, I've got the basic details, the narrative of the chase and some *great* photos, but, for example, do I include the name of the unfortunate officer involved? Pictures of him?'

Hudson glared at her.

'I probably should. That would be good public service journalism, after all. Alerting the public to the presence of a reckless officer in their local force...'

'Don't push it.'

He was tightly coiled and Emilia felt an enjoyable frisson of fear. Would he attack her here? Grab her by the neck? Anything seemed possible after this morning.

'Yes, that's what I should do,' she continued. 'That would be the sensible thing to do. But then again, I could play it another way.'

Hudson said nothing, but he made no attempt to stop her or interrupt. Was he biding his time, working out how to play this? Or was he building up to some kind of eruption?

'I could keep the lead officer's name out of it. Save him some very public embarrassment, which after all would only serve to heap *further* pressure on him professionally... Yes, now that I think about it, I could present the whole episode in a more... positive light. Can't escape the carnage and risk to public safety, I'm afraid, but I could major on the fact that the suspect was arrested, progress made and so forth. And the world need never know who led the operation, who was responsible for the whole debacle...'

Hudson was about to respond, his face pink with anger, but Emilia cut him off.

'For full disclosure, I should mention that I do have photos of you immediately after the crash. Looking a little dazed and confused, I'm afraid...'

This was an exaggeration, but Hudson wasn't to know that.

'Now I would be very happy to include those with the article – it would give the piece colour – but I could also lose them. How I play this is down to you, Joseph.'

'Meaning?'

'Meaning if you keep me up to speed with developments in the investigation, then I can airbrush this morning's incident and help save your career. If you refuse this very reasonable request, then it's open season.'

Hudson continued to stare at her, his colour darkening. Emilia met his eye, refusing to be cowed. She had the power here, not him.

'I'll need some time to think about it.'

He was trying to remain calm, but couldn't conceal his fury.

'Don't take too long. My deadline's in three hours' time.'

She turned, throwing a few parting words over her shoulder. 'You've got my number, Joseph. Don't be a stranger.'

She walked away, hitting the door release and watching the heavy doors open. Turning back, she noticed that Joseph was still staring at her. He seemed determined not to betray his emotions, not to give her a steer as to what he might do next, but Emilia wasn't worried.

He would hate himself for it. He would hate *her* for it. But in the end Joseph Hudson would *have* to play ball.

Chapter 60

A heavy silence filled the room, sapping energy and crushing hope.

'How sure are you?'

Charlie tried to inject some lightness into her question, but it sounded forced.

'As sure as I can be,' Helen responded, barely looking up from the terminal in front of her. 'The suspect's been pretty forthcoming about his activity on the dark web and it checks out.'

She gestured at the screen.

'He *does* have an active correspondence with buyers of rare murderabilia and I think he was telling the truth when he said he made a living from it – there are several very substantial Bitcoin transactions. Why people will pay for this stuff, God only knows, but they do ...'

'And this applies to Justin Lanning and Callum Harvey specifically?'

Helen nodded.

'He had an extensive collection of items – photos of them as they are now, snatched outside their work places, through to signed copies of Pryce's proof manuscript, which he'd obviously stolen from the printers, right up to big ticket items, such as personal possessions from the time of their abduction. He had someone lined up to buy Pryce's necklace – he'd been offered £10,000, but he was planning to auction it once he'd got it.'

'And he's presumably claiming that that's why he was trying to break into Lanning's house, why he was casing the Harvey house.'

'Exactly. Most of the stuff he's amassed has been taken without the owner's consent. He claims that's why he continued running once he realized it was the police after him.'

'Theft, fencing, breaking and entering – he'd be facing a decent stretch.'

'Which would have put a dent in what was proving to be a rather lucrative career.'

'What about his alibi, then? Or should that be alibis...'

'It's true he's got nothing concrete for the night of Lanning's murder, but his offline correspondence suggests he did have a meeting scheduled with a collector this morning. Osbourne looked into it – ANPR places him at an industrial estate on Barnfield Road at the time of Callum Harvey's death. I take it the team hasn't had any joy at the Moon Lounge?'

'Not yet,' Charlie replied carefully. 'Though we haven't spoken to everyone. We've talked to roughly half of the waiting staff, plus the bouncers, of course – nobody remembers seeing anyone specifically matching his description.'

'What about at Wonston Road? Any of the neighbours see anyone suspicious near Harvey's house this morning?'

'Nothing doing, I'm afraid. We're still doing house-to-house, but so far the only people spotted outside the house were our officers attending the scene *after* the call.'

'What about the house itself? Any sign of how Harvey's attacker gained access?'

Charlie desperately wanted to report something positive, but Meredith's initial findings had thrown up nothing.

'The front door was closed but not bolted. There was no sign of forced entry anywhere, though the back door was open when you arrived.'

'So either the killer ghosted in, maybe the back door had been left unlocked ... or Harvey opened the door to him.'

'Possibly, though I can't see Harvey letting our current suspect in. Harvey recognized him when we spoke earlier and obviously would have been on his guard.'

A brief silence followed, one Charlie was keen to break.

'Can forensics help us? The bootprint we pulled from the Lanning crime scene ...?'

'There's no match. That print was a size eight, this guy is a size ten, at least.'

'So have we got it wrong then?'

It was not a question Charlie wanted to ask, but she had no choice given the evidence that now confronted them.

'The suspect *seems* like a good fit in some ways,' she continued, 'but unless we can place him at the scene or discredit his financial motive—'

'Neither of which we can do at present,' Helen retorted.

'—then you'd have to say we're a way off being able to bring charges.'

They both knew this, but nevertheless it helped to say it out loud.

'The possession of a taser is interesting,' Charlie offered gamely. 'But they're readily available if you know where to look and I'm sure plenty of people working in the black economy carry them. Unless we find more, unless we can link him definitively to either of the crime scenes, we're going to have to think again. He'll be under hospital guard for at least another twenty-four hours, which gives us a little time to play with, but I wouldn't bet my house that we'll be pressing charges against him even then.'

Helen couldn't disagree. It was not what she'd wanted, what any of them wanted, after the dramatic events of the morning, but it now looked very much like they'd been barking up the wrong tree. Despite all their endeavours, all their efforts, they were back to square one.

'Do you want me to get the team together, review what we've got...?'

Helen was already shaking her head.

'I'm due at the mortuary shortly and besides, I want all the house-to-house and witness enquiries concluded first. No point going off half-cock on this, not when there's so much at stake.'

'Would you like me to come to the mortuary? Or would you rather I stayed here to assist DS Hudson?'

'Neither, you need to get off home.'

'I don't mind staying.'

'Charlie, you can't miss your own daughter's birthday party. I'm only sorry I can't be there too; I wanted to be.'

'It doesn't seem right, not with everything that's going—'

'It's completely right, so go. We can talk later, if need be.'

Charlie relented, thanking Helen and hurrying off to gather her things. Helen watched her go, thoughts of Jessica enjoying herself briefly raising her spirits. She had been an intermittent presence in her goddaughter's life and would have loved to have been present. But sadly, as so often, she had more pressing duties. Before she set off to see Jim Grieves, she wanted to contact Maxine Pryce and Fran Ward personally. Without alarming them, she wanted to ensure they were taking sensible precautions. She had no evidence that there was a genuine threat to their well-being, but there was no question of taking chances. While a devious serial killer continued to stalk the city, it would be best for them to be on their guard.

Chapter 61

She shut the door behind her, sliding the deadlock across and slipping on the chain. Turning, she listened, straining to hear any signs of movement, a creaking floorboard, a door opening, but there was nothing. She was alone.

Dumping her bag, Maxine moved fast around her flat, darting into both bedrooms, then the bathroom, before hurrying through the kitchen into the living room. Satisfied that she was alone, she tossed her keys onto the table and sank down onto the sofa.

It had never felt so comfortable, so yielding, as it did now. It was tired, she needed a new one, but today she loved the way it engulfed her, wrapping itself around her in a protective hug. How she could have done with the real thing, someone to take her in their arms, but who on earth could have fulfilled that role? Who could she have possibly confided in?

No, this was a burden she would have to shoulder alone. She had faced the danger, made a choice and now she would have to live with the consequences. At the time, it had seemed so simple. It was a straight yes or no. Do or die. And she was embarrassed to admit that she had found the choice easy. Afterwards, she'd told herself that this was only natural. She was a survivor, she was someone who would always make it out, whatever obstacles were thrown in her path. But it wasn't that simple, was it?

Her heart was thumping, her head pounding. What she really wanted to do was wash down a couple of Nurofen with a vodka and tonic, but she didn't have the energy to raise herself from the sofa, so she buried her face in her hands instead, hoping their cool touch might afford her some relief. But the same thoughts kept spinning round her head, the same dull ache of guilt pulsing inside her.

Actions have consequences. She'd always known that but never as keenly as today. She'd hoped that it was an idle threat, that the idea of substituting someone else's death for your own was a wild, baseless fantasy, yet she'd known it wasn't. The voice had sounded so sure, so confident, as if this was a game that would be played at his pace, with his rules. Even so, the news that Callum had been brutally murdered had nearly broken her. She'd woken this morning full of joy, wild, carefree, even optimistic, overwhelmed to have cheated death. How empty and groundless that hope seemed now. Thanks to her, Callum had been murdered. Her old friend, her partner in pain, had been hunted down and strangled.

It was unbelievable, but true. Maxine had stayed hidden in her flat, praying that it would all go away, that she would wake from this awful nightmare, but worse was to follow. Fran had called, asking to meet, refusing to take no for an answer. Maxine hadn't wanted to go – God, she hadn't wanted to go – but she'd had no choice. They had spent over an hour together, during which time she had had to lie repeatedly. About her shock at Callum's grief, about how tragic and unjust it was, about how unreal it all seemed. Worst still, she'd had to look Fran in the eye and tell her she knew nothing about it, that there was nothing to be frightened of. Had she damned Fran by doing so? It didn't bear thinking about – yet it was all she could think about now. What kind of person was she?

A buzzing sound made her jump. For a minute, she thought it was the intercom – fear spiking inside her – but then she realized it was just her phone vibrating on the glass table. Picking it up cautiously, she was relieved to see that it was a number she recognized – the main number for Southampton Central. Perhaps it was DS Brooks following up? Or the main woman – what was her name? Grace? Either way, there was no way she was answering it. Not in the state she was in.

The decision had been made, the deal concluded. There was no point confessing now, giving herself away when the damage had been done. Tonight, she would talk to no one, see no one, scarcely trusting herself not to break down, to blurt out all the darkness. No, tonight, she would stay where she was. Safe. Secure. And utterly riddled with guilt.

Chapter 62

They were ranged in front of her – agitated, excited, expectant. Despite the media liaison officer's best attempts to keep order, the conference had already descended into a free-for-all, questions being fired at Simmons from all angles. There would be no hiding place today.

'Can you identify the suspect?'

'Will you be pressing charges?'

'Have you reopened the case file on Daniel King?'

It was hard to know which one to deflect first. There was normally a predictable rhythm to these events, an etiquette allowing one journalist to ask their question before the next pitched in, but not today. Instead, they were talking over each other, demanding to be heard.

'Was the suspect injured in the collision?'

'Have you disciplined the officers involved?'

'Has the suspect *confessed*?'

Simmons always volunteered to handle the press, leaving Helen to concentrate on the investigation, but for the first time she regretted it. Not that she wanted to offer Helen up to the lions – she was happy to take the brickbats for the team – it was just that today's conference felt out of control. The press pack seemed to be baying for blood and Simmons had nothing to defend herself with, Helen having just informed her that their prime suspect had been downgraded to a 'person of interest'.

Holding up her hand, Simmons appealed for calm.

'Look, I appreciate that you all have questions, but I can only answer one at a time. There is obviously legitimate public concern regarding this case, so let me reassure you that we are working around the clock to conclude our investigation. We do have a suspect in custody, who is helping us with our enquiries and when it's appropriate to do so, I will—'

'Can you give us a name?'

Simmons turned towards the interruption, but she already knew who it was. Emilia Garanita, the ringmaster and chief troublemaker at these events.

'Not at this time. The investigation is ongoing—'

'Do you even *know* his name?'

There was a knowingness, a spiteful glee in Emilia's tone, which took Simmons by surprise.

'I'm not sure that's relev—'

'I've heard rumours that the guy hasn't confessed to the murders – hasn't admitted to *any* involvement in these crimes – and that furthermore you haven't the faintest idea who he is.'

'That's pure speculation—'

'Who is he then?'

Simmons hesitated a second too long, before issuing the standard deflection, prompting the others to jump on the bandwagon. They sensed her discomfort and wanted to drive home their advantage.

'What progress have you made in the case so far?'

'Two people are dead. What are you going to tell their families?'

'Should the public be scared?'

The conference was building to a crescendo, but once more Garanita's voice cut through.

'Were the public put at risk because of poor police work today?'

'Absolutely not,' Simmons countered tersely.

'A high-speed pursuit through a residential area? To capture a man you can't identity, who may have *no relevance* to the current investigation?'

Simmons stared at Garanita, anger flaring inside. The cocky journalist seemed very sure of herself, very well informed.

'The Major Investigation Team are a highly trained, experienced unit who execute their duties to the best of their abilities—'

'They could have killed someone. I take it you've been to the scene? Seen the carnage?'

Perhaps she should have done, perhaps it would have been a good thing to do from a PR point of view, but with everything else going on, Simmons had decided it wasn't a priority.

'I'm aware of what happened.'

'But you haven't seen it with your own eyes?'

The buzz was growing louder in the room, the assembled journalists picking up on this oversight.

'Not yet. I'll be heading there shortly and of course the IPCC will—'

'I was there and let me tell you it was frightening. A major collision on a busy road, young mums and kids about...'

'I understand no one was hurt—'

'More by luck than judgement.'

'Emilia,' Simmons countered, trying hard to retain her cool, 'do you actually have a question or are you just here to pass judgement on—'

'I've got a question and it's a simple one. Who's in control here? DI Grace? You? Because from where I'm standing, the

MIT looks out of control. Floundering, desperate, reckless. DI Grace runs the show – and you have to ask questions about *her* competence – but ultimately the buck stops with you. So can you categorically reassure us that you are in control of the situation? And if not, what are you going to do about it?'

'I can assure you that I am absolutely in control—'

But it was too little, too late. The dam had opened now, questions, insults, accusations raining down on her from all corners of the room. Simmons yearned to fight back, to put them all back in their boxes, Garanita especially, but she had nothing to fight back *with*. Two people were dead and so far they had no bead on a killer who appeared able to ghost in and out of the lives of his victims with impunity. She was on the back foot, rattled and disoriented, and there was nothing she could do for now but hang onto the ropes and take the punishment.

Chapter 63

The tension was high, the excitement at fever pitch, as the package swiftly changed hands. The bouncy castle had been deflated, the birthday tea consumed and now Jessica and her guests were arranged in a neat circle, passing the bulky parcel as a tune from *Frozen II* pumped out.

Steve was in charge of the music, stopping it at regular intervals to ensure everyone got a turn, intervening where necessary to prevent a child having a second go. Jessica and her schoolfriends were totally into it, tearing off the paper with frenzied excitement, digging down to unearth the Haribos concealed within each layer. It was a touching sight – the total focus, the nervous excitement – and Charlie tried her best to get into it. But in truth her mind was elsewhere tonight.

Round and round the parcel went, Charlie clapping and cheering mechanically as each prize was revealed. Normally, she would have revelled in the sight of Jessica having fun with her friends, enjoying the annual celebration. Steve did a lot of the hard yards, organizing the entertainment, getting in the food, but it was Charlie who added the personal touches – decorating the house, sourcing the party bags, laboriously constructing the parcel – and she loved Jessica's infectious enjoyment of her party, even if the whole thing was over in a flash. And there was no question she *was* pleased – things had gone off without a hitch, Jessie was happy – but Charlie's mind had wandered. Physically she was here, handing out cups of tea and chatting to the other parents, but mentally she was still in the incident room.

Despite her protestations to Helen, there'd been no question of missing the fun – she would have been crushed by parental guilt – and on her way home she'd tried to get herself in the party mood, to push the darkness away. But she'd found it hard to shrug off her anxiety, and ignore those persistent, nagging questions. Even now, as she shovelled some more chocolate biscuits onto a plate, unsettling images kept intruding on her consciousness – the livid bruising round Justin Lanning's neck, the desolate, abandoned building site, Callum Harvey lying lifeless and discarded on the living-room floor. Charlie wasn't the best at separating her personal and professional lives, each inevitably bleeding into the other, but after a little decompression she was normally fine. But tonight, even as Jessica squealed with excitement, even as her future sibling kicked in time to the music, her mind kept turning on their difficult day.

The suspect seemed intent on maintaining his anonymity, determined to frustrate them. At first, Charlie had taken this as evidence of his guilt, a desperate attempt to stymie their investigation. Now it seemed less sinister – the fond hope of a man who wanted to return to the murky, faceless world of the dark web, once his innocence had been established. This was unlikely – he might escape serious charges, but would surely still be convicted of theft, breaking and entering and more besides – and at some point he would have to establish his identity, if only to facilitate his eventual release. He was resisting out of pride perhaps, perhaps out of habit, so used was he to living an anonymous, underground existence. But even if they did finally establish his true identity, would it matter? When there was still no concrete evidence linking him to the crime scenes, to the brutalized bodies of Justin Lanning and Callum Harvey?

They'd had setbacks before, of course, during their investigations. Wrong turns, false leads, cases of mistaken identity, but usually there seemed to be other obvious avenues to explore, important leads which had yet to be chased down. But that wasn't the case here. Unlike the children seated in front of her, who knew exactly what to do, the parcel spinning remorselessly round their little circle, like a minute hand around a clock, Charlie, Helen and the others had no clear idea how to proceed. Was it possible that everything they'd done so far had been for nothing? A massive dead end that allowed the real killer time and space to plot his next move? It seemed impossible, but what other conclusion could you draw from a very dispiriting day?

The game had now reached its conclusion. Jessie's best friend Mia was squealing with delight, pulling a bag of gold coins from the heart of the parcel, but for Charlie and the rest of the team there was no such triumph.

Their prize still seemed a long way off.

Chapter 64

She stared down at the corpse, gripped by a familiar feeling of revulsion. The body of Callum Harvey lay on the slab that had only twenty-four hours earlier been occupied by Justin Lanning. And despite their physical difference – Callum was small and slightly plump, where his schoolfriend had been honed and athletic – the similarities were striking. The lifeless, horrified expression, the bloodshot eyes, the heavy bruising and the thin, scabbed line of blood circling the entire neck.

'I presume we're looking at the same injuries?'

Her words drifted away, as Grieves emerged from behind one of the freezer compartments.

'Pretty much identical,' he confirmed. 'Two pinpricks – a taser mark – on the left-hand side of the neck…'

Helen leaned in, spotting the tiny puncture marks.

'…then ligature strangulation leading to asphyxiation and death. Similar width and thickness of wire used. I've had results from the Lanning samples – it's made of galvanized steel, which is the basic component—'

'Of farm wire,' Helen interrupted, concluding his sentence for him.

There was a brief silence, then Helen indicated some dark, purple bruising on the right side of his face.

'What's going on here? Lanning's face was untouched.'

'Yes, that is a point of difference,' Grieves said, brightening. 'Which might give you something to work with.'

In spite of herself, Helen felt a shiver of hope.

'I'm assuming the taser did its job, but perhaps not as well with Lanning.'

'So, he was beaten around the face to subdue him?'

'Not quite. The bruising is quite unusual and distinct.'

Helen now saw that Grieves was right. The bruising wasn't uniform and did have a kind of pattern.

'My guess is your victim was on the ground, but still moving, or still trying to move.'

'So this is … the imprint of a shoe or a boot? Pressing down on his face to subdue him?'

'More likely a boot,' Grieves said, nodding. 'An army surplus or hiking boot, something with hard plastic shapes built into the sole, that could leave their mark on the victim's skin.'

'OK, that's potentially a link to the Lanning crime scene, *if* the boot is the same size and sole pattern, but still, there must be thousands of those types of boots in circulation, hundreds of thousands …'

'It's not the boots themselves that are of interest, it's what was *on* them.'

'Meaning?'

'Meaning there were traces of a fine powder on the victim's cheek. Tiny amounts, but in two distinct places. Assuming there was nothing like that in the house, something that was knocked over during the attack …'

'Not that I saw.'

'Then I think it's quite likely this powder was on the sole of the boot prior to the attack, your killer shaking it free when he stamped on his victim.'

This was Locard's principle, the idea that the killer always brings something – some trace – of himself to the crime scene.

'Any idea what it is?'

'Not yet. I've taken samples for testing, but I'd say it was a mineral of some kind. It's a heavy white dust, odourless, but relatively thick in its consistency.'

Helen's mind rocketed back to Lanning's murder and the thick dust that blanketed the building site. Was it possible the killer wore the same boots to both scenes, leaving a trace of the former on the latter?

'How long?'

She didn't need to expand, Grieves knowing full well the urgency of the situation.

'Meredith should have something for you by midday to-morrow.'

'Perfect.' She turned to go, then checked herself. 'And thanks, Jim.'

The pathologist grunted a response and headed back to work. He'd never been one for protracted goodbyes, so Helen didn't linger, marching towards the exit. It had been a difficult day, full of odd revelations and nasty surprises, but now at the death perhaps they had a reason to hope. Perhaps this residue was linked to the building site, perhaps it wasn't. Either way, if it *had* been left at the crime scene by Harvey's attacker, then it might possibly lead them to him. It was a long shot, Helen knew that, but it was something to work with, something to cling to in a case which so far had left them clutching at straws.

Chapter 65

It had been another excellent day's work. Emilia was not known for her modesty, but today she felt her sense of self-satisfaction was thoroughly justified. Today, she had bossed it.

The press conference had been a train wreck, as far as Simmons was concerned at least. When she'd first arrived in the position, the new station chief had made overtures to Emilia, trying to bring her onside. And initially the journalist had liked her, finding her straightforward and honest. But she had been less visible of late and today's performance was seriously off-key, lacking coherency and, worse, authority.

She'd played straight into Emilia's hands, her uncertain attempt to answer the accusations thrown at her feeding the narrative of police incompetence. It was the cherry on the cake, following the morning's disastrous high-speed chase and the painful lack of progress in the Lanning/Harvey investigation, and Emilia had not held back when writing her article, levelling charges of incompetence and recklessness against the team at Southampton Central. Her crash-scene photos added spice to these charges and for once her editor had even got on board, penning an entertainingly vicious editorial entitled 'Keystone Cops'.

In truth, it could hardly have gone better, but – deliciously

– this wasn't even the best bit. Indeed, she had gained more than a choice headline and a generous slice of column inches today. Thanks to Hudson's rashness and his weakness of character, Emilia had been presented with a golden opportunity, a chance to get back on the inside, and she'd seized it with both hands.

As she'd predicted, Hudson had called her two hours after her unscheduled visit to Southampton Central. He'd blustered as best he could, trying to lay down red lines, but it was all semantics. He'd agreed to help her if she went easy on him now, if she spared him public and professional shame.

This she was happy to do, for the time being. She still had the photos of him, of course, but more than that she had recorded their brief conversation today, during which he'd intimated that he was happy to leak her privileged information regarding the current investigation. In attempting to avoid incriminating himself by sending a message or email, he'd walked straight into her trap. He wanted things to go back to normal, to erase his mistakes today, to be the officer he was before, but in fact he had achieved the very opposite.

From now on he would be dancing like a puppet on a string.

Chapter 66

She stared out over the rooftops, watching the sun slowly slip beyond the horizon. Freshly showered and wrapped in a thick towel, Helen stood silhouetted against the window casement, a cigarette pressed to her lips. Many in her team had switched to vaping and whilst she understood their thinking, Helen wasn't quite ready to relinquish the dirty hit that tobacco gave her. Even now, as she received that familiar nicotine buzz, she could feel her body beginning to relax.

Previously, when deep in a troubling case, she'd resorted to casual encounters, to S&M, to all sorts of reckless enterprises in order to quell the anxiety inside her. Though she still felt the pull of illicit excitement, could still be seduced by pleasurable pain, she'd avoided walking those roads of late, memories of Jake and others still fresh in her mind. Speed now had taken the place of pain, Helen eliciting a thrill from the battering her body took whilst astride her Kawasaki, and in other circumstances she would have been out on the roads right now, seeking adrenalin, seeking release.

Tonight, however, nicotine and a scalding hot shower had had to suffice. She was used to riding alone – she'd been doing so most of her life – but recently had grown accustomed to biking as a pair, of having a competitor racing alongside her. Riding tonight, a solitary figure on those familiar roads, would've just exacerbated the problem, adding personal distress, the sting of loneliness and dysfunction, to her professional tribulations.

This morning already seemed an eternity ago. She'd barely had time to think about Joseph's place in her life, and the discoveries she'd made on Facebook. But now, even as the questions and doubts about the Lanning case continued to fill her mind, thoughts of her lover started to intrude. She'd started the day surprised by his omissions – his lies – about his personal life. The discovery that he had a son had cast a dark shadow over their relationship, not to mention his honesty. Incidents later in the day had called into question his judgement, but also his feelings for – respect for – her. There had been real anger, even venom, in his expression as she'd tackled him following the crash. And while this could probably be excused because of the shock and distress, nevertheless it left her worried.

As she'd stood in the shower, she'd tried to push these worries away. She was too wired to engage with them tonight, she needed to switch off – yet somehow they continued to intrude. Did he have a son? Or could his ex be lying, attempting to smear his character, even elicit money from him? Stranger things had happened and yet the tone of her posts had been sad rather than bitter. Which left Helen feeling unnerved.

Leaving her vantage point at the window, she crossed back into the kitchen. Her laptop was where she'd left it and flicking it open she was once more confronted by Karen Hudson's face, and next to her the beaming Kieran. It should have been a heartwarming sight, but actually made Helen feel sick. Her first instinct was to slam the lid down and walk away, but she knew this would be a mistake. One way or another, she had to know the truth. For the sake of her sanity, not to mention her career, she had to make the call.

Five minutes later she had what she needed. Karen Hudson was a mobile hairdresser in Birkenhead and her contact details were not hard to find. Picking up her phone, Helen hesitated, aware that what she was doing was invasive, provocative even, then dialled the numbers. The call connected, seeming to ring for ages, before a chirpy voice answered.

'Is that Karen?' Helen asked.

'The very same. What can I do for you?'

She had her professional voice on, clearly used to conducting business over the phone. Which made the next bit even more awkward.

'I'm sorry to bother you late. I'm calling from Southampton.'

There was a small but distinct intake of breath at the other end of the phone.

'Is this about Joseph?'

There was suspicion, but also a touch of concern in Karen's voice too.

'Yes, but there's nothing to worry about, nothing's happened. I'm a colleague of his…'

'I see…'

Helen hesitated briefly, then carried on quickly: 'Well, I'm actually a bit more than that…'

Nothing in response. Helen suddenly felt inexplicably tense – and assumed Karen felt the same.

'And I wondered if I could just ask you a couple of questions.'

'What questions?'

She was blunt, but wary. As if this might a trick.

'Look, I feel embarrassed even asking, I know you've been through a lot and probably don't want to talk about it. I'm just trying to get a handle on… on what kind of guy he is.'

Another pause, then: 'What kind of guy do *you* think he is?'

'Secretive.'

The word was out of Helen's mouth before she'd even had time to think.

'That's one adjective for him,' Karen replied. 'Selfish, cruel, heartless might be others.'

Helen took that one on the chin, then continued: 'Can I ask when you last saw him?'

'Eighteen months ago.'

'And the same goes for Kieran?'

'Of course. That man doesn't exist in our lives.'

There was anger there for sure, but a well of sadness too. Helen suspected Karen had tried – and failed – to engage Joseph in family life.

'I'm sorry to hear that, Karen. Genuinely, I am. Can ... can I ask why the relationship ended?'

'Because of the boy, of course.'

She said it as if it should have been obvious, but Helen was momentarily stumped.

'Don't misunderstand me,' Karen now continued. 'Kieran's his, all right. That wasn't the problem.'

'I'm sorry, I'm not sure I—'

'Look, I don't know who you are, or how deep you're into this,' Karen continued quickly. 'But understand this – Joseph is the star of his own movie and everybody else ... well, they're just bit-part players.'

'Right ...' Helen murmured, not liking what she was hearing.

'Joseph and I ... we were more or less OK when it was just the two of us, but as soon as Kieran came along ...'

Helen said nothing – she already had an inkling where this was going. Noises could be heard in the background now – a young boy shouting and laughing – so Karen continued, rushing her words now.

'It happens to a lot of couples. The arrival of a child affects things, affects your relationship. Kieran was a sickly baby, he needed my attention day and night. Joseph said he was fine with that, that he understood and supported me, but he never did.'

'He was ... jealous of you and Kieran?'

'Jealous, angry, frustrated. It's probably my fault.'

'I'm sure that's not true.'

'When we were first together, I doted on Joe, made him feel like the centre of our universe, but once Kieran came along, I couldn't do that. My first loyalty *had* to be to my child.'

'Of course.'

'And that was the problem. Joseph was angry at first, then distant. He started working more, coming late. Then one day ... he didn't come home at all.'

'I see ...'

'I only learnt via a friend – a female colleague of his – that he'd applied for a job in Southampton. He never contacted me, in fact I only "heard" from him via lawyers after that.'

'Does he support you in any way?' Helen said, shocked.

'Oh, he pays what he's obliged to, he's not stupid. But he pays it so he doesn't have to deal with us, not because he wants to.'

Once more Helen was lost for words. Such callousness defied belief. It seemed impossible that Joseph could be so hard-hearted and yet there were elements of what Karen was saying that rang true – the desire to dominate, the frustration at being pushed away, at not being in control.

'Look, I better go,' Karen concluded, snapping Helen out of it. 'I'd prefer it if you didn't call again.'

'Of course, I'm sorry to have disturbed you. And if I've upset you—'

'And don't worry about me, we'll be all right. But watch out for yourself. Do what you need to but be aware that Joe is interested in one person, and one person alone – himself.'

And with that, she hung up.

Chapter 67

The figures were talking, but she wasn't listening. It was some panel show on BBC2, where almost-celebrities and comedians attempted to amuse each other. Fran had thought it might be distracting, might help her relax a little, but it was as if real life – the normal life of working, eating, shopping, watching TV – was happening at a remove, as if she was cut off from it.

Following her conversation with Maxine, Fran had thought about heading home, then on an impulse had decided to head to work. But whilst she was heading there, DI Grace had called, talking her through the situation and urging her to take precautions. The advice was sensible and sane – avoid isolated areas, stay in company, spend the nights with friends or family – and should have reassured her. But actually it had had the opposite effect and soon afterwards she'd got the jitters, convinced some bearded guy on the bus was staring at her, so she had hopped off halfway across the town, summoning an Uber to take her to her parent's house in Shirley. Predictably her mum had smelt a rat – asking if she was having girl trouble, or had been fired from her job, as if Fran was somehow preprogrammed to mess things up – but she'd managed to keep her suspicions at bay. She'd then asked about Justin and Callum, wondering if Fran had heard anything, whether their deaths were linked in any way, but Fran had shut that conversation down, claiming ignorance. This was true, of course, but this hadn't completely assuaged her mother, who'd been fond of the boys and was visibly upset, but it had at least moved the conversation on. A comforting meal of home-made spaghetti bolognese had managed to calm Fran's mood – the three glasses of Chianti hadn't hurt either – and Fran had settled down to watch TV in a slightly better mood.

But anxiety was starting to steal over her once more. She had left her interview with Maxine feeling worried and fearful. Maxine had laboured to reassure her, trying her best to be warm, comforting and calm, but for reasons Fran couldn't put her finger on, she *wasn't* reassured. She couldn't shrug off a nagging suspicion that she wasn't being told everything, that Maxine was concealing things from her. That didn't make any sense, of course – there was no question of Maxine harming Justin or Callum – but still the feeling lingered.

While it did, she would stay put. Perhaps she'd have to invent a problem with her flat, claim illness or – worst-case scenario – confide her real fears to her mother. She didn't want to do that – her mother would go into meltdown if she thought there was the slightest sniff of danger – but it might come to it, if she was to remain in the family home. It was fraught with complications, but suddenly the idea of staying here until the danger had passed until Justin and Callum's killer had been identified and captured, seemed irresistible.

It was the home she'd come back to, after her escape from hell. The four of them had blundered over the Downs, constantly losing, then re-finding the path in the thick fog. They'd barely rested, expecting King to appear at any moment, pursuing them with his vicious dogs in tow, but so disoriented were they that it was several hours later that they tumbled out onto a remote country road, flagging down a startled truck driver. From there they'd been ferried to a petrol station, then to a police station and it was only much later – after a spell in A&E and lengthy questioning by the police – that she'd ended up back in the comfortable semi-detached house in Shirley which had always been her home. Previously she'd been a bit embarrassed by it – the house was small and twee compared to Justin's or Maxine's – but she cried when she crossed the threshold that day. And though it had changed over the years – new sofas, new decor – it was still her safe place. It was still home.

Cheered by this thought, Fran picked up the remote control, firing up Netflix. Perhaps she could find some cheesy movie from the noughties, something comforting and familiar to help her unwind. But as she began to surf, her phone began to buzz.

She shot an angry look at it – she'd already spoken to Helen Grace earlier, had agreed to talk to one of her officers about security measures. Nor did she want to talk to any journalists, several of whom had already left messages on her voicemail. No, she just wanted to shut everything out and wallow in nostalgia.

Thankfully, the phone rang out. Fran continued to flick – *Anchorman*, *Juno*, *Attack the Block* – but then her phone started vibrating again. Cursing, Fran picked it up, flicking a look at the caller ID. Unknown number. Fran hesitated, uncertain. The phone rang out, but almost immediately started ringing again. Irritated, she answered it quickly.

'Yes?'

Silence on the other end. She could hear someone breathing but they refused to speak.

'Who the hell is this?' she demanded.

And now the caller did speak, his soft, sibilant words sending fear arrowing through her.

'Hello, Fran. How nice to hear your voice again...'

Day Four

Chapter 68

It was not her job to talk. She was here to listen.

Chief Constable Alan Peters had summoned Grace Simmons to his office for an early morning meeting. Any hopes that this might be a pep talk, designed to reassure her following her difficult press conference yesterday, were swiftly dispelled. Peters was clearly rattled by the negative press coverage and was determined to make his displeasure felt.

'I'll ask you again. Is DI Grace in control of her team?'

'Yes, sir. I believe—'

'Because the evidence is all the other way. She's a good officer, who's had some exceptional collars, but there's no excuse for what happened yesterday. What if a pedestrian had been hit during the pursuit? Killed even?'

'DS Hudson's actions were regrettable, I admit that, but we did have a suspect in view—'

'Who turns out to be innocent of the crimes we're currently investigating. So, given that they were chasing the wrong man, in a reckless and cavalier fashion, endangering the public, I'll ask the question again.'

Simmons felt sure Peters was feeling the heat himself, that he'd fielded an early call from the Police and Crime Commissioner, hence the verbal onslaught this morning. Peters was allergic to anything that threatened his reputation and, on the face of it, she could see why he was worried. But she had to protect Helen from a man who'd always had doubts about her.

'It was a bad call, sir. And *I will* remind DI Grace of her responsibilities. I will also ask her directly if there are any issues within the team, in terms of personnel or communication, that might have led to yesterday's breakdown in protocol.'

Even as she said it, Simmons wasn't sure she would. Helen didn't need reminding of her responsibilities and Simmons heavily suspected the fault lay with DS Hudson.

'But please understand this is a very fast-moving investigation and, yesterday, it just got a bit ahead of us. Be under no doubt, however, the team *is* functioning well and we are working night and day to bring this case to a swift and satisfactory conclusion.'

This appeared to mollify Peters a touch; he liked fast, neat investigations. But to Simmons' dismay, he wasn't finished yet.

'And what about you?'

'Me, sir?'

'It was hardly your finest performance in front of the press yesterday.'

'Understood. But the questioning was extremely hostile.'

'You're a senior officer, you're trained to deal with situations like th—'

'It was an ambush.'

'Even so, you looked defensive, distracted and, frankly, a little unwell.'

Was this the real reason she'd been summoned here?

'You don't look much better now. *Is* anything the matter?'

This was it then, her opportunity to confess. But could she take it?

A week had passed since the hospital had confirmed she had heart disease. Not a minor problem, fixable through diet and exercise, no, this was a 'make some serious life changes or get your affairs in order' situation. The diagnosis had knocked her for six, so much so that she hadn't told her boys, her friends or her colleagues. But here was a chance to come clean, to ask for help.

'No, I'm absolutely fine, sir. A little tired, perhaps, given the nature of the investigation, but otherwise fighting fit.'

He was eyeing her shrewdly. Did he buy her story? Or was he looking at a sixty-two-year-old woman, knowing that her time was up?

'Now if you'll excuse me, I would like to show my face in the incident room, rally the troops.'

He let her go, but she could feel his eyes on her as she hurried from his office. She wasn't sure he believed her, which left her worried. Not for her own sake, but for Helen's. In a split second, Simmons had made the decision to keep her secret to herself. The right thing to do would probably have been to share her burden – with Helen, then Peters – but it seemed wrong to pile even more stress and worry onto her old friend at such a difficult time. Instead she had lied, determined to shield Helen from her nervous superior. What the team needed now was unstinting support and encouragement. Any questions about Helen's leadership would be hugely undermining and could throw the whole investigation off track. No, it was her job to fend off any such criticism, to soldier on, whatever the personal cost might be.

She had always protected Helen, her best officer and close friend. But how long could she continue to do so?

Chapter 69

The pressure was ratcheting up on all sides.

A restless night had been followed by an unnerving morning. Joseph had nearly come off his bike on the way to work, a courier's van pulling out in front of him without warning as he sped down Exeter Street. It was probably partially his fault – he was distracted and dog tired – but still he'd given the driver both barrels. The release of the tension inside him had felt good for a moment, but he was still unsettled and shaken when he'd arrived at Southampton Central.

The attitude of the desk sergeant had not improved his mood.

'Good morning, DS Hudson. Lovely day for it…'

A few simple words, which would probably be repeated numerous times today. Yet the way they were said riled him. There was an excessive cheerfulness in the greeting that was obviously inappropriate given Joseph's troubles. And was it his imagination or did the sergeant linger on his rank, stressing the 'DS'? Was this a mark of respect? He doubted it, given the glee in the desk jockey's tone. Was this meant to imply that a detective sergeant shouldn't have acted in such a foolhardy manner yesterday? Or even that he might not be a DS for much longer?

Joseph had tried to put these thoughts from his mind as he

made his way to the incident room on the seventh floor. During the long, sleepless night, he had eventually come up with a plan. It was simple enough, but the only way forward. He would do as he was asked, diligently and without complaint, continuing to review the evidence they'd recovered from their mystery suspect's warehouse. He would be dutiful and respectful, keeping his head down and acting in a thoroughly professional way, in the hope of regaining Helen's good opinion, restoring some of his credibility within the team and denying the MIT gossips any further ammunition. And though his heart had sunk at the sheer volume of evidence piled up on his desk, he nevertheless set to it with enthusiasm, pausing only to make himself a strong cup of coffee.

Initially the plan seemed to work, the litany of evidence succeeding in distracting him from his present woes. Their suspect – still in custody, though for how much longer? – had called himself a collector, but this was surely an understatement. He was an obsessive, a hoarder, his stash of murderabilia containing tens of thousands of items. Most of them would be irrelevant – personal items belonging to Ted Bundy and Jeffery Dahmer had no bearing on the current bloodshed – but they would have to sift through them to see if there was anything hidden away that might help inform the investigation. Some items, however, patently *were* relevant, three boxes of carefully bagged Daniel King 'souvenirs' now perched on Joseph's desk.

They had already been labelled and logged. It fell to Joseph to determine whether to bring them to the team's attention. Perhaps they were grasping at straws, perhaps the whole task was pointless, but there was no ducking it. He made swift progress, quickly assessing and dismissing countless items – newspaper articles from the time, a photocopy of a statement made by Fran Ward to the investigating officer, DI Bob Stevenson, a school photo containing all five children, even the brick which their suspect claimed to have taken from the destroyed farmhouse.

A lot of the items were in good condition, others less so. It was clear now to Joseph that their suspect had taken the time to riffle through the charred rubble – unearthing the charred collar of one of his incinerated dogs – as well as the rubbish bins left on site. It was astonishing what lengths he'd gone to in search of personal souvenirs of this twisted individual and though some of them were intriguing – a doctor's prescription for Riluzole and a local number scribbled on a piece of paper without explanation – it was unclear whether they held any salient information for the team. Joseph made these judgement calls as best he could, erring on the side of caution for fear of missing something important, wondering all the time whether his task had any purpose.

He knew it had to be done, that the evidence had to be assessed diligently, and he was determined to be seen doing so, especially as DS Simmons had just popped her head into the incident room to check on progress. But it did feel as if the ship was moving on, the spotlight of suspicion drifting away from their suspect to persons unknown. He'd felt at the time that Helen's decision to assign him these duties might be a punishment – a painstaking dead end that would remove him from the centre of the investigation – and with each passing minute he became more convinced that this was the case.

Whenever a major investigation was running, the number of bodies grew, meaning Joseph had a large audience for his drudgery. It was still early, but already the room was filling up, and Joseph couldn't help but notice the stolen glances, the whispered conversations, the suppressed laughter.

He'd tried hard to become popular within the team but in truth it had been a struggle from the start. Stepping into a dead officer's shoes was always hard and perhaps he had over-compensated, trying too hard to prove himself, to make his fellow officers respect him. He had sacrificed easy popularity in doing so, which now seemed a mistake – there were few who were truly loyal to him, who'd cut him some slack now that he was under pressure. The fact that DC Malik was an amiable, popular officer didn't help either. She'd been discharged from hospital and was back at work, no doubt spreading poison about his behaviour.

He told himself to get a grip, to keep calm and concentrate, but the atmosphere in the room was hard to ignore. He was the most senior officer present, but he felt like the greenest DC, the butt of people's jokes and ridicule. On a couple of occasions, he even caught people staring at him, enjoying his time in the stocks. What right did they have to gawp at him? To gossip at him? What had they ever done?

He had brought multiple murderers to book, broken up drugs gangs, saved innocent children from a lifetime of slavery and degradation. Whereas they had just hung onto Helen Grace's coat-tails, seeking whatever reflected glory they could garner. Their censure now was unjustified and unwarranted and it made him rage.

With each passing second, he felt this sense of injustice more keenly, his antagonism towards his fellow officers cementing and, deep inside him, a burning anger growing too. The big question now was whether he would be able to contain it.

Chapter 70

She roared along the road, weaving her way expertly through the snaking traffic. The city centre was busier than usual today, weekend traffic clogging up the main arteries, but there was no question of delay, Helen keeping her speed steady as she raced towards Briton Street.

She had been crossing the basement car park of her block, intent on heading to the forensics lab in Woolston, when the call had come through. She'd expected it to be Charlie, or Simmons seeking an update, but in fact it was the station operator, asking her to attend the Moon Lounge as soon as possible. She wouldn't divulge details, stating only that the team stationed there needed to discuss an important development with her.

Helen was an experienced policewoman, a CID officer for nearly twenty years, but even so she felt a pulse of adrenalin at the news of a lead. She had no idea what the uniformed officers had unearthed – CCTV footage from a neighbouring property? Witness testimony from a member of staff? – but there could be no doubting it was significant. A rank and file officer wouldn't summon the senior investigating officer unless they had something to say.

Dropping her speed briefly, Helen turned onto Orchard Lane. Seeing the road clear in front of her, she opened up the throttle, roaring away from the congestion. Five minutes later, she was pulling into Briton Street, bringing her bike to an elegant stop outside the popular nightclub. It looked a little lonely in the morning sunshine, the usual queue of underdressed punters absent, but PC Polly Walton was waiting for her, hurrying over to her commanding officer.

'Morning, ma'am,' she said, taking off her hat and smoothing down her hair. 'Sorry to disturb you on a Sunday morning.'

'No worries. What have you got for me?'

The officer paused briefly, before replying: 'I think you'd better see for yourself.'

As she said this, she stepped aside, gesturing towards the open door of the club. Helen didn't hesitate, pulling off her helmet and heading into the gloom.

Chapter 71

'Tell the inspector exactly what you told me.'

They were now huddled together inside the club, Walker flanking the nervous young woman, Helen sitting directly in front of her. The club was sparsely populated this morning, but even so Helen could make out the manager – Chris Bridges – hovering nearby. Helen tried to ignore him, concentrating instead on the witness in front of her.

'I don't know…' the woman muttered, darting the briefest of looks at her manager.

'It's OK, Tatiana, you're not in any trouble,' Helen reassured her. 'We have no interest in you personally.'

The woman seemed slightly reassured by this, but still hesitated.

'If you haven't got your papers yet, or if you're here illegally, we can overlook that if you've got something important to tell us.'

The woman looked at PC Walker, who nodded encouragingly. Taking a deep breath, the young Albanian began to speak.

'I working Friday night. *Very* busy, lot of people…'

'What is it you do here?'

'Cleaning in day. At night, I pick up glasses, clear tables.'

'And that's what you were doing on Friday?'

She nodded.

'They have a handful of them doing it, but Tatiana's area of operation is the VIP area,' Walker elaborated.

Now Helen knew why she was here.

'Go on,' she encouraged.

'I pick up glasses all night there. Lots of girls, lots of drinking...'

'Right...'

'Just before midnight, I see something funny. A man by himself. The VIP section is empty, girls dancing, but he's there. I think maybe he's friend, but he looks strange...'

'Strange how?'

'Nervous? Is that how you say? He looking around a lot... Like he's scared of people watching. But I watch him, I see him—'

'What was he doing?'

'Looking in bags.'

'In the women's handbags?' Helen queried.

Tatiana nodded.

'And then?'

'Then he see *me.*'

She shivered slightly at the memory.

'What happened then?'

'Then he move quick. He pick up empty glass from table, comes to me, gives me... then he go, gone...'

'That's very helpful,' Helen said, trying to conceal her excitement. 'And can you describe this man?'

'Yes, he thin, tall, light hair, down to his cheeks.'

Helen digested this, intrigued now.

'Eye colour?'

The cleaner shook her head.

'What were his features like? Wide nose, thin nose, pointed chin, square chin?'

'Thin, like a woman's.'

Helen nodded, trying to ignore the tension building inside her.

'Anything else?'

Now she saw the woman hesitate. She suddenly realized that she too was rigid with tension.

'One thing,' she eventually continued. 'I see it when he give me glass.'

'Yes?'

The young woman looked up, her frightened eyes locking onto Helen as she added: 'He … he only have four fingers on his hand.'

Chapter 72

'Is it *possible*?'

Grace Simmons was struggling to contain her shock.

'Up until an hour ago, I'd have said no, absolutely not,' Helen answered, still coming to terms with the morning's revelation herself. 'To my mind, Daniel King was yesterday's news, washed up on some remote beach somewhere, or at the bottom of the channel.'

'But…?'

'But we have to consider it now. The witness's description was accurate – height, hair colour, build and obviously his historic injury.'

'Is she credible?'

'Depends on your point of view.'

'Meaning?'

'Well, she's clearly here illegally. Came here to visit friends in Bournemouth on a holiday visa, then promptly disappeared. She's been in Southampton for six months or so, working without papers at the Moon Lounge. So, she wouldn't make an ideal witness if this came to court, but on the other hand I'm not sure she has any reason to lie. What does she stand to gain?'

It was a fair point. The last thing the owners of the Moon Lounge wanted was continued police scrutiny.

'She's risking her job by cooperating and clearly was doing so reluctantly. She's terrified of the police.'

'Could someone have put her up to it?'

'Potentially. But who? And why?'

Simmons stared at her, clearly hoping for something – *anything* – to explain away Tatiana's statement. Helen would dearly love to have delivered, but on the face of it there was nothing suspicious about her testimony.

'Moreover,' Helen continued, 'I'm convinced she had no idea of the significance of her sighting. She'd have been a young girl in Albania at the time of King's crimes, there's no way she would know who he is, or be able to describe him accurately—'

'Unless she'd actually seen him.'

Simmons finished her sentence for her. The two women stared at each other, digesting what this meant.

'Obviously, we'll check this out with other local business, CCTV feeds, et cetera, to see if anyone else spotted him. We've been through them once looking for our former suspect, but we'll do it again. And we're also going to go over the historic sightings of King.'

'Historic sightings?' Simmons queried.

'King has been "spotted" at various times over the intervening years, but none of them were ever verified, and the tip-offs were often anonymous. Time-wasters, hoaxers...'

'When was the last sighting?'

Helen paused briefly, before responding: 'Four weeks ago. Another anonymous tip-off. I'll ask DC Osbourne to chase it down, see if we have a phone number for the caller, or better still, a recording of the call...'

'And this was in Southampton.'

'Yes. Given this, and the fact that the bootprint recovered

from the building site matches King's shoe size, we have to consider the possibility that he *is* alive and active.'

If anything, Simmons was a shade paler than yesterday, shorn of her usual energy and optimism. Once more, Helen was tempted to ask her if she was OK, but Simmons cut her off.

'So what's our first step? I presume you want to keep this under wraps for now?'

'For the time being. Obviously, the team are going to chase down all leads on King – past and present – but first things first I want to get Fran Ward and Maxine Pryce into secure accommodation.'

'You think they're in danger?'

'We have to assume so. Maybe King is alive, maybe it's a copycat. Either way it's possible that all the publicity around Pryce's book, her numerous appearances in the media, have prompted these attacks on Lanning and Harvey. If so, then they are at risk.'

This was not a thought that cheered Simmons, who was nevertheless nodding, trying to be encouraging.

'Clearly, we want to get justice for Justin and Callum, to find out who was responsible for their deaths,' Helen continued solemnly, 'and the team will work round the clock to do just that. But given that a killer is still at large, that we now have a concrete sighting of a suspect, my first priority has to be to the living.'

Chapter 73

'Show me some identification. I'm not doing anything until you show me some ID.'

Fran was trying to keep her voice steady, but she sounded shaky and upset.

'OK, I'm passing it through now.'

The letter box opened, Fran moving aside just in case, then a slim warrant card was pushed through. It would have been a comic scene – the card sliding through as Fran cowered in the hallway – were she not so bloody terrified. Her nerves were shot after a sleepless night, and the sound of the doorbell ringing had made her jump out of her skin. Her mum had risen to answer and had to be virtually dragged away, even as the person outside began to pound on the door. Fran would obviously have to give her mother an explanation now – but that could wait. Right now, her only concern was the identity of the caller.

She took in the warrant card – a round, pretty face next to a name, Detective Sergeant Charlotte Brooks, Hampshire Police. Summoning her courage, Fran moved forward, peering through the spyhole. The same face looked back at her and, convinced that the woman was alone, Fran unchained the door and yanked it open.

*

Two minutes later, they were settled in the living room together. Fran's mother was excluded from the interview, but was no doubt listening at the door. The occasional creak of the floorboard outside made that plain.

'What sort of accommodation?'

'Well, it sounds more dramatic than it is,' Brooks responded calmly. 'But it's basically a safe house. A property we own and can police effectively, providing you with round-the-clock protection.'

Fran stared at her blankly. How had her life come to this?

'It won't be for long,' Brooks continued, speaking as if this sort of thing happened every day. 'Just until this situation is cleared up.'

'This *situation*? You mean the murder of my friends.'

Fran couldn't hide her disdain – how dare this woman suggest that Justin's and Callum's deaths were just another case?

'They were real people, flesh and blood. People who'd already suffered years of torment – depression, anxiety—'

'I know that, Fran, and believe me I feel for them, their families and for you too. It must be terrible to lose two people you were close to.'

Her sincerity was evident, mollifying Fran a little. But still she felt her anger, her emotions, fizzing.

'And we will bring whoever is responsible to justice, but until then we need to make sure you're safe. I know it's going to be a big upheaval, that it'll impact on work and family—'

'It's OK, I'll do it.'

Brooks stopped short, surprised by the speed of her response.

'You can discuss it with your parents, if you want to. I can wait here, whilst you—'

'What is there to say? If I'm in danger, then I should go.'

Brooks said nothing, looking at her oddly. Fran knew instantly that she'd overstepped the mark, that she'd aroused the officer's suspicion, but the truth was that now a sanctuary had been offered, she wanted to seize it. To get herself away from her family, to get her head together, to try and make sense of this crazy sequence of events.

'Well, if you're sure...'

They both rose, but as Fran turned towards to the door, Brooks spoke once more.

'Fran...'

She pivoted to see the officer appraising her.

'Has anything happened?'

'What do you mean?'

'Well, normally people need a bit of time to process something like this.'

'But this isn't a normal situation, right?'

'Of course not, but you also seem very on edge, like something's happened to rattle you.'

Fran said nothing.

'I mean, it's good to be cautious when answering the door, but you were very unwilling to open up, like you were scared of something, of someone—'

'Two of my close friends have just been murdered. How would *you* react?'

Brooks seemed to accept this, but still appeared unsure.

'You're sure nothing's happened?'

This was her chance. This was her opportunity to let someone else into this hideous nightmare. But she knew she wouldn't and was not surprised when she found herself answering: 'No, nothing at all.'

Chapter 74

'No way.'

DC Bentham looked stunned, as if he couldn't believe what he was hearing. But Maxine wasn't going to mince her words.

'I can't possibly drop everything to hide out in some flat in the arse end of suburbia.'

'It's not as bad as you think and, honestly, it'll just be for a short while.'

'The timing's all wrong. I've got a host of media appearances scheduled, not to mention a busy writing schedule.'

'You'd be able to take computer with you,' Bentham persisted, 'though we would suggest you stay off the internet. As for public appearances, I think it would be best to postpone those for now, until such time as we can guarantee your safety.'

'Have you got a suspect then? Someone you're looking for?'

Bentham paused, offering his best attempt at a reassuring smile.

'We're pursuing several lines of enquiry at the moment. Obviously, we'll let you know as soon as we have anything significant to report.'

He was lying, Maxine was sure of that. Justin had been murdered the day before yesterday, Callum just twenty-four hours ago. Yet suddenly first thing this morning it had become imperative to get her to a safe house.

'So you've no one specific?'

'No. Not yet.'

Said too quickly for Maxine's liking.

'Anyway, I can talk you through how things might work, rules of contact—'

'I'm staying here.'

Once more, she silenced him.

'I don't mind having police protection, if you really feel it's necessary, but I'm not being driven out of my flat. This is my home!'

Bentham eyed her curiously, perhaps trying to work out if her bravado was real, or just for show.

'Well, obviously that's an option we can explore. But given everything that's going on, I really do think that—'

'I've said no, don't make me repeat myself.'

Now Bentham finally relented, but his acquiescence was begrudging.

'OK, if that's what you feel is best. We can have officers front and back, round the clock, while you're here, and a separate detail when you need to venture out. But I must reiterate that you should keep public appearances to a minimum and, when you do go out, there will be strict protocols that will need to be followed to the *letter*...'

He continued talking, but Maxine had already tuned out, the words washing over her. It didn't seem real, it didn't seem *possible*. She had been through a terrible ordeal as a child, but she had survived it, she had *grown*, and was stronger and more resilient than she could ever have imagined. But now the carefully constructed edifice of Maxine 2.0 was beginning to crumble.

She had told herself that the awful events of the past had

happened for a reason. She had owned the narrative of her past and fashioned it to a positive end. Maxine was many things to many people, but above all else she was a *survivor*. Someone who could use her experiences, her strength, to inspire others. She had a role, she had a future, but now she was talking to some fresh-faced copper about hiding away from a sinister, creeping danger. This was not how the story was supposed to go, it was not how she'd planned it, and now, as she looked at Bentham's anxious face, she realized that perhaps after all her story wouldn't have a happy ending. The shadow of death was descending upon her once more.

The question was what was she going to do about it? Was she going to stay? Or was she going to run?

Chapter 75

His eyes stared back at her, hard and cruel. Helen took in King's face – the hooded eyes, the twist of his mouth, the cold, blank expression – then turned to face the team.

'Daniel James King. This is the only official image we have of him, a mugshot following his arrest for affray in 2008. It was taken over ten years ago, but it's the best we've got. Tatiana Lucaj is currently working with our e-fit team, which might provide something additional for us, but in the meantime we work with *this*.'

A couple of the team inched forward, keen to drink in the fugitive's features. They had all gathered together in the briefing room – Charlie, Joseph, Osbourne; everyone was present save for DC Bentham, who was still locked away with Maxine Pryce.

'I'm sure you all know the case, but let's refresh our memories. He was the only child of Julia King, father unknown. They lived on an isolated farm on the South Downs, near Chilgrove. It wasn't a particularly profitable business – Julia was an erratic character with a drink problem, qualities that she seems to have passed on to her son. Daniel King was seldom at school, preferring to ride quad bikes and fire his shotguns on the farm. The pair frequently argued and sometimes she'd kick him out of the house. When this happened, or when he had money in his pocket, he'd head to Southampton, frequenting the pubs in the Northam area. It's not your usual party area, but you can buy strong cider for a pound a pint there, not to mention all manner of drugs. It was during one of these occasional trips into town that we became aware of him – he was cautioned on a couple of occasions for being off his face and was also arrested for affray. Now, the phone that was used to contact Justin Lanning sprang to life for the first time in the Northam area. It picked up the signal briefly before disappearing again, used only once later when the threatening call was made. That's all we have currently, but obviously Northam becomes a priority area for investigation. I've asked DC Reid to draw up a list of current clubs and pubs, looking for overlaps with King's old haunts. We should also chase down any known associates in that area.'

Vigorous nods from several members of the team. Everyone seemed engaged, energized, all except Joseph Hudson who loitered near the back of the group, looking oddly distracted. Ignoring her unease about this, Helen pressed on.

'Should any of you need reminding, King was ... is a dangerous individual and should be approached with extreme caution. His record makes it clear that prior to his abduction of the St Mary's kids, he twice attempted to kill, targeting Lorraine Kielty and Amanda Barnes on remote country lanes. Both girls sustained minor injuries – King punched them, before attempting to strangle them – but they managed to fight him off and escape. King was never identified as the attacks occurred a fair distance from the family farm – leaving him free to abduct, murder and kill.'

One of the newer members of the team shuddered slightly, knowing full well what was coming next.

'Having abducted the five kids, he kept them captive in the basement. Initially they were submissive, compliant, and King didn't hold back. He seemed to take great pleasure in torturing the children, beating them with bicycle chains and tyre irons and threatening to strangle them with a length of farm wire.'

Even Charlie looked a little pale now, experienced officers not immune to the terror King could generate.

'The children endured one awful night, but then an opportunity to escape presented itself and they took it. King discovered his mistake and pursued them across the Downs. Rachel Wood was less mobile than the others and fell into his clutches, whereupon he dragged her back to the house and murdered her. Aware that the escaped children would alert the police, he abandoned his dogs, his home, everything – torching the farmhouse and fleeing to the Chichester coast, where he apparently committed suicide.'

A heavy silence filled the room now. Helen knew what question they were itching to ask, so she put them out of their misery.

'Obviously, we now have to question the conclusion of this narrative and ask ourselves whether King could still be alive. Whether he might be responsible for the murders of Justin Lanning and Callum Harvey. Where are we at with the most recent sighting of him?'

'The call was made to the main switchboard from a payphone in a café near the Aldbury estate in Duckworth. The caller was female, but refused to give her name. I've sent uniform down there to ask around. I do know that Tally Greene lives on the estate – she's got multiple cautions for hoaxes, fake bomb scares and so forth, so we'll definitely be talking to her.'

'And the call itself?'

'Nothing in the way of detail, just that the caller thought she'd seen King entering a property in Portswood.'

'Where?'

'They didn't give a road name and to be honest the caller

was pretty vague. The operator put it down to all the publicity surrounding Pryce's book, assuming people would start seeing King's face all over town now.'

'What about the other sightings? The ones going further back.'

'Still chasing those down,' DC Malik replied briskly.

'Quick as you can, please.'

Turning from Malik, Helen addressed the group once more.

'You all have full case files on your desk. Digest them quickly but thoroughly. Anything that strikes you, flag it immediately, to myself or DS Hudson. DS Brooks, I'd like you to get in touch with DI Bob Stevenson, the SIO on the original investigation. I believe he still lives locally. If anyone can give us an insight into King's psychology, he can.'

'Straight away.'

'DC Reid,' Helen continued. 'I'd like you to print up a site map of the Northam area, pinpointing the masts which picked up the killer's phone. I want an exact radius for each mast's reach, plus a breakdown of derelict buildings, doss houses, B&Bs, squats, anywhere where King might be lying low, in addition to a comprehensive breakdown of all the drinking dens in the area.'

'On it,' he said, rising.

'As soon as we have that, we get down there. Pull in uniform if you have to, I want an active presence there, see if we can smoke out any witnesses, any sightings. Cancel any social plans you might have, let your families know you're going to be working late. We have a lead now, a prime suspect, so he must occupy all our thoughts and energies. Let's get out there, find this guy,' Helen fixed her gaze on the team in front of her, 'and end this.'

Chapter 76

She had been out in the cold, braving the bitter wind sweeping through the smokers' area, when her phone had suddenly pinged. Drawing hard on her cigarette, Emilia had fished it out of her pocket with her spare hand, curious to know who was messaging her on a Sunday morning. It was not a number she recognized, but she knew who it was from, silently congratulating Hudson for getting himself a new SIM card. Better to be safe than sorry, given Grace's track record of hunting out moles.

The message was short, but exceedingly sweet. 'Team now actively seeking Daniel King, following possible sighting.'

Emilia laughed out loud, arousing the curiosity of two sports reporters who stood nearby, getting their caffeine fix. Turning away, she read the message again, chuckling with happiness and disbelief. She'd always thought it was possible that King might have survived, assuming he'd spirited himself off to some far-flung country to lie low, until such time as he thought it was safe to offend again. She'd never in her wildest dreams imagined that he might return to the south coast, to the scene of his crimes.

She had hinted at this possibility, of course – it was the subtext of most of her articles about him – but she had never actually come out and said it, fearful of exciting ridicule. But this news changed everything. Now there was nothing to hold her back.

Emilia shuddered, not with cold now, but with excitement. It was a story that was beyond juicy – a famous fugitive returning to wreak his vengeance on those who'd escaped him. It was terrifying, hideous, wonderful and Emilia thanked God that yet again she would be ahead of the game, breaking news of this stunning development before the rest of the nation's news outfits had got a sniff of it. It was as if all her Christmases had come at once, gifting her the story that might yet define her career.

Chapter 77

She felt as if she had the dark mark on her this morning. Everywhere she went, she seemed to inspire suspicion, even fear.

Charlie's conversation with Fran Ward had been awkward and testy and her interview with DI Bob Stevenson had started in a similar vein. The portly retiree had been wary of answering the door, unnerved by the arrival of an unscheduled caller, and was scarcely more welcoming when he found out who she was. He could guess why she'd come and didn't seem minded to cooperate, but Charlie's powers of persuasion eventually won out, which was why she now found herself sitting at the kitchen table in his comfortable bungalow in Fordham.

Between them sat a cardboard box, containing case files, old newspapers, even a battered copy of the posters that had once blanketed Southampton and the south coast, appealing for information on the whereabouts of the fugitive Daniel King. The box, and most of the items in it, were covered in a film of dust, suggesting they hadn't been touched in some time. Out of sight, out of mind, Charlie had thought to herself.

'You're welcome to leaf through this stuff. There may be things there that aren't in the official files, but I don't know how they'll help you. Every major lead, every minor one, was thoroughly investigated.'

'I've no doubt.'

This wasn't just naked flattery. Bob Stevenson had been a respected police officer within the Hampshire force. He'd left with a full pension, several commendations and his head held high, but even so, Charlie could tell from his body language, the way he constantly fidgeted in his seat, that the King case still bothered him. While there was still the possibility that King had eluded them and escaped justice, then Stevenson would never fully feel that he'd done his job. It was the one question mark in an otherwise impeccable career.

'We just want to go over everything one more time,' Charlie continued. 'In light of new information.'

Stevenson had been dismissive initially, not wanting to counternance the idea that King had returned to Southampton. But now he seemed more doubtful, even a touch unsettled.

'How kosher is this witness?' he barked.

'We're still investigating that, but there's no obvious reason to doubt her.'

Stevenson nodded, but looked far from happy.

'And the description was accurate?'

'Very.'

Another small, reluctant nod.

'So what would be really helpful is if you could tell me a little more about King. Nobody spent more time looking into him than you ...'

Stevenson stared at her, suddenly looking tired.

'Believe it or not, I hadn't given him much thought in recent years. I know everyone at the station thinks I obsess about him, but actually I'd managed to put him from my mind. Erica and I have a good life here, I don't need to be dwelling on folk like King. Until that arrived, I'd barely given him a moment's thought.'

He gestured to a package sitting on the kitchen top. Taking it in, Charlie realized that it was a Jiffy bag, on top of which sat a copy of Maxine Pryce's new book.

'She rang me when she was writing it. I took the call, out of courtesy, because of what she'd been through, but I told her I wouldn't be contributing. No point raking over the past…'

Unless there's money to be made out of it, Charlie thought to herself.

'I appear in it, of course,' he said, reaching over to pick up the weighty tome, 'and I suppose I will flick through it at some point, but not yet.'

He said this casually, turning the book round on the table so it was facing away from him, but Charlie could see it unsettled him. Was this just an understandable desire not to go back to that dark place? Or was he fearful of criticism, worried that Maxine might take him to task for failing to bring their tormentor to justice?

'I'm sure it's a fair portrayal of what was a very thorough and effective investigation.'

'I'm glad you think so; not everyone was so charitable.'

Charlie was aware that there had been some criticism in the local press, but in truth such critics had been few and far between.

'Totally,' she said, gamely. 'I know you dissected his life, looked under every rock, which is why any insight you can give me…'

Stevenson shifted in his seat, looking a little more comfortable now that he knew she hadn't come here to accuse him.

'Well, you know the basics. What perhaps doesn't come across in the official reports is just how… strange King was. He hadn't had the best of lives – no father, a mother who was over-fond of the sauce – but while his mum was alive, he just about stayed on the right side of the law. The usual scrapes, drink, drugs, thieving and so on, but she kept him on track. She had some sort of hold over him, I think.'

'What happened to her?'

'She had ALS – motor neurone disease – and it killed her in the end. She'd been going downhill, becoming less physically able, relying more and more on Daniel, then one day she was gone. Suddenly an eighteen-year-old boy was alone in the world, owner of this big, ramshackle farm. Soon after that, things really started to go wrong. Whether it was grief, or the sudden responsibility, or just that he could indulge his vices, who knows, but he went downhill fast. The drinking became heavier, as did the drug use, there was evidence he was downloading vast amounts of illegal pornography, snuff movies and the like. Not long after that he attacked Lorraine Kielty, although we didn't know it was him at the time.'

'And he had no one at all? Nobody to guide him or restrain him?'

Stevenson shook his head.

'Obviously social services tried to get involved, but he was never very welcoming, didn't want to engage. They did…'

Stevenson paused now, a frown creasing his face.

'…they did manage to make him go to a child psychologist a few times. I forget the guy's name, but I remember what he told me. It never went in the file, didn't seem any point after King topped himself, but it's always stuck in my mind.'

He paused, as if genuinely disturbed by the memory.

'He told this shrink that he'd been walking on the farm one day and found an injured bird. A tiny sparrow chick that had fallen out of its nest and injured itself. He picked it up, stroked it, was amused by the way its little beak opened and closed as if seeking food. And then he crushed it. Closed his fist and crushed the life out of the little thing.'

Charlie couldn't help reacting, but Stevenson didn't see, lost in his own thoughts.

'The shrink said he didn't even dress it up as a mercy killing, that he was actually *excited* by what he'd done, that he enjoyed the power he exerted over the bird.'

Charlie digested this, surprised by how upset she was by this image of wanton cruelty.

'That's the type of guy you're dealing with here. Someone who has no respect for life and a...a perverse fascination with death.'

As he said this, he slid the book towards Charlie. Had he decided he wouldn't read it after all? That their chat had decided him against it?

'So, if he is back, if he is genuinely alive, then you'd better find him fast. Because he will kill without conscience. And he'll enjoy doing it.'

Charlie shuddered inwardly, such was the gravity and confidence in his voice. And even as she did so, her eyes fell on the cover of the book, from which King stared back at her, amused, arrogant and cruel.

Extract from One Dark Night *by Maxine Pryce*

This is a chapter I wish I didn't have to write. Dwelling on the indignities, the pain, we all suffered at the hands of Daniel King does none of us any favours. The memories burn strong as do the feelings of terror and helplessness they inspire, but the truth is these injuries are part of us, part of our journey and can't be avoided. If we are to truly know who we are, who Daniel King was, then we have to tell the full story.

At first, we thought he just wanted to hold us captive. Under gunpoint he'd marched us down to the cellar, his dogs barking excitedly and dancing around us. Once we were there, he'd made us tie each other up, attending to the last captive himself, leaving the five of us trussed to two steel pillars in the centre of the room. Then, without warning, he'd departed again.

There was a stunned silence, then an explosion of garbled conversation, but the wiser heads 'decided' that this was a ransom situation. Some of our parents were quite wealthy – it was obvious this guy was going to ransom us for cash, then disappear. This thought didn't cheer everyone – Rachel and Callum's folks didn't have a bean between them – but it made the rest of us feel better. We were convinced our ordeal would soon be over – our parents wouldn't hesitate to cough up.

We were wrong. How badly wrong we had no idea at the time, though we soon found out. Just before midnight, King burst in again, alone this time and high as a kite, slurring his words as he verbally abused us, threatening us with torture, rape and more besides. Then the beating started.

By the light of his paraffin lamp, we could see that the floor was littered with old tools, machine parts and rusty bike frames. King snatched up a discarded bicycle chain and, swinging it above his head, brought it down hard on Rachel's neck. I was next to her and felt the impact of metal on flesh. Rachel groaned, the breath punched from her. Another couple of blows followed. She was mumbling incoherently now, appealing for mercy perhaps, but it made no difference. King's blood was up and he would not hold back.

I'm not sure how long the violence lasted. King circled us, choosing his victims at random, lashing faces, necks, chests, arms. Fran blacked out at one point, her head snapping back into the steel column, Rachel lost a couple of teeth, but nothing seemed to satisfy King's lust for violence. It was as if his whole life had been building to this moment and, now it was here, he was determined to make the most of it.

My beating was sustained, but maybe lighter than most. I was last in line and King had eventually started to tire. I was beaten, bloodied, bruised, but as I peered at our captor, I hoped – prayed – that we were through the worst of it. I tried to engage with him, pleading for our lives, for our liberty.

'You don't need to do this. If you let us go, we won't tell anyone—'

'You're going nowhere.'

'My parents have money, plenty of money. If you release us, you can have whatever you want.'

The chain bit into my cheek. I hadn't seen it coming and was rocked back. For a minute, I was seeing stars, unsure where I was or what was happening. But then I felt someone descending upon me and saw King's sweaty face pressed up against mine.

'You don't get it, do you?' he rasped, flecks of saliva landing on me. 'You're *never* getting out of this place.'

He laughed, straightening up and tossing the bicycle chain

aside, before hurrying over to a rickety table, where he started rummaging for something else. I craned round to look at the others, desperate for something, some show of defiance, but Rachel looked dazed and Fran was sobbing. I couldn't see Callum's face and Justin's was turned from me, so instead I found my gaze drawn back to King who was marching towards me again, a length of farm wire in his hands.

'Please don't hurt me, please don't—'

'Oh, I'm not going to *hurt* you, sugar,' King laughed, unravelling the wire. 'I'm going to kill you. You're *all* going to die tonight.'

Rachel's sobbing increased and I continued to beg, but it made no difference. King moved swiftly, stepping forwards and looping the wire around my neck. I yanked at my bonds, bucked for all I was worth, but I was powerless to stop him, as he pulled the wire tight. Now terror consumed me – I was tethered, couldn't breathe. I knew then – thought I knew – that this was it. That I would die here, in the dirty basement, with this awful sadist looming over me.

'So make your peace with God, sweetheart, because...'

He was revelling in my fear. If I close my eyes, I can still see him, leaning forward, so close that our noses were almost touching, whispering those awful words that still have the power to chill my soul.

'...my face is the last thing you'll ever see.'

Chapter 78

They were up close and personal, Joseph's face just a couple of inches from his target. The scrawny, unshaven figure was scum, a lowlife dealer to the core. Joseph had met his type before, many times over, and usually would have kept a healthy distance from this wraith, with his glazed eyes, track marks and angry tattoos. But today was different. Today they had a killer to catch.

'I asked you a question.'

'And you've had my answer. I don't talk to—'

Joseph took a step forward, his boot 'accidentally' landing on the man's foot. He kept it there, even as his victim struggled to escape.

'I heard you, but I don't like that answer. So I'm going to ask you again. Have you seen this man?'

He held up the mugshot of Daniel King, thrusting it into the man's face. It was still early and the Dagger and Serpent, a filthy backstreet bar which masqueraded as a death metal venue, but was actually a dealer's paradise, was empty, save for Joseph and the unfortunate bartender. Visits from the police were not encouraged and the bar's guardian had so far refused to cooperate, but Joseph wasn't in a mood to be denied.

'No, I haven't,' the bartender countered, without even looking at the photo.

'Look at it,' Joseph demanded, moving it into the man's eyeline.

'Listen, copper, are you deaf or what?'

Without warning, Joseph's hand shot towards the man's groin. Grabbing his victim by the balls, Joseph squeezed hard. The man cried out in pain, but Joseph ignored him, talking over the noise.

'Now listen up, mate. If you want to walk out of here intact, then you are going to look at my photo and you are going to answer my questions, fully and politely.'

The man tried to wriggle out of Joseph's grip, but this only made the pain worse.

'Jesus, get off me ...'

'Look at the photo.'

Tears were pricking the man's eyes now, he was clearly in agony, but nevertheless he now diverted his attention to the photo of Daniel King.

'Look closely ...'

The stricken man obliged, drinking in King's features.

'He used to come in here a lot a few years back, this is where he liked to play. So, tell me, has he been in here?'

The man considered, then: 'No, I haven't seen him.'

'Think carefully,' Joseph intoned, squeezing a little harder.

'I swear I haven't seen him,' the man squealed. 'Honestly.'

'And you're here most of the time?'

'All the time. There's no one else *but* me.'

The man was actually crying now, riven with agony. Without warning, Joseph released his grip, his victim crumpling to the floor.

'Well, if he does come in, call me,' Joseph continued casually, tossing his card onto the prone figure. 'I'll find out if you don't.'

He turned and hurried towards the exit. There were plenty of other dives in the neighbourhood for him to check out and it wouldn't do to linger. He couldn't deny that he'd enjoyed this encounter, but in truth it had yielded nothing and there was work still to do. The revelation that King was still alive had given the investigation – and him – a new lease of life. He had been on the back foot so far – professionally and personally – but if he could unearth a lead that led to the apprehension of King all might yet be forgotten.

Chapter 79

Helen stared at Meredith, adrenalin coursing through her.

'How certain are you?'

Meredith suppressed a smile, amused by Helen's question but unwilling to antagonize her colleague.

'One hundred per cent. It's definitely silica dust.'

'So if we got a sample of dust from the building site for you to compare...'

'I can save you the bother. Justin Lanning's suit was covered in it, so we took a sample and compared them – it's the same substance. That doesn't mean it couldn't have come from elsewhere, of course, every building site has silica dust on it, but it would be a massive coincidence.'

Helen took this in, her excitement rising still further.

'So our killer murders Lanning at the building site. Two days later, he kills Harvey, stamping on his face in the process. Maybe he's tried to clean his boots between attacks, maybe he hasn't, either way he leaves traces of silica dust on Harvey's face...'

'I'd say that's a fair assumption. And the good news is that though silica dust is odourless to humans, it actually possesses a very strong scent, which a sniffer dog would easily pick up. If I were you, I'd get onto the Dog Unit...'

This was precisely what Helen was intending to do.

For the first time in ages, she smiled. Meredith had provided her with several vital leads over the years and this one might prove to be no different. In a case that had been oddly devoid of concrete evidence, finally she had something they could work with. Thanking her old friend, Helen hurried from the Forensics Unit, pulling her phone from her pocket. Now that they had a lead, they mustn't waste a second. It was time for her – for the team – to start the fightback.

Chapter 80

'Drop what you're doing and listen!'

Many heads turned, picking out Charlie who stood in the doorway to Helen's office. The incident room was busy, numerous detectives chasing down leads, but now it suddenly fell silent.

'I've just spoken to the boss and we're shipping out.'

Colleagues were already rising, grabbing jackets and bags, energized by the urgency in Charlie's voice.

'We've got a forensic trace that we need to chase down. We're meeting up with the dog handlers on Hutchinson Street. We will divide into teams and follow individual dogs on a prescribed route – DI Grace wants the entire Northam area covered.'

'What about the Harvey house?'

'And the building site?'

'We will be looking at both of those in due course, to see if we can trace our killer's movements after the attacks. The Harvey residence is more promising – *if* our perpetrator didn't drive away from the scene – but for now we're going to focus on Northam. It's a fairly contained area and cell site mapping suggests our killer has been there within the last three days.'

A murmur of anticipation rippled through the team. Having struggled to find any tangible trace of the killer, suddenly he seemed close.

'If he's still there, if the dogs can pick up a scent, then maybe they'll lead us straight to him.'

Excited faces beamed back at her, cheered by the prospect.

'Well, what are you waiting for? Let's go.'

As one, the team headed towards the exit. Charlie watched them go, buoyed by their energy, determination and optimism. She felt it too and though the idea of confronting this phantom made her uneasy, she couldn't deny her excitement at the prospect of bringing him in.

If the dogs did their work, if the gods were on their side, then soon they would be face to face with a killer.

Chapter 81

The door sprang open and he leapt out, landing elegantly. The sprightly black Labrador strained at the leash, desperate to get going, his handler fighting hard to restrain him.

'Who's this?' Helen asked, approaching quickly.

'Wilbur. He's good, but he's young, overzealous...'

'We were all like that at one point.'

'I'll have to take your word for it,' DS Francis responded, puffing. 'Now, what have you got for me?'

'Silica dust,' Helen replied, handing the clear plastic bag to her colleague. 'It doesn't look like much, but...'

Francis examined the thin layer of dust in the bag, then bending down, opened it for his charge. Wilbur didn't hesitate, shoving his nose into the opening.

'How many dogs have we got?'

'Six in total,' Francis replied quickly. 'Wilbur, Jonty, Alice, Rose, Max and Oliver. Trained them all myself.'

'And you think they'll be able to help? The traces we're talking about are probably minute...'

'Don't worry, Inspector. A dog's sense of smell is a thousand times more powerful than ours. If your man's left a trail, our team will find him.'

Wilbur was tugging at the leash, so Francis handed Helen back the bag.

'Go on, boy.'

He didn't need telling twice, fastening his nose to the road surface, searching for the scent. His progress was slow and meandering, zigzagging from side to side, under the careful guidance of his handler. Helen watched the performance, excited but oddly tense. Would they find something? Or would this prove to be yet another wild goose chase?

On they went, drifting towards the intersection at the top of the street. Helen knew she needed to be patient, that these things took time, but still she yearned for the dog to snap into action, fastening onto a bona fide scent. Their progress in this case had been extremely limited so far – this forensic breakthrough the only concrete lead they'd managed to unearth, and Helen was desperate to make it pay. She knew though that the trail would be faint, the quantities of dust falling from the suspect's boots infinitesimal – and that was if he walked these streets at all, rather than driving to some remote lock-up or hideout.

He had been in Northam – that was the slim hope Helen was clinging to. Six routes had been marked out, covering the major thoroughfares and side roads, six routes that were now being pored over by Wilbur and his kennel mates. Helen had no doubt they could find a trace if there was one, but there were a million ways in which it could be obscured by rubbish, passing cars, footfall and the passage of time. All they could do now was wait and hope.

They had reached the end of Graham Street – another section of their route completed – so turned into York Road. This was a side road, leading to Millbank Street, the last major artery in this part of town. Once there, they would have completed the majority of their route, with only a few cut-throughs left to explore. With each passing minute, the knot in Helen's stomach tightened. What would she do if this came to nothing? How would she keep the team energized and optimistic, with so few other leads to pursue?

Now a sound made her look up. Wilbur was barking, circling a spot on the pavement. Helen hurried over, as DS Francis turned to her.

'Definitely got something…'

The dog was tugging at the lead, eager to continue. Helen took in the road – it was a cut-through, badly lit and unremarkable, full of parked cars and vans. Perhaps their suspect had stopped his vehicle here, where Wilbur was now sniffing. She nodded at Francis, gesturing to him to continue.

'Come on…'

Wilbur set off fast down the street, Helen dogging his heels. They covered the ground fast, heading swiftly towards the next intersection. But just as they were nearing the end of the street, Wilbur paused, circling once more. It looked for one terrifying moment as if he'd lost the scent, but then he darted left, disappearing down a side road. Helen followed, watching Francis closely for signs of frustration or disappointment, but the handler seemed as focused and energized as his charge. On they went, eating up the yards in this gloomy, rubbish-strewn road, until eventually it came to a dead end, opening out into a wide yard. Chain-link gates formerly guarded the entrance to this strange oasis of space, but not any more. They hung open and Wilbur hurried through them, completing a circuit of the yard, before coming to a halt, sitting down once more and emitting two soft barks.

'This is as far we go for now,' Francis said, lowering his voice. 'We could search the buildings, but we'd need the rest of the dogs, plus a proper police presence.'

'It's OK, we can handle it from here.'

As Francis bent down to give the dog a reward, Helen took in the scene in front of her. The yard, which was littered with sodden cardboard boxes and rotting packing cases, formed the main entrance and car park to a rambling industrial estate. There was a scattering of buildings – large, two-storey units and warehouses. The industrial estate had once been a hive of industry and activity; now, however, it was a stale, forgotten place, the buildings abandoned, the doors chained up, the windows dirty and cracked. Taking it in, Helen shivered – it would be the perfect place for a phantom to hide – and she hesitated to approach the nearby buildings. But there was no need to worry – Helen wouldn't be facing this ghoul alone.

It was time to summon the cavalry.

Chapter 82

They came from all parts of the city, clogging the small yard and adjacent roads with patrol cars and unmarked vehicles. Uniformed officers, plain-clothes detectives, even a handful of bodies from the local Traffic unit, all descending on the area, summoned by Helen's call to arms.

One of the dogs had followed a scent to this lonely industrial estate, and a painstaking search was now under way. They may have lost the element of surprise, but such was the speed of the response that Joseph Hudson felt sure that anyone hiding inside wouldn't have had time to escape. The odds were now further stacked against him, given the sheer number of bodies present, but they couldn't afford to take any chances.

'Spread out, twenty yards apart, but keep your neighbour in sight,' he barked at the line of officers that flanked him. 'We do this systematically and we do it *together* ...'

Joseph had been nearby when he got the call. Obeying Helen's instructions, he'd hastened to Northam Road, which effectively formed the rear boundary of Gerrards Industrial Estate. It was never a place that vehicles would have used – the narrow entrance was employed by workers and pedestrians as a cut-through – but it *would* make a discreet escape route now. Taking the lead, Joseph had ushered the officers through it, before organizing them into a wide defensive line, spreading out in front of the first building that came into view.

It was a shabby affair, a battered tyre fitters' sign hanging limply off the wall, a testament to past industry and purpose. Now the building seemed of interest only to bored kids, the windows shattered, graffiti covering every available brick. Discarded cigarette butts and empty cider cans completed the picture – Joseph taking pleasure in crushing one with his foot.

They had now reached the doors to the building. Perhaps they had been chained up once, like the other buildings on view, but there was no sign now of any restraint, the padlock mooring having been ripped clean off the door. Testing the handle, Joseph found it opened easily. Pausing on the threshold, he turned to see a bevy of eager officers waiting to follow him. This was it then. A chance to bring in their prime suspect. To make a bit of history. An opportunity for Joseph to redeem himself.

Taking a deep breath, he tugged the door open and stepped inside.

Chapter 83

The first thing that struck her was the smell. Musty, moist, rank; it was the sweet scent of decay.

Helen was convinced something had died in here and even now, amidst the gloom, her eye alighted on the culprit, a sticky mass of feathers that had once been a pigeon. Though long dead, it was seeming to move, crawling ants giving the illusion, then, as Helen stepped around it, the devastated bird suddenly came alive, darting away past her. Helen froze, confused, only to see a long, fat tail disappearing behind a packing case.

Passing the corpse, Helen took in the sad interior of the building. It seemed to be some kind of storage facility, flattened boxes, foam pellets, even a list of dockets lying discarded on the ground. It had probably never been the most glamorous of workplaces, but it looked truly grim now, the windows thick with grime and the floor coated in slick, dirty water, thanks to the numerous holes in the roof. Choosing her path carefully, Helen moved forward, searching for signs that the building had been recently occupied – food wrappers, water bottles, sleeping bags, but there were no signs of life. Rounding the discarded trash, Helen moved on, flanked by three uniformed officers. Their perpetrator was violent and unhinged – there was no question of Helen facing him alone, however good her track record of survival had been thus far.

They had reached the back wall now, where some stairs led upwards. Helen mounted them swiftly, the other officers falling into line behind her. Reaching the top, Helen tried to peer through the small glass window into the space beyond, but it had been shattered, distorting the view. Unable to see what was facing them, Helen slid her baton from her belt, extending it to its full length. Then, nodding to the others to follow, she pushed through the doorway.

Immediately, there was a response, a pair of startled pigeons taking flight. Helen was momentarily startled by them, but as she followed their crazy progress around the room, colliding with both the ceiling and the walls in their panic, she saw that they were alone. There was no more life here than there was downstairs – it was just an empty, forgotten space.

Frustrated, she marched across the slick concrete surface, kicking a cardboard box out of her path. She covered the floor in ten seconds flat, heading now for a door that led out onto some kind of fire escape. Reaching it, she tested the handle. It was stiff and unyielding, rusted over, so Helen put her shoulder to it and the door sighed open. A rush of cold air hit her and Helen embraced it, stepping out onto the metal walkway.

Now the full extent of the industrial estate became apparent. Standing twenty feet or so above the ground, she could see seven, eight, nine different buildings. They were all in various states of disrepair but the site itself was unusually active, dozens of officers fanning out to explore the forgotten shells. Why had such a large site been abandoned? It seemed criminal at a time when businesses and charities were screaming out for space, when there were folk sleeping rough. Surely some use could be found for this extensive site?

Turning away from the edge of the balcony, Helen was about to address her companions when suddenly her radio squawked into life.

'DS Hudson to DI Grace, over.'

'This is Grace,' Helen answered. 'What have you got? Over.'

'Smoke,' he answered, breathlessly. 'Smoke coming from an old printing press towards the rear of the site. Over.'

Helen spun round, directing her gaze in that direction.

'I'm sure it wasn't going when we arrived. Someone's just started a fire.'

A dozen possibilities presented themselves – was their suspect here? Destroying evidence? Destroying himself? – but Helen didn't stop to consider them. She'd now spotted the tiny plume of smoke coming from a building about two hundred yards away, so she didn't hesitate, sliding down the fire escape and sprinting towards it.

Chapter 84

There was no time for subtlety, now it was all about speed. Skirting a couple of small sheds, Helen raced towards the building's main entrance, arriving there just as Joseph and his team of officers came into view. Already the uniformed men were fanning out to surround the building, but Helen's focus was purely on the door in front of her, which was locked, seemingly determined to keep her out. Swearing under her breath, she took a step back, then lashed out with her foot. Her steel-capped boot smashed into the lock, the door springing open, just as Joseph Hudson appeared at her shoulder. Gesturing to him to follow, she darted inside.

The interior was gloomy but in better nick than the other buildings they'd investigated. A scattering of photocopiers and scanners stood behind the till counter, but it was clear that the smoke was not emanating from anything on this floor, so vaulting the counter, Helen hurried towards the stairs, Joseph hot on her heels. Reaching the bottom of the staircase, they raced up it. Helen was straining every sinew, determined to catch their suspect, determined to be in at the death.

Exploding through the doorway onto the second floor, she scanned the room in front of her. There were larger units here, printing presses that must be of considerable value, which a fleeing suspect might hide behind, but that was not what drew her eye. Instead, it was the sight of an oil drum at the far end of the room, belching thick smoke into the air, that grabbed her attention.

Careless of her own safety, Helen sprinted forwards, eating up the yards to the drum. At any moment, she expected King to leap out at her, but she made it across the floor unmolested. Grabbing the rim, she waved her hand frantically, trying to disperse the smoke. It was hard to tell exactly what was in the drum, the smoke and the strong scent of lighter fluid making her eyes water, but she could see some kind of fabric burning, as well as newspapers and what looked like some kind of map.

'Put that out.'

Joseph was by her side and instantly obliged, yanking the drum sideways and over, so the flaming contents spilled onto the floor. Instantly they reacted to the sudden burst of oxygen, flaming even higher, but Joseph was already onto it, using his jacket to scatter the remnants and dampen down the blaze. Helen paid him no heed, turning to take in the rest of the room. Other officers had now reached the second floor, spreading out to look behind the presses and in the scattered cupboards, but Helen barely noticed them, her attention fixed on the fire escape, which hung open, swaying back and forth in the growing breeze. If their fugitive had just fled the scene, then this was the route he would have taken.

Helen was there in seconds, pushing through the door. Now she had a choice, down to the yard, or up to the roof. The yard didn't seem a viable escape route, it was already filling with uniformed officers, so instead she burst upwards, hammering the metal stairs. Her lungs were straining, her legs burning with exertion but she ignored her protesting body, climbing ever higher, before grasping the rail and hauling herself onto the roof.

It was a flat roof that seemed in decent condition, save for the odd hole through which thin plumes of smoke now crept. Nevertheless, Helen took care as she picked her way towards a sizeable substation that formed the only cover. If their suspect was hiding out, then this was where he would be. Helen reached it quickly, circling it carefully, before grasping the handle. Taking a breath, she raised her baton and tugged the door open, ready to strike.

There was no one inside, just a mass of ancient circuitry. Swearing, Helen turned away, hurrying back towards the edge of the roof. Planting her foot on the ledge, she stared down into the yard, but was met by faces of her officers below, looking up at her expectantly. Turning away she hurried to the other side, but here too she found only her team, maintaining a defensive circle around the building. Helen couldn't believe it. According to Joseph the fire had been set *after* they arrived. Helen was inclined to believe him, as some of the contents had not yet been destroyed. Yet in spite of that, despite straining every sinew to bring him in, their prime suspect had eluded them once more.

Standing on the edge, looking down at the ant-like humans below, Helen felt a crushing sense of disappointment. Meredith's breakthrough had led them here, to what Helen assumed was King's centre of operations. They had had the advantage of surprise, weight of numbers and a determination to bring their prime suspect to book. Nevertheless, they were left empty-handed.

Once more, this phantom killer had vanished into thin air.

Chapter 85

'Did anyone see anything?'

There was a note of incredulity in Simmons' voice.

'Doesn't look like it,' Helen replied. 'We had forty officers on site, we've talked to them all.'

'So what happened?'

'I think we surprised him and he fled. He presumably knew the site well, better than us, at least.'

'But how did he do it? How on *earth* did he get away?'

'There are multiple ways out of that place if you know your way around. We had the front and back entrances covered, but there are numerous holes in the fencing bordering the site. We're currently doing house-to-house on the surrounding roads. People may have noticed the smoke, or seen someone slipping through the fence...'

It sounded like a forlorn hope and probably was.

'And you're sure it *was* our man? Not some random drug user or squatter?'

'We believe so. It's a great space to hide out, plus the contents of the oil drum suggest this might have been some kind of nerve centre for him.'

'Because?'

'There was lots of detritus – the remnants of juice cartons, food containers – which suggest someone had been living there for a while. Those are not of interest in themselves, but DS Hudson managed to save some other items which are more intriguing.'

'Go on.'

'We found a map of Southampton. Not an A to Z, a bigger Ordnance Survey one. Most of it was burnt, of course, but DS Hudson did manage to rescue a fragment, on which an address in Lordswood is clearly circled – Callum Harvey's house.'

'Right...'

'We also have the remnants of a Mercedes key fob. It's badly melted but the insignia is still visible, so it could have belonged—'

'To the car Lanning was abducted in,' Simmons interrupted. 'Can we get any forensics off these items, anything that might confirm King's presence there?'

'We'll try. They *were* badly burnt, but if anyone can find something, Meredith can.'

'And that's all there was in the drum?'

'Barring fragments of local newspapers. Whoever has been living there has obviously been keeping up with the news, which suggests it's probably not a homeless person or an addict.'

Simmons nodded firmly, trying to appear positive, but it was clear mention of the press had lowered her mood still further.

'You'll be aware that Emilia Garanita has already broken the news that King is our prime suspect. Any idea how she got hold of that information?'

'Not yet. But I'm going to make it my business to find out. I can't imagine any of the team would be so reckless but I'm not blind to that possibility.'

'And how would you like to play it, with the media, I mean?'

Helen considered this for a moment, then replied, 'I don't

think we can duck this one. It's on the *Evening News*'s feed already, it'll be in the national papers tomorrow...'

'You want us to confirm that we're looking for King.'

A tiny second of hesitation, then Helen nodded.

'He's clearly organized, determined and adept at evading detection. So far, we haven't had a single confirmed sighting. I don't know how Emilia got hold of this information, but perhaps this leak might help us. Our best resource now is the eyes and ears of the public.'

'Despite the inevitable false sightings?'

'We'll have to live with those. I think we should come clean, put out an appeal and see what comes back.'

'People will be scared...'

'I appreciate that, but we have no choice. King is a highly dangerous, highly motivated individual, who will kill without conscience. We have no reason to think he'll target members of the public, but people should be on their guard.'

Simmons accepted this, buoyed by Helen's decisiveness and sense of purpose.

'I'll get onto it straight away,' Simmons confirmed enthusiastically, picking up her phone.

Thanking her, Helen took her leave, marching back along the seventh floor to the incident room. As ever, she left the meeting feeling motivated and purposeful, but the truth was that unless they got a lucky sighting or a further forensic break, then they were no nearer to catching Daniel King. They had traced his movements, discovered his lair, even taken the ruthless killer by surprise, but still he had eluded them. Meaning he was out there right now, free, unrestrained.

And ready to strike again.

Chapter 86

There was no question about it. She *had* to run.

At first, Maxine had toed the line, listening to Bentham's lectures, handing over her schedule and generally behaving like someone prepared to sit tight until the danger had passed. But once she was away from prying eyes, safely ensconced in her bedroom, she'd snapped into action, ignoring the ban on online activity to devour the local news feeds.

She'd immediately wished she hadn't. The secret that Bentham had been so keen to keep from her was out – Daniel King was back in Southampton. She wouldn't necessarily have believed it – Emilia Garanita was a notorious rumour-monger – but Hampshire Police had confirmed the news via their Twitter feed *and* scheduled a press conference for later that day.

Furious, Maxine's first instinct was to burst out of her bedroom to confront Bentham. How on earth was she supposed to make informed choices about her safety – her *life* – if people concealed things from her? She had suspected, no, she had feared – that King might be involved, given the taunting nature of his phone call, and the awful manner in which Callum and Justin had been killed, but she had clung to the idea that it might be some sicko, some copycat, desperate for their fifteen minutes of fame. Now, however, there seemed little doubt. Daniel King was back in town, determined to claim the schoolchildren who had evaded him all those years ago.

The obvious thing to do was to stay put. To hunker down and wait for King to make a mistake. But would that keep her safe? He had already murdered two people and got away scot-free. Did the police have a bead on him? Any sense of where he was now or what he was planning? Or was he one step ahead of them, even now planning his next attack?

It was impossible to know while they refused even to confirm that he was a suspect, and it made her blood boil. The police had not done their job all those years ago – it was the kids themselves who had engineered their escape from the farmhouse – and there was little prospect of them doing so now. That was a different force, of course, and there was no doubting Helen Grace had a reputation for bringing in vicious killers, but still... Callum had summoned the police and where had that got him? No, there was no question of staying here, in a flat King might have already scoped out. She would be a sitting duck, King biding his time, waiting for a lapse in security, when he could seize his opportunity for a deadly reunion...

It was time to go. She had already thrown some clothes into a holdall, gathered what cash she could and stowed her car keys in her pocket. Her beloved VW Golf was a stone's throw from the back of the house, stationed in a private car park. If she could make it there undetected, she would be away. She had told Bentham that she intended to stay in town, to honour her work commitments, but there was no question of her remaining in Southampton now. No, she would get in her car and keep driving until she was safely at Heathrow. She would make calls en route – she could visit her parents in Florida, or even Vanessa, her old uni pal, in Melbourne. It didn't matter as long as she was miles away from Southampton. Miles away from Daniel King.

Heartened, Maxine tugged her holdall shut. It felt good to be taking action rather than sitting still, slowly going mad. It was tempting to make a break for it now, but she knew that would be madness. Better to wait until it was dark, until there was a change of the guard outside. She would know when the moment had come and she would have to seize it.

Her life depended upon it.

Chapter 87

'Will you be staying?'

It seemed an odd question. Why a woman whose life was in serious danger would want the protection of a cumbersomely pregnant officer was beyond Charlie, yet despite her initial caution, Fran had warmed to her, finding comfort in her gentle, attentive manner.

'Well I can stay for a bit if you like, while you get settled in,' Charlie responded carefully. 'But I'm a detective, I don't work in Special Protection, so your point officer will be DS Grainger, as we discussed.'

Fran nodded absently, as if uninterested in the answer, now she'd learned that Charlie wasn't going to babysit her. Despite her willingness to embrace Special Protection, Fran had seemed fidgety and dissatisfied with the process, first arguing that she should be told where they were going, then finding fault with the house – which was by turns too depressing, too airless, too exposed. In reality it was none of these things, just an ordinary suburban house, save for the reinforced doors and the uniformed officers stationed in the hallway and kitchen, but Charlie hadn't pointed this out, sucking up Fran's fretting and dissatisfaction with good grace. This place, ordinary though it might be, was the safest place for Fran to be right now. In time, she would come to realize this, but Charlie could understand why the young woman was on edge and was happy to roll with it, doing what she could to put her at her ease.

'I could send someone out, if there's anything you need. Magazines, books, snacks or sweets...'

But Fran shook her head, dismissing the idea.

'There's no internet here,' Charlie continued, 'but there's a TV and DVD player downstairs, with a decent selection of films.'

Another curt, baffled shake of the head, as if the idea of entertaining herself was crazy.

'Look, Fran, I know it's hard, being away from your family. And that you're probably feeling very disoriented and scared, but the best thing you can do is go with this. Try and find a way to relax, to distract yourself. That way, the time will pass quicker, which means you'll be home quicker...'

'It's not me that needs to be doing stuff, it's you lot,' Fran shot back, her voice quivering slightly.

'And we are, trust me. We're pouring huge resources into this and we've got the best of the best working on it. Our priority now is to bring the perpetrator in – and we will do – but in the meantime we need to keep you safe, comfortable and as happy as you can be. So if there's anything you need, something you can work on whilst you're here...'

'That's going to be pretty tough, unless I can hold my gym classes in the living room.'

'That might be tricky,' Charlie said smiling. 'Though I do know an overweight mum-to-be who could do with a good workout...'

Now a brief smile from Fran, the tension easing slightly.

'You look great,' she offered.

'I look like the Michelin man,' Charlie countered. 'With swollen feet and stretch marks to boot.'

'Well, maybe when this is all over,' Fran offered tentatively, 'you can come to the gym, get you back in shape.'

'I'd like that,' Charlie said genuinely. 'Though I warn you, it won't be easy. I've got these two old friends, cake and chocolate, that I can't seem to shake off...'

Fran nodded, smiling, but her relief was temporary, as if the thoughts of a carefree future only served to remind her of the difficult present.

'You will get him then?' she asked, her voice suddenly quiet and fragile.

'Yes, we will. And then you and Maxine can get on with the rest of your lives.'

'Is she in one of these places too?'

Charlie hesitated before responding.

'Yes, she is.'

'Have there been ... have there been any attempts on her life? Has she been in danger at all?'

'No, not that we're aware of. Special Protection is just a precautionary measure, for both of you, until we can resolve this.'

'If anything had happened to her ... would you tell me?'

It was a strange question, but Charlie could understand her concern. They had to withhold some information from their charges and she could tell Fran had picked up on this.

'Yes, we would. It's only fair you know what we're dealing with, but please try not to worry.'

Fran turned away from her, walking over to the frosted window.

'Maxine is in safe hands, guarded day and night. No harm will come to her, so set your mind at rest. There's no need to be upset or scared—'

'Oh, I'm not scared, not for Maxine anyway...'

'Because?'

'Have you met her? She's ... she's armour-plated, I'm not sure anyone could kill her, even if they wanted to.'

It was said with humour, but there was a bitter edge to it that surprised Charlie. She had expected Fran to express concern for her old friend, but this sounded more like ... contempt.

'Be that as it may, she will still be well looked after, as will *you*.'

'Fair enough, but it's a waste of time and money. Bad things don't happen to people like Maxine, not really. Misfortune just seems to bounce off them, like they are somehow entitled to success, money, happiness, status, while the rest of us have to scrabble around.'

'But if something had happened to her? Say, it was she who had been targeted now, rather than Justin or Callum ...'

Charlie was genuinely curious now, surprised by the hardness that had crept into Fran's expression.

'Then maybe I'd start to believe that there *is* a God.'

It was offered unapologetically, but still Fran couldn't miss Charlie's reaction.

'Oh, I know she presents well – she's strong, in touch with her feelings, a campaigner and an inspiration ... but let me tell you she's none of those things, not really. And if something does happen to her, then so be it.'

Fran paused, before concluding: 'That bitch deserves everything she gets.'

Chapter 88

'Hi, this is Maxine. Please leave a message.'

Emilia punched the red button, ending the call. This was her third unsuccessful attempt to raise Maxine Pryce. The professional survivor, who'd been so keen to court the media of late, had suddenly become very shy.

Peering through the windscreen, Emilia looked up at her flat, with its nondescript door and discreetly frosted windows. It was not Emilia's first visit here – all roads seemed to lead to Pryce these days – but now there was a difference. A uniformed officer could be seen loitering by the front door and Emilia had no doubt there was one out back too. Intriguingly, she'd also snatched the odd glimpse of DC Bentham, ghosting around the interior, bolstering her conviction that Maxine was within.

Yawning, Emilia glanced at her watch. She was used to stakeouts, knew they took time, but still she was impatient for results. The response to the news of King's presence in Southampton had been electric – a mixture of shock, panic and excitement – already dozens of people had contacted the paper with 'information'. These leads would prove to be groundless, but that wasn't the point: it was the scale and fervour of the reaction that counted. There was little now that could top the latest headline, pronouncing King's return, save for the arrest of the man himself or an interview with one of his terrified targets.

Fran Ward was a possible, but there was no doubt in Emilia's mind that Maxine was the real prize. She was the famous one – the face of their tragedy and the one who had done most to trumpet their experiences. Had she unwittingly kick-started this process? Goaded King into returning to Southampton? It was an intriguing question and one Emilia was keen to put to the author. Maxine was so sure of herself, arrogant almost, but what was she feeling now? Regret? Sadness? Fear?

Picking up her phone, she tried the author again, but Maxine's voicemail kicked in once more. No matter, Emilia would wait. Maxine would have been told to keep her head down, stay put and initially at least she would heed that advice. But how likely was it that she would stay inside long term? Emilia knew Maxine – she was headstrong, arrogant, seemingly desperate for recognition and success. Sales of her book were already going through the roof, according to her publisher's Twitter feed – hardly surprising given the news of the past few days. Maxine was the woman of the hour; this was all she'd ever dreamt of. Even given the alleged threat to her security, was it conceivable she would pass up her opportunity to embrace her celebrity? She had been in and out of the media for nearly two years now, following her first tentative regurgitation of her teenage trauma on BBC South. Was it possible that she would shun the limelight now?

No, she wouldn't wear it. She couldn't. Whatever the police had said to her, Maxine would emerge at a time of her choosing.

And when she did, Emilia would be waiting for her.

Chapter 89

She eased open the window, letting the cold night air flood in. Pausing, Maxine listened, straining to hear if her movement had been detected, but all seemed calm. Summoning her courage, she poked her head outside. As she'd hoped, the back garden was temporarily unguarded. She'd heard the new shift arrive and was pleased to hear the gentle lilt of conversation coming from the kitchen as the officers exchanged notes during the handover.

Maxine tugged harder, the window sliding fully open. It was a blessed relief – it had taken a long time to get the locks out, she'd had to resort to using a nail file in the end to unscrew them – and she was determined to press home her success. Even so, she paused now, peering outside. There was no fire escape, no drainpipe, no easy means of descent. She would have to jump.

This wasn't in itself a disaster – she was only one floor up and there was a large flower bed to aim at. But what would happen if it went wrong? If she sprained, or broke, an ankle? What would happen if her escape was detected? How would she explain that away? In truth, Maxine had already debated these questions and decided the reward was worth the risk. So, ensuring the holdall was securely on her back, she slid onto the ledge, placed her feet on the brick work and pushed off.

The air rushed past her as she fell, the ground rising up to meet her. She landed heavily, the breath knocked from her, even as her feet sank into the soft soil. Gathering herself, breathing heavily, she looked around. There were no sounds, no signs of movement within, so picking herself up, she hurried down the garden path. The high back gate was bolted top and bottom, but wasn't padlocked, so sliding the bolts across, Maxine slipped through the gateway, closing it gently behind her.

Beyond the gate was a narrow alleyway, running along the back of all the houses. It was supposed to be for access, but was now a dumping ground for cardboard boxes, garden waste and abandoned prams. It was dark and lonely and Maxine shivered as she peered along it. The clouds were scudding over the moon, throwing strange shadows onto the ground below, making the alleyway alive with menace.

Maxine stared into the darkness, trying to penetrate the gloom, then back up at the flat. Anyone stationed here would have a great view of the property, it would be a great place to lie in wait. Once more she scanned around her. *Was* there anyone there? Or was her mind playing tricks? Either way there was no point lingering, so turning up the collar of her coat, she hurried off into the night. To her great relief, there was no movement, no sounds in the alley behind her and a minute later she was free and clear.

She marched along the darkened street. The car park was just around the corner and she would be there in under a minute. It had been an extravagance to pay for her own dedicated parking space, but one she'd willingly stomached, given how careless the lorries and vans were on her road. Now it gave her comfort, knowing that her pristine Golf would be exactly where she'd left it, waiting for her as she made her escape.

Rounding the corner, her eyes fell upon it. Shiny, silver, new. Her heart leapt – the VW seemed to promise safety, release, even happiness – and she hurried towards it, her feet crunching over the loose gravel. Tugging the keys from her pocket, she zapped it open, hauling open the boot. Tossing the holdall inside, she slammed it shut, the sound echoing through the deserted car park, even as she rounded the car, heading for the driver's door. Her hand grasped the handle and she was about to tug it open, when suddenly she ground to a halt.

'What the fuck...?'

She couldn't believe it. She blinked twice, as if she was seeing things. But there was no doubt about it. The front tyre was flat. How could that be? She'd used the car only two days ago and it had been fine.

A nasty thought now started to take hold and Maxine bent down to examine the tyre. She was praying she was wrong, that she was being paranoid, but her fingers now traced out a long, dark gash in the rubber. This was no accident, someone had deliberately slashed the tyre.

Her heart pounding, she rose, a hundred thoughts spinning around her head. But even as she did so, she heard a noise. Footsteps in the gravel behind her.

Maxine froze, paralysed by fear. And now she became aware of something else. The sound of someone breathing. It sounded like he was right behind her, like he was almost *on top* of her, but still she refused to look, her mind scrabbling for answers. What should she do? How could she save herself?

But before she could answer these questions, a voice spoke. A voice from her worst nightmares.

'Hello, Maxine.'

Chapter 90

She stood on the threshold, her body rigid with tension.

Somebody was inside her flat. There could be no question of that, she could hear movement within – footsteps? – and a faint light was visible, sliding under the crack of the kitchen door. For a moment, Helen hesitated, wary of stepping inside. Should she call for assistance? Tackle the intruder herself? She opted for the latter – the arrival of backup would only alert the intruder to their presence, perhaps creating greater problems – so sliding her baton from her belt, she stepped inside, pushing the door to behind her.

Darting a look inside the living room, she padded along the corridor to the kitchen. There was definitely someone in there, but they seemed to have gone quiet. Had they detected her presence? Were they even now lying in wait? Helen marvelled at how quickly, how surprisingly, life could kick you in the balls. She had been looking forward to returning home and relaxing, having a shower, trying to process the difficult events of the day – and now she was creeping down the hallway of her own flat, braced to defend herself.

Pausing at the door, she listened intently. There was no mistaking it, someone *was* inside and it sounded like they were riffling through her drawers. She didn't have much of value, but she was damned if she was going to let somebody root through her possessions. So, grasping the door, she flung it open and stepped inside.

Joseph Hudson spun around, just about managing to hang onto the cutlery in his hand. Laughing, he placed one hand on his fast-beating heart, holding the other up in mock surrender. 'I know, I know, apologies for the intrusion, but I wanted to surprise you.' He gestured to the neatly laid table, on which sat a steaming bowl of linguini. 'I wanted to say sorry.'

Chapter 91

There was nothing for it. She would have to call and apologize. Charlie knew she should be at home – should have been there over an hour ago, in truth – but there was no question of her leaving yet. She would call Steve, try to placate him, buying herself a little more time. The data technicians were hard at work and Charlie was resolved to remain in the incident room until they had either found what she was looking for or exhausted every avenue trying.

She had been back at Southampton Central for over two hours now, but her mind continued to turn on her conversation with Fran Ward. The latter had refused to elaborate on her feelings for Maxine, seeming to regret her harsh words. This was not, Charlie sensed, because she felt bad about having spoken disparagingly of her schoolfriend, but more because Fran was annoyed at herself for having allowed someone else to see behind the veil, to glimpse her true feelings. It was just a flash – a brief, surprising moment of honesty – but it had struck home forcefully with Charlie, who was convinced that it might be important in understanding this strange case.

Right from the off, from the moment the unfortunate schoolchildren had stumbled to safety, the overriding narrative had been one of solidarity, of a close group of friends sticking together through thick and thin. It was a line that had been oft repeated in the media, most recently by Maxine herself. Charlie had been struck when reading her book by the emphasis Maxine had placed on the group's *togetherness*, putting their survival squarely down to the support and affection they gave to each other.

But subsequent events had revealed this to be a fiction, at least in part. There was no doubt they had managed to endure their ordeal together, stumbling through the fog to safety. This should have fostered an enduring bond, but actually the group had only seen each other fleetingly since that awful time. Furthermore, real tensions had become evident: Maxine clashing with Justin over money and Fran displaying real contempt for the narrator of their shared trauma. Was this all about money? About Maxine's regurgitation of past suffering? Or was there something else going on?

Charlie longed to know, to unearth the root cause of this apparent division. But Fran had clammed up and Maxine was hardly likely to elaborate – she had already given her version of events, in great detail, in her book. Charlie had skim-read it and knew Pryce had a party line on this, which majored on unity and resilience, on affection and ties of loyalty. It seemed to be going down well with the paying public, so what chance was there now of Maxine contradicting her own narrative?

No, if Charlie wanted more, she knew she would have to find other means of casting light upon the nature of their friendship. Which in the modern era meant social media. Daniel King's victims were children of the digital age, happy to record every detail of their lives on Facebook, Instagram and other sites, living out their friendships online as much as in person. The small-change and big dramas of their existence would be found there, so Charlie had tasked the data technicians with a sweep of the schoolchildren's digital lives.

Initial investigations had thrown up little – the group seemed to be an oddly pleasant bunch of teens. There was one unpleasant post from Maxine, suggesting that Fran might be short for Frank, a not very subtle dig at her schoolfriend's masculine physique. But it was never followed up and didn't seem sufficiently weighty or venomous to poison a friendship. On the face of it, there seemed little to suggest a fracture in the group.

As the minutes ticked by, Charlie paced up and down, casting an occasional eye over the technicians, at other times stealing glances at the clock. As ever she was torn, keen to be back home with Steve and Jessie, yet determined to leave no stone unturned. She felt sure they were missing something obvious, something that would help steer their investigation, but as yet they'd turned up little of note. Was it possible they should be looking elsewhere? Going back to the victim's families, perhaps, digger deeper in their pasts? It hardly seemed appropriate, Callum Harvey and Justin Lanning's families reeling, lost in grief, but perhaps it would be worth it, if it threw up something concrete? Charlie shivered at the prospect, however. She hated intruding on people's pain.

'You might want to take a look at this…'

Wrenching herself from her thoughts, Charlie hurried over to the technician's desk.

'Just been looking at Pryce's Facebook posts. All sweetness and light generally. If a little self-regarding…'

'But…' Charlie replied impatiently.

'But about a year ago, she deleted a lot of posts.'

'A digital clean-up…'

'Exactly. These were historic posts, mainly from when she was still at school.'

'Were any of the deleted posts created *before* their abduction by King?'

'Yes, the majority of them.'

'And?' Charlie replied, properly intrigued now.

'And they're not very pleasant. She sounds off at a number of people, a few kids I haven't heard of, but also Fran Ward. They seemed to fall in and out of friendship. But her fire is mostly saved for Rachel Wood. She *really* didn't like her...'

Clicking on a tab, the technician pulled up a post, dated 16th March 2012. There was no text, but the image said it all – Rachel's face had been crudely photoshopped onto a pornographic image. It was unpleasant, vindictive and faintly ridiculous, the heavily made-up, yet essentially innocent schoolgirl's face completely at odds with the contorted, surgically enhanced body it graced. As amateurish and unconvincing at it was, however, its intent was clear. Maxine wanted to humiliate and embarrass her schoolmate.

'There's a couple more like that, but this is the most significant one, the one that got the most traction anyway.'

Charlie looked down at the number of likes and shares the post had received, angry at the petty callousness of the attack.

'OK, run off copies of these and anything else you unearth. I want the whole team across this.'

Nodding, the technician returned to her work, as Charlie headed back to her desk, a spring in her step. It was not a smoking gun, but it *was* a clue, giving the lie to the fiction of unity Maxine Pryce and her friends had created. Charlie had been acting on instinct, hoping a deep trawl would yield results, and she had been proved right. Whatever positive spin Maxine put on things, whatever myths Fran and the others were happy to foster, Charlie was now convinced that the full story had never been disclosed.

Chapter 92

'How did you get in here?'

Joseph shrugged, smiling as he said, 'I've learned a few tricks in my time.'

'Set a thief to catch a thief?'

'Something like that. You should get that lock looked at, it's shocking.'

He lifted another forkful of linguini from his plate. The food was delicious, but Helen had eaten little so far, unnerved by his sudden appearance in her flat.

'You're lucky nobody dialled 999.'

'Oh, I wasn't sneaking around. I said hello to your neighbour as I was getting the shopping in. Jane, is it?'

'Joan.'

'She was friendly enough, has seen me around. Guess I'm becoming part of the furniture.'

It was said lightly – cheekily – but sounded forced. Joseph was working hard to create a nice, easy vibe between them, but in truth there was so much that was going unsaid, so much bubbling beneath the surface, that Helen was finding it hard to relax.

'I'll have to have a word with her about that. She's way too trusting.'

Joseph seemed to take this with good grace, smiling as he resumed his assault on his pasta.

'Any word from Meredith?' he asked, his mouth full.

'Nothing yet. She and the team are on site. There's nothing obvious in the main building, but perhaps we'll get lucky elsewhere.'

'What about uniform?'

'Still doing house-to-house, but there's lots of industrial units around there, not much in the way of residential property or footfall.'

'Something will turn up.'

'I hope so. Because right now it looks like we don't know our arse from our elbow. Something Emilia Garanita has been only too happy to point out.'

'Tomorrow's chip paper,' Joseph replied, dismissively.

'Chip paper that's read by the police commissioner, local politicians and a whole load of others who can make our lives very difficult if we're not seen to be doing our jobs. It doesn't help that Garanita's obviously got the bead on someone at the station, has access to sensitive information that she's willing to use, despite the danger it might pose to Maxine Pryce or Fran Ward.'

Joseph said nothing, finishing his pasta and laying his fork aside. But Helen noticed that he wouldn't look at her, his beaming, confident peacemaking faltering just for a moment.

'It's not the first time she's wormed her way into our investigations, but we've managed to keep her at bay recently.'

'She'll come a cropper soon enough, her sort always do.'

'It's weird though,' Helen persisted. 'Why now? How has she suddenly managed to get a handle on who our suspects are, what we're planning? If she finds out where Maxine and Fran are, I wouldn't put it past her to try and doorstep them or somehow gain access to the property.'

'She wouldn't do that.'

'She *would*. There are no depths to which that woman wouldn't sink.'

Joseph nodded, conceding the point, taking a small sip of beer. But there was something in his eyes – concern? tension? – that intrigued Helen. .

'You haven't had any dealings with her recently, have you?'

'Of course not. I'm not that stupid.'

'No contact *at all*?'

'I'm not fresh off the boat, Helen. Give me some credit.'

His body language was defensive, his tone slightly strained. Helen was convinced he was lying to her, though why she wasn't sure. Surely he wouldn't be so foolish as to get into bed with Emilia? What would he have to gain? No, it seemed crazy, ridiculous.

'Are you OK, Helen?' Joseph enquired, cutting across her thoughts. 'You haven't eaten much.'

'I'm fine, just a lot on my mind, that's all.'

'If you don't fancy the pasta, I've got *pudding*,' he said, brightening once more as he rose from the table.

'Actually, do you mind if we leave it? I don't have much of an appetite.'

Joseph paused, regarding her carefully. Despite his best attempts to get things back on track, the temperature in the room had suddenly dropped.

'Helen, I'm trying my best here...' he said, exhaling heavily. 'I know I fucked up, that I behaved foolishly and I'm trying to make amends.'

'I know that.'

'We're a good team, a good fit, so tell me what I have to do to get things back on track. If you want me to say sorry, I'll happily—'

'It's not about that.'

'Then what?'

Helen looked at him. Did she really want to get into this? Tonight of all nights? Yet what choice did she have?

'It's ... it's about trust.'

'I understand that. Going after our suspect alone ... I accept that it was out of order, I've said as much—'

'I didn't mean at work, though, yes, it was reckless *and* dangerous.'

Joseph was staring at her, aggrieved but also curious now.

'What's going on, Helen?' he demanded, an edge to his voice. 'What have I done to make you doubt me like this?'

The words hung in the air, demanding an answer.

'This is none of my business, I totally accept that,' Helen said quietly, getting her apologies in first. 'But ... but you told me you didn't have any kids.'

'I don—'

But the lie died on his lips, Helen staring directly at him.

'You have a little boy. Kieran.'

Joseph didn't try to deny it, continuing to stare at her.

'I asked you about kids and you told me categorically that you didn't have any.'

'I know and I'm sorry ... but it seemed such a big thing to bring up so early in—'

'He's your *son*, Joseph.'

Joseph continued to meet her eye, refusing to break eye contact.

'A boy who should be part of your life. Who you turned your back on.'

'Who the hell have you been talking to? What do *you* know about my son?'

Helen hesitated. Joseph's fury was clear, but there was no point ducking it.

'Look, I shouldn't have done it, but I called Karen.'

'You did *what*?'

'It wasn't my place, I know that, but I needed to know what was going on.'

'You don't want to go believing anything she's got to say...'

'Why not?'

'Because she's an angry, bitter woman.'

'And why's that? Because of something she did? Or because of something you did?'

Now there was no mistaking it, raw anger flaring in Joseph's eyes.

'You two have got it all worked out, haven't you? I bet you had a lovely time—'

'It's wasn't like that, Joseph—'

'—gossiping about me, running me down—'

'No, absolutely not—'

'—feeding off her lies, sticking the knife in.'

'I wanted to find out the truth.'

'And she told you the truth, did she?' he spat back, scornful.

'I don't know. Did she? Did you walk out on them? Did you turn your back on your own son?'

Her question hit home, Joseph silenced by the strength of the accusation.

'A yes or no, Joseph. That's all I need.'

But instead of answering, Joseph took a step towards her. Immediately, Helen rose, primed to respond. Suddenly she had no idea what he was going to do, what he was capable of.

'You have no right,' he rasped. 'You have no right.'

His face was contorted with anger. For a moment, Helen thought he was about erupt, lash out at her, such was the livid emotion in his expression. But then he turned from her, marching out of the kitchen without a word.

Seconds later, the front door slammed shut, the perfect full stop to another awful day.

Day Five

Chapter 93

'You're not welcome here, so bugger off.'

PC Dan Meadows wouldn't usually have been so blunt, but his patience had run out. He'd tried three times to get the journalist to move on, but still she was camped on the doorstep.

'Look, we both know she's here, so can we cut to the chase?' Garanita countered. 'Let me talk to her, for five minutes, then I'll be on my way. I just want a comment.'

'Are you mad?' Meadows shot back, desperately trying to keep his volume down. 'She doesn't want to talk to anyone, least of all *journalists*…'

'You make it sound like a term of abuse,' Garanita replied teasingly. 'Look, mate, I can hang around all day if you like, she's going to have to—'

'And I can arrest *you* for obstructing the police in the execution of their duties.'

But the journalist just laughed.

'If I had a pound for every time one of your lot has threatened me with that… and I'm still here.'

She opened her arms in a gesture of victory. Worried, PC Meadows shot a look down the road. It was early morning and people were starting to emerge on the quiet suburban street, hurrying off to work, ushering kids out of the house. The last thing he needed was a stand-up row with the unrepentant journalist.

'I'm sorry, but the answer's no.'

Garanita was about to respond, but Meadows didn't give her the chance, shutting the door in her face. Immediately, the knocking resumed.

'For fuck's sake...'

He shot a look down the hallway to his colleague, who shrugged helplessly. There was little they could do, they were trapped, yet there was no question of them remaining here, not with Garanita publicly drawing attention to Pryce's current whereabouts. Where did that journalist get off, sacrificing others' safety to boost her own career ambitions?

With a heavy heart, PC Meadows mounted the stairs to the first floor. It was very possible Pryce had heard the altercation and knew what was going on, but if not, he would need to put her in the picture. He didn't relish the task, but summoning his courage, he knocked on the door.

'Miss Pryce? It's PC Meadows...'

No reply from within. It was early, it wasn't impossible she was still asleep, so he knocked again.

'Miss Pryce? I was wondering if I could have a word. Something's come up.'

There was no question that she could hear him, but still there was no movement within. Surely her curiosity would be aroused now, so why wasn't she responding? He knocked once more, his anxiety growing.

'Is everything OK? I really *do* need to talk to you...'

Still nothing. He teased the handle, half expecting the door to be locked, but it opened easily.

'I'm coming in, Miss Pryce...'

Cautiously, he stepped inside. He was fearful of finding her half naked, of arousing her anger, but to his surprise, the room was empty. There was no sign of Pryce at all.

Worse still, her bed hadn't been slept in.

Chapter 94

She had hardly slept at all. Thoughts, anxieties, fears had swirled around her brain, even as the baby kicked and wriggled. Having a new life inside you was a unique, wonderful experience, yet sometimes it felt as if you were under constant attack, your baby fighting you every step of the way. It was a little like that this morning, Charlie having to dig deep just to summon the energy to put one foot in front of the other.

Rising early, she had consumed two strong cups of tea before finally galvanizing herself. She'd asked Osbourne to contact friends and, where appropriate, family, searching for nuggets of information about Fran, Maxine and the harmony of the group as a whole. She, however, wanted to go back to the beginning, to find out more about the dynamic between the schoolchildren, following their discovery of Pryce's vindictive posts.

She'd called in, letting Helen know what she was planning, then squeezed her unwieldy bulk into her Renault, making her way across town to Fordham. Parking up, she'd completed the short journey on foot and was now standing outside St Mary's comprehensive school.

Students streamed past, circumventing her as they hurried through the school gates. Charlie had had a happy education and the sight of a busy school always cheered her – so much energy, so much noise, so many possibilities. In her day, there had been plenty to do, but nothing like the myriad of clubs and courses the kids could take now: teaching themselves to make animated films, to become DJs, to record and distribute their own music. Part of Charlie wished she could go back to that time, to be a teenager again, yet she wasn't naive. She knew that for many, school was no picnic – academic pressure, bullying, drugs, even gang violence intruding on the students' lives. And that was over and above the friendship problems – fractured loyalties, loss of status, exclusion – that came as standard. Every student had their issues, every school had its secrets, which was why Charlie was here. If there *was* a serious problem amongst Fran, Maxine and the others, someone in this school would know about it. Plucking her warrant card from her bag, Charlie headed for the school office, waddling forwards as fast as her baby would let her.

Chapter 95

She was the first in, which was how she liked it. After a disturbed night, Helen had headed to the office early, keen to get ahead of the day. En route, she had fielded a call from Charlie. Despite her audible exhaustion, her old friend was heading to St Mary's School to do some further digging, determined to leave no stone unturned. Helen knew she must do the same.

Shutting herself in her office, she spread the case files out in front of her. From here she had a good sight line to the murder board, the smiling faces of Justin Lanning and Callum Harvey staring back at her unnervingly, so she could easily cross reference between the two. She hoped that by poring over every detail, alone and undisturbed, she might unearth some clue, some important link, which had so far eluded them.

Certain important facts were not in doubt. Two murders had been committed, carried out in a way that had struck fear into the hearts of the victims. Even before the witness from the Moon Lounge had identified him, Daniel King was an obvious suspect – because he loved to terrorize his victims, because the two victims were only connected through him, because the MO for the attacks – ligature strangulation – was the same as before. The fact that the killer was haunting Northam was another important clue – it was a place King knew well and would feel comfortable hiding out in. Overwhelmingly, the available evidence pointed to King, yet there were still questions that had to be answered, gaps to be filled in.

Motive was key. There was no doubt King would have fantasized about having those schoolchildren at his mercy once again, but he was taking a massive risk in returning to finish the job, when the world thought him dead. And why strike now? Why wait over eight years to target them? Yes, Maxine Pryce had put the case back into the public eye, perhaps provoking him, but surely that would make King's task *more* difficult, given the attention Pryce and her fellow victims were now attracting?

More pressing still was the manner of the attacks. Lanning had been duped, his killer posing as his driver. But what of Callum Harvey? He had called Southampton Central, convinced his life was in danger. He'd promised to lock all the doors, to wait patiently until Helen arrived, yet still he had met a grisly fate – this despite the fact that there seemed to have been no forced entry or even a struggle. If King *was* his killer, how had he managed to gain access? Was it possible he was already in the house when Harvey made the call?

It was an intriguing thought, King lying in wait to ambush Harvey, but if this was the case, why hadn't Harvey fought to protect himself? Was he simply *surprised* by his attacker? Or ... was it possible that Harvey knew his attacker and trusted them, had perhaps even let them in willingly? Could it be that Maxine or Fran were somehow involved?

It seemed improbable, but then the precision and care with which these killings had been carried out suggested that the perpetrator had something to hide, or something to lose at least. On the face of it, these killings didn't have the hallmark of King, who was by nature impulsive and impetuous, but then who knew what might have happened to him in the intervening years? Was it possible he'd grown in sophistication, honed his 'craft'?

Keen to dig further into his psychology, Helen opened up his file, leafing through his charge sheet, notes made by the social services of the time, even local newspaper cuttings from the time of his mother's funeral, but there was little here that she didn't already know. So instead she turned to their more recent discoveries about King. Here, too, concrete evidence was thin on the ground, but there was the material they'd recovered from the warehouse, the items Joseph Hudson had sifted and collated. There were plenty of curiosities here – a brick taken from the wreckage of the torched farmhouse, a dog collar that their dark web collector claimed belonged to one of King's Dobermanns, both of which had died in the fire – but little in the way of clues. Flicking through the inventory, Helen saw that Joseph had flagged a couple of items and she took a closer look at them now.

The first was a Southampton phone number, scribbled down in King's uncertain hand on a scrap of paper. Without hesitation, Helen rang it, but was not surprised to find that the number was discontinued – Joseph, for all his faults, would have checked *that*. They would need to dig deeper, see if BT had a historic listing, a name they could chase down, in case the connection was important. Could it be the number belonged to a friend of King's? A confidant? An accomplice?

Putting the scrap of paper to one side, Helen investigated the other item. This was a prescription, never used, seemingly, for a medicine called Riluzole. Helen wasn't familiar with it, so examined the rest of the label. It was stained and ripped, the prescription having been culled from the farmhouse bins, yet Helen could still make out some of the details, notably the name of the GP and the name of the patient. Daniel King.

Now Helen paused. She knew that King's mother had suffered

from motor neurone disease and had assumed this prescription was for her. But looking at the date of issue – a few weeks *after* her death – and the name of the patient, it was clear this had been made out for her son. This was interesting, as there had been no mention of any illness in anything she'd read about King.

Intrigued, Helen fired up her computer, searching for information about Riluzole. Now she was in the zone, drinking in the information on her screen, totally oblivious to the members of her team who were filtering into the office. Indeed, she was so lost in what she was reading that her phone made her jump, buzzing on the desk next to her. With one eye on the screen, she picked it up.

'DI Grace.'

'It's DC Reid, ma'am. I'm sorry to bother you, but we've got a problem.'

Immediately he had her full attention, such was the note of alarm in his voice.

'Maxine Pryce is missing.'

Chapter 96

'Maxine?'

Her cry drifted across the car park, slowly dying amidst the silence.

'Maxine?'

Louder this time, but again Emilia's enquiry yielded no response. Had Maxine hatched a different plan to escape? If so, where was she now? Leaning on the silver Volkswagen, Emilia considered her options, for once stumped as to what to do next.

Following her unsatisfactory conversation with PC Meadows, Emilia had considered heading back to the office, but ultimately had decided to stay, intrigued to see whether they might try to spirit Pryce away to a different location. Emilia was prepared for a lengthy stakeout, but in the event, she hadn't had to wait long, the harassed police officer suddenly bursting from the flat a few moments later in a state of high anxiety. He desperately scanned the road, talking nineteen to the dozen into his radio. This fevered dumb show gave Emilia a good clue as to what had happened and the snatched snippets of conversation she overheard confirmed it. Maxine Pryce had fled.

It seemed counterintuitive, a reckless thing to do, but Emilia wasn't surprised. Had Pryce run because she felt trapped? Or had she simply decided that it was crazy to go into hiding when everyone wanted a piece of her? Either way, she was gone.

The police were now frantically searching the vicinity, calling for backup, but Emilia hadn't lingered, hastening to the corner of the street before disappearing from view. Maxine had a new VW Golf, her pride and joy, which she secreted in a private car park to keep it safe from careless drivers. She had boasted of her new purchase in their phone interview – the car and the private parking space evidence of her newfound wealth – and Emilia hurried there now. There was no way Maxine would hang around, waiting to be caught, she would have a purpose, a plan. First stop would be the car park. From there, she could go anywhere, presumably planning to put as much distance between herself and Southampton as possible.

Yet, to Emilia's surprise, Maxine's car was still there. It sat helplessly in the parking bay, its airless front tyre now totally flat. Emilia's frustration was building; if anything, her desire to seek out Maxine had increased, now that the story seemed to be growing: a young woman in danger, fleeing her flat to take her chances, or perhaps refusing police protection in order to pursue her career – either way, there was a concrete development in the Daniel King story which she wanted to pursue. But first she needed Maxine. A comment and a snatched picture would do nicely. But where was she?

Grabbing her phone from her pocket, Emilia dialled Maxine's number. It was done more in hope than expectation, yet to Emilia's surprise she now heard the phone ringing. Not just in her earpiece, but the actual phone trilling nearby. What was going on? There was no sign of Maxine. Had she dumped the phone before fleeing? It was possible, of course, but why would she come here and *not* take the car? Perhaps the flat tyre had stymied her escape attempt, but even so, why would she ditch her phone?

The call rang out and Emilia was directed to voicemail. The journalist redialled, listening intently. And now she noticed something. The trilling was audible, but it was muffled, the sound dulled. Straining to hear, she picked up something else. The melodic sound seemed to be coming from the boot of the car.

Now Emilia hesitated. Should she continue her investigations or retreat to alert the authorities? She shot a look behind her, but she was quite alone in the deserted car park, so sliding her hand into her sleeve, she tugged at the handle, wrenching the boot open. Cautiously, she peered inside, but immediately her hand went to her mouth, a soft gasp escaping her lips.

She had found Maxine Pryce, but too late. The woman lay lifeless in the boot of her own car, a ring of livid purple bruising encircling her slender neck.

Chapter 97

'Why do you want to know about Maxine Pryce?'

There was suspicion, but also concern, in the woman's voice. Charlie knew she would have to allay her fears, to bring her onside if she were to gain anything meaningful from this interview.

'We're doing some background digging on the relationships between Maxine and the other children who were abducted. I assume you knew them all?'

Donna Parks, the school's long-serving deputy head, nodded briefly.

'Yes, they were all good kids, with plenty to offer. I can't believe that Justin and Callum...'

She couldn't bring herself to say the words, visibly upset, so Charlie leapt in, quick to capitalize.

'It's a terrible tragedy and we're *determined* to find out who did this and bring them to justice.'

Parks seemed pleased by this, her sense of loss clear.

'In order to do so, it's vital we understand the connections between the abducted children, to get a sense of their relationships – fallings-out, romances, shared hobbies and so on. How well would you say you knew them?'

'Very well. I taught them all at one stage or another.'

'It must have been hard for you, for the school, when they went missing.'

Parks shuddered at the memory.

'I can't really describe it... It was *awful*. We encourage lots of our students to do the DoE awards. It's a brilliant experience and looks great on their CVs, but what happened to them... well, it was our worst nightmare come true.'

It was a phrase that Charlie had often heard in connection with Daniel King.

'What that man did to Rachel, what the others endured,' Parks continued, shaking her head angrily, tears once more pricking her eyes. 'We did what we could to support the parents, to assist with the search... and we were so relieved that they turned up. I think we all felt that we might lose them.'

'And what happened after they were found?'

'They were checked out at South Hants, then interviewed by the police. The headmaster and I were there, of course, offering what support we could. We were hopeful then that they would all come back to St Mary's, finish their education, but... it didn't quite work out like that. Some stayed, others decided a change of scenery was required. I tried to stay in touch with them, of course, but it was hard...'

'And for those that stayed? Did they remain close?'

'In a way. They had a shared grief, a shared experience that nobody else could understand, but I... I got the sense that they avoided each other. When they were with other people, they could almost forget about it, be someone else...'

Charlie digested this, scribbling down a couple of notes.

'And before their abduction, what were they like? Were they a tight unit? Did they socialize together? Were there any romances?'

This was what Charlie had really come for and the experienced deputy head seemed to sense this.

'Is this off the record?'

She seemed oddly tense.

'If you'd prefer. Whatever you say can remain strictly between us for now.'

Parks considered this, weighing up her options, then finally she spoke: 'Well, they were a mixed bag. Callum and Rachel were from difficult, volatile backgrounds, Justin and Maxine were from more stable, affluent families.'

'And Fran Ward?'

'Somewhere in between.'

'And the dynamic between them?'

'It varied. Justin and Maxine were close; they were the leaders in the group. Callum was everyone's friend, the joker. Fran was the reliable one, solid, sensible, practical. And Rachel, well, she was new to the school and was still finding her place. I think doing DoE was her way of trying to fit in.'

'So Maxine and Justin ran the show?'

'Pretty much. I think Maxine liked the idea of the pair of them bossing things, like king and queen of the Prom.'

'Were they ever in a relationship?'

'No, though I suspect Maxine wouldn't have said no. She – we – didn't know Justin was gay back then. It wasn't something he broadcast.'

'And were there any specific tensions between them? Any fallings-out?'

Now Parks hesitated, as if searching for the right way to respond.

'I'm particularly interested in what people felt about Maxine Pryce.'

Charlie had said it gently, carefully, but immediately saw a reaction.

'Anything you can tell me would be very helpful...'

'Well, Maxine... was a girl who always knew what she wanted. I'm not surprised that she's the one who managed to... to cull something positive from what they went through. She was always very ambitious, very determined. Perhaps felt the world owed her something...'

'Because of her privileged background?'

'And her personality. She was one of those kids who had to be top in everything, couldn't bear being at a disadvantage.'

'What would happen if she was?'

Parks shrugged, then: 'She'd react.'

It was an obvious attempt to avoid the question, but there was no way Charlie could allow that.

'In what way?'

'She'd... she'd redouble her efforts to come out on top. And if that didn't work, she'd try... other means.'

Again, Parks paused, as if wary of speaking ill of her former pupil.

'Meaning?'

'Well, I'm convinced she cheated in her coursework, perhaps even in exams. And there was no question she lied – about herself, about others...'

'In what way?'

'She'd puff herself up, whilst denigrating others. Spreading lies, rumours, getting them into trouble...'

'Can you think of any specifics?'

'I can remember she accused Fran Ward of copying her work once, when I know for a fact she didn't. And she was pretty brutal to Rachel.'

'Why?'

'It seems silly now,' Parks continued, shaking her head. 'But I think she got it into her head that Justin had a thing for Rachel. Rachel came from a difficult, violent background, hence why she'd suddenly moved to this school, this area. Maxine got wind of this, found out Rachel's mum was usually drunk by noon and ensured the rest of the school knew. That was typical Maxine – a massive overreaction to something fairly petty.'

'Because she has to win?'

'Partly that,' Parks continued, sadly. 'And partly because she enjoyed it, enjoyed making mischief.'

'It sounds like it was a little more than mischief.'

'You're right, it was,' Parks corrected herself. 'It was vindictive, premeditated and cruel. Of course, Rachel never found out who was spreading those rumours. There's no way she would have done the DoE trip if she had.'

'And that behaviour, that malevolence, was par for the course for Maxine?'

The question hung in the air. For a moment, Charlie thought the deputy head wasn't going to respond, but then dropping her eyes, she replied: 'To be honest, yes. Maxine had some good qualities, was nice enough when she was happy, comfortable. But when she was angry or upset, well, then... then she was pure poison.'

Chapter 98

The car was still rolling to a halt as she grasped the door handle. Hauling herself out, Charlie flashed her warrant card at the approaching officer, then lifted the police cordon and hurried towards the car park.

Her baby was on the move this morning, constantly changing position as she scuttled over the gravel surface. Charlie felt breathless and uncomfortable, hesitating now as she approached the silver Volkswagen. Part of her wanted to find out what was inside, part of her really didn't, but she had no choice, having been summoned by Helen. Her old friend was standing by the open boot, grim-faced, and as she peered inside, Charlie could see why. Maxine Pryce lay there, her neck badly bruised, a look of abject horror on her face.

'Who found her?' Charlie muttered.

'Garanita,' Helen replied, shaking her head in disbelief. 'She was loitering outside her flat. When it became clear that Maxine had done a bunk, she came here hoping to intercept her... but she got this instead.'

'Did she see anyone?'

'She says not and I believe her. The body's stone cold.'

Charlie looked down at Maxine. She was no pathologist,

but she could tell that rigor mortis already gripped the young woman's body.

'She's giving a statement now,' Helen continued, 'but I don't think anything useful will come of it. We don't even know when Maxine left her flat.'

Charlie took this in.

'Scene of crime should be here within the next ten minutes or so. I'm going to have to ask you to hold the fort until then.'

'Sure ...' Charlie replied slowly, surprised that Helen was leaving the scene.

'DS Hudson's organizing house-to-house. Once the scene is secure and Meredith's team are in place, I want you to pull the rest of the team back to base and start looking at Maxine's movements, her calls, her financial transactions over the last day or so. If she received a threatening call last night, if that's what made her run, I want to know.'

Helen turned her attention to the corpse once more. 'She still has her phone on her, but I want forensics to run the rule over it, so contact her mobile provider and get a full call history. Buzz me the minute anything comes up.' She stepped away from the car.

'How long do you think you'll be?' Charlie responded, fishing.

'Couple of hours or so.'

Clocking her friend's curiosity, Helen added: 'There's somewhere I need to be.'

She departed without elaborating, leaving Charlie alone with the body. She stared down at it, disbelieving. She'd known that Maxine and Fran were potentially in danger, but still it didn't seem possible that this woman, this vital powerful woman whom she'd spoken to not two days ago, was dead. Maxine, whose face had graced numerous newspapers, whose voice had been heard on radio and television, had been brutally murdered. It was a reminder of the fragile hold we all have on life, how all our energy, purpose and strength can be snuffed out in an instant. With immaculate timing, her baby now gave another powerful kick, slamming down on her pelvic bone once more. But this time Charlie didn't feel any pain.

Now she just felt numb.

Chapter 99

He only glimpsed her out of the corner of his eye, but he knew it was her. Nobody moved quite like Helen – powerful, graceful, athletic – nor with such purpose. Some of the officers were distracted by her sudden appearance, darting glances at their SIO, but Joseph Hudson was determined not to react. He wouldn't give her the satisfaction, appearing like some faithful dog mooning after her, not now things had taken a decisive turn.

He'd spent another restless night pondering how to handle things. He was the one who'd been wronged, yet she had the rank, the influence, the credit in the bank. If she wanted to move him on, perhaps by ensuring the investigation into his recent crash was sufficiently damning, then she could probably do it. Everyone said she had Grace Simmons in her pocket, could do what she wanted ... but why *should* he move on? He had worked hard to get this posting and he was damned if he was going to be frozen out because of Helen's paranoia and snooping.

But how best to respond? Should he say nothing, hoping the potential embarrassment of their relationship becoming public would be sufficient for Helen to let things lie? Or should he go on the offensive, letting her know his position clearly and challenging her to go against him? He'd erred towards the latter and had thought about doing it this morning, but then events had taken matters out of his hands.

Bentham had called him just after nine. He was alerting all senior detectives, summoning them to join the team to the private car park near Pryce's flat. Joseph hadn't been expecting an attack on her, questioning whether King would be so reckless, so rash, now that they were under police protection. Yet he had struck once again, somehow luring Pryce out of her flat to her death. Privately, he marvelled at the killer's efficiency and expertise; he seemed forever one step ahead of them, able to strike at a time of his choosing, seemingly with no risk to himself. It defied logic, but the facts spoke for themselves. Three dead bodies and not so much as a sniff of a sighting. He was laughing at them and Joseph wondered now if there was anything – or anyone – who could stop him completing his vengeance.

'You know the drill,' he barked, concealing his fears from the group of officers gathered in front of him. 'We want a comprehensive door-to-door and will stay on site until we have spoken to every resident. Maxine Pryce was last seen alive by PC Dan Meadows at 9 p.m. last night, so we're after any sightings between then and nine o'clock this morning, either in her road or near the car park. Strange noises, sounds of a struggle, unfamiliar figures in the road, suspicious vehicles idling or speeding away from the scene…'

The officers nodded, digesting his words.

'Find out if there's a Neighbourhood Watch group, anyone who might have footage of the local streets – on phones, CCTV cameras, bike or car cams. DC Reid is currently checking for sightings from couriers, cab drivers and food delivery firms. If any of these prove significant, I'll be looking for volunteers to chase them up.'

He carried on giving out orders, the assembled throng nodding purposefully with each directive, but slowly his mind started to drift. He'd done this plenty of times, could do it in his sleep, his attention now drawn back to Helen, who had once more come into his field of vision. To his surprise, she was leaving the scene, climbing onto her bike. She was only twenty feet from him, but was not surprised that she didn't look in his direction, didn't even acknowledge he existed. A house-to-house operation was vitally important with a crime like this so, on the face of it, it was no obvious slight that he'd been tasked with running it. Yet Joseph was sure it was yet another punishment, a menial task which would keep him away from the good stuff, the scene of crime. The honour of running that show had predictably fallen to Brooks, Helen's old friend and comrade.

Helen was revving her engine, preparing to depart. Her ability to come and go as she pleased underlined how powerless he was. Brooks and he were of equal rank, but it was the unspoken rule that Brooks was the SIO if Helen was absent. It hadn't always been that way, but there was no doubting it would be from now on. If he'd ever hoped to audition for the role of her deputy, Joseph had burnt his bridges now. He would not be trusted now, nor his suit advanced by his former lover.

Professionally stymied, he *could* nevertheless take the initiative in his private life. Helen might think she had the whip hand, able to use, abuse and accuse him as the mood took her, but there was no way he could let that happen. He would be no one's whipping boy. Their relationship might be crumbling under the weight of Helen's baseless hostility and suspicion, but he would not wait patiently for her to deliver the final cut. No, he would this end on *his* terms.

Chapter 100

The bike roared past, speeding away down the road. Helen Grace seemed utterly intent on her task, her eyes locked on the road, oblivious to all around her. Oblivious to the fact that she was only a few feet from Maxine's killer.

The figure loitering on the street corner followed the bike's progress, watching with admiration as Grace weaved in and out of the traffic, slowly receding from view. There was no doubt that she was an impressive figure – dynamic, powerful, determined – but today such admiration was tinged with concern.

She was obviously heading somewhere in a hurry. But where? And why?

So far, everything had gone to plan. Pryce's death had been extremely satisfying and no more difficult than the others. In fact, in some ways, it had been easier. Justin Lanning had at least tried to fight, whilst Callum Harvey had had the presence of mind to beg. Pryce had done neither, terror robbing her of the power to speak, to act. She had simply submitted to her fate.

The journalist's discovery of the body had not been planned, but it was no matter. Someone – the cark park attendant, another motorist – would have found the body before long. After that, events had followed a familiar pattern, Grace and her circus of detectives descending on the scene, desperately searching for clues, for witnesses, anything that would give them a lead on the perpetrator. It was amusing to watch them scurrying around, so determined, but so blind, clueless as to how to stop this.

With the first two murders, Grace had spent considerable time on site, keen to unearth some lead, some steer, however minor. But not this time. This time she had arrived, passed the baton to her colleague, then taken her leave. She'd virtually run to her bike, leaping on it and roaring off, diverting around the police roadblock before speeding past the growing crowd of bystanders and gawpers. Several amongst them had turned to watch her go, but their curiosity was minimal and insignificant by comparison. For them, it was just a minor diversion rather than a matter of life and death.

Where was Grace going? Why such urgency? She wouldn't wilfully abandon the crime scene unless it was something of the gravest importance. But what? The end was so close now, was it possible that Grace might yet stymie things? It seemed impossible, but doubt gnawed away, breeding suspicion and even fear. Grace had brought in dangerous killers before, single-handedly on some occasions, and had always appeared a dangerous foe. So far she'd been kept at bay, but now as curiosity festered and concern grew, an awful possibility presented itself. Was it possible that she would stem the bloodshed? That Maxine Pryce would be the last to die?

It didn't seem credible, it didn't seem right. But where previously there had only been certainty, now there was only doubt.

Chapter 101

'How did it happen?'

The officer in front of her shifted uneasily on his feet, avoiding her eye.

'I don't know, to be honest. I've just had the bare facts so far. DS Brooks will be in touch shortly, she should be able to tell you m—'

'Was she murdered?'

Fran didn't care how rude she sounded. She just wanted the facts. Cooped up in this stuffy, depressing house, she had been slowly going out of her mind, even before her awkward companion had entered to deliver his grim news.

'Like I said—'

'Was she murdered?'

Her tone was harsh and as she said it, Fran took a step towards the officer. She would shake the information out of him if she had to.

'Yes, she was.'

'Strangled?'

The officer paused, obviously torn. He needed to follow orders, but he was also a human being and understood Fran's need to know. Slowly he looked up, then nodded briefly.

Fran felt the air go out of her, a groan escaping from her lips.

Stricken, she crumpled down onto the bed, hiding her face in her hands. Awful images pulsed through her mind – Maxine having the life choked out of her, slowly, painfully – and the world started to recede. She felt surrounded by darkness, by suffering, by death. It had been years since she'd experienced anything like this, but now she was right back there, stuck in that awful farmhouse, with King looming over her. She could picture his face perfectly, see the awful relish with which he informed them all that they were going to die.

'As I said, DS Brooks will call you shortly.'

Fran jumped, the words startling her. She had been so lost in her own thoughts that she'd momentarily forgotten that the police officer was still present.

'Don't bother, I don't want to talk to anyone.'

Nausea consumed her, fear assailing her. She just wanted to bury her face in her pillow and pretend none of this was happening.

'I do think you should talk to her. I'm sure she has some information th—'

'No calls.'

Her tone was defiant, determined.

'OK, then. Maybe in the morning. In the meantime, I'll be outside and my colleague's on the front door, so you're quite safe.'

If it was meant to reassure her, it missed the mark. How could two officers hope to resist the remorseless power of Daniel King, a man hell-bent on destroying those who had escaped his clutches?

The officer was moving away now, retreating quietly. But as he reached the door, he paused, the floorboard creaking noisily as he turned back to her.

'And, once again, I am very sorry for your loss.'

Fran could have laughed, so wide of the mark was his attempt to console her. It was not grief she was feeling, nor even sadness. She abhorred everything about Maxine – her callousness, her duplicity, her bloodcurdling selfishness – and she was sure the world would not miss her. There was no sympathy for a life lost here, no pain at her passing. No, it wasn't a sense of loss that was crippling Fran now. It was anguish. It was terror.

But, above all, it was guilt.

Extract from One Dark Night *by Maxine Pryce*

I think it was Justin who first spotted our opportunity.

We had endured a hellish night of torture and terror – the verbal abuse, the beatings, then the promise that we'd all die in King's filthy basement. I was convinced I would be first, King pulling the wire so tight that I almost blacked out. But then suddenly he released me, loosening the wire and pulling it away with a flourish. I can still picture the excitement on his face as he drank in my terror.

King was enjoying himself, there was no question about it. None of us had any doubt that he was going to kill us. He marched round and round, eyeing us each in turn, gripping the wire between his clenched fists.

'Ssso,' he lisped. 'Who wants to go first?'

I was too traumatized, too sore to speak, even if I'd wanted to. The others obviously felt the same, maintaining a despondent silence.

'No takers? OK then, I guess *I'll* have to decide.'

I felt physically sick. Was this it? Was this the beginning of the end?

King continued to circle us. He was humming to himself, happy and carefree, then suddenly started to chant, rehashing a children's rhyme to hideous effect.

'Ip, dip, doo . . .'

With each word, his attention moved from one potential victim to the next.

'The cat's got the flu . . .'

Broken as we were, we were hooked to his every word.

'The dog's got the chicken pox...'

It was tempting to count ahead, to work out where he would end up, but I couldn't bear to, in case it ended up on me. Closing my eyes, I braced myself for the final line of the rhyme, but to my astonishment, King suddenly stopped.

I opened my eyes. He was standing in the middle of the basement, his body rigid with tension. He was listening intently and now I understood why. There were noises coming from upstairs.

I couldn't make out what it was at first, then suddenly I realized. It was the dogs. King's Dobermanns were going berserk, barking furiously. King swore, angry that his enjoyment had been curtailed, but he couldn't ignore the warning signs. If the Dobermanns were barking at an intruder, a car perhaps, then it meant someone had turned up uninvited. Someone who might be looking for us.

Worried, he hurried up the stairs, slamming the door behind him. We heard the key turn in the door, then footsteps hurrying away. I wasn't quick enough, alert enough, to register what that meant, but Justin was. Previously when King had left the room, he'd locked the door before sliding two bolts across for extra security. This time, in his haste, he'd forgotten to. Meaning that there was one rusty old lock between us and freedom.

'Come on, guys. This is it...'

What happened next was extraordinary. Having been so down, so defeated, suddenly we all came to life, Justin urging us on. We were tethered to the water pipes, but Callum's bonds were nestled up against a metal bracket, which held the pipes in place. He had been gently rubbing his ropes against it for some time but now he renewed his assault.

'Please,' Rachel begged. 'Please hurry...'

Callum redoubled his efforts. Each second felt like an hour. The dogs were still barking, but any second we expected King to return.

'Come on . . .'

This time it was Fran, but she was speaking for all of us. Now that we had a glimmer of hope, a thin chance of escape, we had to seize it. Suddenly, without warning, Callum's bonds broke. Now he was on his feet, hurrying over to Rachel. Now she was free. It didn't seem possible but it was true. Moments later, we were all on our feet, staring at each other.

Energy coursed through us. It was tempting to race up the stairs, but Justin counselled caution. He led us up slowly and carefully, fearful of alerting King to our attempted escape. Each step was agony, the boards groaning horribly. I fully expected the door to fly open, King in front of us, shotgun raised, but we made it to the top undetected. Justin had picked up a rusty chisel from the floor and now slid it into the gap between the door frame and the lock. Steadily, he increased the pressure. It was awful to watch – what was taking so long? Why wouldn't it give? – then suddenly the lock flew off, the door falling open.

Instinct now took over, Callum rushing out and lunging for the front door, but Justin caught hold of him, dragging him back. We were shocked at first, but then we realized why – King was out front, shouting at his dogs. Heading that way, we would run straight into him. So instead we hurried down the gloomy corridor to the rear and there – to our amazement and delight – was another door. Lifting the latch, I grasped the handle and pulled. Moist, night air flooded in, cool and refreshing, but we didn't linger, pushing through the door and out.

The backyard was littered with junk and our route forward was perilous. If anything, the fog was even worse than before, we could barely see two feet in front of us. Suddenly the whole enterprise seemed hopeless. How could we possibly know which way to go? Which way to head?

'Let's just keep going straight,' Rachel whispered, urgently. 'Eventually we'll hit a road or something...'

'But how do we even know which way is straight?' Fran shot back. 'We could go round and round in circles.'

'We don't have a choice, we'll just have to judge it as best we can.'

King's voice, piercing and cruel, ended our conversation. The dogs had quietened now and he was berating them for barking at shadows. It was now plain that there was no rescue party, so we didn't wait around, lurching into the thick fog.

Right from the off, the going was tough. We managed to make it off the farm, but immediately encountered problems. The ground was soft, boggy and uneven. Callum caught a rabbit hole, plunging to the ground, and behind him Rachel was already starting to struggle, her swollen ankle hindering her progress. We buoyed her up, supporting her over the softer ground, urging her to keep moving.

'Come on, Rach. I know it hurts, but we have to keep going...'

As we encouraged her, we continued to shoot anxious glances over our shoulders. There was as yet no sign of King, however, no sign that he'd discovered our escape, but we knew it wouldn't be long, so we stumbled on, swearing, crying, even as our feet sank ankle deep in the watery soil. We had been through so much, endured so many indignities, but this truly felt like we were in the middle of a nightmare, running through fog that seemed as impenetrable as it was endless. I had a sickening feeling that any minute now we'd end up back on the farm, but I kept this to myself, helping Rachel and Fran forward, both of whom were now struggling.

There was no question of stopping, of giving up, but even so we all froze as we heard it. King was shouting their names, cursing them viciously, his dogs joining in, barking wildly. We ground to a halt, listening intently. Was the sound growing weaker, moving away from us? Or was it getting louder?

We stood there, swathed in mist, straining to hear. King's voice *was* getting louder. Was it possible the dogs were following their scent? Or was King acting on instinct, plotting a random course? Either way, we had to run.

We renewed our efforts, powering forward. All of us, even the boys, were whimpering now, determined to keep going, though riven with fear. We were all fit enough but our punishment had sapped our spirit, our stamina, and we stumbled haphazardly on. Still King's cursing grew louder. Could he tell we were close by? Could he see us?

A small cry made me turn. To my horror, Rachel was on the ground, seemingly unable to move. The boys paused, even as Fran and I sprinted over to her.

'Rachel, you can't stop now . . .'

'I have to . . .'

'You've got to get up, we have to keep—'

'I can't take another step.'

Tears were streaming down her face. I crouched down to look at her ankle, which was hideously swollen. Rachel must have clocked my reaction, because she now said: 'You go on.'

'No,' we said, hauling her to her feet. 'We're not done yet.'

Swallowing her agony, Rachel summoned her reserves of courage and we pressed on. We were relieved but not surprised, she'd always shown her best in adversity. We were supporting her, taking some of her weight, propelling her forward. Happily we were soon making good progress again and before long she was able to carry on under her own steam, half hobbling, half running to keep up with us. I think we all felt a shot of energy, of optimism then, as if perhaps it would still be all right.

I tried to keep my thoughts on happy things. I thought about my parents, my cat, my cosy bedroom. And I thought about my friends, about the happier times that lay ahead for Callum, Justin, Fran, Rachel and myself. God knows, we'd earned them.

'Where is she?'

It was Fran who'd asked the question. Wrenching myself back to the present, I turned, my heart tumbling into my boots as I did so. Rachel was nowhere to be seen.

'She was right behind us,' I breathed. 'I swear she was right behind us.'

I took a step forward.

'Rachel?'

My cry drifted away through the mist, eliciting no response.

'Rachel?'

I screamed it this time and now I heard something. A faint answering cry.

'We've got to go back.'

I said this to Fran, whilst turning back to look at the boys. But they had now vanished. Fear consumed me now, but even so I grabbed Fran by the hand.

'Come on.'

She seemed reluctant, but in spite of her terror, despite the proximity of King and his dogs, we stumbled back through the fog, back towards where we thought we'd last seen Rachel. But our hands clutched at thin air, even as our feet sank into the earth.

'Rachel, please,' I moaned. 'Where are you?'

But we could only hear King's dogs now. We were scrabbling, clinging to each other, desperately searching for our friend. It seemed impossible that we would lose her, plucky irrepressible Rachel, now that we had made our escape. We would find her, we *had* to find her, everything would be OK...

But then we heard it. A shrill, sickening cry, Rachel's anguished voice ringing out, before suddenly being stilled.

Chapter 102

She sat at her desk, buried in her own thoughts.

When she'd arrived back at the office, Emilia had been the focus of everyone's interest and concern. Disbelief fused with curiosity as colleagues who'd never shown the slightest interest in her peppered her with questions.

'Are you OK?'

'Do you need to go to the hospital?'

'What had happened to Maxine?'

'Why don't you go home, rest up?'

'What did you actually *see*?'

'Was it King?'

Emilia endured it for twenty minutes, then called time, insisting that she was shocked but fine and had work to do. Hurrying to her work station, she'd fired up her computer and prepared to write this evening's headline, but for once words failed her. 'Maxine Pryce found dead'. 'Maxine Pryce murdered'. Nothing seemed to cut it, nothing captured the full horror of what she'd just experienced.

She had no strong feelings for Pryce, she seemed no better or worse than anyone else. Emilia had admired her spirit, her independence, her determination, even if this was tinged with envy and a certain territorial hostility. Emilia had already written two books about her own life, her own sufferings, but she had never received the amount of attention and media coverage that Pryce had – she wouldn't still be working for the local paper if she had. She had met Pryce once, spoken to her on the phone a couple of times, and until that final appearance at Waterstones, the ambitious young woman had seemed in control of her destiny.

But looking back it was clear that Pryce had sensed she was in danger. Her erratic, fearful performance at the bookshop confirmed that. Was she looking for King? Expecting him to rear up in front of all those people? If so, she'd been well off beam, King waiting patiently until she was alone before claiming her.

Emilia had seen dead bodies before, but the sight of Maxine, lying in the boot of her own car, had really struck home. This was partly because of the contrast between her usual dynamism and her lifeless corpse, but also because of her injuries – those hideous purple bruises and that awful crimson line, where the wire had cut into her flesh. Could there be any more terrifying way to die, the life literally squeezed out of you?

It made Emilia shudder and looking down she saw that her hands were shaking. It *was* hard to put this morning's experience into words, because she was still in shock, because the memory was so awful, because what was happening was so unbelievable. It was possible to relay the bare facts in a headline, Maxine Pryce, the professional survivor, had been killed, but that didn't come close to summing up the full horror, the full meaning of her death. For it wasn't just that another young person had died, that a twisted killer had struck again. Now it was something more terrible and more awesome. What it really meant was that events were now reaching their bloody conclusion, that this ghoul was close to having his lust for vengeance sated.

Daniel King was close to finishing the job.

Chapter 103

This was where he'd last been spotted, the last place he was seen alive.

It had taken less than an hour for Helen to make it here, crossing county lines as she sped to the small village of West Ashling. She was on the edge of the South Downs, in unfamiliar territory, and normally would have called her opposite number in West Sussex's Major Incident Team to alert him to her presence, but there was no time for that today. She would have to move fast if she was to avert more bloodshed.

The village was a picture of quiet, English country life. Pulling up outside the handsome village store, with its plentiful baskets of fruit and veg, it seemed an unlikely setting for high drama, but eight years ago it had been at the epicentre of the local police force's hunt for Daniel King.

Following the schoolchildren's escape, King had set upon Rachel Wood, dragging her back to the farmhouse, exacting a terrible revenge on the injured girl, but he knew the game would soon be up. Torching the house, he'd fled, over the Downs, through the mud and, briefly, back into civilization. He had emerged from the wilderness in West Ashling, caught on CCTV hurrying away from a petrol station on the fringes of the village. But it was not this sighting that interested Helen – she'd seen the footage previously and knew it was grainy and brief – it was the witness who'd spotted King in the village itself which intrigued her now.

She had rung ahead, wanting to check that the greengrocer's was still in business, thus was not surprised to see Peggy Turner standing in the doorway of the shop, surveying her.

'You can't park there, dear. You'll get a ticket for sure,' the elderly shop owner warned, a smile on her face.

'I'd like to see them try,' Helen countered warmly, displaying her warrant card. 'DI Grace. We spoke on the phone?'

'Indeed, we did. Come on in.'

She moved to the side, ushering Helen into the shop. Five minutes later, they were ensconced in the back room, perched on armchairs with steaming cups of tea. Helen had little time for pleasantries and her hostess seemed to sense the urgency, getting straight to the point.

'Danny used to come in here quite regularly,' she said, casting her mind back.

It seemed strange to hear her say his name like that. It was always 'Daniel King' or 'Daniel King, killer'; the use of his abbreviated first name made him seem ordinary, normal even.

'His mother wasn't very mobile, so he did most of the grocery shopping. I think he favoured the Sainsbury's near Chichester, but he wasn't very organized. He was always forgetting things and frequently had to call in here for emergency rations.'

She smiled at the memory, but it soon faded as darker thoughts intruded.

'I always thought he was an odd one, but he was loyal and attentive to his mother. I never thought he'd end up ... doing what he did.'

'What did he buy?'

'Just the usual. Eggs, bread, milk, cigarettes and alcohol, of course. Towards the end there was a lot of that. I probably shouldn't have sold it to him, but he didn't have much in his life after his mother died and I didn't have any grounds to refuse him.'

Regret was writ large on her face, despite her protestations. It was as if the elderly shopkeeper feared that the beer and spirits she'd sold King had somehow contributed to the schoolchildren's ordeal.

'So he was a fixture in the village?'

'Not a fixture, but we saw him around. He was ...' She hesitated, as if fearful of sounding foolish. 'A bit of local joke, to be honest. You'd see him marching along in his long wax coat and hat, his Dobermanns at his heels, like he was lord of the manor, rather than the owner of a rather decrepit farm. I felt a little as though he were searching for something ... status, respect, I don't know what ...'

'I see,' Helen replied, intrigued now. 'And that morning, the morning of the children's escape, the fire at the farmhouse, you were opening up as usual?'

'Yes, it's just as I told Bob Stevenson. I was up just before six in the morning. I'd come down as normal and was outside, putting out the fruit and veg.'

'And that's when you saw him?'

'Yes. I noticed him straight away because there was nobody else about ... and because it was strange to see him in the village so early.'

'Tell me exactly what happened.'

The old woman paused, regarding Helen curiously as if it might be a trick question. But Helen's expression bid her carry on.

'I was putting out the baskets and I looked up. And there he was on the other side of the road, marching off in a real hurry. I only learnt later what had happened, that he was on the run—'

'Can you remember what he was wearing?' Helen interrupted, keen to keep things on track.

'I've said all this before, it should be in the files...'

'Humour me.'

'Well, as I said at the time, he was wearing his normal outdoor gear. A long wax coat, boots, his hat...'

'Where was he in relation to you? Opposite you or...?'

'He was a little further on down the road, hurrying away.'

'So you couldn't see his face?'

Turner paused now, thinking back.

'No, but it was definitely him. You could tell by his size, if nothing else. He was tall...'

'Could you see anything of him? Hands? Legs? The back of his neck?'

'Well, no, I don't suppose I could really...'

'Did you speak to him? Try and engage him?'

'Yes, yes, I think I did,' the shopkeeper confirmed, casting her mind back. 'I called out to him, I often did that when I saw him around.'

'And did he respond?'

'No. He was in hurry—'

'Did he turn at all when you called him?'

'No.'

'Was that usual? Would he usually ignore you?'

'No, I suppose not. He didn't have many friends, people were a bit suspicious of him, so he normally said hello.'

'So it was out of character?'

'Well, yes, but he was on the run, wasn't he? He was fleeing for his life...'

Her tone was defiant, her testimony definitive, but the strain in her voice betrayed her. Peggy Turner had been a key witness in the original investigation and had enjoyed a certain celebrity because of her brush with a killer. But it was clear now to Helen that the elderly shopkeeper was unsure of herself, fearful now that she had made a terrible mistake.

Chapter 104

DC Osbourne tore down the corridor, the precious parcel tucked under his arm. He was used to receiving urgent summons from DI Grace, but this latest seemed more significant than usual. He hadn't been able to make out everything she said – she was in West Ashling and the reception was pretty poor – but he'd got the thrust of her instructions, racing back to the forensics lab at Woolston.

He'd reached the end of the shiny corridor now, skidding to a halt by the lab doors. Rapping on them, he peered through the glass, holding up his warrant card for the approaching lab assistant. Pushing the door release, she ushered him inside.

'I'm looking for Emma Barton?'

Meredith Walker, the lab chief, was still at the car park, crawling over Pryce's vehicle, so Osbourne had been directed to her deputy instead.

'Over there,' the assistant responded, singling out a tall, slim figure in the bowels of the lab.

Thanking her, Osbourne hurried over, the lab technician turning to greet him.

'You must be DC Osbourne.'

'Nice to meet you,' Osbourne replied, shaking her outstretched hand.

'You said you had something important for me?'

'Urgent request from DI Grace,' he replied, handing her the bulky package. 'For the King investigation.'

Barton nodded soberly, her smile fading a touch. 'I see.'

'These are from the original investigation. DI Grace will ring you shortly to confirm her instructions, but basically we want a comprehensive forensic trawl ...'

Barton was already studying the package intently, checking the seal, noting the label, which confirmed that the items inside hadn't been touched for eight years, having been stowed away in police storage pending a satisfactory outcome to the case.

'Any skin cells, hairs, blood, mucus, any and all sources of DNA are to be examined and logged.'

'By when?'

'By an hour ago. Those were her exact words.'

'Well, I'll do my best, but if she wants it done properly ...'

She had already turned away from him, sliding on gloves and carrying the package over to a sterile search area. There, she carefully broke the seal, retrieving the items inside, before laying them out in front of her.

Osbourne watched her, transfixed not only by her gentle, methodical approach, but by the items themselves; items which seemed to bring a missing phantom back to life. Ranged on the table in front of Barton were Daniel King's hat, boots and mud-spattered wax coat.

Chapter 105

She spread the pieces of paper over her desk, taking in the endless rows of numbers. As promised, Charlie had secured the scene, waiting patiently for Meredith Walker, but had made good use of her time – charging one of their data analysts with obtaining the full call history of Maxine Pryce and Fran Ward.

As soon as Meredith had arrived, Charlie departed, racing back to base and hurrying up to the seventh floor. She was pleased to see that the task she'd set was well in hand and moments later she had the data spread out in front of her. Hunkering down, she ran her finger along the rows, drinking in dates, phone numbers, call duration and more besides. In complex cases like this, the devil was usually in the detail.

Immediately, she hit a stumbling block. Maxine Pryce had been killed in a virtually identical manner to Justin Lanning and Callum Harvey, but with one critical difference. The first two victims had both received a phone call, warning them that they had one hour to live. Pryce had not. It was hard to know the precise time of her death, but it must have been late yesterday evening, given her current body temperature and the extent of the rigor mortis. She had been seen alive at 9 p.m., fleeing her flat shortly afterwards, perhaps. Charlie had assumed she'd received a threatening call and decided to make a break for it, heading home to get her car, money and so on – yet her phone history revealed that she'd received no calls at that time.

Prior to that, her phone had been busy, with the run-up to publication and the fall-out from Lanning's death. But after 4 p.m. yesterday she'd received no calls at all. Perhaps her agent had warned people away, perhaps Maxine had followed police advice and turned her phone off. Either way, there had been no threatening call, no advance warning of what was about to befall her.

Why? The perpetrator of the bloody crimes had been so clinical, so precise, so sadistic in his enjoyment of his victims' terror, revelling in their knowledge of their impending death, so what was different about Pryce? Why had she been spared this psychological torment?

Convinced that she was missing something, Charlie pored over the rows of numbers. It was perhaps possible that their perpetrator had deliberately gone quiet, following his narrow escape from the industrial estate in Northam, but did this fit with his serene self-confidence thus far? Certain that he would have tried to contact Pryce somehow – she was, after all, the most prominent, most outspoken of his survivors – Charlie decided to go further back, checking out the preceding days, weeks even, to see if she had been targeted.

Ignoring familiar numbers, she looked for calls from a phone number that was blocked or withheld. The threatening calls to Lanning and Harvey had been precise, each lasting approximately one minute, so Charlie cross-referenced call duration with call source, desperately searching for something that would explain this strange anomaly. But there was nothing; she had received no calls either on her landline or on her mobile.

Perplexed, Charlie was about to call Helen when a thought struck her. DC Reid had mentioned that Maxine had been spending time at a flat in the city centre, borrowed from a friend of her agent. It was a place where she could write unmolested, where she was *alone*. Sensing a breakthrough, Charlie dug out the address, before running a phone and utilities check. Moments later, she was on the phone to BT, impressing upon them the urgency of her enquiry.

And now she found what she was looking for. For weeks now there had been no calls at all to the flat's landline, either incoming or outgoing, as the owner was away in the States. Last Friday, however, there had been a call. It was received at 6 p.m. from an unregistered mobile and lasted exactly one minute.

Charlie exhaled heavily, pleased to have found the call, but confused by the timing. Maxine Pryce had been killed late on Sunday evening, yet had received the call a full forty-eight hours earlier. Checking the timeline on the murder board, Charlie realized with a jolt of surprise that actually the call had come before Harvey was targeted and killed. Why hadn't the killer struck? Maxine would not have been hard to target, either in the flat or walking alone to Waterstones. Why wait two days before making good on his threat? And why target Callum Harvey instead, the morning after the original call to Pryce?

It was possible that something had occurred to make Harvey an easier target, but this killer was resourceful, bold, determined – he didn't seem the type to run shy of a challenge. Which made Charlie wonder – was it possible that Pryce had somehow postponed her fate, shifting the killer's attention to Harvey? It seemed improbable, yet she wouldn't have put it past Pryce to do exactly that, if given the choice.

If given the choice. This thought lodged deep in Charlie's brain and suddenly she was scrabbling through the paperwork, searching for Fran Ward's call history. If Maxine had somehow postponed her date with death, shifting attention to Harvey, was it possible that Fran Ward had done something similar? Was *that* why Pryce wasn't contacted in the hours before her death?

Her finger sped down the line of calls, working backwards from today. She ignored the landline – Fran was living at her parent's house – concentrating on her mobile instead. And in less than a minute she had it. Fran had received a call on Saturday night from an unregistered mobile at about nine thirty p.m. And, as with the others, the call had lasted exactly one minute. Within twenty-four hours Pryce was dead, Fran seemingly having cheated death.

And now, for the first time during this troubling case, Charlie sensed the pieces beginning to slide into place. She had no doubt that Fran would have willingly directed the killer's attention away from her towards Pryce – she had no time for her former schoolfriend; in fact she appeared to despise her. An awful image suddenly presented itself – Charlie's mind shooting back to Jessica's party. It suddenly seemed clear to her that Fran, Pryce and the others had been involved in some kind of game, a cruel version of pass the parcel, which unravelled friendships, tempting the participants with the opportunity to avoid their fate.

Instinctively, she felt that Pryce had seized her opportunity, condemning Callum Harvey to death. Fran Ward had presumably done likewise, hence Pryce was now dead. But what did that mean for Fran? There was no one left for the killer to call, no one left for Fran to pass the buck to. Did that mean she would be spared? Or would she be this brutal killer's final victim?

Alarmed by this thought, Charlie snatched up her phone, intent on calling Helen. But as she did so, the woman herself burst into the incident room, heading directly towards her.

Chapter 106

'It can't be her, can it?'

DC Reid spoke for many in the group, whose shock was evident. They were gathered together in the briefing room, crowded around Helen. DS Simmons had joined the throng, to offer encouragement and support, but she too was struggling to hide her astonishment.

'She died in the farmhouse fire…'

'We *thought* Rachel Wood died in the fire, but there was never DNA confirmation of that, as the body was completely consumed by the flames – bones, teeth, the lot,' Helen corrected him. 'A large concentration of human ash *was* found in the basement, as were Rachel's earrings, her necklace, even traces of her shoes. So it's easy to see how the mistake was made. The other kids had been tortured there, King was bigger and stronger than Rachel, who was injured anyway.'

'But King was spotted hours after the fire hurrying through West Ashling.'

'A witness thought she'd spotted King, but we've now established that she never actually saw his face.'

The team digested this bombshell, looking ashen. Was the phantom they'd been searching for really just that?

'The investigating team went with the obvious narrative: King captures Wood, kills her, torches the house and then flees, but we now know there are problems with that scenario. First off, the dogs. They were fiercely loyal to King and he to them, so why were they abandoned, left to die in the fire? Bob Stevenson speculated that King sacrificed them, as they would hinder his escape, but I'm not sure that stacks up. They were King's only friends in the world, the only things he cared for. If it was *King's* body in that basement, however, the presence of their remains with him makes a lot more sense. Loyal to their master until the end…'

A couple of the team nodded, Helen's version of events starting to make grim, logical sense.

'More important, however, is the evidence DS Hudson recovered from the warehouse,' she continued, gesturing briefly in Joseph's direction, the latter dropping his gaze to avoid hers. 'A prescription made out to Daniel King for Riluzole. This is what made me think we were on the wrong track. Riluzole is prescribed for ALS, motor neurone disease. ALS is an incurable, muscle-wasting condition which can be genetic. His mother died of it – it now looks like King had it too.'

'Why didn't we know this before?' DC Osbourne queried, his temper flashing through. 'Why did Bob Stevenson's team not find this?'

'You'd have to ask him,' Helen replied calmly. 'But my guess is they weren't looking for it. As far as they were concerned, they were hunting a fugitive, who'd either killed himself or hot-footed it to the Continent. Their focus would have been on finding him – tracking his phone, his bank account, chasing down any friends or accomplices, not in visiting his GP for an exploratory chat. Plus our "collector" stole this prescription from the destroyed farmhouse before the search team had managed to go in, so the investigating team would never have found this evidence—'

'But what does it mean?' DC Bentham asked, daring an

interruption. 'The prescription was made out, what, eight years ago now...?'

'As I said, ALS is a wasting disease. There is no known cure and life expectancy after diagnosis is short – three, four years at the most.'

'So odds on he'd be dead by now?' Charlie responded.

'Yes, or if not dead, then severely incapacitated. In a wheelchair, in hospital. Given this, it's inconceivable that he could have carried out these attacks. Which is why I asked Meredith Walker to look again at King's wax jacket, boots and hat.'

The team were silent now, hanging on her every word.

'They weren't tested first time round, not properly anyway, as they were just the discarded clothes of a fugitive – his keys, wallet, phone were in the pockets and that was enough for Stevenson. But Meredith's taken a new look at the wax coat today and she discovered a single black hair, caught in a popper on the inside of the collar. As you know, King had fair hair, so Meredith obtained a DNA sample from it and ran it through the system. It's a match for Rachel Wood.'

This time there was an audible gasp from the group, but Helen pressed on.

'We can't be certain what happened, but I'm guessing Rachel somehow overpowered her attacker in that basement, torched the farmhouse, either accidentally or deliberately, then fled. Fragments of her clothing – the fastener from a bra strap, a buckle from her belt – were found in that basement back room, which would fit with King stripping her, before attacking her. If she was fleeing from the burning house, into the fog, naked, cold and vulnerable, then it's perfectly possible, probable even, that she grabbed the first things that came to hand – King's coat, boots and hat – and threw them on. I think the reason King didn't turn to say hello to Peggy Turner that morning in the village was not because he was on the run, it was because it was actually Rachel Wood.'

'But what about the sighting at the night club? Two nights ago?'

Joseph had bided his time to intervene and had chosen the trickiest, most pressing question.

'I've no idea,' Helen replied honestly. 'But we need to find out. Perhaps Tatiana was mistaken. Perhaps she was deliberately misleading us. Either way, we need people down there *now*, getting answers. If she deliberately lied to us, then it cost Maxine Pryce her life.'

'And what about the phone calls? Lanning and Harvey both said they were contacted by a *man*...'

'Absolutely, but voice distorting apps are very sophisticated these days and ten a penny. If Rachel wanted to disguise her gender, it wouldn't be hard.'

'Even so, if Rachel *had* escaped the farmhouse,' Joseph insisted, provoking curious looks from other members of the team, 'why would she not just go to the police and bring her ordeal to an end *that* way? Why vanish? What could she possibly stand to gain?'

Helen wasn't sure if Joseph was attacking her version of events to test it or to undermine it. Either way, Charlie jumped in before she could respond.

'Perhaps she spotted an opportunity,' she said, as the team now turned to her. 'I've been looking at Rachel's life over the last few days and it doesn't make for pleasant reading. She was new to St Mary's, placed there a few months before her ordeal under an Emergency Protection Order. She and her mother Vanessa had been victims of domestic abuse for years prior to that, at the mercy of a controlling, violent partner. Things were better for them down here, but money was tight, Vanessa had alcohol abuse issues and Rachel was the butt of school jokes because of the way she dressed, the way she spoke, her lack of money...'

'So... what? You think she deliberately took the opportunity to disappear, to reinvent herself?'

Joseph was persisting with his interrogation, but sounded less bullish now.

'Think about it,' Charlie confirmed. 'She kills a man, stumbles from the farmhouse, spends a long night wandering the Downs. She could go to the police, *should* go to the police, but she must assume that the other kids have already made it home, alerted the authorities. What will the result of that be? A big police investigation into King, into *her*, and huge press interest in the children. There's no way her name wouldn't feature in the papers, on TV—'

'Alerting her violent father to their new whereabouts,' DC Reid added.

'Exactly. Now she could have been rehoused, given a fresh identity even, but she would still be left in a difficult relationship with a mother who was both neglectful and an alcoholic, with no money, no prospects... *Whereas*, if she took the opportunity to vanish, to start over when the world thought she was dead, then she could never be found by her father, by her mother, by *anyone*. Nor would she have to answer for her actions in the farmhouse, for killing King...'

It was a seductive theory, one which, on the face of it, made perfect sense. But still the team had questions, DC Osbourne now interrupting.

'Even if all this is true, why now? Why would Wood strike now after all these years? What was she trying to achieve?'

All eyes turned to Helen once more.

'It's a fair question, DC Osbourne' – she had been expecting this question and was ready for it – 'but I'm not the best person to answer it.'

Chapter 107

Fran Ward paced back and forth, her eyes turned to the floor. Helen watched her closely, shooting a quick glance at Charlie, before repeating her request.

'If there's anything you can tell us, anything that might explain why Rachel would target you and your friends, now's the time to share it.'

Ward didn't look up. She was still reeling from the revelation that King might *not* be responsible for these awful murders. That in fact it might be her old friend, a girl she'd mourned and shed tears for, who was now wreaking a terrible revenge.

'I just... I just don't see how it's possible...'

'I know and I understand your shock,' Helen continued, gently. 'But we've checked with King's local hospital. They've confirmed they made the ALS diagnosis. That's why he was slurring his words when you met him, the disease was already destroying his muscles, his balance, even the ability to speak. There's no way he can be responsible for *any* of this.'

The words seemed to knock the wind out of Ward, who stopped pacing, slumping down on the bed.

'So, if Rachel is responsible for these crimes,' Charlie added, 'can you tell us why she might do something like this? What she has against Justin, Callum, Maxine, you...?'

Fran dropped her face into her hands. Charlie shot a look at Helen, fearful they were losing her, but then the young woman spoke.

'It's *her* fault.'

The words shot out, anguished and bitter.

'Rachel?'

'*Maxine*,' Ward corrected her. 'It's all *her* fault.'

'I don't understand...'

Ward took a deep breath. It was as if the words were being dredged from her soul, as she continued: 'What she said on TV... what she wrote in that book...' Ward could barely contain her disgust, even now. 'It wasn't true.'

'Some of it must have been,' Charlie protested. 'Your abduction, the ordeal you went through...'

'The basic shape of it was, yes, she couldn't lie about *that*,' Ward carried on. 'But the rest of it was bullshit. We were never the Famous Five... We were never a happy group...'

'Why? What happened?'

'Rachel happened.'

'Meaning?' Helen queried, curious now.

'She was a late addition to the team. Justin's suggestion. We were all fine with it – thought he was trying to be kind – but Maxine hated the idea.'

'Because she thought Justin had feelings for Rachel?'

Ward nodded dully.

'Maxine was at Rachel from the word go, finding fault with her clothes, her equipment, her attitude. It wasn't Rachel's fault that she'd had to beg and borrow her stuff, that she wasn't as athletic as us. And it was true she didn't look the part, with the glossy black hair, the fake eyelashes, the make-up, but still there was no need to be so *cruel* to her...'

Even after all these years, the memory of Maxine's vindictiveness was fresh.

'Of course, after Rachel hurt her ankle, things got even worse. In her book, Maxine claimed that we blamed Callum for losing the map and so on, but that wasn't true. It was *Rachel* that Maxine blamed – for losing our way, for going to the farmhouse, for meeting King...'

Ward shivered, wrapping her arms around herself.

'When we were down in that place, waiting our turn, waiting to be tortured, raped, killed, God knows what, Maxine wouldn't stop. Goading Rachel, blaming her for our misfortune... We tried to stick up for her, well, I did, at least, but Maxine wouldn't be silenced.'

'So what happened? When you escaped, did Maxine deliberately abandon her? Leave her behind in the fog?'

Ward faltered now, tears filling her eyes.

'She...'

It was almost as if she couldn't bear to say it.

'She never made it out the basement.'

Helen stared at her, utterly wrong-footed.

'But Pryce said that you all escaped, that Rachel got lost in the fog.'

'It wasn't like that *at all*.'

Still she wouldn't look at Helen.

'Tell me, Fran. Tell me what happened that night.'

There was a tenderness in Helen's voice, but steel too. They had to know. Fran Ward took a deep, tearful breath, before eventually responding.

'King... he... he had us tied up in the basement. He was walking round us, chanting that dreadful rhyme, trying to work out who... who to kill first.'

'Which is when the dogs started barking—'

Ward shook her head vigorously.

'That never happened. They were in the room with us the whole time.'

Charlie shot a concerned look at Helen, but she ignored it.

'King ... King didn't make it to the end of the rhyme, but not because of those awful dogs. *Maxine* stopped him.'

'What do you mean?'

'Maybe she'd counted it out, knew it would land on her. Maybe she was just scared. Either way, as he reached the end, she just blurted it out ...'

'Blurted what out?'

'She told him ... to take Rachel.'

For the first time, Helen was silenced, stunned by this callous act of cruelty. The room was now silent, save for Ward's soft sobbing. She seemed hollowed out, a shadow of her former self.

'What happened then?' Charlie coaxed, hanging on her every word.

Nothing from Ward. It was as if she hadn't even heard the question.

'Fran, please ...'

Ward shot Charlie an anguished glance, then continued, faltering and grim.

'Rachel ... Rachel begged for her life, telling King to take *Maxine* instead. So ... he asked the rest of us what we thought. That's when Maxine went for it, reminding us that we hardly *knew* Rachel, how she'd been a problem from the start, how *she'd* got us into this mess ... I didn't want to hear it, knew that this was what King wanted us to do, but then ... then I heard Justin agreeing with her, telling King to take Rachel. Callum too – he didn't say anything, just nodded, but still ... After that I didn't have much choice, what I said wouldn't have made any difference anyway ...'

'So you let him take her?'

Ward didn't respond, breaking down into deep guttural sobs.

'What happened then?'

Helen knew Ward wanted to stop, but there could be no question of sparing her now.

'I couldn't bear to watch. I closed my eyes, but I could still hear it. Hear Rachel being dragged into a back room, hear her screams as he tore at her clothes, hear her agony as he beat her, over and over. I cried. I cried and cried, wanting it to be finished, wanting to die there and then ... but suddenly I realized – *sensed* – that someone was standing in front of me.'

'Who?'

The answer was perhaps obvious, but Helen needed to hear Ward say it.

'Maxine. In the book, she said that it was Callum who broke free, but it was *her*. She must have loosened her bonds before King started his awful game.'

'Hence why she was so keen for him to take Rachel, because it would provide a distraction, buy the rest of you some time to escape.'

Ward nodded dully, confirming the awful truth.

'What then?'

'She ... she untied us all.'

'And then?' Helen urged, impatiently.

'I ... I wanted to help Rachel, of course. There were four of us, perhaps we could overpower King? But Maxine wouldn't have it, said we owed her nothing, that she was no friend of ours. Callum was terrified, Justin suggested it would be better to go and seek help elsewhere. Anyway, they both followed her up the stairs and started working on the door. A minute later ... they were gone.'

'And you?'

'What could *I* do?'

Ward looked up, staring directly at Helen. Her expression was beseeching, heartfelt, but guilt-ridden.

'I wanted to help Rachel, I really did. I couldn't bear the thought of leaving her there. But I was on my own, a seventeen-year-old girl against a grown man ...'

She turned to Charlie, as if pleading for forgiveness. But she received none.

'So?'

'So I ran ...'

Dropping her face into her hands once more, Ward sobbed. Huge, racking sobs. Helen laid a comforting hand on her shoulder. She felt sorry for her, for the young girl put in an impossible situation, but she was angry too. At the lies, the omissions, the callous betrayal of a vulnerable young woman. To spare themselves, to make the world think well of them, the survivors had connived in a terrible fiction. But their deception, their cruelty, had cost them dear.

'Is that why all this is happening?' Ward now blurted, through tears. 'The phone calls, the ...'

'We believe so.'

The sobbing increased. Ward was obviously devastated, wrung out by her awful confession. In other circumstances, Helen would have been tempted to leave it there, but there was one more question she *had* to ask.

'Fran ...'

The sobbing subsided just long enough for Helen to be heard.

'When you received the threatening phone call, was it just a direct threat to your life? Or were you given a choice? The opportunity to cheat death?'

Ward looked up, the colour vanishing from her tear-streaked face.

'Fran?'

She stared at Helen, stupefied, then hung her head.

'I ... I was told that I had one hour to live. But ... but that I could avoid that ... if I chose ... chose Maxine to die in my place ...'

As Fran resumed her crying, Helen turned to Charlie. A clear picture was now starting to emerge. Rachel Wood could have revenged herself on her betrayers in a simpler fashion, attacking them when they least expected it. But that wasn't enough for her. No, she wanted them to *know* that awful fear of death, wanted them to be crushed by the impending sense of doom that she'd experienced at the hands of King. More than that, she wanted to toy with them, to *undo* them. By offering them the chance to nominate another to die, she was unmasking the quartet, revealing how thin the bonds of their so-called friendship were, in a cruel game of pass the parcel. Callum Harvey and Justin Lanning had perhaps redeemed themselves, refusing to play her sick game. Pryce and Ward had not acquitted themselves so well, sacrificing another to save themselves.

Wood was determined to reveal the moral bankruptcy of her former friends, whilst exacting a comprehensive, terrible revenge. Which meant that though the picture was now clear, the story was not over yet.

Whilst Fran Ward was still alive, Rachel Wood would not rest.

Chapter 108

She stared at herself in the mirror, taking in her reflection.

The glass was cracked and dirty, hanging on the wall in a public toilet she'd been forced to use since Helen Grace discovered her base in Northam, but it served its purpose, allowing Rachel to take in her sharp features, her pallid face, her piercing blue eyes. Even as she stared at the glass, a smile stole across her features, bringing light and life to her expression. This was her – unadulterated, exposed – and it pleased her greatly.

It hadn't always been this way. Her looks hadn't always pleased her. As a child, she'd thought she was odd-looking, overly tall, with broad shoulders and a boyish, asymmetrical face, and that was before her dad started to rearrange it for her. She used to gaze at herself in the bedroom mirror, looking at the bruises on her neck and cheeks, wondering how best to conceal them. Her mother had always said nobody could know, that the beatings were *their* fault, so from an early age she had been allowed to use her mother's make-up.

Looking back, it was so messed up, the make-up a reward for the beating, and she remembered now that she'd once thought the violence might actually be a *good* thing, given the rewards and the cossetting that followed. Her father eventually put paid to that warped notion, nearly killing her mother one night in his drunken fury. Shortly after that their lives had changed forever, the pair spirited from Manchester under the cover of darkness to begin a new life in Southampton, but her love of make-up lingered. Her new schoolmates, even some of the teachers, thought the fake tan, the lip gloss, the preposterously long eyelashes were a northern thing, scarcely guessing at the root of Rachel's desire to disguise her true face. She didn't care, was happy to go along with their casual snobbery, especially as some of the boys liked the look of her.

How ugly Rachel appeared to her now. What a painted whore she was, preening and pathetic, dishonest and cowardly. She had traded off her looks for years now, especially during those years of exile in Brighton, Bournemouth and elsewhere, but when it came to it, when the moment came to *act*, she'd revelled in dispensing with her former self. The long black tresses were hacked off, a short back and sides taking their place. The eyelashes were binned, the fake tan too, leaving a thin, pale, boyish face looking back at her.

Her teenage self would have rebelled against this sexless figure, but now her reflection brought only happiness. Gone were the attempts to please, the attempts to appease. Now there was just this, the unvarnished truth, and it thrilled Rachel to the core.

Her transformation was complete. Previously she'd been a puppet, a hideously decorated doll, despised and pitied by all who encountered her. Now she was an object of terror, of awe.

Now she was an angel of death.

Chapter 109

'I want us to double the security detail on Ward. Four officers on hand, *day and night*...'

Helen marched away from the house, pausing only to let a struggling Charlie keep up. She was aware that she was talking too fast, that her tone was harsh, but she was deeply alarmed by what she'd just heard.

'Of course, I'll phone it in now,' Charlie confirmed, pulling out her phone.

'We've been one step behind the whole way,' Helen continued, shaking her head. 'But if we can save one life that will be something...'

'Absolutely,' Charlie responded, keying in the numbers and raising the phone to her ear.

'Text me once you've done it. I'll see you back at base.'

Charlie's call now connected and she turned away, so Helen carried on, marching fast towards her bike. Their visit to Ward had been informative – Helen now had concrete progress to report to Simmons – but this didn't make her feel any better. From the off they had been looking the wrong way, pursuing an innocent collector, then a phantom who was long dead, allowing the real culprit to carry out her murderous scheme unhindered. How many lives could have been saved if she'd worked harder, faster, *smarter*? They were already facing three funerals and Helen feared that, despite their best endeavours, the worst was yet to come.

She knew she was being hard on herself, on the team. Nobody had had an *inkling* that Rachel had survived the inferno. Yet if they had not been distracted by other faces, other suspects, they might have got to the truth in time to save Maxine Pryce. They had uncovered the collector's trove of material relating to King nearly forty-eight hours ago – had Joseph and Helen been working more closely together, had their personal issues not impeded their professional relationship, would they have processed that vital piece of evidence, King's prescription, sooner? Once again, Helen berated herself for crossing the line, letting herself be distracted by her own selfish needs. Hadn't she realized by now that relationships always ended in heartache and failure? This time her mistake may have cost a life.

Right on cue, her phone bleeped. Looking down, she saw that it was a message from Joseph. Short, but not particularly sweet.

It's over. Trust is the minimum.

She would have laughed at his cheek, if she wasn't so angry. If he had been in front of her now, she would have taken his head off, enraged by his self-serving, pompous arrogance. *He* was the one at fault, the one who'd lied, but still he postured as the aggrieved party. How she'd misjudged the situation, misjudged him so badly, was beyond her – she'd thought they might be kindred spirits, but actually he was a man of straw.

It should have been her calling time on things, bringing the whole sorry episode to a close, but of course his ego wouldn't allow that. He had made his point and made it clearly. For men like Joseph it was important to be in control, even at the last. He would decide when and how the story ended.

Chapter 110

There is always a price to be paid for your actions.

Emilia had learned this as a child and learned it the hard way, the victim of an acid attack by her father's criminal associates, men she refused to smuggle drugs for. She'd never regretted her actions, the arrest of her attackers freeing her family from their thrall, but her resistance had come at a price, mentally and physically. At a tender age, it was a valuable lesson, one she hadn't forgotten.

Others had been slower to learn, however, believing that their entitlement, their position in society, their sheer good fortune somehow absolved them from this reckoning. Occasionally, it was Emilia's job to rebalance the scales and she'd enjoyed doing this with DS Hudson. He wasn't a bad police officer, neither especially incompetent nor corrupt, but he was arrogant, aggressive and dismissive. In other words, a classic male. He had resisted Emilia's overtures at first, trying to get what he wanted without paying a fair price, but he'd soon discovered the error of his ways. Maybe he could behave like that with Grace and Brooks, but not with her. When she made a bargain with someone, she expected them to honour it.

He'd griped, of course, suggesting he'd done enough already, and there was no denying he *had* been useful. But his service was not yet at an end, not while this investigation was ongoing, and she would need to call on him again now. Her attempts to root out Maxine Pryce had paid off, but not in the way she'd expected. It had delivered another sensational development in the case and thrust Emilia back into the spotlight, as both a key witness and chief reporter, but it had not given her the inside track, personal testimony from those most closely involved. This was what Emilia really craved – a sense of what they'd been going through, a sense of what it was like to feel death stalking you.

Maxine Pryce was dead, like Justin Lanning and Callum Harvey before her. Which left only one person who could give Emilia what she needed, who could complete the picture for her. For obvious reasons, Ward's current location was a closely guarded secret, hence her need of Hudson's assistance. He would refuse, of course. He would claim that he would be putting her life in danger, compromising the investigation ... but he would play ball in the end, when he realized that the alternative was his exposure and disgrace.

This was the way it had to be, the only way it *could* be. Five days ago, the world knew of Lanning and his friends only as survivors, four young people who'd bravely pushed through tragedy and heartache to a new life, a new future. Now three of them were dead, brutally and efficiently executed. The killer was still alive and there was only one prize left to play for now, only one person who could give him the satisfaction he craved and Emilia the scoop she needed. All roads led to Fran Ward now.

And Joseph Hudson would help Emilia find her.

Chapter III

'What do you mean she's gone?'

The words exploded from him, saliva flecking the air.

'Just what I said: she hung around for a few hours after you lot spoke to her and then that was it ... pooofff!'

Lisa McGee flicked both hands up in the air, gesturing a puff of smoke. The deputy manager of the Moon Lounge wasn't pleased to have the police back in her club and seemed intent on letting Joseph know it.

'This is what happens,' she continued. 'I find decent workers like her—'

'Illegal workers,' Joseph corrected.

'Decent workers, who are happy to graft, to do long hours, earn their money, then your lot come along, asking her all sorts of awkward questions. And guess what, we don't see her for dust afterwards. Took off without even collecting her wages—'

'Then you're quids in, aren't you?' Joseph countered, as irritated by her tone as by the news she was relaying.

'Hardly! Where am I going to find another hard worker like her at short noti—'

'Do you have any idea where she might have gone?' Joseph interrupted. 'Do you have a forwarding address, a phone number, any idea where she's staying?'

But McGee was already shaking her head.

'It was cash in hand. She turned up, she got paid. That's how it worked.'

'But how did she come to be working here in the first place?'

'A friend of hers, an Albanian girl, Ajola, recommended her. And before you ask, she doesn't work here any more either. So I'd love to help you ... but my hands are tied.'

She gestured at him once more, holding her hands up together. Joseph was sorely tempted to slap some cuffs on them, drag her down the police station and charge her with obstruction, but there was little point. She was clearly telling the truth. Thanking her tersely, he headed on his way, cursing his luck. He had come here, hoping to get to the bottom of this mystery, to try to understand *why* Tatiana had lied to the police, but was leaving empty-handed. What chance was there of finding her now? Presumably she would simply reappear somewhere else in the black economy, meaning it would take weeks to track her down, if they ever managed it. It would be like looking for a needle in a haystack, given the way things were in Southampton these days.

Perhaps they'd never know why she fled. Had she disappeared because she was an illegal, frightened of the police reneging on their promises and reporting her to the immigration services? Or had she been frightened off by someone? Was it possible that the whole thing was a ruse, that this vulnerable witness had been pressured into lying to the police by someone with a hold over her? Or had she simply been mistaken about what she saw? Was it even possible she'd read some of the stuff in the newspapers about King, seen the stuff on the TV, and somehow convinced herself she saw him?

Joseph barged through the doors out into the sunlight. His anger was growing, his frustration spiking and he stalked back to his bike in a dark mood, wondering how to break the news to the team. Despite the fracture in his personal relationship with Helen, he was determined to show her, and the team, that he was still an effective officer, a valuable asset. Yet how could he when life kept frustrating him? How could he show them that he was worthy of their respect?

He had reached his bike now, but as he made to mount it, his phone started ringing. He tugged it quickly from his jacket – had there been developments? – but on seeing the caller ID, his face fell. Emilia Garanita. Anger flared in him; the last thing he needed now was her tugging his chain. He wanted to smash his phone, smash *her*, and even now he found that his arm was raised, ready to hurl his iPhone to the ground. But at the last minute he caught himself, common sense just about managing to rein in his fury.

Rejecting the call, he slid the phone back in his pocket. He was on the back foot, with Helen, with Emilia, with the team, but losing control would not help him now. He needed something big, something impressive to wrest the initiative back in his favour and petulance would not help him achieve that. No, he needed to be smart, canny, successful. The endgame was now in play and he needed to be in at the death, to somehow snatch victory from the jaws of defeat.

Even so, as he turned the ignition, he could see that his hand was shaking. He needed to control his rage, to be resourceful and effective, but it would not be easy. The adrenalin was pumping, his emotions in riot, his sense of grievance growing. And though he might try to lie to himself, there was no denying that he was perilously close to the edge now.

Chapter 112

'There's no "Rachel Wood" on the electoral register in Southampton, Portsmouth or anywhere in Hampshire for that matter.'

Helen was not surprised by DC Reid's assertion. It would be odd if their prime suspect had established herself as a bona fide, voting citizen, having made the decision to disappear all those years ago.

'What about bank accounts, credit cards...?'

'There are scores of accounts with that name nationwide,' Reid replied. 'But nothing locally. And no debit or credit cards bearing that name have been used in Southampton in the last eight weeks or so. We could go back further...'

But Helen was already shaking her head.

'She's probably been operating under a new name for years, possibly several *different* names. Besides, she's not going to make such an elementary mistake. These murders took serious planning; she's gone out of her way not to be seen, not to leave a single forensic trace, she's not going to be caught through any conventional means.'

A hush settled over the assembled knot of officers. Helen and Charlie were back in the incident room, flanked by Joseph

Hudson and a posse of DCs. Having secured Fran Ward, the priority now was to bring Wood in.

'What about an e-fit?' Charlie asked. 'See if anyone recognizes her.'

Helen glanced at the murder board. A photo of Rachel Wood aged seventeen, taken just before she was abducted, had recently been added. Helen took it in – the long, glossy hair, the lustrous lashes seemingly at odds with her narrow, angular features and a certain suspicion in her narrow blue eyes.

'It might be worth putting something together, concentrating on the features, the shape of the face. The rest – hair, make-up, eye colour are easy to change. But even that will only get us so far – we don't know what style she favours now, what clothes she wears, where her area of operation is...'

'We could head back to Northam,' Reid offered.

'She's long gone from there.'

Helen hadn't meant to sound dismissive but she was worried by their inability to get any sort of handle on this elusive killer. Where was she? What was she planning? She had the feeling they were running around in circles.

'What about if we go even further back?' Charlie said, snapping Helen out of it.

'Meaning?'

'Well, when she was at school, Rachel and her mum were living in a flat in Townhill Park. There must have been places she went, after school, when her mum was out of it, places she felt safe. Somewhere familiar, where she knows the lie of the land, how to blend in. Could be a park, a shopping centre, shops, a café. If we had an image of what she might look like now, it could be worth asking around, see if anyone's seen her.'

It wasn't much, but it was something. Charlie was right – killers did tend to gravitate towards places that were familiar to them. Townhill Park was not a fashionable area of Southampton, so you wouldn't have much footfall beyond the folk who lived and worked there. It might be a good place to hide out.

'OK, detail a handful of officers there. Let's talk to local residents, but also be on the lookout for abandoned properties, squats and so on. There are plenty of vacant commercial properties out there that she might take refuge in.'

'It's weird though, isn't it?' Osbourne observed. 'She's from Townhill Park, went to school in Bitterne, yet throughout this she's based herself in Northam.'

Helen knew he was trying to be constructive, that he wasn't trying undermine Charlie's suggestion, but he had a point.

'Northam was King's area of operation, he went to the pubs and clubs there, not her.'

'We don't know that for sure, she could have gone there...' Charlie countered.

'But she wasn't much of a drinker, because of her mother. Plus, Lanning, Harvey and the rest of that crew used to go to Portswood to drink, to the Jolly Sailor pub. I've not seen anything that suggests they went to Northam.'

'So maybe she was deliberately trying to mislead us,' Helen replied. 'The phones used to contact Lanning and Pryce first pinged in Northam, her base was eventually found there, maybe she wanted us to think that King was behind all this.'

'Possibly,' Osbourne replied. 'But that would suggest it was her who put Tatiana up to lying, wouldn't it?'

It was certainly a possibility, though on the face of it, it seemed a ridiculous suggestion. Why would the young Albanian tell such a whopping lie for a total stranger? Could she have been bribed by Rachel? Threatened by her?

'It's impossible to know for sure,' Helen said quickly, determined not to get sidetracked. 'For now we should send officers to Townhill Park, but also to all the places we know Rachel has been in the last few days. Lordswood, Shirley, Wickham. Previously we were looking for a lone male. The fact that we're now searching for a known female changes things completely. Let's sort copies of her original photos, plus an e-fit of what she might look like now and get out on the streets, talk to possible witnesses, go back over CCTV feeds, try anything and everything we can to find her.'

The team rose now, energized and ready to carry out Helen's orders, but as they did so, DC Bentham intercepted them. It was clear that he had something urgent to impart, so Helen held up her hand, stopping the team in their tracks.

'Sorry to intrude, but I just had a call from the comms team...'

Helen was listening intently, suddenly tense, hopeful.

'The phone that was used to call Maxine Pryce... it's just become active again.'

Chapter 113

'Where is she?'

Helen and Charlie were now in the communications room, flanked by DC Bentham. Rose Richardson, who spent most of her day tracking phone signals, sat in front of them, a digital map of Southampton filling her screen.

'Currently,' Rose replied, pointing to a red dot at the bottom of the screen, 'she's in Bitterne.'

'When did the phone come on line?'

'About ten minutes ago. There are a good few masts down there, so the signal is pretty strong.'

'Is she stationary or on the move?' Helen asked, hoping desperately that it was the former.

'Stationary.'

'Right,' Helen said, turning to Bentham. 'Alert uniformed officers in the area. Once we've got a more specific location, we'll direct them to her.'

Bentham didn't need telling twice, hurrying to the door and yanking it open. As he did so, Joseph Hudson appeared in the doorway, filling the space. Instinctively, Bentham stepped aside to let his superior in, before heading on his way.

'Osbourne said you had a lead on Wood's location.'

It was said plainly, professionally, as if nothing had passed between them in the last couple of days. Helen was determined to respond in kind, refusing to let anything distract them at this critical moment.

'Phone signal's back on.'

'Where?'

'Bitterne,' Helen replied, before turning to Richardson. 'Can we get a more exact location?'

'Well, it's hard to be precise. The signal is triangulating between these three masts, which means she could be anywhere within this radius.'

She drew an imaginary circle on the screen with her finger.

'How big is that area?' Charlie enquired.

'About half a mile or so.'

Helen shot a look at Charlie. It was a bigger area than she'd been hoping for, but what choice did they have?

'Hold on,' Richardson now continued. 'She's on the move.'

'Shit.'

The word slipped from Helen before she could stop it. Odds on, Wood would elude the local uniformed officers ... unless they could somehow cut her off.

'Which direction is she heading in?'

'North.'

All eyes were on the screen, following the progress of the dot, which moved jerkily up the screen.

'She's moving pretty fast, isn't she?' Helen observed, intrigued.

'She must be in a vehicle of some kind.'

'Where is she now?'

'She's moving into Bitterne Hill. Looking at the direction of travel, I'd say she was probably on Woodmill Lane ...'

Helen angled another look at Charlie, but she was already picking up a phone to call Bentham.

'Hold on, she's stopped again.'

424

Helen moved in closer, looking intently at the dot, which was now stationary. But only briefly, the small red circle starting to edge north once more.

'Why did she stop there?' Joseph asked. 'There are no traffic lights or crossings there.'

'What's the traffic like?'

'Should be clear at this time,' Richardson said, turning to another monitor.

A few frantic seconds of typing, then live feeds from Woodmill Lane sprang up, showing that the traffic was indeed flowing freely.

'Yup, she's making good progress, heading north...'

'Towards Eastleigh.'

Another interjection from Joseph and this one got everyone's attention. The safe house where Fran Ward was being held was in Eastleigh.

'Hold your horses, she's stopped again.'

'What the hell?' Joseph muttered. 'The roads are clear.'

Helen stared at the screen, puzzled. Then: 'She's on a bus.'

She turned to Joseph and Charlie, who'd now rejoined them.

'There's no other reason for that stop–start pattern of movement and look there...'

Helen was pointing at the screen. A Bluestar No. 12 bus was clearly visible, moving away from the bus stop.

'She's on the move again,' Richardson confirmed.

'That's it, then.' Joseph turned to Helen.

'Shall I let uniform know?' Charlie asked. 'Tell them to head there—'

'Better if we do it ourselves,' Joseph interrupted. 'We can't leave anything to chance, not now. I'm happy to take a detail down there, intercept the bus—'

'We should tell Traffic, coordinate with them,' Charlie persisted, aggravated at being talked over.

'No time for that,' Joseph countered. 'Besides, they can't handle something like this. If they want to set up road blocks, fine. But they can't face Wood on their own, they've got no concept of what they're dealing with.'

'DS Hudson's right,' Helen replied. 'We need to get down there now, but with a tactical unit in attendance. If there's any danger to life, we neutralize Wood. Understood?'

'Absolutely,' Joseph replied, looking positively cheerful at the prospect. 'And you're happy for me to lead?'

Now, finally, he did look at her. His expression was neutral, but there was something in the eyes – a challenge – which Helen couldn't fail to pick up. Charlie was looking at her, fully expecting her to swat him down, and she was sorely tempted to do just that.

'Yes, you lead. Let me know as soon as you have eyes on her.'

Joseph didn't bother replying, hurrying from the room in his eagerness to get started. Helen didn't linger either, thanking Richardson for her help and following Joseph out the door. She could sense Charlie's shock, and could tell that her old friend wanted to question her, but she wasn't ready for the postmortem. Not yet.

Chapter 114

She stared out of the window, but saw only darkness.

Night was stealing over Southampton now, consuming houses, landmarks, the places Fran knew and loved. Her home town seemed alien and unfamiliar, as if it were somehow cutting her adrift. Fran was used to being on her own, but she'd never felt so isolated as she did tonight.

She'd decided against making polite conversation with the officers downstairs, retreating through another reinforced door to her accommodation on the second floor. Now she questioned the wisdom of that decision. She was stuck... stuck in this small airless bedroom. The walls seemed to be closing in on her and, as she was forbidden from using her phone or the internet, her only distraction was to peer through the net curtains at the city below. But the cityscape was lost to her too now, hidden in shadows, meaning she was utterly alone with her claustrophobia, her regret, her fear.

With each passing minute, her anxiety ratcheted up a notch. She had a pounding headache, was finding it hard to breathe, was convinced she was slowly losing her mind. Perhaps the sensible thing to do would be to call for the officers and head out of this tiny prison for a few minutes, to talk about the weather, the football, anything. Yet she knew instinctively that she wouldn't.

She wouldn't feel safe outside this stuffy room and, besides, what would they talk about? What was there to say while Rachel was at large? Nothing mattered until she was captured, until this whole hideous nightmare was over.

How she rued the day she'd met them – Justin, Callum, Maxine. In reality, Fran had never truly been part of the group. She was more popular than Rachel – that wasn't hard – but she was never one of the cool kids, never funny or sporty or pretty. She was just Fran – reliable, responsible, capable Fran, a useful person to have around. She'd accepted Maxine's invitation to join their DoE group, happily welcoming Rachel to it later, pleased that she had found some purchase in a school year that had not always been kind. She knew Maxine wasn't happy at the make-up of their troupe, could sense her hostility, her paranoia, but felt sure that they could get through the two days unscathed. How wrong she'd been.

Since it happened, since those awful days, she'd spent much of her time hating Maxine, fantasizing about telling her exactly what she thought of her, telling the world what they'd done, how gross their betrayal had been. These waking dreams gave her temporary relief, but little more, and soon she was back in the grim reality, crippled with guilt once more. She had replayed that moment, the second she'd turned to run, multiple times, imagining different scenarios in which she stuck with Rachel, saved her even. But the thought of King descending upon her, *murdering* her, always brought her up short, giving the lie to her thoughts. She was a coward, plain and simple. Someone who had put herself first, when she should have helped her friend. Who was to say she wouldn't do exactly the same thing again now, if put in the same situation?

Yes, they had all betrayed Rachel, sacrificing her to save themselves, and all had now paid the price. It was terrifying to think that her schoolfriend was out there now, watching, waiting, choosing her moment to strike. Rachel's vengeance was obscene, sickening, cruel, yet could Fran say, hand on heart, it was unwarranted? If *she* had been abandoned to King, how would she have felt? If she had been forced to live in the shadows, while others traded off the experience? Telling lies, fabricating stories, appearing on TV, preening and posing for the cameras. How Rachel's bitterness must have grown as she saw them all prospering, making their way in life, even as Maxine regurgitated their suffering for profit, lying about her sadness at Rachel's loss, feeding off the corpse of her old 'friend'. She understood the anger, understood the bitterness, but still it chilled her blood, sending fear arrowing through her. They had betrayed Rachel, and all but she were now dead. What possible alternative ending to this story could there be now, while Rachel continued to elude the police, striking at will? Suddenly her power, her reach, seemed inescapable. Perhaps after all it was only a matter of time.

Gripping the sill, Fran stared out into the night. She'd hoped to find comfort in the view, but tonight saw only desolation and danger. There was nothing to do, nowhere to go, no way to distract herself from the sentence that had been passed down to her. So, she stood motionless, staring out into the inky black, wondering if she would ever see another dawn.

Chapter 115

The car purred along the darkened street, keeping pace with its quarry. Joseph Hudson was in the driving seat, DC Bentham alongside him, with DCs Reid and Malik in the back. Conversation had been brisk and plentiful at first, but the quartet were now silent, intent on the task in hand.

'Check the ETA of the tactical unit.'

Bentham did as he was asked, radioing the armed response unit that was on its way to them.

'Three minutes, four tops.'

Joseph nodded, keeping his eyes fixed on the bus in front. It was fairly full, plenty of stops left before its terminus in Eastleigh, and it was hard to make out individuals, but he felt sure Wood was on there, hidden amidst the bodies. How he would get his hands on her was another matter. They would have to stop the bus before Eastleigh, but when? When would the bus start to thin out, reducing the number of targets? Even if they did chance upon her, would they recognize her, so much time having passed? And if they did, would they persuade her to come quietly? Or would it be a fight to the death?

Joseph should have been scared by this prospect, perhaps excited too. But he was neither. The whole experience felt strangely natural, even inevitable, as if everything had been building to this moment. After everything he'd been through, after all the wrong turnings and setbacks, this was his time to shine, his opportunity to bring this troubling case to a conclusion.

'One minute away.'

Joseph nodded, before responding.

'OK, guys, saddle up. We'll let the bus go on one, maybe two stops more and then, if circumstances allow, we'll execute a hard stop. The firearms boys will go in first, then us. We've got a better handle on who Rachel is, what she's capable of, so we need to be on that bus, but I want you all to exercise extreme caution. I don't want any of you getting hurt.'

He couldn't resist picking out Malik in his rear-view mirror. She had been passed fit to resume duty and it was strangely apt that she should be here, in the car with him once more, as they brought this case to a close. Perhaps she would gossip less, bitch less, once he had Wood in cuffs.

'Here we go ...'

Looking in his side mirror, Joseph saw a blacked-out Audi estate overtake him, pulling easily past the bus in front, before gliding back into lane. This was it then. The bus was now boxed in, tactical support was in position, the team was ready. They were minutes from having Rachel Wood in custody.

All he had to do was say the word.

Chapter 116

She closed the door behind her, cutting herself off from the world. She knew she would have to face Charlie soon, perhaps even confide a little of what had passed between her and Joseph, but now she needed to be alone.

Joseph, the team, pretty much the whole station was energized by the unfolding drama in Bitterne. At last, after days of fruitless searching, it appeared they would finally come face to face with this elusive killer. To some extent Helen shared their excitement, hoping against hope that this difficult case would soon be at an end, but part of her was troubled, unable to enjoy the adrenalized atmosphere in the incident room.

Charlie might chastise her for letting Joseph take the lead, but Helen's generosity of spirit was not entirely without strategy. Like the others, she would be more than happy if he brought Wood in, but instinct told her to be cautious of an early resolution. She couldn't have said this to Joseph, nor probably to the team, but the whole thing seemed too easy. Wood had been so cautious when targeting her victims. She used a different phone each time, using it just once to call the unfortunate recipient before disposing of it. Every step of the way Wood had taken great pains to conceal her tracks – with the phones, by assuming a male voice, by basing herself in Northam, perhaps even strong-arming a vulnerable witness into lying for her. She had proved adept at misdirecting the police, happily leading their eye wherever she wanted it to fall. Was it not possible, probable even, that she was doing the same thing now? Yes, the signal was heading in the right direction, towards Eastleigh, but why turn the phone on? There had been no activity on it so far, no attempt to contact Ward, so why risk turning it on when she wasn't using it? Unless she deliberately wanted to lead them into a cul-de-sac? To distract them from her real target?

Pacing her office, the blinds down, Helen's mind went back once more to Osbourne's earlier words. Wood was a master manipulator, someone who knew King well, who knew the public's interest in this ghoulish phantom and was able to harness this knowledge to her own ends, making the world believe a dead man had risen again. Her attention to detail, her knowledge of the hunt for Northam was such that she'd even managed to set up camp in his former stomping ground, with the result that even when they discovered her lair, they still remained in the dark, pursuing a pointless manhunt for a man long dead.

How she had escaped them then defied belief, unless she truly did have the luck of the devil, but then there was much about this case that was inexplicable. How had Tatiana been pressured into lying to the police? Why had Callum Harvey seemingly welcomed his attacker in his house? How was Wood so knowledgeable, seemingly always to be one step ahead of the investigation? Helen's mind rocketed back to their first suspect, the gaunt taser-wielding collector, who knew everything about Daniel King. He would have been a good suspect, but there was obviously no way Callum would have let him into the house and it was clear now that he hadn't set foot in the Moon Lounge. No, whoever targeted Tatiana must have spent time at the club, must have seen her as the weak link and had the means to persuade her to play ball. How she'd have loved to have the illegal immigrant in the interview room now, guiding the young woman to a confession, to the revelation of who had strong-armed her...

And now a thought struck Helen, a thought so shocking, but so persuasive, that she actually stopped in her tracks. Frozen, her mind went back to Sunday morning, to an interview outside the Moon Lounge. And now another memory intruded, the recollection of a tiny anomaly in the evidence, something she'd clocked at the time, but never really processed.

Hurrying back to her desk, Helen pulled open her files, ripping out pieces of paper until she found what she was looking for – the witness statements taken from Harvey's neighbours after his murder. She leafed through them, soon finding what she was looking for. The first statement was made by a Mrs Frances Lang, recording what she glimpsed at 10.08 a.m. The second was by a Mr Dan Crowther, detailing what he'd witnessed at 10.14. Their testimony was similar but had one crucial point of difference, which told Helen all she needed to know.

Shoving the papers back into the file, Helen raced to the door. Throwing it open, she was surprised to find Charlie on the other side. Her old friend looked a little awkward, formal even, as if she had a speech prepared. But Helen didn't give her the chance.

'Come with me.'

Chapter 117

'Everyone stay where you are.'

Joseph had mounted the bus and was facing a sea of startled faces. There were about twenty people seated before him – people who moments earlier had been heading north to Eastleigh, enjoying a thoroughly unremarkable day. That had all changed in an instant. First, an armed response vehicle had come to a sudden halt in front of the bus, forcing it to stop. Then four officers, wearing body armour and wielding semi-automatic weapons, had boarded the vehicle. Now a detective was standing in front of them, warrant card in hand, barking orders. They looked stunned and, more than that, they looked scared.

'My name is DS Hudson, this is a police search operation. Please stay in your seats until you are cleared to leave.'

Already he was marching up the aisle, casting an eye over the faces that presented themselves. An elderly white woman, a young Asian boy, a young black woman. His heart was beating fast – he felt adrenalin, fear, anticipation. On he went, the face of another elderly woman, wrinkled and accusing, passed before him, but he pressed on. Two teenage boys, looking excited by what was unfolding, a pregnant woman who was looking thoroughly pissed off. Joseph strode on, but his conviction was already faltering. He was convinced Wood was on this bus, but

435

scanning forwards he could see that there were only a handful of passengers left. None of whom looked remotely like Wood.

Had he missed someone? Reaching the back of the vehicle, he turned and marched back down the aisle, rechecking his first impressions to ensure he'd not been duped. But to no avail. Wood was not on the bus.

'What do you want to do?'

Bentham was by his side, looking downcast. His junior was whispering, trying to spare their blushes, but Joseph had no such compunction. Turning to the passengers, he roared: 'I want ID on display *now*. I want bags open, pockets turned out ...'

He fixed them all with a furious glare.

'...and nobody gets off until they have been thoroughly searched.'

Chapter 118

They stared intently at the photo, scrutinizing the image in front of them. They were searching for familiar features, hoping to feel the warm glow of recognition, but it was apparent from their faces that they'd found nothing.

'No, I'm sorry... We don't know this person.'

Mrs Walker handed the photo back to Helen. As she did so, her husband slipped his hand into hers, sensing emotion was not far from the surface.

'Nothing to be sorry about, you've been very helpful,' Helen said, comfortingly.

'And you say,' Mr Walker replied, falteringly, 'that this person...' he gestured to the photo of the smiling woman, 'has borrowed Polly's name, her identity...'

'That's right. This picture is of WPC Polly Walker, a serving member of Hampshire Police. When she applied to join the force two years ago now, she gave details which she obviously "borrowed" – she put both your names as her parents, used Polly's date of birth, appropriated details of her schooling—'

'But she looks nothing like her. Polly's got red hair, for God's sake. Don't you do ID checks?'

'Of course we do. Every recruit is rigorously scrutinized, but it is possible for people to cheat the system. If they've managed to obtain someone's passport, for example, doctored it with their own picture...'

Mr Walker turned to his wife, Helen spotting the silent communication.

'Can I ask when you last saw Polly?'

The question seemed to bite, Mrs Walker dropping her eyes to the floor, as her husband sought a response.

'Three years ago, possibly slightly more. Polly's our only child and we love her to bits, in spite of everything. But we were never able to reach her, to control her. She had unreliable friends, unpleasant boyfriends and once the drugs got hold of her...'

'Do you have any idea where she is now?' Charlie enquired gently.

'None at all.'

The pain was evident, in the way his voice shook, the way he gripped his wife's hand.

'Occasionally, we hear tell of her. Friends, acquaintances spotting her. Once in Brighton, once in Portsmouth. They... they try to put a positive spin on things, but we think she's basically living rough, surviving hand to mouth...'

'And is it possible she had her passport on her?' Helen asked.

Another silent exchange between husband and wife.

'When Polly left for the last time... she took everything that might have some value. Jewellery, iPads, laptop, even the television. We only realized later that her passport was missing too. She'd taken it from the filing cabinet without our realizing...'

'And would it be in character for her perhaps to sell it, to fund her drug habit?'

'Totally.'

It was said definitively, powerfully, but still the desolation shone through. It was hard not to feel desperately sorry for the couple who had loved and lost.

'And when was the last sighting of her? The last time she was spotted?'

A long, pregnant pause, then finally Mr Walker answered.

'Nearly a year ago now. Honestly... we've... we've no idea if she's alive or dead.'

And there it was. As Charlie moved to comfort Polly's father, who himself was now crumpling with sadness and grief, Helen dropped her eyes to the photo once more. Having disappeared from the Downs, having faked King's death, Rachel Wood had remained below the radar, but had clearly stayed close, haunting the south coast. Maybe she'd lived on the streets at first, maybe in hostels, perhaps she'd even had addiction problems herself, like her mother before her. Whatever, somehow she had come into contact with Polly Walker. Who knew what state the poor girl was in when she sold Rachel Wood her passport, or had it taken from her, but Helen suspected the latter didn't care. Rachel had what she wanted. The ability to become someone else.

Staring at the smiling face in front of her, Helen berated herself for her stupidity. The taser should have been a clue, all officers issued with one as standard. As should the fact that Callum willingly let his attacker in. Who else would he trust in those circumstances, having just summoned *the police* to help him? And then there was the small matter of Tatiana's testimony, WPC Polly Walker standing next to her as she recited her lies to Helen. It seemed clear now that Rachel/Polly would have threatened the young woman with prison, with deportation, returning later to order her to vanish. A young woman, with no friends, no power, would have had no choice but to comply, scared by this alarming brush with officialdom.

It was the uniform, her role as a bona fide police officer, that had shielded Rachel Wood, allowing her to execute her deadly plan, to keep a close eye on the team's hunt for the killer, whilst hiding in plain sight. That, and her ability to shape change. Justin Lanning had not recognized his old friend, with her short hair, broad shoulders and anonymous driver's uniform. Callum Harvey had probably not recognized her either, until it was too late. And Helen hadn't spotted her either. She had been face to face with her on a number of occasions, but had seen nothing. Her hair had changed, her long tresses replaced by a short back and sides. Her eye colour had altered too, presumably thanks to tinted lenses. She wore no make-up and even the shape of her face had altered, being slightly fuller now, but for all this, the oddly angular features, the thin nose and mouth, looked at with a fresh eye, were unmistakably her. It seemed incredible, but it was true.

Perky, committed WPC Polly Walker, was actually Rachel Wood.

Chapter 119

His emotions were in riot, his mind clouded, his frustration at boiling point. None of this made *any* sense.

The gaggle of passengers had been herded off the bus one by one, under armed guard. They had had to provide ID, before submitting to a search. At first, this had just been bags, coats and pockets, but when no sign of a phone was discovered, the searches had become more thorough, to the consternation of several passengers, whose shock was turning to anger.

Ignoring their recriminations, Joseph had remounted the bus, stalking up and down the aisle, desperately searching for the missing phone. He was sure one of them must have dropped it on the floor, or hidden it down the side of a seat, but however hard he probed, he found nothing. His fingers were black with dirt, but still he pressed on. They had had a bead on Wood, she was here, travelling towards Eastleigh... yet suddenly she'd disappeared in a puff of smoke. What the hell had happened?

'Anything?'

Bentham had boarded the bus now and was hurrying towards him. Hudson shook his head; he'd done an initial sweep of the bus and found nothing.

'Do you want us to check the bottom of the bus, the wheel arches...'

'Why not?' Joseph said absently, descending to his hands and knees.

It wasn't dignified, but Joseph had no choice. So, as Bentham left the bus, Joseph proceeded to crawl along the aisle, checking the undersides of the seats, the hidden recesses, poking and probing with his dirty fingers. There was no way he could return to the station empty-handed. He accepted that they had failed to locate Wood, but to return without any explanation at all was unthinkable. Somehow, he had to make sense of the evening's strange turn of events.

Now he saw it, three rows ahead of him. Scrabbling over the grimy surface, he peered under the seat. And there it was, a mobile phone crudely gaffer-taped to the underside of the seat. Cursing, Joseph just managed to restrain himself from tearing it off, livid at his own stupidity. He'd thought they'd finally got sight of Wood, that they would be able to intercept and bring her in. But as her artful diversion proved, Wood remained resolutely one step ahead of them.

Chapter 120

She ceased pacing, flicking a brief glance at the uniformed officer before returning to her vantage point at the window. The WPC was carrying a tray of food, but Fran had no interest in the sad-looking chicken salad. In truth, she had little appetite for anything tonight.

She heard the officer put the tray down, then return to the door, shutting it gently behind her. Teasing the curtains open once more, Fran peered out into the gloom, looking at the empty suburban street below. But as she did so, she heard something else. The soft creak of a floorboard.

Someone was in the room with her. Out of the corner of her eye, she glimpsed the dark black of the officer's uniform. So, she hadn't left after all, despite appearing to do so, despite closing the door. What was she playing at, loitering there like that? And why had she closed the door? Why the need for privacy?

And now a horrifying thought took hold of Fran. But before she could register it fully, before she could open her mouth to speak, a voice rang out. A voice that was shockingly familiar.

'Hello, Fran.'

It was impossible. Spinning, Fran saw the officer remove her hat, tossing it casually onto the bed as she approached her. Fran stood there, paralyzed. She was sure she must be mistaken

– Rachel didn't have short hair … But it was unmistakably her – the expression, the slender features and those piercing blue eyes.

'Rachel …'

She breathed the word, unable to muster any volume, any conviction. It was as if she'd been punched in the stomach, robbed of speech, energy, even the ability to gather her thoughts. Rachel was dead, killed by that monster Daniel King, yet here she was, alive and well. Where had she been all these years? What had happened to her? And what about King? If Rachel was alive, he must be …

Now she saw the weapon in Rachel's outstretched arm. In a split second, it all became clear. This was no loving reunion, this was her appointment with death.

She opened her mouth to scream, but it was abruptly cut off as the teeth of the taser slammed into her chest. A moment's shock, then suddenly her whole body convulsed, wracked by the most awful pain. Gasping, she stumbled, then fell, colliding heavily with the wooden floorboards. She remained there writhing, insensible to anything but the agony that consumed her, her limbs jerking hopelessly on the floor. Even so, she now became aware of Rachel bending over her, removing the probes from her chest. There was no need of them now, Fran was powerless to resist. Her attacker clearly knew this, crouching down beside and running her finger gently over her cheek, as she said: 'How nice to see you again.'

Chapter 121

'We need to call it in now.'

Helen was tearing down the stairs outside the Walker home. For once, Charlie was matching her stride for stride.

'Contact the house, nobody has access to Fran Ward until I get there.'

Charlie had pulled out her phone and was scrolling through her recent calls.

'How was it even possible, how did she slip through the net?' she murmured, finally finding the number she was looking for.

'She recreated herself,' Helen replied simply. 'She's been living at an address in Portswood for the last two years. The references her landlady and co-tenant gave us were genuine, as were the details she provided about her early life. To all intents and purposes, she *was* Polly Walker...'

Charlie raised the phone to her ear, but still her mind was turning on the day's shocking revelations.

'She must have been planning this thing for two years at least...'

'Which was about the time Maxine Pryce started appearing in the media. Must have been hard to swallow if you were living on the streets, having been sacrificed for your friends...'

They had now reached Helen's bike and she swung her leg

over it. Having secured Fran Ward, the priority was now to find WPC Polly Walker and bring her in. So far, she'd managed to stay hidden, using her privileged access to the investigation, to police records, to the King case, to artfully misdirect their attention. Helen had no doubt it was she who'd called in the anonymous sightings of King, carefully laying the foundations for her plans even as she completed her training. Everyone thought she was a rookie – green, eager but inexperienced. In fact, the opposite was true. She had shown wisdom and experience beyond her years; coldly, callously murdering those who'd betrayed her.

For the first time, however, they had an advantage. Nobody knew where Charlie and Helen had gone, as she'd decided to keep the rest of the team in the dark until she was certain what they were dealing with. Wood presumably still thought her bus diversion would keep them busy and Helen would have to use her ignorance to their advantage.

Firing up the engine, Helen flicked off the brake, her wheels inching forwards. She was about to deliver a parting shot to her old friend, but before she could do so, Charlie turned back to her, the phone still clutched in her hand. She looked ashen, stricken.

'Wood's at the house. They've ... they've just let her in.'

Chapter 122

PC Jack Bullen tore up the stairs, officers Marsh and Thomas just behind him. They had been chatting in the hall, dissecting last night's football, when the call had come through. As DS Brooks had relayed her latest findings, his blood had run cold. The prime suspect, the woman responsible for three brutal murders, was a serving police officer. Someone he knew and liked. Someone he'd just admitted to the house.

Her appearance hadn't raised any concerns, the uniformed officers rotating regularly in a strict shift system. Walker had been pencilled in for tonight, so he'd welcomed her, as he would any other officer. She'd seemed in good spirits, keen to help out, offering to take Ward's dinner up to her. She'd even suggested she might linger for a while, see if she could raise her spirits. He'd even wished her luck in her task, little realizing her true intent.

Reaching the top of the stairs, he grabbed the handle. The first floor, where Fran Ward was based, was secured from the downstairs area by a reinforced door. Bullen pressed down hard on the handle, but as he'd expected, the door refused to budge, secured from within.

Turning to his breathless companions, he ushered them back, making some room for himself. Then, with a sudden burst of speed, he threw himself at the door. His shoulder cannoned into the shiny metal, but made no impact, the bar sending arrows of pain up and down his left flank. Shaken but determined, he hurled himself at the obstacle again. The door frame shook, the staircase vibrated, but still there was no tangible effect on the door itself.

'Here, let me have a go.'

Thomas now took over, barrelling into the door, once, twice, three times, before he too withdrew, clutching his shoulder. PC Marsh took this as his cue, stepping forward and kicking out at the lock with all his might. Again, the door shook, but held. Again he tried, again he was repelled.

'Let's do it together.'

Nodding, Marsh lined himself up next to Bullen.

'On the count of three. One, two, three...'

They surged forward, slamming into the door.

Nothing. They had made an indentation on the surface, but the door had held. Exhausted, hurting, Bullen exhaled an expletive. Delay meant danger. A vicious killer was locked inside with Ward, who even now might be fighting for her life. Time was of the essence; the odds were against them and they were doing everything they could.

But still the obstacle in front of them refused to yield.

Chapter 123

Fran lay on the floor, unable to resist as Rachel slipped the wire around her neck. She wanted to lash out, to grab her friend by the hair, to scratch her eyes out, but her limbs felt heavy and useless, her body quaking from the shock of the taser. She was prone, defenceless, utterly at the mercy of her attacker.

'Can you imagine what it's like,' Rachel said quietly, completing the loop of the wire, 'to *know* you're going to die?'

It was said not with relish, but with a grim bitterness. As if anger still burned inside her. Fran nodded to indicate her understanding, but her actions were awkward and erratic.

'No, you don't. You don't have the faintest idea. I looked into that man's eyes, that *monster's* eyes, and I knew that he was going to kill me. That I was going to die, naked and alone, on that hideous bedstead.'

Fran shut her eyes, tears seeping from them. This was the scenario she'd feared, the scenario she'd often imagined. Rachel dragged into that awful back room, abused, tortured, then killed…

'What's more, he was going to enjoy doing it. Do you remember what he used to say to us? "My face is going to be—'

' "—the … the last th-thing you see." '

Fran just managed to get the words out. Her tongue felt fat

and unwieldy, like it was fighting her. She knew she had to get control of it, if she was to have a hope of saving herself. She needed to talk to Rachel, reason with her, beg for mercy.

'You *do* remember...' Rachel cooed, brightening. 'He said it to me that night. I can still feel his hot breath on my face as he said it. Except it wasn't *me* that died that night.'

To Fran's surprise, a smile stole across her attacker's face. Rachel's experiences had cost her – up close she looked older than her years – yet Fran could see pride there. A supreme confidence too, as if everything was proceeding exactly as Rachel had foreseen. Her attacker seemed completely unconcerned by the commotion on the stairs – the shouting, the hammering on the door – calmly going about her business, as if nobody could touch her.

'He thought I was at his mercy, that he could do what he wanted with me,' she continued, the smile fading now. 'But there was a nail loose on the bedstead. And while he beat me, whilst he tried to *break* me, I used it to loosen my bonds and then, when he came in for the kill...'

Her eyes seemed to glaze over, lost in the memory.

'...I drove that dirty nail right through his eye.'

Fran shivered violently, repelled by the image. She could see the nail penetrating King's skull, the blood spurting onto young Rachel.

'He wasn't expecting *that*,' Rachel laughed. 'He made a right mess of the place, banging into stuff, knocking things over...'

'It... it must have be-been aw-wful...'

But Rachel appeared not to hear her.

'I wasn't sure what I was going to do... whether I'd have to finish him off or... but then his legs went. That was when he knocked over the paraffin lamp and after that I knew *exactly* what I had to do. I've never run so fast in my life...'

Coming to, Rachel returned her attention to Fran. Grasping the ends of the wire, she prepared to tighten the noose.

'I got out, Fran. I survived that fire. But I never forgot that feeling... of helplessness. Knowing that I was going to die, that I only had *minutes* left on earth.'

'Please, Rachel...'

'That's what I want you to feel, Fran. It's what I wanted *all* of you to feel.'

'I... I... don't deser... deserve thi—'

'Don't fight it, Fran. This is the way it was *meant* to be.'

Her attacker loomed over her, looking directly at her, righteous anger igniting her cold, blue eyes.

'Time's up.'

Chapter 124

Helen tore along the road, the wind battering her body. Behind her she could hear the sirens, a dozen patrol cars descending on Eastleigh. Normally she would have waited for them, arriving with the cavalry in tow, but there was no question of that now. Wood was in the house and every second counted.

Helen wrenched back the throttle, roaring along the tarmac, praying she wouldn't be too late. They had been playing cat and mouse with this killer for days, slowly piecing together her horrific design, but now it all came down to this. A race against time to save Fran Ward's life.

All the schoolchildren had suffered. And all had stains on their conscience. But none had felt their guilt more keenly than Fran. She had no animus against Rachel, had felt sorry for her, in fact, trying to befriend her. And when it came to it, lost in that awful fog with King in hot pursuit, she had tried to save Rachel. She'd *wanted* to save her, until fear had mastered her. It wasn't a nice thing to, it wasn't the *right* thing to do, but she didn't deserve to pay for her actions with her life. That, however, was exactly what Rachel Wood intended – to terrify and execute the girl she felt had betrayed her.

It was late now and the roads were clear. Helen took full advantage of this, roaring north past the exit for Southampton

Airport. She could see the signs for Eastleigh now, directing her towards the train station and leisure centre, but she wasn't interested in these local landmarks. The safe house was hidden amidst the rows of terraced properties in Eastleigh's suburban heart – it was there that this final battle would take place.

She was speeding along the main road, the railway lines just visible now to her right, but she changed direction, upping her speed as she leaned into a sharp left turn, swinging off the main drag and onto Derby Road. This too was clear, so she cut along it, before once more diverting, this time spinning off to the right. She barely braked, her wheels squealing in protest at the sudden change in direction, skidding across the gravelled road, sending tiny stones spinning up into the air. Grantham Green, a tiny communal garden, lay in front of her, empty now except for an amorous couple on one of the benches. For the second time in as many days, Helen found herself roaring through one of Southampton's open spaces, skirting the lovers, then the children's playground, before emerging on the other side.

Killing her speed, she descended the pavement, checking for speeding cars. But luck was on her side and she sped on, racing into Wilmer Road. This quiet residential street was usually empty, the definition of sleepy suburbia, but tonight something was up. Helen could see a small knot of people, hovering on the pavement in dressing gowns and coats, looking discomfited and concerned.

Helen roared up to them, fearful of what she might discover. They parted as she approached, looking at her with undisguised curiosity, before turning their attention back to the house. On the face of it, there was nothing unusual about the property. It was a neat, unremarkable terraced house. Nor was there anything to see, no struggle, no arrests. But the noise from inside was arresting – the front door was open and hammering and shouting could be heard from within.

PC James Marsh rushed to meet her. Helen had hoped – prayed – that they would be able to save Fran, that they would be in time, but his face told her the news was bad.

'She's locked the access door. We've tried everything, but we can't break it down…'

Anxiety spiked through Helen as she shot a look at the first-floor window. What was going on in there? What was Wood doing to her? The curtains were drawn and it was impossible to see, the horror within shrouded from view.

'One of the patrol cars is bringing a barrel charge. Once they're here, we should be able to get in, but they'll be another five, ten minutes at least…'

As he spoke, Helen's hopes turned to dust. There was no way in, no way to get to Fran Ward. They had tried their best, but they were too late.

Chapter 125

The wire was tight around her neck, digging into her skin. Fran was fighting to breathe, gasping for air, her attacker delighting in slowly, deliberately, pulling the noose taut.

'Please...'

It was barely audible, a faint, pathetic appeal to a pitiless killer. Fran's vision was starting to cloud now, it felt like her windpipe would crack at any minute, and she was still powerless to lift her arms. She knew there would be no mercy here, no reprieve, but she had to try.

'Rachel...'

Her attacker seemed not to register her own name, lost in the moment, as she pulled the wire still tighter. Whatever had remained of the young, troubled girl that Fran knew was long gone, Rachel showing no emotion now as she prepared to take her life. She had become the monster she once feared.

'I... wanted to save you...' Fran gasped. 'Please believe m—'

But the word died on her lips, as Rachel tugged the wire harder, cutting off her air supply. Panic seized Fran – she couldn't *breathe*, couldn't drag any oxygen into her lungs. Her legs were jerking back and forth, some feeling coming back into them as adrenalin and fear flooded her system. But her attacker seemed not to care, kneeling on her arms as she gave the wire one, final tug.

'No, you didn't,' she whispered, resting her nose on Fran's. 'You abandoned me. And now you must *pay*.'

Chapter 126

'What do you want to do?'

Helen's gaze was fixed on the first-floor window, barely hearing the anxious chirping of PC Marsh next to her.

'We have to do something, ma'am.'

His voice was shaking, paralysed by anxiety and fear, but Helen ignored him, desperately searching for a means of reaching Fran. The first-floor window was too high to access by standing on the bins and there was no drainpipe nearby to climb. If they could get a ladder, they might be able to reach the sill, but that would take time to source and even then it would a perilous manoeuvre, involving smashing the window while perched on the narrow ledge. Easy for Wood to fight back, to push the intruder down onto the concrete below.

PCs Thomas and Bullen now emerged from the house, exhausted and defeated. They hastened towards her, but had no good news to share.

'We've tried everything, but we can't shift it.'

Helen's eyes flicked to the house, to the stairs leading up to the reinforced door.

'Until we get the barrel charge, something that can give us a bit more bite …'

And suddenly Helen knew exactly what to do.

'Stand aside.'

She revved the throttle and the two men jumped out her way. She pulled it back, once, twice, three times, the engine roaring as the wheels spun furiously on the pavement. Then without warning, Helen kicked off the brake. The bike sprang forward, through the open doorway. Helen hit the bottom stair hard and momentarily the bike left the ground, the wheels rotating crazily in the air, before they bit the carpet once more, propelling her upwards. If she hesitated now, if she wasn't fully committed to this madness, she would fail. The bike roared forwards, the locked door rushing towards her. Closing her eyes, Helen gripped the handlebars and braced herself for the moment of impact.

Chapter 127

She jerked her head up, shocked by the violent crash outside. Thus far, her fellow officers' attempts to reach her had seemed distant, strangely muted, as if their hollering and banging were taking place in another world. But there could be no mistaking *that* sound – someone had just smashed the reinforced door off its hinges.

Fear and uncertainty gripped Rachel Wood. Everything had gone to plan over the last few days – *everything* – and she was so close to completing her mission, snuffing out those who'd sentenced her to death. But now all that was in jeopardy.

Returning her attention to Fran, she tugged on the wire with all her might. Fran's face was puce, her eyes bulging. Death could only be seconds away, so Rachel redoubled her efforts, determined to finish the job. But now she became aware of something else. A hand was tugging at her hair, pulling her back. Puzzled, she darted a look in that direction, to discover that the feeling in Fran's limbs had returned. She was starting to fight back.

Brushing it off, she tugged once more at the wire, but she had loosed her grip for a moment and Fran twisted away from her. Rachel grabbed her victim by the hair, forcing her to face her once more, but now she heard movement outside. There had been a strange roaring outside – something loud and mechanical – but that had been stilled now – replaced by footsteps, hastening towards her.

Now Rachel didn't hesitate, releasing her grip on the wire and running. She had no intention of being caught, of spending the rest of her life festering in a cell; she had come too far, done too much to end her days that way. Haring across the room, she flew through the door – just in time to see Helen Grace hurrying towards her. She froze for a moment, taking in the helmeted figure who appeared to be limping slightly, then turned and fled, swinging round the banister and sprinting up the stairs to the top floor.

Bursting through the door, she found herself in a modest loft conversion. There were no more stairs, no fire escape, but there was a pair of French windows leading onto a small balcony. Grace was scrambling up the stairs behind her, so racing forward, Rachel unlocked the doors and flung them open, hurrying outside.

Stumbling out onto the balcony, she looked around. There was no way she could climb down and it would be suicide to jump, which left only one option. Grace was only a few feet from her now, so Rachel didn't hesitate, climbing over the railing onto the ledge beyond. Even as she did so, her pursuer spilled out of the doors onto the balcony, so now Rachel jumped, bridging the small gap between the houses and landing on the tiled roof opposite. Immediately, she started skidding downwards, but reaching out a hand she grabbed hold of the metal flashing. Her body jerked to a halt, then slowly, carefully, she hauled herself upwards, eventually cresting the apex of the roof.

Here there was a thin line of flat tiles decorating the ridge, forming a perilously narrow pathway. Scrambling onto her feet, Wood shot a look behind her. Grace was preparing to jump, so turning, she hurried along the ridge. It was twenty centimetres wide and extremely awkward to traverse – the tiles were uneven and slick with the evening dew – but with police cars screeching to a halt below, she had no choice but to risk it.

It was do or die.

Chapter 128

Joseph skidded to a halt, vaulting off his bike. He had not been summoned directly, but as soon as he'd heard the call, he had raced towards Eastleigh. It was clear that the phone on the bus had been a deliberate diversion, a trap they had walked into, allowing Wood a free run at her final victim. If there was a way he could atone for this error, if he could help bring this sorry saga to an end, then he had to seize it. For him, for his career, the next few minutes might be crucial.

He was already halfway down the path, his baton extended, his body tensed and ready for action. But as he neared the anonymous safe house, a cry nearby made him stop. One of the attending PCs was pointing at the roof, shouting frantically. Puzzled, Joseph slid to a halt, angling his gaze upwards – just in time to see Helen launch herself into the air, landing with a bang on the roof of the neighbouring house.

'What the fuck...?'

It was a crazy thing to do. Even now, the desperate figure was sliding down the slippery tiles on the front of the house. In a second, she would plunge off the roof, plummeting two storeys to the ground below. Helen had a reputation for bravery, for recklessness, but even by her standards, this was madness.

His heart was in his mouth, watching her descent with

anguish, but then suddenly, mercifully, her foot caught on the guttering and she managed to still her progress. Now she was on the move again, scrambling back up the tiles to the apex of the roof. And now he saw why – just ahead of her, making her way carefully, gingerly forwards, was Rachel Wood.

It was a bizarre sight – a uniformed police officer being pursued by a female biker – but nothing in this case had been ordinary or straightforward. Each new development, each new twist in the investigation, had brought fresh problems and disappointments. Joseph had hoped he might be in at the death, able to cull something from the wreckage of this investigation, some shred of triumph, but it was now clear he had arrived too late. There was nothing he could do but shadow Helen, as he always seemed to do, hoping against hope for a positive outcome.

Rachel Wood's fate was now in Helen's hands.

Chapter 129

Helen grasped the edge of the tile, pulling herself upwards. As she did so, her fingers slid off the slick surface and for a moment she felt her body sliding downwards again, but throwing out her other hand, she managed to regain her grip, hauling herself onto the top of the roof.

Turning, she saw Wood nearing the edge of the roof. This house was connected to its neighbour, so the fugitive hurried on, wobbling momentarily before righting herself. Regaining her balance, Helen set off in pursuit. She was already short of breath, her ribs aching from where her Kawasaki had cannoned into her on impact, and she knew she had damaged her right knee. She could run – *just* – but it was a lumbering, fast limp, ungainly if effective. Nevertheless, she had no choice but to carry on. Wood was intent on escaping capture, hoping perhaps to vanish as effortlessly as she had before, but there was no way Helen could allow that.

She didn't dare look down, couldn't allow herself to be distracted by the circus below. If she was to come out of this alive, if she was to have a chance of bringing Wood in, she couldn't let her concentration waver for a second. The path she was walking along was narrow, no more than a few inches wide, so she had to tuck one foot carefully in front of the other, keeping her arms spread to maintain her balance. It was a cool night, slippery dew starting to form on the tiles, and the wind was picking up. Occasionally, a strong blast would whip over Helen, rocking her off balance, threatening disaster. But on she went, maintaining her momentum as she hopped onto the neighbouring property.

She could see Wood up ahead, moving remorselessly forward. She seemed to be utterly fearless, careless of the danger, determined to escape. She moved effortlessly over the tiles, keeping her pace steady, her arms outstretched, as if she was riding the wind. Helen marvelled at her confidence, her poise, wondering if she had a ghost of a chance of catching her. Wood seemed oddly invulnerable, as if the usual dangers, the laws of physics, did not apply. She seemed determined to escape, whatever obstacles lay in her path.

Helen upped her speed – she daren't risk losing her – but as she did so, she lost her footing again. Her right foot slid sideways and she tumbled with it, pitching head first down the roof. Screaming, she flung out an arm, and somehow she found traction, grabbing hold of an old TV aerial attached to the nearby chimney. For a moment, she hung in the air, suspended from the groaning metal pole by one hand, her legs kicking frantically. She could hear shouts below, but cut them out, focusing on the task in hand. Now her feet found the tiles once more and she scrabbled gratefully back up the roof.

Breathless, her heart pounding, she turned back towards Wood. She'd expected to see the fugitive in the middle distance, free and clear, but actually she was just thirty feet ahead, having inexplicably come to a halt. Helen seized the initiative, clearing the small gap to the neighbouring house and hurrying along the narrow ridge towards her. She was eating up the distance between them and, as she neared her quarry, she saw the reason for the delay.

The gap between the house they were on and the neighbouring property was unusually large, a wide side-access path dividing the properties. It couldn't easily be bridged and in normal circumstances you would never attempt a jump. Wood clearly felt she had no choice and, hearing Helen coming up fast behind her, let fly.

Such was the power in her leap that for a moment Helen thought she would cross the gap easily, but as Wood neared the neighbouring house, she seemed to lose momentum, plummeting downwards. Helen cried out, but suddenly Wood's descent was arrested, the desperate fugitive clinging to the guttering at the edge of the roof. She had saved herself and even now was scrambling back up to safety.

Taking a few steps back, Helen prepared to jump. She allowed Wood to get clear, then found herself sprinting towards the edge. Success depended on fine judgement and just as Helen had almost run off the roof, she pushed down hard with her front foot. Now she was sailing through the air, the roof hastening towards her. She had judged it better than Wood, but still landed on her knees, skidding along the narrow ledge. Pain flared through her, the skin ripped off, but Helen was already struggling to her feet, powering on.

Wood was twenty yards ahead of her, tiring perhaps, but doggedly determined. On she went, lumbering from house to house, straining every sinew to stay ahead. Helen matched her, stride for stride, finally feeling she had a chance in this race, a slim hope of bringing this pitiless killer in. Slowly, inexorably, the gap between them was narrowing.

Without warning, Wood ground to a halt once more. They were on the last house in the row now and even from her limited vantage point Helen could see that patrol cars and a ring of officers were gathered below. Even if Wood could descend to ground level, there would be no escape. She had run out of road.

Wood clearly sensed this, turning now to face her pursuer. Helen had dropped her pace, now walking slowly and carefully towards the suspect. Wood was scanning about her, looking for some means of escape, but it was clear that this was pointless. The chase had come down to this, the two women facing off against each other on top of a slippery roof.

'That's enough, Rachel. It's time to end this.'

To her surprise, her adversary smiled.

'I'll say when it's time.'

'You've nowhere to go. So let's head down together—'

'So you can lock me up? Throw away the key?'

'So we can *talk*.'

Wood snorted with derision.

'Sorry, *ma'am*, I'm not going to be locked up like an animal, put on show for everyone. I won't be a victim again.'

'It's not like that, I know what you've been through, which is why I—'

'I'm not *that* person any more,' Wood spat back. 'I'll never be that person. This is me now.'

A blast of icy wind roared over them, unbalancing Wood temporarily. This seemed to decide her and she took a step towards Helen.

'Perhaps you're right, Helen. Perhaps this is the end of the road. For both of us.'

She took another step towards Helen, then another, her pace rising all the time.

'Rachel, listen to me. I know you've suffered, I know what you've been through, but it doesn't have to be like this.'

Wood was smiling, Helen's words bouncing off as she started to run.

'I don't mean you any harm. I want to *help* you.'

But it was too late. Wood had made up her mind and was now sprinting towards her. There was nothing that Helen could do now but brace herself for the impact.

Chapter 130

Charlie craned her neck backwards, staring at the figures above.

She'd tried to keep up with Helen as they raced towards Eastleigh, but it had proved a hopeless task. She'd lost her before they'd even passed Southampton Airport, arriving at the safe house far too late to be of any assistance. By the time she'd scrambled out of the pool car, Helen was already inside, having battered the door into submission, fearlessly pursuing their prime suspect.

In spite of her condition, in spite of the danger, Charlie had been determined to join her, to offer what assistance she could. But her progress was halting and slow – her belly was suddenly cramping ominously – and even as she'd struggled towards the house, two figures had appeared above her, scrambling across the roofs. Charlie was stunned, riven with fear, unable to do anything but follow the frenetic chase from a distance. On more than one occasion, Charlie had cried out, first as Helen slid down the roof, then as Wood misjudged the gap, nearly plummeting to her death. And she watched on in horror now as the fugitive charged directly at Helen, determined to bring her down.

Charlie was convinced that Helen would do something, that she'd have a trick up her sleeve. But in truth, Helen had nowhere to go, no way of avoiding the onrushing Wood. And now Charlie saw the impact, Wood flinging herself forwards and wrapping both arms around Helen, knocking her clean off her feet. The impact carried both women forward and now they were tumbling downwards, sliding quickly over the tiles. It all happened so fast that Charlie barely had time to cry out, the sound dying in her throat as she watched the pair fly from the roof, plummeting through the air before hitting the ground with a sickening crunch.

Chapter 131

She stared up at the sky, her eyes glassy and still. Her face, that moments before had been rosy, was already leaching colour, the pallor of death claiming her. She had fought, fought to survive, but the battle was over, the final breath escaping from her now, as she lay on cold, hard ground.

Helen had seen people die before, but seldom at such close range. She was lying directly on top of her adversary, nose to nose, and almost saw Wood's soul escape as the light died in her eyes. In spite of everything, Helen wanted to capture her essence before it could depart, breathing life back into this troubled young woman. But there was little chance of that – even if Wood could have been saved, Helen was in no condition to help her.

She had been convinced that this was the end. Wood had smashed into her, then suddenly they were falling, spinning wickedly around, plunging towards the earth. Then it was over, Wood crashing into the ground, still clutching Helen to her breast. The impact was awful, shocking, barrelling through Helen, even as a long, slow groan escaped the killer's lips, but the protection Wood provided must have saved her. She was alive.

Her whole body was reacting, shaking violently. Her vision was swimming, but even so she could make out a widening pool of blood, crowning the back of the young woman's head. For a moment, Wood's face swam into focus and Helen saw a look of surprise, as if she'd never expected her scheme to end this way. But that was all Helen would be allowed to make out – hands were now grasping her, turning her over. She slumped onto her back, next to the prone figure, staring up at the sky, then into Charlie's anxious face as it appeared above her.

'Helen? Helen, can you hear me?'

Helen wanted to nod, but found she couldn't, her whole body starting to seize up. So instead she smiled, provoking tears of relief from her friend.

'Jesus, Helen … Why do you do this to me?'

Charlie was laughing through tears, clutching her belly. Helen wanted to answer her, to reassure her, but had no breath to do so, so she squeezed Charlie's hand a little tighter instead. Even if she *had* been able to speak, what would she have said? She didn't know why she'd risked her life to bring Wood in, why she constantly put herself on the line. All she did know was that she felt compelled to do so and was glad of it. She had saved Fran Ward's life and, though Rachel Wood had died in the process, this awful chapter in their lives was now drawing to a close.

'It's over …'

The words slipped from her, barely audible. Charlie had turned away, attempting to master her emotions, and Helen wanted to reassure her old friend, to let her know that despite appearances, everything would be OK.

'We did it …'

Now Charlie did turn back to her. Helen was still clutching her hand and hoped to see relief, even happiness in her expression. But to her surprise she saw concern, even fear. It took Helen a moment to compute what was going on – why was

Charlie so anxious? – but then she spotted her hand clamped to her bump. And even before she spoke, Helen knew what Charlie was going to say.

'I think the baby's coming.'

Day Six

Chapter 132

'How long is this going to take?'

Helen was lying on the hospital bed, the very image of frustration.

'Nearly done. Now, if you could just follow my pen with your eyes...'

Helen submitted, watching the repetitive motion, the pendulum-like back and forth of the pen, praying it would be over quickly. She'd been at the hospital for several hours now and despite her protestations that she was fine, they refused to discharge her. Dawn was breaking – Helen could see the dirty pink glow of the sun through the blinds – but there was no let-up, Helen enduring a battery of tests to ensure that there were no broken bones, no concussion, no internal bleeding. Helen was convinced there was no need – she was battered and bruised, but unharmed – but she had no power here.

'Right then, last one...'

The doctor put down his pen, taking Helen's hand in his. Seeking out a pulse, he consulted the watch pinned to his coat, silently counting as he pressed his fingers into her flesh. The room was quiet, even the sounds outside the room strangely muted now, and as Helen's eyes settled on the doctor's watch, to the second hand ticking remorselessly around, her thoughts were drawn back to the extraordinary events of the last few days.

Even by Helen's standards, it had been a bizarre and disturbing case. After eight long years, Rachel Wood's desire for revenge burned so fiercely that she'd been determined to put the fear of God into her former schoolfriends, giving them advance warning of their impending death, before delivering the coup de grâce. It was hideous, it was cruel, but there was a perverse logic to it, given the callousness of their betrayal and her awful experiences at the hands of Daniel King.

His motivation was harder to discern. Previously, Helen had assumed that King was a sadist, a twisted loner whose grip on reality had been irreparably fractured by alcohol and drugs. But now she had the full picture of his lonely, troubled life, she wondered whether there might have been something else at play. King had watched his mother die, her body slowly destroyed by motor neurone disease, and he knew the same fate awaited him. His diagnosis must have felt like a death sentence, given what he'd already witnessed, so was it possible that he gained some relief in terrorizing others, in making *them* feel death's cold hand? Was this, perversely, the only time he felt truly *alive*?

It was an intriguing possibility, one Helen instinctively felt made sense, but they would never know for sure. According to Fran Ward, Wood had confessed to killing King in that grim basement. King, however, had taken his secrets to the grave. All they could do now was speculate – no doubt many books would be written on the subject of Daniel King and Rachel Wood in the years to come.

Helen looked up to find the doctor smiling at her.

'Sorry, did you say something?' Helen asked, snapping out of it.

'I said that, in spite of my better judgement, I'm going to discharge you.'

Helen was already on the move, but Dr Macdonald laid a gentle, restraining hand on her arm.

'But I want you signed off for *at least* a week. No work of any kind and definitely no heroics. OK?'

Helen happily consented, sliding off the bed and signing her discharge forms. She looked a mess, wrapped in an ill-fitting hospital gown, but she didn't care, grabbing a nearby robe and throwing it on as she hurried to the door. Over her shoulder, she thanked the doctor for his care, but she wasn't going to linger.

There was somewhere she needed to be.

Chapter 133

It took Helen ten minutes to find the maternity unit – the hospital was a perfect maze – and longer still to gain access. Official visiting time hadn't started yet and as Helen wasn't a relative, the midwives were reluctant to admit her. Helen was more touched than she could say when Steve took charge of the situation, insisting that Helen *was* family and should be admitted without delay.

'How are you feeling?'

'Fighting fit,' Helen lied, noting Steve's tactful decision to ignore her ungainly limp. 'How are *you*?'

To Helen's delight, Steve broke into a beaming grin.

'Top of the world. She's...'

He hesitated, as if lost for words, then gestured towards the room.

'Well, why don't you see for yourself?'

Smiling, Helen tentatively rounded the door, to find Charlie sitting up in bed, cradling her newborn. Instantly, tears pricked Helen's eyes – Charlie was the closest thing she had to a real family and she was delighted to see that mother and baby were safe and well.

'You look like I feel,' Charlie joked wearily as Helen approached her bedside. 'Are you sure you should be up and about?'

'Probably not, but I couldn't resist.'

Responding to the cue, Charlie shifted her position, affording Helen a glimpse of the pink, puckered face of her sleeping infant. Helen took in the baby's soft features, the tiny little fingers poking out of the top of blanket, and once more felt emotion flood her. The simple beauty of an innocent new life was breathtaking to behold.

'We've decided to name her Orla. After Steve's grandmother.'

'Orla,' Helen repeated softly, running a finger gently over her little cheek.

'Can't fight that Irish heritage ...'

It was said with a smile and Helen responded. It was a huge relief to her that both mother and baby had come through fine, given the inauspicious, premature start of Charlie's labour. And after the awful events of the last few days, it was a powerful reminder to her that there were good things in the world, that some stories do have a happy ending.

'How long have I got?' Helen asked, shooting a look at the clock.

'There's about an hour or so before they're going to weigh her.'

Even as she spoke, Charlie shifted once more, gesturing to Helen to take the baby.

'Go on, lighten my load.'

Helen obliged, carefully extracting Orla from her grasp and cradling her in her arms. The sensation, the warm bundle pressed against her chest, was exhilarating. Suddenly Helen was filled with energy, with strength, with optimism. Things had been so tough of late, so dark, but now finally she could be at peace. Only last night she had been involved in a fight to the death, but already that bitter struggle was receding from her mind, replaced by something better, something *good*. This was Helen's time now – one perfect hour which she could spend with this beautiful baby.

And she intended to enjoy it to the full.

Chapter 134

Helen meandered back through the hospital corridors in a contented daze. She was exhausted, she was in pain, but she was happy. She would treasure the memories of Orla's arrival and hoped to experience many more such times over the years. Somewhat to Helen's surprise, Charlie had asked her to be godmother again, an honour she didn't feel she deserved, given her fleeting appearances in Jessica's life thus far.

Walking swiftly through the hospital, Helen vowed to do better. Whatever life threw at her, she was determined to be a more active presence from now on. She would be signed off work for at least a week, time enough to spoil Jessica and Orla and help Charlie and Steve get to grips with their enlarged family. It would be a great opportunity to get to know Jessie better – the years seemed to be racing past – the fact that she was already at school beggared belief – and if Helen wasn't careful, the young girl would be a young woman before she knew it.

Determined not to delay, Helen hurried back to her ward, intent on gathering her clothes, phone and keys. She would head home, grab some sleep, then re-engage with the world, re-engage with *life*.

Grabbing the door handle, she pushed inside. Such was her momentum that she almost barrelled into a tall figure standing by the bed, clutching a bouquet of flowers. Pulling up just in time, she was surprised to see Joseph Hudson standing in front of her.

'They said I'd find you here.'

Helen nodded, but said nothing, wrong-footed by his sudden appearance.

'I thought that perhaps you'd done a bunk.'

'I went to see Charlie,' Helen muttered, feeling uneasy, caught off guard.

She pulled her robe around her, trying to hide her flimsy hospital gown, but Joseph seemed not to notice her discomfort.

'Yes, she's next on my list. Talking of which, the team wanted you to have these.'

He offered her the flowers. Helen took them mechanically, but didn't look at them.

'They'll be pleased to hear you're up and about.'

'I'm fine, really ...'

'Of course, you are. So when can we expect you back at base? Are you going to take a well-earned break or is it straight back to the coal face?'

She stared at him, lost for words. His cheerfulness and energy should have been heartening, yet it seemed totally misplaced, wrong even, given everything that had passed between them. It was as if he felt a confident smile could somehow wipe out the lies, the arguments, the fractures.

'I haven't decided yet, not really, but ...' Helen hesitated, uncertain how frank to be, 'but I'm not sure this is going to work, Joseph.'

He continued to smile at her, but his eyes narrowed.

'Us being part of the same team, after everything that's happened.'

'What are you saying, Helen?'

His tone was calm. Helen had the strong feeling he was being deliberately obtuse.

'Charlie will be on maternity leave now and, well, I'm not sure having you as my deputy is a great idea, for either of us.'

Joseph didn't respond, regarding her curiously. Once more Helen paused, but... what was the point of beating about the bush?

'I think it would probably be best for everyone if we shook hands and moved on. I'm happy to help you find a new position, something fitting your rank and experience. I know it's not what you wanted, or what *I* wanted for that matter, but the way things are—'

'No.'

One word, shot at her with sufficient venom to bring her up short.

'That's not how it's going to be. I'm sure you'd like it that way – sweep me under the carpet and move on – but that's not going to happen. I have worked *too* hard to get this position, sacrificed *too* much, to have it stolen from me.'

He spat the words out, fury in his eyes. Even as she did so, he took a step forwards, his chest pressing into the flowers that were still clutched to hers. Instinctively, Helen took a step back, then another, but Joseph kept coming, boxing her into a corner. For a moment, Helen thought he might grab her, strike her even, and she braced herself for the attack. But instead he moved in close, pushing his face into hers.

'If you want to move on, that's fine,' he rasped, 'but know this. I am not going *anywhere*.'

He held her gaze, challenging her to respond, before slowly disengaging, walking around her towards the doorway. Seconds later, the door slammed shut, leaving Helen alone.

And there she remained, a solitary figure in the quiet, sunlit room, the bouquet of flowers still clutched to her thumping heart.

Credits

M.J. Arlidge and Orion Fiction would like to thank everyone at Orion who worked on the publication of *All Fall Down* in the UK.

Editorial
Emad Akhtar
Lucy Frederick

Copy editor
Liz Hatherell

Proof reader
Clare Wallis

Audio
Paul Stark
Amber Bates

Contracts
Anne Goddard
Paul Bulos
Jake Alderson

Design
Debbie Holmes

Joanna Ridley
Nick May

Editorial Management
Charlie Panayiotou
Jane Hughes
Alice Davis

Finance
Jasdip Nandra
Afeera Ahmed
Elizabeth Beaumont
Sue Baker

Marketing
Tom Noble

Publicity
Leanne Oliver

Production
Ruth Sharvell

Sales
Jen Wilson
Esther Waters
Victoria Laws
Rachael Hum
Ellie Kyrke-Smith
Frances Doyle
Georgina Cutler

Operations
Jo Jacobs
Sharon Willis
Lisa Pryde
Lucy Brem

*Read on for an exclusive
sneak peek at the new
D. I. Helen Grace thriller*

TRUTH OR DARE

There is everything to play for…

Day One

Chapter 1

He didn't want to move, but he knew he had to. He had come too far, risked too much, to back out now. Steeling himself, he crept forwards, his eyes scanning the gloomy yard. If there was any movement, any possibility of being detected, then he would turn and run without a second thought. But there was nothing, no sign of life at all, so he pressed on.

The portacabin lay directly in front of him, lonely and isolated in the darkness. A dull glow crept from beneath the blinds, the sole indication that it was inhabited. Anyone stumbling upon this yard might easily have missed the anomaly – this was a place where things came to rot and die, a dumping ground for abandoned cars and household junk. Curiosity was not encouraged, the entrance gates were chained and, though he had snapped the padlock easily, he was sure no-one else had been tempted to try. You wouldn't set foot in this place unless you had to, nor would you assume that a treasure trove of secrets lay just beyond the stained door of the portacabin.

The ground was littered with rusting exhaust pipes, empty packing cases and abandoned white goods. It would be easy to kick something amidst the darkness, alerting his victim, so he moved forward carefully, teasing his way through the detritus. In the distance, a siren wailed, startling a bird who took flight, squawking loudly, but he ignored it, grimly focused on the task at hand.

Reaching the portacabin, he paused, pressing himself up against its filthy carapace, craning around to peer through the window. The glass was grimy, coated in bird mess and dirt, so his view was blurred, yet he could still make out the figure inside. Overweight, sprawling, a bottle of Jack Daniel's clamped in his hand, he could see the significant form of Declan McManus, slumbering on a tired sofa. The man seemed totally out of it, utterly at peace with the world, which seemed profoundly odd given the grave danger he was in. Surely he wouldn't have been so relaxed had he known that his hiding place had been discovered, that someone *else* knew his secret?

He counted silently to ten, wanting to be *sure* that McManus was asleep, then quietly stepped up to the door. Still there was no sound within, so reaching out a gloved hand, he turned the handle. His heart was thumping, his hand shaking, as he teased it downwards. This was the point of maximum risk, when his approach was most likely to be detected, but the handle slid down easily. Cautiously, he eased the door open, preparing to cross the threshold. As he did so, however, the aged hinge started to protest, screaming out in alarm. Horrified, the intruder froze, uncertain what to do, then acting on instinct, he yanked the door fully open. The hinge squeaked briefly, then was silent once more. Stepping inside, he cast an anxious eye towards the sleeping man, but McManus hadn't stirred, the near empty bottle of bourbon having done its work.

He closed the door, the sounds of the night suddenly dying away. Now it was just the two of them, cocooned inside this sad space. It was even more unpleasant and odorous than he'd anticipated, a fitting backdrop for the grubby individual in front of him. This was where McManus hid his spoils, conducted his business, brought young girls. He shuddered to think what had occurred within these four walls, but he was not here to dwell on past crimes, he was here to do a job. To do what was *necessary*. Many lives had been blighted by this man, but perhaps after tonight he would do no more harm.

Stepping forward, he looked down at the comatose figure. Part of him still expected McManus to rear up, wrapping his sweaty palms around his neck... but he lay still, undisturbed and unsuspecting. There was nothing stopping him, no imminent danger, no chance of detection. This was it.

It was time to kill.

Chapter 2

The pale face stared up at her, tranquil but lifeless. Detective Inspector Helen Grace had encountered many bodies in Jim Grieves' mortuary, but this one brought a lump to her throat. They always did when they were young.

The girl lying half-hidden beneath the crisp white sheet was only sixteen years old. Eve Sutcliffe, a gifted student at the prestigious Milton Downs Ladies Academy, still awaiting the results of her GCSEs. Long auburn hair framed a pretty face still touched by teenage hormones, a cluster of spots decorating her left cheek. The beauty in her features, the serenity of her expression, however, hid the brutality of her murder.

'Blunt force trauma,' Jim Grieves growled. 'From the shape and size of the impact wound, I'd say we're talking a hammer. Was anything recovered from the scene?'

Shaking her head, Helen leaned forward, Jim Grieves turning the deceased to reveal a bloody mess at the back of her skull. The young girl's half-naked body had been found in bushes in Lakeside Country Park five days ago. No weapon had been discovered, no witnesses unearthed, nor did they have any offenders under consideration. Helen had been hoping Jim Grieves would give her something to work with, but he quickly put paid to that notion.

'Not much more to tell you, I'm afraid. She was struck eight, possibly nine times, with considerable force, fracturing her skull and leading to massive internal bleeding. She probably wouldn't have been conscious after the second blow, but even so ...'

'Any hairs? Sweat? Blood?'

Grieves shook his head.

'Nothing under her fingernails, no sign of a struggle. I imagine that she was approached from behind and subdued before she had a chance to fight back.'

'What about semen? On the body, on the clothes?'

'You'll have to ask Meredith about her clothes, but there's nothing on or in the body, in fact there's no sign of sexual assault per se, no scratching or bruising around the genitals. She *was* sexually active, but not in the days, possibly weeks leading up into her death.'

Already Helen's mind was turning. Was there a boyfriend on the scene? Someone she'd recently broken up with? Someone who felt angry and spurned? Or was this a random act of violence, a young girl falling victim to a vicious, sexually-motivated stranger?

'So, her attacker was intent on assaulting her, but lost his nerve? Got frightened off?'

'You tell me, you're the detective ...' Grieve fired back, with grim relish.

Helen took the hit, privately acknowledging that the title had never felt more like a millstone. So much bloodshed, so much heartache of late, yet so little to go on. Recently, Helen had felt like she was swimming with one hand tied behind her back, drowning in a rising tide of violence and brutality.

'I've got a couple more bits and pieces to do,' Grieves continued, in conciliatory mode, 'and if I find anything significant, I'll let you know. I just wanted to give you my initial findings ...'

'Thanks, Jim. I appreciate it.'

And she did. But it didn't help her. The memories of Eve's devastated parents – their desolation, their agony – were still fresh in Helen's mind. It was a case that *demanded* to be solved, not just for Eve's sake, but for others who might yet be in danger from this violent offender. But so far they had nothing. Staring down at the girl's innocent face, Helen was filled with guilt and sadness – for the loss of all that Eve might have been, all she might have become.

For a young life brutally snuffed out.

Chapter 3

The lighter sparked in his hand, then died. He wanted to scream, to spew out his rage and anxiety, but there was no question of that – his victim lay only a few yards from him, docile but dangerous. If McManus awoke now, if he took the fight to his assailant, there would only be one winner.

He tried again, the lighter clicking out its quiet, hopeless rhythm. Still it didn't catch, remaining lifeless in his hand. It made no sense, he had bought it only yesterday, it was *full* of fuel. He'd used it on the way here, one last cigarette, and it had worked perfectly. So what was the problem now? Yes, his hand was shaking, but surely not enough to disable the device?

He tried again, aggressively, persistently. It sparked, more encouragingly this time, but the flame burnt only briefly before going out. And now McManus stirred, snorting and rubbing his nose, disturbed by the click, click, click of the lighter. He was moving, shifting his substantial weight on the tired faux leather sofa, which squeaked loudly in response, disturbing him still further. A frown, a cough and then he dropped the bottle of bourbon, which landed on the floor with a heavy thunk. Now his body shivered, as if juddering back into consciousness. There was no doubt about it – he was about to wake up.

Trying to calm himself, the intruder stared at the lighter,

willing it to work. He pressed the small metal wheel and pushed down hard. Once, twice, three times and now – miraculously – a flame sprang up. A strong, steady flame. His breath hissed from him, tension flooding from his body, and he didn't hesitate, raising the flame to the milk bottle he was clutching in his left hand. The dirty rag hung, moist and heavy, in the bottle's mouth, asking to be ignited. Carefully holding it to the flame, he watched with excitement as the homemade fuse took. Now the fire was working its way up the primed rag towards the petrol inside.

Taking a step back, he looked down at the man in front of him. His eyelids were flickering, he was only moments from consciousness, so raising his arm, he hurled the bottle down. Smashing on the hard floor, it exploded into flame, greedily latching onto the spilt whisky, the aged sofa, the man's clothes. The ferocity, the heat, was far greater than his attacker had expected and he stumbled backwards, away from the conflagration, suddenly fearful for his *own* safety.

Retreating, he grasped the door handle gratefully, yanking it open. He was about to run through the open doorway – run away as *fast* he could – but now something, some semblance of calm, some fragment of his planning – made him pause. *Refusing* to look backwards at the scene of horror, he gathered himself, reaching down to pull the key from the lock. Then, moving swiftly and silently, he stepped out of the portacabin, shutting the door behind him and turning the key in the lock.

Stepping out into the cool night air, he hurried down the stairs, desperate to be away from this awful place. But even as he did so, a sound from within the burning cabin stopped him dead in his tracks.

A single, agonized scream.

Chapter 4

He hurried down the alleyway, eagerly searching for his prize. A sharp-eyed constable had spotted it half an hour earlier and Detective Sergeant Joseph Hudson had wasted no time in responding. Running to the bike park, he'd raced across town, determined to have something to show for the day.

The officer now came into view, standing guard over the abandoned BMW. Hudson was convinced the stolen car would have been stripped, then dumped, and his instinct had been proved right. Here was the prestige vehicle he'd been seeking, the proud status symbol that someone had been prepared to kill for.

'I haven't touched it,' the constable ventured quickly, as Hudson approached. 'I just clocked the number plate and called it in.'

'Thank you, Constable ...?'

'Atkins, Sir.'

'Well done, Atkins,' Hudson responded, giving him a hearty slap on the shoulder. 'Good work, but I can take it from here ...'

The constable nodded, pleased with the compliment, then headed off. Hudson watched him go, gratified to have cultivated another foot soldier, then turned his attention to the abandoned vehicle.

Unsurprisingly, it wasn't locked. In fact, it wasn't even secured, the driver's door hanging ajar. Donning a pair of gloves, Hudson teased it open, crouching down to peer inside. It was a BMW 5 Series, four years old, but top of the range and, before it had been stolen, it would have had a state-of-the-art entertainment and navigation system to complement the hand-stitched leather interior. Now, however, it was a mess. From the outside, with its striking, metallic paint and tinted windows, it still looked impressive, but the view from the inside was very different. It had been cannibalized – the screen ripped out to leave hanging wires, the main armrest removed, even the chrome handles had been lifted. He was surprised to see the leather seats still in place, but perhaps the thief was an amateur, keen to make a quick buck. If so, he hoped he'd got a good price. The cost had been high and the reckoning would be severe.

Hudson's eyes were now drawn to the dark stains in the driver's footwell, then to the rust-colored smears on the window next to it. Up until ten days ago, this prestige vehicle had belonged to Alison Burris, an administrative manager at Southampton Children's Hospital. It had been an extravagant anniversary present from her besotted husband and it was her pride and joy. She always parked it in a discreet car park, a couple of blocks from the hospital, and it was there that she was targeted, late on a Wednesday night.

It was perhaps foolish of her to be alone in the car park so late at night, but still she should have had every reason to feel safe. As it was, she was set upon by a carjacker as she attempted to drive home. A struggle ensued – her clothing was torn, a clump of hair ripped out – as Burris battled to fight off the thief. It had proved a bad call, the young professional stabbed twice in the heart, before her attacker made off with her vehicle.

Alison Burris was found by a businessman just after midnight, but by then she was long dead. Hudson was the SIO on the scene and was quick to put the pieces together. There had been a spate of luxury car thefts in Southampton of late, another front in their battle against rising crime in the city, though few of them had been as violent as this one. As Hudson had crouched down over the poor woman's body, his eyes had been drawn to the narrow, cylindrical wounds in her flesh. He was still waiting on the post-mortem – Jim Grieves had a backlog of bodies – but Hudson had a pretty good idea of what killed Burris. She had been felled by a sharpened screwdriver, rammed into her heart at close quarters. It was a sickening way to die and for what? There was a thriving market for black-market car parts in Southampton, had been ever since the post-Covid downturn, but even so, what would the thief have got for the parts he lifted? Five thousand pounds? Six? It seemed a paltry payback, but in these troubled times perhaps it was about right. Looking down at the brutalized interior of the car, the blood smears on the window, Hudson reflected that of late one thing had become abundantly clear.

Life was cheap.